DANGEROUS MISTAKES

DANGEROUS MISTAKES

A Leah Nash Mystery

BY SUSAN HUNTER

Cover Design by Nancy Fetters Beach
Layout by Penoaks Publishing, http://penoaks.com

For Sara and Brenna

CHAPTER 1

"ALL OF US ARE DYING."

"Well, yes, I guess I can't argue with that, Betty," I said to the slight, white-haired woman seated behind my desk in the newsroom. I had come barreling in to pick up a new notebook, late for my next assignment.

"Oops, sorry, if I could just get into that center desk drawer there." I gently rolled her away from the desk, edged my drawer out a couple of inches, and stuck my arm into the depths until I felt cardboard. I tweezered out the spiral-bound notebook between two fingers.

"All of us. Dying. It's not right."

I slipped the notebook into my purse and moved to scoot Betty back into position, mentally cursing our receptionist Courtnee for sending her back to the newsroom. Again. Betty Meier was a retired nurse in her 80s. Years ago, during my first stint at the *Himmel Times Weekly*, she often stopped by to drop off an ad for a garage sale, or a press release for the Sunshine Girls bazaar, or to put in a notice for one of the many other groups to which she belonged. But now she suffered from Alzheimer's, and when she came to the office it was because she'd wandered away from home. This was the third time in the past two months that she'd ended up here. As I reached round her to slide the chair, she grabbed my arm, clamping on with almost desperate strength.

Startled, I looked down into her upturned face. The spark of life in her faded blue eyes caught me by surprise. I swallowed the placating answer I'd been about to give.

"No, Betty, it's not right. It doesn't matter how old we are. No one wants to go into that good night." I pulled up the visitor's chair and sat down so we were eye level.

"No, no, no! It's us. Everyone is dying. Where's Max? I want to talk to Max." The bright light had gone out as quickly as it had come, and her eyes took on a cloudy cast again. Her fingers released their grip, and her voice became querulous.

"Max isn't here any more, Betty." Max, the former owner of the *Himmel Times Weekly* wasn't just gone, he was dead. How and why he died was something I didn't like to talk about, but never really stopped thinking about.

Just then a harried-looking woman in her early 40s burst through the door.

"Mom! I've been looking all over for you. Sweetheart, what are you doing here?" She knelt down and patted her mother's arm. In an aside she said to me, "I'm sorry, Leah. The caregiver didn't show up. Mom's next door neighbor went over, but then her dog got hit by a car and she had to leave. I rushed out of work. It was only 10 minutes, but when I got there Mom was gone."

"Don't worry about it, Deborah. It's OK."

"Sometimes she seems fine, you know? The other day, out of nowhere, she said 'How was work, Debbie?' It almost broke my heart. She hadn't initiated a conversation in weeks, and then for a second, there she was. My mom. And just as quickly she was gone, and there was a confused old lady who doesn't know who I am."

"I'm sorry," I said, awkwardly and inadequately. Two things I specialize in, awkward and inadequate. "She keeps saying all her friends are dying."

She nodded. "I took her to a funeral a month or so ago. I knew she'd want to be there, but I shouldn't have. She's been upset ever since." She turned to her mother again. "Mom, let's go home. Tandy's coming over tonight, and we'll have dinner and watch some family movies. That'll be nice, won't it?" She slid her arm under her mother's and helped her up. As they left she turned to me. "Leah, again, I'm so sorry. I know we can't go on like this. It isn't safe for her."

"It's not easy," I said, though in truth, and thank God, I knew nothing about the pain of the parent–to–child reversal Deborah was experiencing. My mother—maddening, bossy, loving, funny woman that she is—still has full control of all her faculties, and would happily take charge of mine if I'd let her.

I followed Deborah out the door on a run, but I was already 15 minutes late for an interview with the incoming principal at Himmel High School.

"Really, Courtnee? Betty Meier sitting in the newsroom? At my desk? Why did you take her back there?"

It was nearly five when I got back to the office, and I was a little on the pissy side. Make that a lot. My interview with the principal didn't go well. He was unhappy because I was late and even madder when I left early. I had to, or I'd have missed shooting a ribbon cutting ceremony at the new McDonald's franchise. That's the kind of cutting edge journalism we do here at the *Himmel Times*. On the way back to the office, the iced tea I'd bought at the drive-through tipped over, and half of it ran into my purse. In fairness I couldn't blame Courtnee for that, but I think that fairness is far overrated.

Looking up from her Facebook account, Courtnee gave a shrug.

"I'm a receptionist, Leah. It's my job to receive. So I received her into the newsroom. You were gone, and Miguel is out, and Rebecca wasn't here, and like always, I had to take care of things myself. She likes sitting at your desk."

Miguel Santos is the other full-time reporter, and Rebecca Hartfield is the publisher and micromanager at the *Times*.

"The next time she comes in, if there is a next time, 'receive' her in reception. Sit her down—out here—and call her daughter. OK?"

"Okaayy." She gave a flip of her silky blonde hair and turned to read the text that had just pinged on her phone. At the same time a loud static-filled squawk came from the scanner in the newsroom. I couldn't make out the words, but I didn't need to, because Rebecca was already out of her office to translate. She's a cool blonde—calm, measured, methodical. And oddly, not that crazy about me.

"Good, you're still here. There's a working fire at 529 Halston. A residence. I need you to cover it."

"But I've got a Parks Committee meeting. Miguel is—"

"He's still in Milwaukee. You can do a phone follow-up on the meeting. Is there a problem?"

"No. Nothing," I muttered. I grabbed the camera and headed out.

My name is Leah Nash, and in the exciting, competitive, high-adrenalin carnival that is journalism, I operate the merry-go-round. I'm a reporter for a small-town weekly in Himmel, Wisconsin. It's where I started 11 years ago, and it's where I landed 18 months ago, after a series of bad career decisions. I had an exit strategy, but it hadn't come together quite yet.

The fire assignment was no big deal. Except it was. Though I wasn't about to confide my darkest fears to Rebecca, who as far as I can tell has the empathy and emotional range of a Popsicle. The truth is, I'm afraid of fires—to the point of hyperventilating and quaking in my shoes. Have been since I was 10 years old. I never willingly cover one. But sometimes I have no choice.

My hands were sweaty on the wheel, and I was repeating *"breathe in, breathe out"* in a frenzied mantra as I pulled up. Smoke billowed from the back of a small two-story house. Here and there yellow flames shot red-tipped tongues out the windows. Gray ash snowflakes floated through the air as firefighters wrangled hoses, flooding the fire into submission. Still I sat in my car, unable to open the door and move closer to the burning house. Hard as I tried not to let it, my mind hurtled back to another fire, a long time ago. I squeezed my eyes tight to shut out the images. A second later they popped back open in surprise at the sharp rapping near my ears. I rolled down the window so that David Cooper could lean in.

"Hey, Coop."

"Hey. What are you doing here? Where's Miguel?"

"Rebecca sent him out of town. So it's me." I struggled to put on an air of professionalism as I opened the door and hauled out my camera bag. Coop is my oldest friend and a lieutenant with the Himmel Police Department.

"So what's the story? Anyone hurt? What are the damages? Do they know how it started?" I fired off questions, determined not to let him know how hard it was to force myself to walk closer toward the heat of the fire, to hear the snap and pop as it ate through dry wood, the crash as a section of roof gave way.

I didn't fool him. Coop doesn't say much. But he sees a lot. Which I find quite irritating when it's me he's looking at.

"Al Porter's over by the ladder truck. He thinks it's just about under control. I'll point him in your direction when he gets off the phone. No sense you going over there and getting in the way."

I try not to let my weaknesses show. If anyone sees what hurts or scares you, it makes you vulnerable. And in my experience, that's not a good thing.

I shook my head. "I'm going over to talk to him."

He looked at me, but didn't say anything.

"Look, I'm fine."

"Yeah, I know."

"Don't patronize me. I hate it when you patronize me."

"I'm not. Just saying it's wet and slippery and crowded over there. Call Al over here, and you'd be out of the way. Suit yourself."

"I will."

"Oh, I know."

We could have gone on like 10-year-olds forever—at least I could have—but the fire chief walked up just then.

"Leah." He nodded and paused to wipe a rivulet of sweat running down the side of his face, smearing ash across his cheek. He had pulled off his yellow helmet and I could see that his gray hair was wet and curling in wisps. Pushing 60, and about 30 pounds over fighting weight, Al isn't going to be September in anyone's *Fire Fighters Calendar*. But he knows how to run a crew, keep them safe, and put out the fire, and no one is in any hurry to tell him to hang up his turnout gear.

"You're a little late to the party. But Matt McGreevy got some good shots and video too."

I could've kissed Al and Matt both, but I played it casual. "Oh? Sure, that'd be great. Whose house is it?"

"Old gal by the name of Betty Meier."

Al picked up on the shock I felt right away.

"It's OK, Leah. You know her? She wasn't home. Nobody was. Well, except for one pretty mad cat, but we got her out all right. The old lady was at her daughter's, the neighbor said. I guess she's got some dementia issues. Might have left on the gas burner on the stove. But don't print that," he hastened to add. "We're gonna have the state fire marshal in."

A loud whoosh of water hit the house just then, spraying the charred remains. No flames were visible, but I knew that didn't mean the fire was out. Some of the crew would be on the scene for a couple of hours to make sure the blaze didn't start up again.

"She's wandered away a few times and come to the paper, asking for Max. I talked to her daughter today. I think she's probably going to move her to a nursing home." Poor Betty. Losing all her friends, her memories, and tonight it could have been her life. It's true. Old age isn't for sissies.

"Yeah. I'd say it's past time for that. Fire can move so damn fast. People don't realize how—" He stopped. Looked at me. Looked embarrassed. I helped him roll on past a subject I didn't want to delve into either.

"For sure. So, who called it in? What's the damage estimate?" I went through the standard reporter's litany of who, what, when, where, why questions, and when I had all the information Al could give me at the moment, I asked Matt to email me his photos and video.

Then I packed it in and went to back to the office to post a few pictures and a news brief on the *Times* website. I stopped by the front desk and checked the spike on the corner of Courtnee's desk for messages. At 6:30 p.m. she was long gone.

I pulled off the notes for me and gave them a quick glance. Nothing looked urgent, so I stuffed them in my purse to read later. In the newsroom, I didn't bother to flip on the light, just turned on my desk lamp and used the blue glow of the computer screen. It was kind of nice there in the semi-dark. There was no jangle of Courtnee's unanswered phones in reception, no tap-tap-tap of other keyboards, no repeated clunking of cans of soda coming out of the Coke machine.

Before I started writing, I texted Coop and Miguel to see if they wanted to meet up for a beer and a burger at McClain's, then I filed a quick story. I uploaded two of the photos Matt had sent to my iPhone and a short video clip. When I finished, I leaned back for a long, satisfying yawn and stretch, my chair tilted and my arms reaching as far back as possible. I was right at that almost orgasmic point of satisfaction, when every muscle was extended and just on the edge of relaxing, when the light clicked on.

"Leah."

I all but tumbled out of my chair.

"Rebecca! Geez, how about some warning when you creep in on little cat feet?"

"Did you get the story?" Her eyes, the color of a blue-tinged icicle, blinked behind her black-framed glasses.

"Already written. Nobody hurt. Betty, the woman who owns the house, wasn't there. Property's totaled though."

"Photos?"

"Yep."

"All right, good. Pull the commission story from the front page and run with the fire above the fold—if the pictures are any good. Are they?"

"Matt McGreevy took them. They're great. It was really nice of him to share them, especially since you fired him last month."

"I did not fire him. Stringers aren't employees. They're independent contractors. Why didn't you take the photos?"

I flashed back to my near panic attack at the fire, my dithering around the edge trying to get my nerves under control. The shaming fear that had gripped me. "I got there too late. Matt rolled out with the fire department—he does their videography. And he's a good guy, so he shared them, even though you 'not' fired him."

"I don't cut costs for fun. It has to be done. That's my job." She spoke slowly, as though explaining something to a small child.

I gave in to the urge to get a rise out of her. "I thought you went to journalism school. Not bean counting academy."

"I was hired to get the *Times* in better financial shape, and that requires the counting of some beans. It might be easier if you didn't take every decision as a personal affront."

Something in her voice made me look up from putting away my stuff. She had taken off her glasses and was rubbing the bridge of her nose. Her shoulders had sagged a little, and for a minute I saw her as a woman with a tough job, who didn't have the luxury of casual banter with her staff or after-work drinks at McClain's. Her role was to be the bad guy, the nay-sayer, the buzz-killer. That had to be pretty lonely. She was only 36, just a few years older than me.

"Rebecca, would you like to—"

She cut me off before I could invite her to stop by McClain's with me. "Don't forget to turn your mileage in tomorrow. It's the cutoff, and you won't get paid this month if you don't get it in. I've already told Courtnee that."

As part of the general cutbacks and reassignments in Rebecca's lean and mean vision for the *Times*, Courtnee had been assigned the task of processing mileage and expense reports. It had proven to be one of the more effective cost-saving measures, because half the time Courtnee didn't finish the reports in time for us to get paid for the month, which she always insisted was our fault. The other half of the time, she screwed them up, and they didn't get processed correctly until the following month. I suspected there was some method to Rebecca's madness in giving the job to Courtnee, in that to some degree, expenses were always deferred.

"Right." I gathered my things and left before saying something I'd regret. Working at the *Times* wasn't exactly a step up the career ladder, but when Max was here it was fun. I missed the camaraderie, the kidding around, the messy, lively, frustrating, fulfilling business of putting out a paper. When Rebecca first started, I thought we might be friends. She's near my age, she's from Wisconsin like me, and she'd even worked at the *Grand Rapids Press* in Michigan, like I had, though at a different time. It just seemed like we'd have a lot in common. Instead, Rebecca sucked the happy right out of the air. If it weren't for Miguel, I might have done something stupid like I did at the *Miami Star Register*. Namely leaving one job without having another waiting. I wanted to play it smart this time. But she was making it awfully hard.

CHAPTER 2

I HADN'T HEARD from either Coop or Miguel by the time I got to the parking lot, and I didn't really feel like going to McClain's Bar anyway. So instead I drove my car to the north end of town and parked it in front of the wooden posts that form the boundaries of Riverview Park. The lights on their old fashioned poles shone on the deserted park with its weather-beaten picnic tables and forlorn wooden benches. I turned off the engine and looked at the empty acreage, repopulating it with my memories.

As a little kid I spent hours on the swings and the jungle gym with my sister, Annie. Later, in the middle school years, Coop and I would rendezvous here to ride our bikes at breakneck speed on the gravel path that circles the park. Sometimes we'd make forbidden treks across the railroad trestle spanning the Himmel River at the edge of the park. It was a shortcut to JT's Party Store, which held a child's mother lode of candy. Later on, when I was a teenager, I'd bring my youngest sister, Lacey, here too. We'd feed the ducks down by the river, and I'd spin her around on the merry-go-round until we both were dizzy with laughter.

As an adult, whenever I came back to town, I was drawn to this space. If the weather was fine, the park was filled with families. Parents pushing strollers, kids running and shouting, heady with the sheer joy of a bright, sunny afternoon. I liked to watch and listen to the happy hubbub all around me. Once upon a time, our family was like that. My mother, my father, Lacey, Annie, and me.

But then Annie died in a fire when she was eight and I was 10. Lacey was just a baby. My dad left shortly after that. Lacey died five years ago at 17. People know about her, because of the story I did last year. Most people forget about Annie. It was so long ago. When they do recall it, like the fire chief Al Porter had tonight, I change the subject. If pushed into a corner by someone more curious than kind, I usually offer an Oscar Wilde paraphase. *To lose one sister may be regarded as a misfortune; to lose both looks like carelessness.* All but the most dense retreat then.

I'm pretty good at keeping others at bay, but I have a tougher time with my own thoughts. That's why I don't like to be near a fire. When I feel the heat, see the flames, hear the crash and crackle of burning wood, a pain I can't stop rises with choking force. It takes all I have just to breathe. When Annie died, it was the end of my family as I'd known it. Everything changed.

I stared blankly at the bleak early winter landscape in front of me, willing my mind to settle, to forget, to achieve the numbness that was gradually creeping into my toes and fingers as I sat in the unheated car. Finally, I turned on the engine and left the park to drive down Himmel's mean streets.

Leaves that only a few weeks ago danced gaily in the trees, sporting vivid orange, red, and gold colors, now lay scattered, curled and brown, on the pavement. They crunched under my wheels or skittered onto the windshield, borne up by gusts of wind in the cold November night. A shiver ran through me. We were going into another Wisconsin winter. My second one since moving back. I was determined to make it my last.

Himmel, like a lot of upper Midwestern towns, is a faint copy of its former self. The empty store fronts downtown and the shrinking memberships in churches and social clubs tell a story that long-time residents are tired of hearing. A changing economy brought about factory closings, small stores gave way to big box operations, and people who expected to live here forever had to move to find work. The population had dropped from the bustling 20,000 of my youth to its current 15,000. Even the Chamber of Commerce has a tough time keeping a straight face when it promotes Himmel as a little piece of heaven on earth.

I wasn't one of the people who never wanted to leave. I couldn't wait to get away and get started on my "real" life when I graduated from college. I'd been gone for 10 years when my progress up the career ladder was halted by my own impulsive stubbornness. After clashing with an editor at my last job at a midsize daily, I made the grand gesture and quit. That didn't work out so well. In the struggling world of print media there weren't a lot of newspaper openings. During a long, fruitless job hunt, I realized that smart and smartass aren't the same thing. I'd like to say I changed my ways, but I'm kind of a slow learner.

I finally had to take the lifeline tossed to me by Max Matulka, my old boss at the *Himmel Times*. I had planned to be there for six months. Just enough time to get myself back on track. But I got caught up in an investigation with some serious personal stakes—the accidental death of my sister Lacey years earlier. By the time it was over, I had discovered that Lacey had been murdered.

The articles I wrote for the *Himmel Times* got a lot of play in the online media and on cable news. Pretty soon I had a publisher, a $10,000 advance, and a book in the works. It wasn't enough to quit my day job, but I was hoping the book would help me transition from reporting to writing true crime books. That way I'd have everything I loved about journalism—researching, investigating, finding leads, making sense of things, writing—and none of what I didn't—cranky editors, impossible deadlines, workplace politics, and compromises in quality caused by shrinking news budgets.

The manuscript was in page proof stage, the final step before printing. *True Crime: Unholy Alliances* was set for a February release. Who doesn't like a little murder for Valentine's Day?

In the meantime, I still had to eat and pay the bills, so I was still at the *Times*. It had changed a lot since the death of Max last year. His wife sold it to a hedge fund that specializes in sucking up the life force of small town papers until they're dried husks of their former selves, then selling them. Or shutting them down. So far, Rebecca had cut staff, cut overtime, micromanaged coverage, and increased our workload. I just wanted to hang on long enough to get my book off the ground.

As I pulled in the driveway of our house, a red Toyota pulled up behind me. Miguel.

"Chica! I've been following you since you turned the corner onto Main Street. Don't you ever look in your rearview mirror?"

"Hey, you. Come on in."

I hit the kitchen light as we came through the door, grabbed a couple of Supper Club beers and some sliced turkey and bread from the fridge, and put them on the kitchen table.

Miguel took off his brown leather jacket and laid it over the back of his chair. Under a dark green v-neck sweater he wore a shirt with tiny green checks and a skinny burgundy tie. Well polished brown shoes poked out from under his gray pants.

"You look cute." If he weren't 10 years younger than me—and gay—I'd seriously think about taking our friendship to the next level.

"Gracias. Just got back from Milwaukee. Buenas noticias! Good news. My uncle Craig, he made it. He's on the transplant list; we got the OK from the Kidney Transplant Team." His smile made me smile.

"That's great. Now what?"

"Now we wait. But at least we know if a kidney match comes up, he's in line."

Miguel had lived in Himmel since he was 16, when his mother sent him to stay with his aunt and uncle, to keep him safe from some nasty gang bangers who had it in for him in Milwaukee. He took to small town life and stayed on after college, when he got a job at the *Times*. I met him last year when I came back. If I had a younger brother and I got to choose, it would be him.

13

I reached over and rubbed the top of his head—I can never resist a chance to mess with his perfect hair. He laughed and pushed my hand away.

"Now, dígame, tell me about your day."

I told him about the fire—not the near panic attack part, just that I got there late, but we still had some good pictures thanks to Matt McGreevy. When I went to rummage in the fridge for mustard and mayo for our sandwiches, I knocked my purse off the bar. The entire contents spilled out, and as Miguel scrambled to help me pick it up, I grabbed the handful of pink message slips I'd meant to look at before leaving the office.

I stopped and read through them. A reminder call from my dentist's office, a request to speak at career day at Himmel High School—given the state of my own career, that would not be a very inspirational talk—and then something odd in Courtnee's well-rounded handwriting.

4:30. She called about murder. And of course because it was Courtnee, there was no phone number, or any clue who "she" was.

I tried to determine whether this was a request for me to kill someone, an inquiry about the murders I covered last year, or an invitation to a philosophical discussion on the taking of human life. I shared the message with Miguel.

"Murder? We can investigate again. Just like last year, chica." His dark brown eyes lit up.

I shook my head. "Think about it. Courtnee took the message from someone called 'she.' Who probably didn't say murder, more like burger, as in the burger eating contest on Saturday. Someone probably wanted us to take photos."

"Come on, chica—Courtnee's not that lame."

"Oh no? Last week she told me she bought an argyle for her mother's garden. She meant a garden gnome. She got the word gnome mixed up with gargoyle, and then somehow made it come out argyle."

He grinned. "You're like a Windtalker. You and your amiga Courtnee, you speak a language only you understand."

"I'll try my translation skills out on her tomorrow. But don't start counting on a big story. Good thing, too. I'm barely keeping up with regular stuff, and I'm behind on my book. But after it's published, all the big stories in Himmel—the Farm Bureau meeting, the Highest Butterfat Content Milk Award, the sewer repair on Maple Street, even the burger eating contest—all those front-pagers will be yours, Jimmy Olsen." I smiled, but instead of smiling back, his face became serious.

"Chica, it won't be the same when you go. *Estoy tan triste*—I'm so sad when I think about it."

"You should be thinking about moving on yourself. The writing's on the wall. That soulless hedge fund Rebecca works for is not going to leave anything standing. You've got a year or two at the most, I'd say."

"I can't do anything now. I can't leave my Tía Lydia now, with Uncle Craig so sick."

"Yeah, I know you can't. Well, I might be hanging on right along with you. Who knows what will happen with the book? Maybe I'll be at the *Times* until Rebecca kicks me to the curb. Which could be any time, actually. She hates me."

"No she doesn't, chica. She just doesn't show her feelings. She's not so bad."

I stared at him in astonishment. "You're kidding, right?"

"She's not that bad. She's had a hard life. Her mamá committed suicide; she never knew her papá. Her adopted parents were *muy mal*. Very bad. She was in foster care; she had no family!" As part of a large extended family with millions—or so it seemed—of cousins, aunts, and uncles, Miguel couldn't seem to wrap his head around Rebecca's aloneness.

"Hey, I'm sorry she had a Jane Eyre childhood, but that doesn't give her the right to make my life miserable now. She's impossible to work with, and the room temperature drops 10 degrees whenever she walks in."

"She'll warm up to you, if you let her."

I raised an eyebrow, but before I could comment the doorbell rang, and my mother and Paul Karr came in from the living room laughing and doing a disco move to *Stayin' Alive*. My mom installed a digital doorbell that plays tunes from her MP3 player, and she changes it up so often you never know if the *Barber of Seville* or the BeeGees will start up when you hit the buzzer.

"Miguel!" She grabbed his hand and executed a few quick dance steps with him, while Paul came over and gave me a side-shoulder hug. Then they both sat down and joined us.

"What have you two crazy kids been up to?" I asked.

"Carol and I went to dinner and a movie, and then we stopped by McClain's for a drink." Paul was talking to me, but his eyes kept straying to my mother, who was laughing at something Miguel had said to her. Paul has been our dentist forever and my mother's "special friend" for the past few years. He's definitely smitten—and why wouldn't he be? My mom is great-looking, small and trim, with spiky black and silver hair and the same dark blue eyes my sister Lacey had. She's smart too, but pretty bossy. Though Paul doesn't seem to mind.

"Guess who we saw at McClain's? Ben. With a date," my mother said.

"You and Ben broke up? Why didn't you tell me?" Miguel asked.

I shook my head. "We didn't 'break up.' We weren't ever a couple. We just went out for awhile, that's all."

"What am I gonna do with you? I find you a smart, good-looking boy and you throw him away. You know I can't go shopping for you every day, chica. I have to look out for myself, too."

"Don't worry about it. I'm fine, he's fine, we had fun and now we're done."

He and my mother exchanged resigned glances. They'd both had high hopes for Ben, an IT consultant I met last year through Miguel. But as time progressed, I discovered he never listened to cheesy pop songs, he didn't like old movies, and he had no idea who Jack McCoy was. It just wasn't meant to be.

"OK, OK, that's enough discussion about my love life."

"You mean lack of it, don't you?" my mother said.

Miguel came to my rescue and abruptly changed the subject. "Leah got a message about a murder today."

"What?"

"Miguel is exaggerating. Courtnee took the message, so it could be about anything." I shoved it over to my mother and Paul.

"She? Who's that? There's no phone number or anything."

"This is my life. I keep telling you. Courtnee was sent here to drive me mad."

"It doesn't seem like she could mean an actual murder, does it? I mean, aren't we past our quota for the decade in Himmel?" Paul asked, referring to the events of last year.

"I would think," my mother said over her shoulder. She was carrying out my original mission to make Miguel and me turkey sandwiches. As she set them down in front of us and pulled up a chair for herself she added, "Garrett Whiting's suicide last month was bad enough."

"Yes, that was terrible. Marilyn and I were friends with him and his wife Joan years ago," Paul said.

Marilyn was Paul's ex-wife. Anyone she befriended was suspect in my book.

"They had a couple of kids, too," my mother said. "The Whitings were clients when I first started working for Karen." My mother had been a paralegal at a law firm that closed last year. "The son's name was Jamie, really sweet little boy. And the daughter—now what was her name? She was gorgeous."

"Isabel," Miguel said around a mouthful of turkey sandwich.

"You know them?" I asked.

"*Un pocito*. A little. She was in my class. Jamie was a few years behind."

"Well, I'm sure she knew you. You can't walk into Aldi's grocery store without all the cashiers shouting hello."

"Hey, if you got it, chica, you can't help it." He grinned before taking an enormous final bite of his sandwich, then washing it down with a swig of Supper Club.

17

"Isabel must be what, 23, then? And Jamie can't even be 21 yet. It's so hard. Especially for the daughter," my mother said.

"Why do you say that?" asked Paul.

"She's the one who found the body," Miguel answered for her.

"That's really rough. I didn't know that," Paul said. "Joan and Garrett divorced years ago," he added. "Joan moved out west somewhere after the divorce. The kids were still pretty young. She died a few years ago, and from what I've heard, she never saw Jamie and Isabel again."

"Nice mother," I said.

My mother frowned. "Don't be so judgmental. Being a mother is tough, and Joan had other problems."

"Like what?"

"She had a prescription drug addiction. She went to rehab to kick it. Maybe she couldn't, so she didn't come back. Or maybe she did, but she felt too ashamed, or too guilty, or maybe her kids wouldn't have anything to do with her. Not everyone is as forgiving as you, Leah."

I made a face at her sarcasm. "My sympathy's with the kids, not the mother who ran out on them. Well, look, it's been a long day. You guys can rehash Himmel history some more if you want, but I'm going to bed."

"I gotta go too, chica," Miguel said, then bent to give my mother a quick kiss on the cheek and waved to Paul and me. "See you later."

I changed into a T-shirt and sweats, washed my face, then flopped down on the bed and fell into total coma sleep. It took me awhile before I realized that the annoying giant bumble bee buzzing my dream was actually my phone bouncing and vibrating on the night table next to my bed. I fumbled around for a second, then found it and answered without looking at the caller ID.

"Hello?" I said, following it with an involuntary and really loud yawn.

"I'm sorry, were you sleeping?" The voice was female, light and pleasant, but agitated.

"What time is it?"

"Um, it's, let me see. Oh no, it's 11:45. I'm sorry. I didn't realize it was so late. I shouldn't have called. Go back to sleep."

"Oh no. Hold on. You don't get to wake me up and then do a hang up. Who is this?"

"My name is Isabel Whiting. I left a message for you at the paper today, but you didn't call me back. And I—oh, this was a bad idea. I'm so sorry. I called Courtnee at home and got your cell phone."

I was fully alert now. "I got a note about your call from Courtnee, but the message was—" I hesitated. "A little ambiguous. And she didn't leave a phone number."

"I feel really bad calling you. It's just that I don't know what to do. And it's all I can think about. I thought maybe you. You know. Because of your sister. I'm sorry."

"OK, quit saying you're sorry for starters. I'm awake now, so talk to me."

"It's my father. Garrett Whiting. The police say he killed himself. But he didn't. I know he wouldn't do that."

In my experience, families of suicide victims often think that. They usually try to convince themselves that it was an accident. Sometimes the medical examiner helps them think that, usually when it's a solo hunting "accident." That wasn't the case with Garrett Whiting.

"Look, Isabel, this is a really bad time for you, I know. But I talked to the sheriff's department at the time it happened. There wasn't anything to suggest anything but suicide. It was pretty cut and dried, from their perspective."

"I know that, but he didn't kill himself. No one will listen to me. Somebody killed my father."

"OK, what makes you so sure?"

"Can't we just meet in person? I know you'll understand if I can just talk to you face to face. Please. If you don't, then there's no one. I've tried, but I don't know how to do this by myself."

It can be pretty lonely out there on a limb. I know, because I've been there myself more than a few times.

"OK, how about this? I could do coffee at the Elite tomorrow, around 10? We can talk and—"

"Oh, thank you, thank you so much. I'll be there. I'm sorry I woke you, but thank you."

"All right but—" Before I could finish my cautionary words against expecting too much she had hung up.

I sat staring at the phone in my hand for a minute, wishing I hadn't given her false hope. I was just delaying the inevitable. More than likely, Isabel was going to have to accept that there were things about her father she hadn't known. There always are.

CHAPTER 3

FIRST THING IN THE MORNING I went straight to an 8 a.m. Board of Supervisors meeting at the county courthouse, which also houses the Grantland County Sheriff's Department. It was, as usual, way longer than necessary as they debated restrictions on a private airfield owned by Grady O'Donnell, a farmer who rented hangar space to a handful of private pilots in the area. It was nice extra income for Grady, but some neighbors were complaining about flight noise and lights at night. No decision was reached, also as usual, and I was not in the best mood when the aimless meeting meandered to a close.

Out in the hall, I ran into Charlie Ross, a detective with the sheriff's department. I mean "ran into" literally. He stopped short just ahead of me to adjust khaki pants that were losing the battle between his belly bulge and his belt. I was looking at my phone for messages, and I hit him from behind with a soft thunk. It barely shook his solid bulk.

When he turned and saw it was me, his pudgy red face got even redder.

"Nash. I already know you can't hear. Leastwise I guess that's why you're always buttin' in when people tell you to stay out. Looks like you can't see either."

"Sorry, Ross, you're hard to miss, I agree."

"I hear the *Times* isn't doin' so hot. Tryin' to make the sheriff's department look like a bunch of screw-ups didn't work out so good for your paper, huh?"

"Not the sheriff's department. Just you, Ross. You're the one who screwed up the investigation of Lacey's death. But don't worry, you can read all about it, all over again, when my book comes out."

Now why did I say that? Yes, Charlie Ross is an ass. Yes, his incompetence helped keep the truth about Lacey—and a lot of other really bad things—hidden for years. And yes, he'd come after me with both barrels blazing for something I didn't do. But in the end the facts came out out, Lacey's killer was found, I was exonerated, and he was still stupid. Couldn't I ever resist antagonizing him? Apparently not.

His close-set mustard brown eyes narrowed. "Always got a smart answer, don't you, Nash?"

"That reminds me, I'm looking for some answers from you. I need a copy of the case file on the Garrett Whiting investigation."

"I already gave you the information last month. It was suicide. End of story."

We don't run suicide stories in the paper, unless the death occurs in a public place or the victim is a public figure. The obituary usually uses something vague like "passed away unexpectedly." And I'm OK with that. Some things should stay private. But Isabel had piqued my curiosity and a look at the file would be helpful.

"Whiting's daughter Isabel is pretty adamant that her father didn't kill himself."

"Yeah? Well, facts are facts. You find a guy sittin' in a chair, he's got a hole in his head, powder residue on his fingers, and a gun sittin' on the floor beside him. It doesn't take a genius to see he blew his own head off. Autopsy confirmed it."

"He didn't leave a note, right?"

"No. Lotta times they don't."

"Isabel seems to think—"

"Nobody wants to think their old man offed himself. She was a little hysterical when we got there. It happens. Family, they don't think so clear when somethin' like this happens. Maybe they don't want to. He's drinking his rum and Coke, mixin' it with some pills. He's got financial problems. His son's a druggie. Life don't look so good. So he takes the easy out and pulls the trigger. If it walks like a duck and quacks like a duck, it's a duck. And this duck is quackin' suicide. Plain and simple. Take my advice: You try to make somethin' outta nothin', all you're gonna do is look stupid. You don't want that, do ya? 'Specially with your big important book comin' out and all."

"It's an inactive investigation. I can get the file."

"Not from me you can't."

"I'll go to the sheriff."

"Knock yourself out."

What I wanted to do was knock him out—or at least on his well-cushioned butt. What I said was, "OK then. I'll see you around."

"Not if I see you first."

As I walked through the front door of the *Times* Courtnee greeted me.

"So, did Isa-bitch get hold of you last night?"

"Who?"

"You know, Isa-bore Whiting? So last night she calls me up. Right in the middle of Sheer Delight Make-up Value Hour on the Buy network. Before I could get her off the phone, they ran out of the Pre-Prep Foundation Magic in Alabaster. I hope you're happy."

"Deliriously." Looking at her carefully filled-in eyebrows, heavily mascaraed lashes, and shiny pink lips, it was hard to imagine there was any make-up product not already in her arsenal.

"Why didn't you just put her name on the message you left me? Or her phone number? That would have been helpful. And why are you calling her such mean fourth-grade names?"

Her full lips started to protrude in a pout. If at 20 Courtnee represents the next generation of American workers, we are all in a lot of trouble. Self-confident without any basis, incompetent without any awareness, unencumbered by any sense of responsibility, she is perpetually aggrieved and slightly perplexed by job duties that pull her away from Tweeting, Tindering, and Yik-Yakking.

"You don't have to get all up in my grill. She's just like #I'm Awesome. She thinks she's like this, this Queen of Switzerland or something. I can't even."

Queen of Switzerland? Interesting, but I didn't have time to explore that peculiar turn of phrase.

"You know her father did die just a month ago."

"Oh. I know. Everybody does. She is such a drama queen."

"What have you got against her? She wasn't even in your class at school, was she?"

"No, but my brother Jared wanted to hang with her, and she totally burned him. Like she thinks she's so lit. She's not."

Ah. Never forgive, never forget. The Fensterman code.

"Well, it would have saved me a midnight call if you had just written down her name and number."

"It's not like I'm your, like, personal assistant, Leah. I do the best I can."

Sadly, I think that is true.

"And she was all like freaking and talking about how her dad didn't kill himself, and no one would listen to her, and could she talk to you and yada yada yada. So I told her you'd call. Only you didn't." She glared at me, and suddenly her inept job performance had become my dereliction of duty.

"Courtnee, you—"

I was just about to launch when Rebecca came into the reception area. She fixed on me, and a frown crossed her face. Time for me to exit, stage left.

"What happened at the Board of Supervisors? Anything change with Grady O'Donnell's private airport? Did you lay out the editorial page yet? Make sure you put the letters below the fold."

I started edging toward the door. "No big action at the board. No ordinance on the books, neighbors are SOL on their noise complaints about the airport. Might be some interest in changing county regulations, if the neighbors get fired up, or they may just let it drop. That's all there was. As usual, the board didn't take any action. The pages are almost laid out. I'm just going to check out a lead. I'll be back before lunch."

"What lead?"

"She's going to talk to Isa-bi—Isabel Whiting. She thinks her dad was murdered."

Rebecca moves with surprising speed for a person with such a calm demeanor. She had one hand on the door and the other on my arm, so I had no choice but to turn around.

"This is the doctor who committed suicide last month?"

"That's what the sheriff's department and medical examiner said."

"Then what's this about?"

I really didn't want to get into it with Rebecca before I even knew what "it" was. I glared at Courtnee, but it bounced right off her guilt-proof armor.

"I got a call from the daughter. She's convinced her father wouldn't have killed himself, and the police are wrong. I'm meeting her for coffee at 10."

I was ready for her to tell me to forget it, that it wasn't an efficient use of my time or the paper's resources.

"I'm going to be out for the rest of the day. Make sure you're back by noon. And I want full disclosure after you meet the Whiting daughter."

"OK, sure." And I left remembering what Miguel had said about Rebecca's mother—that she had committed suicide. Maybe it made her feel sympathetic to Isabel. Wait a minute, Rebecca, sympathetic? No. Had to be some other reason.

CHAPTER 4

THE BELL HANGING OVER THE DOOR jingled as I walked into the Elite Cafe. I scanned the room looking for Isabel, though I hadn't thought to get a description from Courtnee. Clara Schimelman, the owner, was bustling around the small wooden tables, a white tea towel tossed over her ample shoulder.

"Leah, you looking for your friend? She's over there." She pointed toward the corner to a table half-hidden by a large, somewhat shopworn artificial fern. "She won't take no rugelach. She only wants the black coffee. But you have chai and rugelach, or maybe raspberry linzer, is good today. Yes?"

The Elite Cafe and Bakery isn't very imposing to look at, but the menu of bakery treats and the deli case are to die for. Everyone comes to the Elite. It's like Rick's in Casablanca, without the gambling and the Nazis.

"Rugelach sounds like heaven." I moved toward the counter, but she waved me away with a flutter of her damp towel.

"No, you go sit with your friend. I bring to you."

The person who stood up to greet me was tall and slender with dark blonde hair cut in an elfin style. She looked at me out of thick-lashed brown eyes.

"Hi. I know you're Leah. I'm Isabel Whiting. Thank you so much for coming. You must have thought I was crazy last night." She was wearing a light pink sweater of some soft, fluffy yarn and a pair of faded jeans. A tiny gold bell on a delicate chain hung on her neck. She had a good handshake, firm and cool. She smiled and I smiled, and before it turned awkward Mrs. Schimelman delivered my rugelach and chai latte and Isabel's coffee.

"You sure you don't want the rugelach?" She turned hopefully to Isabel.

"No, no thank you. I'm fine." She seemed anything but—uptight and nervous.

Mrs. Schimelman shook her head, sending a bobby pin flying and freeing several strands of gray hair. "You come back again, you try my poppyseed cake. Off the hook." Though she hasn't lost her German accent after more than 40 years, or learned the more subtle points of English grammar, Mrs. Schimelman delights in collecting and using bits of slang, usually several years out of date.

As she moved away, Isabel shifted her coffee from the right hand side to the left.

"You're a lefty, huh? So's my Aunt Nancy." I was trying to ease into things, maybe take her tension down a notch. Nervous people are hard to interview.

"I'm the only one in my family, so I've had to adapt." She started sliding the little bell charm on her necklace up and down its chain.

Clearly, my effort to set her at ease was not working. Might as well jump in then. Maybe she'd relax as she told her story.

"So, Isabel, why don't you tell me why you think your dad didn't commit suicide."

She took a breath, let it out slowly, then leaned back in her chair and wrapped both hands around her coffee cup.

"OK. My dad died last month. I found him." She stopped.

"I heard that. I'm really sorry."

"I'm not asking for sympathy. I just want the truth."

"Isabel, according to the sheriff's department, the truth is pretty clear. Your father shot himself with a handgun." I tried not to sound too harsh.

"But it isn't clear at all. My father would never have killed himself. Never."

"People do some inexplicable things sometimes. We can't know what's going on inside someone else's head."

She gave me a frustrated look and then tried again, gripping her cup tightly in her hands.

"Look, I was adopted when I was only three. My parents had Jamie the same year. My mother left when I was seven. So you see, I already lost a parent twice, my real mother and my adopted mother. There is no way that my dad would do that to me again on purpose."

She couldn't have hit the mark harder with me if she knew my whole history. My dad left when I was 11. I knew what it felt like to be abandoned by a parent. And I understood her need to believe that her father hadn't let her down, whatever his own situation. But maybe the kindest thing I could do was to try and lay it out for her and help her start to accept reality.

"I get why you feel like that. But I talked to Detective Ross. He said your dad had a lot on his mind—financial issues, your brother's drug problems. That night he was drinking, he mixed it with medication, and he decided he wanted out. Do you know what kind of money problems he was having?"

"He invested a lot of money in what turned out to be a pyramid scheme. Kind of like that man in New York. Bernie Madoff. Only not as big. My dad did lose a lot, but it's not like we were poverty-stricken. He knew he could recover. Money wasn't that important to him. He wouldn't kill himself over something like that."

"Isabel, one thing that's really hard to get around is the way he was found."

"I know. He was in his study, slumped in a chair. The gun dropped beside him on the floor. I can still see it when I close my eyes." She shuddered. "I understand how it seems. But there were other things. Things the police wouldn't pay any attention to."

"Like what?"

She let go of her cup and leaned forward.

"There was no suicide note. And he had appointments scheduled for the next day—a haircut, a massage."

"People don't always leave notes. And haircuts or massages, they could be standing appointments."

She plowed on, determined to make me see.

"There's more. He ordered a book online that night. It came three days later. I have the receipt. He printed it out and put it in his file. Who orders a book, files the receipt, then shoots himself? And that night he even took a pound of Hook's 15-year-old cheddar out of the refrigerator and set it on the counter. It was still on the cutting board when I went into the kitchen. If it was some kind of 'last meal,' like the sheriff's detective said, wouldn't he have eaten it?"

OK, she had me at cheese. In Wisconsin we respect our cheese. To set out a hunk of Hook's cheddar and not even take a taste of it, that was sacrilege. Especially when it goes for $50 a pound.

"All right, maybe there are some inconsistencies. But remember, he had both Klonopin and alcohol in his system. He probably wasn't thinking all that clearly, and he may have been more worried than you knew."

"He wasn't drunk, if that's what you're saying. At least he wasn't when he called me. And he didn't use Klonopin."

"Wait a minute. Your father called you?" That was a detail Ross had declined to share.

She nodded.

"Where were you?"

"I was east of Cleveland, driving home from the Adirondacks. I'd been visiting my old roommate at Blue Mountain Lake, at her family's cabin. We were supposed to stay until Monday, but on Saturday night Lauren's grandmother had a stroke and she left right away. I took off Sunday morning. I got as far as somewhere outside of Cleveland when it started raining so hard I stopped for the night. Dad called me around quarter to 12. Well, 11, Wisconsin time."

"What did he say?"

"He was worried. About Jamie."

"Why?"

"Jamie had a problem with prescription drugs in high school, but he's been really good for a long time. My dad sent him to this therapeutic boarding school in Maine his senior year. You know, a school for kids with substance abuse issues. He did great there. Then he enrolled at Himmel Technical College after he graduated, to get his grades up. This fall he started at UW. He even decided to stay at home for the first semester, just to, you know, stay grounded. Everything was good. I thought."

"So what made your dad worried?"

"Jamie was starting to behave like he used to, sleeping a lot, taking off, acting kind of out of it. When Dad told me that, I asked him to look in my medicine cabinet. The Klonopin I had last year for anxiety was gone. I didn't use it, because I didn't like how it made me feel. I should've dumped it, but I forgot about it. I felt terrible, like I'd, I don't know, tempted Jamie. I told Dad I'd come straight home. He didn't want me driving that late at night that far, but I knew I wouldn't be able to sleep.

"I left right away, but I had to get gas and it was still raining pretty hard, so I didn't make as fast time as I wanted to. I got home around 8:30 in the morning. Jamie's car was in the driveway, and there was a light on in Dad's study. I went right in, and…" For the first time she lost her composure. She gave a shudder and her voice trailed off. After a minute she took a drink of her coffee and started again.

"Don't you see? My dad wouldn't call, ask me to come home, say we had to help Jamie, and then kill himself. He knew I was coming home and I'd be there by 8:30. He'd never, never make me be the one to find him. He wouldn't."

I felt sad and sorry and unsure I could offer her anything but the pity that she didn't want. She read my expression.

"It's no use, is it? You're not going to help me."

"I want to help you, Isabel. But I'm not sure helping you believe your father was murdered is the way to do it. You realize, the way he was killed, it would have to be someone he knew, someone he trusted. Someone who could get very close to him. It wouldn't be a random killing."

She looked surprised then, as though she'd been so determined to prove that her dad didn't shoot himself that she hadn't really considered who else might have. But she rallied.

"Well, sure, of course. I mean, you said it yourself. We can't know what goes on inside people's heads. Maybe it was a patient or a friend even, or maybe, I don't know, a neighbor?"

"All right, who then? Who might have had a reason to kill your father? Did he have problems with a business deal, or a patient who died, or a relationship that ended badly? Someone who envied him, or resented him, or blamed him for something?"

She put both hands to her forehead and rubbed her temples, all the while saying, "I don't know. I just don't know."

"What about your brother Jamie? You said his car was there. Where was he?"

"He was passed out cold in his room. Didn't even know anything had happened, could barely remember getting home. Dad must already have been dead when he got there."

"He didn't see anything? Didn't he go by your father's study?"

"No. He always comes in through the kitchen and up the back stairs to his room on the third floor. Dad's study is at the front of the house, on the opposite end from Jamie's bedroom."

"What does Jamie think about things?"

"It's hard to tell what Jamie thinks. He doesn't want to talk. I think he feels guilty, because he and Dad weren't getting along, and he was in the house and didn't even know Dad was dead. I'm having a hard time communicating with him right now."

"And you've told all this to Detective Ross? You didn't hold anything back?"

"I told him. I told the sheriff. I even tried to get Mr. Timmins, the district attorney, to talk to me, but I never even got past one of his assistants. Everyone thinks I'm just a hysterical daughter who can't let go. You do, too, don't you?" Her voice held both frustration and accusation.

I didn't answer, thinking about Charlie Ross investigating Lacey's death, and how he had been content with surface appearances. And how he had resented me trying to dig deeper. And how people's patterns are hard to change. Maybe he had done the same with Garrett Whiting. I tried to talk myself out of what I already knew I was going to do, but I didn't succeed.

"OK. I'm not saying that you're right, or that I can do anything about it. But I will poke around a little. That's all I can promise."

She jumped out of her seat and came over to hug me, just as Mrs. Schimelman came by with coffees and an order of linzer for another table. Long years of experience allowed her to swerve her large frame with a ballet dancer's grace. She set the pastry and drinks down without incident.

"I'm so sorry," Isabel said.

"It's OK. No worries. You need to chill. I bring you a rugelach. You say you don't want none, but you skin and bones." She shoved the pastry in Isabel's direction.

Isabel sank back into her chair, smiled the first really happy smile I'd seen from her, and took a bite of the crescent-shaped cookie filled with apricot jam. Satisfied, Mrs. Schimelman moved on.

"Do you want to come to the house? Do you want to meet my brother?"

"Well, to start, I'll need to talk to some of the people who knew your father pretty well. See what their take is on his mental state, anything he might have confided that could shed light on his death. Any ideas?"

"I suppose Dr. Bergman. He's my dad's associate in the surgical practice. I don't really know him, but he's worked pretty closely with my father for the past couple of years."

"OK. Who else?"

"Ummm, maybe Frankie Saxon? She's a counselor at Himmel High School. Maybe you know her?"

I shook my head. "Must have been after my time." Which now that I thought about it had been 15 years ago. How did I get so old so fast?

"She helped my dad a lot when Jamie got into trouble with drugs. She found the place for him to get straight. I don't know, but Dad might have called her about Jamie, too."

"Her name is Frankie?"

"Francesca, actually, but she goes by Frankie."

"Anyone else?"

She thought for a minute. "Not really. Dad didn't have a lot of friends. He was always so busy with his practice. Oh, probably Miss Quellman could help, too. She was my father's office manager forever. And then there's Miller Caldwell, the lawyer. The one who used to be president of the bank? He knew Dad for a long time."

I was familiar with Miller Caldwell. He'd been pivotal in my sister's case, and I was pretty sure he'd give me any help he could. "That sounds like a good start."

"Thank you, Leah, you have no idea what this means to me." She reached out and put her hand on my arm. I gave it a squeeze with my other hand. There was something about her that got to me, I had to admit.

"I'll be in touch."

CHAPTER 5

"CHICA, I DON'T KNOW ABOUT THIS."

Miguel stretched his long legs out from under the scarred wooden table. It was Thursday night, and the paper was put to bed. We were having a post-production dinner and drinks at McClain's, an old-school bar I love. It's filled with duct-taped vinyl booths, rickety tables, and the faint acrid smell of cigarettes gone but not forgotten. The waitress doesn't kneel beside your table, introduce herself, and then interrupt you every 10 minutes to ask how everything is. At McClain's, they don't care how everything is. I respect that.

"What don't you know?"

"Dr. Whiting. The suicide. Isabel, sure, she doesn't want to think her papá killed himself. But..." his voice trailed off.

"But what would be his reason for committing suicide?" Nothing like an opposing viewpoint to throw me into devil's advocate mode. "Garrett Whiting was worried about his son. He wanted to help him. And he talked to Isabel that night and asked her to come home. He knew she was leaving right away. What kind of father would shoot himself in the head and leave his daughter to find him?"

"But how could someone else do it? And make it look like Dr. Whiting did it himself?"

I'd been thinking about that ever since I left Isabel.

"I have a theory," I began, but then I felt two large hands clamp down on either side of my neck and give a squeeze. My shoulders shot up and I gave an involuntary shiver.

"I'll bet you do."

I looked up at Coop looming over me.

"Quit it."

He let go and sat down in the chair next to me, shrugging out of his leather bomber jacket and pulling his HPD cap off his short black hair. Before he could say anything else a waitress materialized at his side.

Short and curvy with curly brown hair and round brown eyes, Sherry Young had a crush on Coop that had lasted through high school, marriage, two kids, and her divorce.

"Hi, Coop. Leinenkugel? You want a cheeseburger basket?"

"No thanks. I'll just have a beer, Sherry. I've got somewhere to go."

"Oh, that's too bad. I get off in a little while. I thought maybe you'd like to play in the dart tournament with me," she said, giving him a big smile and touching him lightly on the arm. He ignored the amused looks Miguel and I exchanged, and as Sherry walked away he asked, "What's your theory about?"

"She thinks Dr. Whiting was murdered," Miguel said.

"How did you come up with that?"

"What if someone staged Whiting's murder to make it look like suicide?"

"That seems pretty unlikely. You've been watching *Law & Order* marathons again, haven't you?"

"No, listen. What if Whiting was kind of out of it? You know, he had his evening rum and Coke or whatever, and maybe he was anxious, upset about his son, so he took some Klonopin. Maybe more than he should have. That stuff can knock you out. I slept right through the dental surgery Paul did on me last month. And you know my primal dental fear. Sleeping in the dentist chair is not something I do."

"Yes, but you didn't shoot yourself in the head, did you?"

"The point is, I don't remember anything about it, from the time I sat down until they shook me on the shoulder and said it was over. And they had me turning my head and lifting my tongue and they were jabbing things into my mouth. They could have put a gun in my hand if they'd wanted to. Isn't it possible that if Whiting was under the influence of Klonopin plus alcohol, someone he knew and trusted could put the gun in his hand, move it up to his head and pull the trigger? And there's another thing, Isabel says her father didn't use Klonopin."

Then, before he could raise the objection, I did it myself. "I know, it wouldn't be hard for a doctor to get some if he wanted to. But it also wouldn't be hard for someone to give it to him, if *they* wanted to."

I could tell Coop was turning it over in his mind before he shook his head. Lots of times Coop and I don't agree, but I have to admit he usually gives my ideas a thorough think through before he shoots them down. "I haven't seen the report, but if you think Occam's Razor here—the simplest explanation is usually the right one—Charlie probably got it right."

"Occam's Razor is about probability, not fact. Shouldn't we make sure all the facts are present and correct before deciding on the probable explanation?"

"She's got a point, yes?" Miguel asked with a wink at me.

"Don't encourage her."

"Here you go." Sherry had arrived with his beer. She leaned in as close as she could without falling into his lap as she put the drink in front of him.

"Thanks." He moved almost imperceptibly to the left.

"Sherry, mi bonita, you are killin' it tonight. New highlights in your hair?"

"Thanks, Miguel, I'm glad somebody noticed. Can I get you a refill?"

"No, gracias, I'm good."

"Hey, what about me?"

"What about you?"

"A refill? Another Jameson please."

"Drowning your sorrows, Leah?"

"What are you talking about?"

"Oh, I get it. Good for you. Who cares if your boyfriend was in here last night with a really hot redhead, and they were all over each other." She smiled sweetly.

"Yay for Ben. I'm glad he found somebody."

"If that's your story." She shrugged. "Another shot and you might even believe it."

I considered my range of rejoinders, but she left before I could get one out.

"I didn't know you and Ben broke up."

"We didn't. We weren't together. Not really. Not a big deal. Maybe I should have written it up for the paper." I returned to the main issue. "Whether it's probable or not, admit it's possible that someone staged Whiting's death to look like a suicide."

"Maybe. What about the victimology?"

"What?"

"Victimology, you know, looking at the victim's life, relationships, reputation, habits. Did he have future plans? Was he in financial trouble?"

"I don't know enough yet. I haven't seen the file, and when I ran into Ross he wasn't too keen on me getting my hands on it."

"I doubt that will stop you," he said. "When you do get a look, pay less attention to the weapon and the body—the sheriff's department and the M.E. will have that covered. You're not likely to see anything they didn't. But if Charlie made assumptions because it looked like suicide, he might not have asked all the questions he could have."

"Oh, I'm sure he made assumptions. Isabel said she tried to point a couple of things out to him, but you know what a dolt he is."

Coop shook his head.

"What?"

"It's not your job to ride to the rescue for this Isabel. And it's not going to make your life any easier if you get on the wrong side of the sheriff's department again. Do you really want to tangle with Ross?"

"I'm not rescuing her. I'm investigating her story. And the only reason I might 'tangle' with Ross is if he got it all wrong again. I'm just asking questions, that's all."

"Are you sure? Sounds like you already have your mind made up."

"Yes, I'm sure. I just don't think Isabel Whiting's concerns should be dismissed."

"Now you're mad."

"No." And I wasn't. Well, maybe a little.

As Sherry set my refill down he said, "What does Rebecca think about it?"

"I haven't told her yet. I have to figure out a way to swing her to my side first."

"Your boss? I'd be careful if I was you. You just might get yourself fired again," Sherry injected.

"And if I were you, I'd be talking to customers who cared. But oh, you're not me. So you'll probably just stand here annoying us."

"C'mon, Leah," Coop said, as Sherry sniffed and walked away. He finished his beer in one long swallow and set it on the table. "Well, I gotta go. Just think about it, will you? Make sure you're not just following up on this to piss Ross off."

"Why are you in such a hurry?"

"Maybe he has a mystery date," Miguel said.

"No mystery. Just places to go." He stood up and put his jacket on, then put some money on the table for his bill. "See you later."

"Right. See you."

Something was up with Coop, but I figured I'd find out sooner or later. After he left I finished my Jameson. "Time for me to go, too."

"Chica, hey, I'll give you a ride."

I started to protest, but two whiskeys in an hour and the level of tired I felt made me reconsider. I definitely didn't need a DUI.

"OK, thanks."

"Why are you always so hard on Sherry?" Miguel asked as we got into his car.

"I'm not."

"Sí, you are. Do you want Coop for yourself?"

I shook my head.

"Coop's my best friend. Since we were 12. That's how we like it, you know that."

"Then why do you always hate his girlfriends?"

"I don't," I said in surprise. "Why would you say that?"

"Sherry has a crush. So? Coop's a man steak, you know, lots of ladies want to eat him up."

"Well, I just think he could do better than Sherry, don't you?"

Miguel didn't answer.

"OK. OK. Maybe I do come on too strong with her. She just irritates me. I guess I could ease up. A little."

He smiled. "So you don't want Ben, and you don't want Coop, who do you want?"

"I want a man I know I can't have." I raised an eyebrow in his direction to make my point.

"You have my heart, chica. It's just my body you can't get next to."

I laughed.

"As long as your heart's in my corner. You know I'm not just out to get Ross, don't you?"

"I know. What can I do?"

"You could tap into the gossip grapevine at your aunt's salon." Miguel's Aunt Lydia owns Making Waves, a trendy hair styling place with a wide-ranging clientele.

"Sure. I'm helping out there tomorrow while Aunt Lydia goes to Milwaukee with Uncle Craig."

"Another doctor's appointment?" Since his uncle's kidney issues had worsened, it seemed like all Miguel's aunt and uncle did was an endless round of doctor and dialysis appointments.

"No, not this time. He's feeling OK. They're going to visit friends. They have to take the good days when they come."

"I guess that's true. So what are you going to do at the salon? Wax eyebrows, do some highlights, a few makeovers?"

"What? You think I can't handle it? Oh. I can. I'm the best shampoo boy north of Chicago. Believe it."

"I do, I do. Now listen good while you're massaging that conditioner through some Himmel matron's hair. See if you can find any Garrett Whiting gossip to give me."

"That's violating shampoo boy/client confidentiality. But for you, I'll do it."

"I appreciate it."

"Why don't you stop by?"

"Oh, no. Don't start," I said, as he reached over and lifted my baseball cap off my head, causing my hair to tumble down on my shoulders.

I leaned away and picked up a strand of my own hair. In an exaggerated version of Miguel's speech patterns I crooned, "Oh, chica, some copper highlights. A little green eyeshadow, a wash of brown—your hazel eyes will spark."

"I don't sound like that."

"Yes. You do. I've only heard you say it to me about a hundred times. Why don't you love me the way I am?"

"You know I love you. But you could look so fierce. You just won't try. How can I get you with somebody if you won't even try? I'm not giving up."

"Oh yeah you are. Let it go. Hey," I said as we buckled in and he pulled on to the street, "how did you get Rebecca to let you off tomorrow?"

"I keep telling you. She's not so bad."

"Not how I see it, my friend. She just doesn't like me. How can that be? I think I'm very charming, don't you? Don't answer that."

As we rounded the corner I saw a red SUV parked next to the curb in front of my house.

"Expecting company?"

I started to shake my head, but stopped when the door of the SUV opened. Illuminated by the cab light was a figure I knew very well. What I didn't know was what the hell he was doing here.

"I can stay, chica," Miguel said, seeing my shocked expression. I was already unbuckled and had my hand on the door handle.

"No, that's OK." I tried to slip away without further comment, but Miguel was not down with that.

"No. I'm not leaving you alone in the dark with a stranger," he said as he unbuckled his own seatbelt. Since I definitely didn't need a third party at this meeting, I came clean as I leaned my head back in.

"It's OK, Miguel. It's my husband. My ex-husband that is, Nick Gallagher."

Miguel's eyes widened and his mouth was working, but nothing came out. Before anything did, I said, "Thanks for the ride. I'll talk to you later. Bye."

CHAPTER 6

I TURNED TO MEET Nick as he walked up.

"What are you doing here?"

"Nice to see you, too."

We had tripped the light sensor above the garage door, and as it came on I saw that six years after the fact—the fact of our divorce—he looked just the same. A piece of fine, wheat-colored hair fell across his forehead in a way I'd once thought endearing. His sea-green eyes held a familiar glint of amusement, as though he were in on some joke the rest of us weren't. When he smiled, his eyes crinkled at the corners and he revealed a set of perfect teeth. He looked like a man confident and at ease with his place in the world. The only thing that betrayed a hint of discomfort was the way his hand slid the zipper on his open jacket up and down, making a faint sawing sound. Suitable background music to our conversation. He tried again.

"Leah, it's great to see you."

"Really? Why?" I opened my purse and started digging for my house key.

"Don't be like that. We're divorced. We don't have to be enemies." He reached out and touched my arm. I felt the involuntary little shock I used to get when he touched me unexpectedly.

"I'm not your enemy, Nick. But I don't want to be friends. So, thanks for stopping by and goodnight."

"Wait. Leah, come on. Can't I come in? Just for a minute. I've been waiting here for over an hour, and it's pretty cold. Just a cup of coffee, and I'm on my way. OK?"

Curiosity warred with my instinctive urge to say no. Curiosity won.

"All right." I pushed the door open, and over my shoulder added, "For a minute."

I turned on the light, dropped my purse on the table and hung my jacket on the hook near the kitchen door. As I put the coffee on, Nick took his coat off and draped it over the back of a chair, then went to the cupboard and took out two mugs and set them on the counter. Something about the easy way he moved around the kitchen annoyed me. Nick always made himself at home. No matter whose home it was.

He walked past the bar that separates the kitchen and living room, picked up a photo or two on the mantel and looked at them, then came back and sat down at the table.

"Looks like your mother has done some redecorating. The living room's a different color, isn't it?"

"She's had a hard time finding a job since Karen's law firm closed. She's been channeling her energy into fixing up the place. But you didn't come all the way from Michigan to have a Martha Stewart moment with me. What do you want?"

I added creamer to his cup of coffee and set it down in front of him, then took the chair opposite, my arms folded across my chest.

"Oh-oh. I know that Leah look." He slipped into a Ricky Ricardo accent. "You've got some 'splainin' to do, Nicky."

I didn't crack a smile.

"You're not making this easy, you know."

"That's not my job description anymore. Making things easy for you."

"Are you really still so angry at me?"

To buy some time, I got up and poured myself a cup of coffee. When I sat back down, I spoke slowly, trying to figure out my truth as I talked.

"I'm not mad at you any more, Nick. I'm surprised to see you, and a little curious. And a little annoyed, maybe, that you think you can just drop back into my life without notice. I guess I just don't care enough about you anymore to be angry with you."

"A little harsh. But honest as always, that's my Leah." His smile was so warm it reminded me of all the things I liked about him. Then he started talking again and reminded me of all the things I didn't.

"How did I let you get away?"

"You didn't let me get away. You cheated on me, and you lied to me, and then you blamed your affair with Seraphim or Cherubim or whatever her name was on me. I was too intimidating, I was too intense, I expected too much from you." I knew perfectly well what her name was. Seraphina. A tall, exotically beautiful graduate assistant in the psychology department where Nick had been a temporary faculty member. "You knocked me down. I got back up. But there's no need to cover old ground. Just tell me what you want."

"I want to say I'm sorry. I'm sorry I wasn't good enough for you. You were always so strong, so absolutely sure you knew the way things should be—the way I should be. You never needed my approval. But maybe I needed yours, and when I felt like I couldn't get it, I looked elsewhere. I'm sorry."

"A pro tip for you: When asking forgiveness, it's not a good move to tell your victim it was really all her fault."

"Victim? That's not something you ever were."

"Oh yeah. I was."

I didn't elaborate. No way was I going to admit that I was a victim of my own insecurities. That when I met Nick, I wanted him to love me so much that I surrendered whole parts of myself. I pretended to be less smart, less vulnerable, less strong-willed, less driven. At the same time, I wanted him to see me as more than I was—more confident, more giving, more patient—more worth loving. Because I didn't believe then that anyone could really love me as I was.

I still have my doubts, but I'm a lot more attached to my sense of self now. My real self. That doesn't mean I don't realize there are things I need to change. Only now I try to change them for myself, not for anyone else.

"Wait. This isn't going the way I wanted it to. I'm not saying it right. Let me try again. You know, you really can be a little terrifying. I did some terrible things, Leah. Whatever the reasons, there are no excuses. I hope you can forgive me."

I had once longed to hear those words, to feel the satisfaction of Nick admitting he was a liar, a cheat, a hypocrite. Now though, when he uttered them, or came as close as he probably ever would, I didn't feel the thrill of victory I'd imagined. Instead, I felt the urge to back away from the moment, to retreat from the emotions threatening to burst to the surface. So I did.

"You drove seven hours to ask forgiveness for something that happened seven years ago?"

"I didn't come here from Michigan. I've been teaching a class on Thursday nights at Himmel Tech."

"You're living in Himmel?" I certainly don't know everybody in a town of 15,000, but it was hard to believe if Nick were here, somebody wouldn't have run into him and mentioned it to me.

"Not in Himmel. I have a tenure track position at Robley College in Clarkson. I'm covering a class at Himmel Tech for a friend of mine. He's out for the semester, and I can use the money."

"Tenure track? That's good, I'm glad for you."

During our brief marriage Nick had been frustrated by his temporary faculty status at Grand Valley State University outside of Grand Rapids, Michigan, where I worked for the *Grand Rapids Press*. Tenure track positions aren't easy to come by, and he was always worried he'd be a temporary for life.

"You are? Really?"

"Yes, really. I know it's what you always wanted."

That smile again. "That's great to hear. But I need you to hear what I'm saying, however badly I've been saying it. I own what I did. I'm sorry I hurt you. I apologize."

"All right. All right. OK, I forgive you. I wasn't perfect either—though I never cheated on you." I couldn't resist adding that.

"I know. You wouldn't. If I had it to do over again, I wouldn't either, but, well, here we are."

"Yep. Here we are."

We were both quiet for a few seconds and drank our coffee as though that simple act took all of our attention. Then he spoke again.

"So, how are things going for you? I read about Lacey and everything last year, and I wanted to call, but I didn't have the courage. I didn't think you'd want to hear from me, and I didn't want to make things any worse for you. I didn't know what to say."

"That's OK. There really wasn't anything to say. I'm glad we know the truth, that's all."

Another strained silence ensued, during which we both focused on our coffee again, as though it were a magic elixir to promote small talk.

Finally I said, "I got a book deal. I'm working on the final proofs now. Supposed to come out in February."

"A book? Really? That's great. So you're not going to be staying in Himmel? I was surprised when I heard you were back here. You're too good to be stuck at a small town paper."

"Yeah, well, thanks. I kind of blew things at my job in Miami and bounced back here to regroup. Hopefully the book thing takes off. We'll see."

"That's great," he repeated. "Really great."

"So, what about you? Do you like teaching at a small school?"

"Yeah, sure. Robley's a really good liberal arts college. We get a lot of top students. I've only been there a year, but I can see a future for me there."

"That's good. What about family? Are you married, kids?"

"No, not married. How about you?"

"No, nothing to report."

"Still love 'em and leave 'em, Leah?"

"Yeah, right."

"What about your friend Coop? Where's he these days?"

"He's back in Himmel, too. He's a lieutenant in the police department."

He nodded. "I'm not surprised. He seemed like a basic good guy."

"You say that like you think being honest, and reliable, and trustworthy is dull. Oh, that's right. You do."

"Hey, that wasn't a criticism. I mean he seems like a capable, nice, guy. Seriously. So, how's life at the *Himmel Times?*"

"Oh, you know. A lot of meetings to cover, Cranberry Queen pageant, local elections, zoning board controversy, that kind of thing."

"Sounds pretty deadly."

"It's a living. Though I just started looking into something that could turn interesting."

"Really? What?" He lifted his eyebrows just a little and raised his cup to his lips.

And then, for reasons unclear to me—maybe I wanted to show off a little, impress him with my investigative know-how, make my life sound a little more exciting than it was—I started telling him about Isabel Whiting, and Garrett's death, and the odd things surrounding it.

"I might be a little dense, but how do you think someone could kill him with his own gun and not leave traces? Walk me through it." He leaned forward a little, as though nothing was more interesting to him than whatever I had to say. Nick could be a great listener when he wanted to be. And I find it hard to resist a receptive audience.

"It would have to be someone he knew, someone he trusted, OK? Maybe an old friend stops by to see him. Suggests they have a drink, maybe he offers to make it. Or," I said, warming to my subject, "maybe the friend brought a bottle laced with Klonopin with him. He makes a drink for Garrett, has something else himself. When Garrett gets woozy from the drug and alcohol mix, the friend slips on the gloves he has in his pocket, takes the gun out of the desk, puts it in Garrett's hand, holds it to his head and presses the trigger. Then he takes his bottle, washes out his own glass, puts it away, and goes. Doesn't matter if his fingerprints are in the room. He's someone Garrett knows, and it wouldn't be unusual to find his prints there."

"But how would he know Garrett had a gun in his desk? And that it was loaded?"

"He's a friend. Friends know things."

"What about motive?"

"That's what I have to figure out. You're a psychologist. Do you think a man like Garrett Whiting, who had a son who needed him, and a daughter who'd already been abandoned by her mother, do you think he would just suddenly kill himself and leave them totally alone?"

"Leah, I don't know anything about Garrett Whiting. It wouldn't be professional—or helpful—for me to guess at what motivated him. Not to get too technical on you, but people do crazy things."

True that. Before I could say anything, my mother came bursting through the door.

CHAPTER 7

"I'M TELLING YOU, if Bernard Magnuson winds up dead, you can put me at the top of the suspect list." She had half-turned to slip off her coat and hang her keys on the hook by the door, and was so wound up she didn't notice Nick's presence.

"We had a knockdown drag out at parish council tonight. He's the most intolerant, self-righteous, hypocritical so-called 'Christian' I've ever seen. Everyone knows he can't keep it in his pants, but he thinks he can pass judgment on a woman who made a mistake, then worked her butt off to turn her life around. He doesn't think it's 'appropriate' for Kim Granville to serve on the school board. Because she has a son and she's never been married. He should be—" By this time she had turned back to face us.

"Nick! What are you doing here?"

"Still like mother, like daughter I see. Hi, Carol. I was just leaving. I stopped by to see Leah for a minute. I'm sure she'll tell you all about it." As he spoke, he'd risen, slipped on his jacket, and moved toward the door.

"Just think about what I said, Leah. I really mean it. Call me if you want to. Good to see you, Carol." And he was gone.

"Well, you are absolutely not calling him. Are you?"

"No, Mom. I'm not planning on it."

"What was he doing here? Why did you let him in?"

"Take it easy." I filled her in.

"I hope you're not going to fall for that man again. You had to move all the way to the ends of the earth to get over him."

"North Carolina is hardly the 'ends of the earth.' Don't worry, he wants me to forgive him, not get back together with him. I was pretty hostile when I first saw him—"

"Hold on to that feeling."

"No, I don't think I will. I'm glad he came by tonight, because while I wasn't looking, I guess I really did get over it. I'm not mad anymore, because I don't care any more. And the time we were together taught me something important. That's it's never worth giving up who I am."

She looked at me the way she used to when, caught with crumbs on my mouth, I had vigorously denied any knowledge of missing cookies. "I hope that's true. But you know, if a nice, not-Nick man comes along, you could just disguise a few things, couldn't you? You know, like your smartass remarks, and your need to win every argument? I would like to have grandchildren before I'm too old to play with them."

"Not listening. Let's move on." I had to give her something to get off Nick, so I filled her in on Isabel.

"You're all in already, aren't you? No matter what you're saying to me or telling yourself, you've made up your mind that Isabel needs you."

"Don't say it. Don't tell me Isabel isn't Lacey. I know that."

"That isn't what I was going to say."

"Oh really?"

"I was going to say that Isabel isn't you. You're drawn to her because she's on some hopeless quest and no one will believe or help her. Just like you were with Lacey."

"Yeah? And look what happened. Look what I found out."

She sighed. "You're responding to how bad she hurts. You know how that feels. I'm not saying don't help her. All I'm saying is know why you're doing it, and know when to stop."

"Don't worry, I've got this. I know what I'm doing and why. Like I know I'm going to bed now. I'm exhausted. See you in the morning."

Shortly after I got into bed, I heard my mother's door close, and about 10 minutes later the muffled sound of her regular deep breathing, just shy of a soft snore. I tried to sleep, but I couldn't. Too much going on in my head. Finally I got up, threw on jeans and a sweatshirt, and headed over to the place I go when I need help thinking.

"How are things at work?"

It was 11:30 p.m. and I was sitting in the warm and cozy kitchen of the Reverend Gregory Lindstrom's brown brick bungalow. A little late for conventional visiting, but our friendship has never been conventional. He's a Roman Catholic priest; I'm a non-believer—or at least a skeptic. He's thoughtful, patient, and wise. I'm, well, not. But he listens, he doesn't judge, and he doesn't give advice unless I ask for it.

"Ugh. Same as they have been since Rebecca showed up. More work, less help. Rebecca's job is to cut costs, and boy has she ever. A friend of mine from J school works at a paper where they send all their copy to a 'pagination hub.' In Malaysia. They got rid of local copy editors and proofers and graphic designers and do all the editing and layout out for a bunch of papers from there. That's not us yet, but it could be, if Rebecca or her corporate overlords decide that's the next step."

"I suppose that's more efficient, to centralize things."

"Maybe, but copy editors in the hubs don't know the towns, the issues, the people being reported on. My friend said when his town's basketball team won the state championship, the hub copy editors misspelled the team name—twice. Local people don't like it. They want

51

their local news, and they want it right. When they don't get it, they cancel. And when enough people cancel, the paper folds. That's what I see in Himmel's future. A town without a paper. And Rebecca couldn't care less."

"Aren't you being a little hard on her?" His pale eyes blinked behind his glasses.

I considered. "Possibly. I mean I get that it's her job to tighten things up. But how can she like a job where her whole purpose is to prepare the paper for slaughter? The hedge fund that owns us and a lot of other papers—they just want to suck us dry, then sell or shut us down."

"Maybe she doesn't like it. Maybe she doesn't have another option. You know very little about her and the struggles she may have faced."

"I'll take favorite Gregory Lindstrom quotes for $250, Alex. 'Remember that everyone you meet is afraid of something, loves something, and has lost something.' Am I right?"

He nodded and took a sip of tea from his favorite *X-Files* mug. I felt a rush of affection for the compact little priest with his fluffy white hair and kind eyes. He always listened as though nothing I had to say, not any of my secret shames, or sorrows, or regrets, shocked him, or angered him, or moved him to anything but quiet compassion.

"OK. I don't know what she's going through, or has been through, or why she acts the way she does. I shouldn't personalize it." I waited. "Is that it? Is that what you're trying to get me to see?"

He smiled full-on then. He really has a lovely smile. It starts in the corners of his mouth and slides on up his chubby little cheeks until it rests right in the center of his light blue eyes.

"You'll see what you need to when the time is right, Leah. I have every confidence in you."

"I wish a few more people did."

He raised an eyebrow and gave me an inquiring look.

"I'm starting work on a story, and I'm the only one who thinks it could be a story. I got this call from Isabel Whiting, Garrett Whiting's daughter. You know, the doctor who died last month."

"And?"

I explained Isabel's conviction that her dad hadn't killed himself and her reasons.

"Garrett's behavior is a little odd, I agree. But I find people, especially troubled people, can do very inexplicable things."

"You say 'Garrett' like you know him. Were the Whitings part of St. Stephen's parish?"

"No. I knew Garrett years ago, when he was a young doctor in Milwaukee. I worked part-time as a chaplain at St. Cyprian's Hospital. But I haven't even had a conversation with him in many years."

"Was he the kind of person to get someone mad enough to kill him?"

"One could argue we're all that sort of person, depending on what someone else wants or needs from us, and what we're willing to give."

"Well then, do you think he was the kind of person who would kill himself?"

"That was a long time ago, and I certainly didn't know him well enough to judge. Suicide is a complicated affair."

"You sound like Nick." The words were out of my mouth before I could stop them. I hadn't come here to talk about Nick. Or had I?

"That's your former husband?"

"That's the one. He stopped by to have me grant him absolution."

"I see. And did you?"

"Yeah. Pretty much. I guess so."

Father Lindstrom is really good at the silence trick. You know, don't comment, just let the silence hang there. Most people can't stand it and will start babbling. Myself included.

"It's not like I think he's fundamentally changed. He'll always do what's best for Nick, but maybe it's best for me to let that anger go."

He nodded.

"I mean, how long can you stay mad at someone? We're not exactly BFFs now. He has his life, and I have mine. And now I feel like I can actually wish him well. That's all."

"That sounds like quite a lot."

I stood up and put my mug in the sink.

As he walked me to the front door I said, "Who knows? Maybe I'm turning into a brand new me. All forgiveness, all the time."

He smiled, and just before he closed the door he said, "I like the old you just fine, Leah."

I love that guy.

CHAPTER 8

THE NEXT MORNING I tapped lightly on Rebecca's office door with the hand that held a pastry bag containing two rugelachs from the Elite. In the other was a cardboard holder with a chai latte and an extra large, extra bold cup of coffee, black. Rebecca's favorite poison.

"Come in."

It still took me aback whenever I entered her lair. The office that my old boss Max had inhabited for almost 40 years was now unrecognizable. Gone were the teetering stacks of files, the dusty bowling trophies, the jar of M&Ms, the occasional petrified remnant of a bygone feast. Instead there were freshly painted walls in a neutral beige with bright white moldings, wooden floors restored to their golden oak glory, and a sleek glass and metal desk. Even Max's favorite rocking/rolling cushioned office chair had been replaced by an ergonomically correct and aggressively modern version. The desktop was so clean I hesitated to put my tributes on it.

I sat down without waiting to be asked.

"Hey. I got you a treat at the Elite. Coffee, just the way you like it. And rugelach fresh this morning."

"Thanks for the coffee. I don't snack. I have a high protein breakfast at home and nothing else until lunch."

I almost said, "Of course you do." But I held it in. *Keep your eyes on the prize, Leah.*

"Healthier, I'm sure."

"So, what do we have, Leah? A suspicious suicide or a delusional daughter?"

"I'm not sure yet." I gave her the rundown, and while I talked she made notes on a yellow legal pad she'd pulled from a side drawer.

"Well, what do you think?" I sat on the edge of my chair, poised to launch a fusillade of reasons why it warranted further investigation.

She didn't answer right away. Instead, she steepled her fingers and looked at me, her eyes slightly narrowed. As I waited, I tried to figure out what was going on beneath the polished exterior. But I couldn't get past the surface: straight white-blonde hair that swept the top of her shoulders, every strand falling into perfect alignment. A long, thin nose offset by a generous mouth. A faint v-shaped wrinkle between her eyebrows that deepened when she concentrated. I noticed it was just beginning to leave a permanent trace even when her forehead relaxed. But it was her eyes that demanded attention. A glacier blue rarely warmed by a smile. Her unwavering gaze warned a person not to trespass, not to get too close. What had happened to make her so wary? I wondered. Then with a start I realized she was talking to me.

"Sorry, what?"

"I said all right. Go ahead. But keep it low key. You can do low key can't you, Leah?"

"All right? You mean start interviews, get the file?" I had expected her to reject the idea, initially anyway, because it might upset people, hurt the bottom line, make waves, any of the things that a good, true story can do.

"That's what 'go ahead' means, isn't it?" She permitted herself a small smile, but it was gone in seconds, a flash of sunlight overwhelmed by a leaden sky.

"OK. Just so we're clear. You're saying I can ask for the case file, I can interview Ross or the sheriff. I can follow up on any leads I come up with. Is that right?"

"What's the matter, you can't take yes for an answer?"

"No. I mean yes. I just don't usually hear 'Go for it,' from you, that's all."

"Don't make me regret it. You did hear the 'low key' part, right?"

"Oh, yeah. Right. Absolutely." I stood up to go before she changed her mind.

As I reached the door she said, "Leah."

I turned back to look at her. "Yeah?"

"Don't take any unnecessary pokes at Charlie Ross, all right?"

"Sure, OK. And, uh, thanks Rebecca."

So that just happened. But why?

It had been easy to get an appointment to talk to Grantland County Sheriff Lester Dillingham. His secretary Jennifer Pilarski (née Naseman) is always in a sunny mood. She and I had been academically and alphabetically linked from kindergarten through high school. Almost everything about Jennifer is soft—her comfortable round body, her wavy shoulder-length brown hair, her warm brown eyes, and her soothing voice. Everything except her laugh, a joyous, whooping, belly-shaking blast that causes an irresistible spasm of laughter in everyone around her. Everyone except teachers, principals, and other assorted authority figures. She thought I was hilarious, and I love a good audience. As a result we spent a lot of quality time together in disciplinary settings ranging from the kindergarten time-out corner to the high school assistant principal's office.

"Hey, Jen. How's Lester's quest for true love going?"

She giggled. "Not good. He keeps asking me to set him up with my mother."

"I've got one of those. Do you think 10 minutes of heaven with Carol Nash could get me access to the unredacted Garrett Whiting file?"

Jennifer knows my mother well. The thought of Carol and Lester together set her off, as I knew it would.

I couldn't help but respond in kind, and within seconds we were laughing so hard I could hardly stand up. Is there anything more fun than laughing 'til your cheeks hurt with someone you really like? We didn't hear the door to Lester's office open.

"What's the joke, girls?"

I attempted a quick recovery.

"Hey, Sh-Sheriff, noth—, no, nothing," I said in a half-gasp, half-giggle. "You know, just 'girl' stuff. I had the funniest thing happen when I was at the gynecologist—"

His face turned red with the kind of embarrassment some men still feel at the mention of women's sexuality in any context other than a dirty joke. I glanced at Jennifer, who was fighting to achieve sobriety, and I took pity on them both.

"Never mind. On second thought, not that interesting. Or funny. Actually, if you have just a minute, I was hoping to talk to you about Garrett Whiting."

He ushered me into his office. His broad face, with its ex-hockey player's bent nose and thick gray mustache, was still slightly flushed from his near encounter with "female issues."

"I heard you might want to take a look at the Whiting file."

"You talked to Ross?"

"Yeah. He did mention it. You know, Leah, we got some things wrong on your sister's case, and I'm still real sorry about that. I told your mother and you both. But we're not a bunch of Barney Fifes over here. The Whiting case was suicide."

"I'm not saying it wasn't. I just want to see the file. What harm could that do?"

"No harm to us. None at all. Everything was by the book. But that's not exactly what Charlie said you were doing."

"Well, Detective Ross and I don't communicate all that well, I'm sorry to say."

"I've noticed. Now, how can I be sure you're not just going to try to find something in the file because you have it in for Charlie?"

The old boy tone that had crept in put my back up a little, and I responded in a way that Rebecca probably wouldn't like.

"Look, I can file a Freedom of Information Act request and get it."

"Yeah, you could. And I could redact it so you wouldn't wind up with much of anything. But I'm not gonna do that."

"You're not?"

"Nope. Matter of fact, I already told Jennifer to get a copy made for you. Course the *Times* is gonna have to pay for it."

"Sure, of course," I said, but I was uneasy. I'm wired to expect things to go wrong. When they don't, it throws me off balance.

"Wait a minute. What's really going on here, Sheriff?"

He shook his head and chuckled. "You're sure not like your old dad. He was a real easy going guy. Yeah, Tommy was always ready for a laugh. He was a heck of a guy. We played on the state championship football team back in 1973. Last time Himmel fielded a winning team."

If he was trying to throw me off my game, he did. I never talk about my father. To anyone. I didn't answer, and he returned to a favorite theme.

"Charlie Ross is a good investigator. He made some mistakes in the past. We all do. Even you. I'd hate to see you tryin' to make him look like an idiot again."

So many possible responses. All of them so unwise. I restrained myself.

"Thank you, Sheriff. I don't plan to." Whether that happened or not was in the lap of the gods. Sure to be dropped there by Charlie Ross and his own fumble fingers.

He picked up the phone and buzzed Jennifer, asking her to get the file for me. As I thanked him and left he said, "You give my best to your mother now." Which made me wonder what else I might have gotten hold of, if I'd played the mother card.

CHAPTER 9

FRIDAY IS ALWAYS A PRETTY SLOW DAY at the paper. The latest edition is out, and the next deadline isn't for another six days. I went back to the office feeling pretty good about having a nice chunk of time and, with Miguel off, relative quiet in the newsroom to go over the Garrett Whiting file.

I looked at, but didn't linger over, the photos of the body. Dr. Whiting had been found sitting in an armchair, one of a set of two that flanked a small table holding a reading lamp. An empty glass with the remnants of a drink sat on its polished wood surface. The gun that shot him was on the floor, next to the chair. My untrained eyes saw nothing that the experts hadn't recorded.

I focused on the other photos of the room, hoping to get some sense of the person that he was, from the things he chose to have around him.

In front of an arched window on the north wall was a sparely elegant wood desk. A small extension on one side held a PC, its computer mouse neatly aligned on the left. A note in the file indicated that taped to the bottom of the keyboard was a list of passwords— Garrett's email account, Amazon account, pin numbers—the kind of stuff my mother keeps stashed near her computer in case of a "senior moment." Nothing exciting like the combination to a hidden safe or a Swiss bank account number.

In the center of the desktop was a leather portfolio and just above it a Meisterstuck Mont Blanc pen in a silver and onyx holder. I recognized the high-end writing instrument only because I'd done a feature story once on a pen collector. Who knew you could drop $1,000 on a pen? A black phone sat within reach of anyone sitting in the well padded black leather chair behind the desk. On the right-hand corner was a framed photograph. A close-up showed it to be a picture of Garrett Whiting, looking very JFK on a sailboat. There was nothing else—no photos of his kids, no desk art, no expensive paperweights.

The rest of the room was just as anonymous. The walls were painted a sage green, the floor was dark wood. A set of shelves holding books that looked more of the scholarly than best-seller variety was built into one wall. All that the furnishings and the room itself allowed me to deduce was that Garrett Whiting was a very tidy man who enjoyed a solitary drink in his study. Sadly, the crime scene evidence team had found no muddy footprints, no dropped cufflinks, no tell-tale bits of fiber to indicate the presence of anyone other than Garrett.

I put the photos aside and started scanning the reports. Isabel told police she'd found the body at 8:30 a.m. She'd called 911. She told Ross she had spoken to her father around 11 p.m. the night before. I flipped through the phone LUDs—the local usage details—for Garrett's landline. The details for Sunday showed the call Garrett had placed to Isabel. The one Ross didn't think to tell me about. There were no other calls from or to the Whiting house that night, and no calls at all on Sunday on Garrett's cell phone records.

Isabel's brother Jamie had told the detectives that he wasn't sure when he got home, but it was pretty late. He had spent the weekend at the family cabin near Eau Claire. He had planned to stay another night and go home Monday morning, but changed his mind when his cell phone died and he didn't have a charger with him. When he got back to Himmel around 11 p.m., he stopped to fill up his car and ran into a friend who invited him to a party. It turned out to be a "pharm party," where kids bring a variety of pills, throw them in a bowl and everyone at the party grabs a mystery drug. He wasn't sure what he'd taken, but with the weed he smoked, the pills, and the beer, he was in pretty bad shape.

He didn't notice anything when he got home, just went to his room and crashed. He didn't wake up until Isabel came in that morning. He said the friend who invited him was Keegan Monroe and he might remember more. When police contacted Keegan later that day, he verified inviting Jamie, and said they'd left the party around 4 a.m. He was certain, because he wasn't as 'f'd up' as Jamie, and he remembered a neighbor banging on the door, saying it was almost 4 a.m. and he was going to call the cops if they didn't shut up. The party broke up then, and Keegan walked home. Jamie drove off.

Ross had noted that Jamie's bleary eyes and the lingering odor of stale beer and marijuana seemed to support the story he and Keegan had told. The housekeeper, Evelyn Godfrey, said she came in at 9 a.m. Monday through Friday and had the weekends off. The last time she saw Dr. Whiting was the Friday before he died. He seemed fine to her. He had stayed in his study all day working. She had fixed dinner and left the house as usual at 5 p.m. Jamie wasn't home. Dr. Whiting told her his son was away for the weekend.

The next thing I read was the autopsy. The medical examiner put time of death between 11 p.m. and 3 a.m., based on stomach content analysis, body temperature, and rigor mortis, and the fact that Isabel had spoken to her father shortly before 11 p.m. Then I found something I didn't expect. Something that cast a whole new light on things. I closed the file and made a couple of calls. An hour later I was on my way to the Whiting house just outside of town.

"Leah! Hi, come on in. What are you doing here?" Isabel's smile faltered when she saw my stormy expression. No one has ever accused me of having a poker face, and I wasn't taking any pains to hide my anger as she led me into the formal living room.

"What's wrong?"

I sat down on the edge of a cream-colored couch and waited until she had taken the chair opposite me.

"You lied to me."

The force of my words caused a physical reaction. She jerked back and her eyes widened. "I don't understand. I didn't lie to you. I wouldn't—"

I didn't let her finish. "Why didn't you tell me your father had Parkinson's disease?"

"I—"

"He had a reason to kill himself, Isabel. He was a surgeon. His career was over."

"He told me about the Parkinson's the night he called. But he wasn't suicidal. He was worried about Jamie. I thought if I told you about it, you'd dismiss me, too."

"Didn't you know I'd look at the case file, talk to the medical examiner, talk to the investigator?" Not that Ross had told me anything. Or the sheriff either. They were trying to teach me a lesson. That every case wasn't Lacey's, and I wasn't as smart as I thought I was.

Isabel had raised her hands to her mouth, her fingertips poking out from the overly long sleeves of the pale yellow sweater she wore. "Please, don't be so angry, Leah. You're the only one who can help me."

"After I read the autopsy, I called Detective Ross. And then I ate a big, rancid helping of humble pie." It had been an excruciating call to make. He was gleeful, and I knew that he had set me up. Ross isn't as dumb as I thought. He figured out there's no better way to get me to move full speed ahead then to tell me not to do it.

So I walked right into his funny little joke, and he couldn't stop laughing and insulting me. And I had to take it. In this case, he was right, and I was stupid. He was so happy, now that he had a story to spread to all his cronies. How that smart mouth reporter wasn't so smart. He even gave me a bonus to show how extra dumb I was.

"But wait. There's more. Detective Ross told me that your father had a life insurance policy. One that pays you and Jamie $1 million when he dies. Except oops, it has a suicide clause. You don't get anything if he kills himself within two years of the policy taking force. No wonder you were so anxious to prove he didn't commit suicide. You missed cashing in by six months."

"No!" She had found her voice and she spoke so loudly it broke my rhythm. I shut up for a minute.

"No, you're wrong. I don't care about the insurance. I tried to get the sheriff's department to investigate before I even knew there was insurance or a suicide clause. It's not about the money! Please, you have to believe me. I know I should have told you everything. But I thought you'd start investigating, like you did for your sister. You'd find more about my father, and you'd know he didn't kill himself. And then it wouldn't matter. I could tell you then."

Tears had welled up and started running down her cheeks. She didn't even brush them away. I suppose I should have felt bad, maybe given her a little pat, or at least handed her a Kleenex. I didn't.

"Look, I can't help someone who can't be straight with me. I went out on a limb for you, and you sawed it off. That's it. We're done."

I stood and walked out, leaving Isabel quietly weeping on the chair. I yanked hard on the door and almost tumbled into the guy who was standing on the other side, arm up to open it from the outside.

I had the impression of someone young, late teens or early 20s, but he was wearing a red hoodie that concealed his hair and shadowed his face.

Jamie, I assumed. He stepped back as I lunged out.

"Excuse me." I brushed passed him. I heard the front door close as I reached my car. Snow, which had been falling sporadically as I arrived, had picked up speed and the driveway and my car were covered under a light layer. I backed out with the windshield wipers screeching across the screen and fishtailed a little as I pulled onto the blacktop.

It's not like a source had never lied to me before. They do it all the time to protect themselves, or to point you in the wrong direction, or because they don't want to get involved, or sometimes, the weirdos, just because they can. But I had invested something in Isabel. All right, maybe it was more accurate to say I had projected something onto her. I did see a little of myself in her. I knew how it felt to have everyone against you. And I had identified with her so strongly that I lost my objectivity. I hate it when my mother is right.

I was so focused on my thoughts that I didn't notice until the last minute that the big, white, grandma Buick coming toward me had crossed the center line. I swerved and she missed, but the sickening scrape and thump on my car door told me I'd just taken out someone's bright red mailbox. This was turning out to be a grade A day.

CHAPTER 10

I PULLED MY CAR into the driveway that the mailbox belonged to and walked up to the door of a neat white farmhouse with a wrap around porch and green shutters. I rang the doorbell a couple of times before it was answered.

The woman who appeared wore a peach-colored T-shirt, knee-length black yoga pants, and a sweatband that could have been lifted from a 1980s Olivia Newton John video.

"Hi. My name is Leah Nash. I'm sorry, but I just took out your mailbox."

She frowned, but not because of her mailbox.

"I'm sorry, dear, I'm a little hard of hearing. Come in, won't you?" She opened the door wider. A work out DVD was blasting in some corner of the house. It explained why she hadn't come running when I crashed into her mailbox.

"Just a minute, I'll turn that off. Go on into the kitchen." She pointed vaguely to her left, but I followed my nose, which told me that somewhere nearby were freshly-baked chocolate chip cookies. Music has nothing on cookies when it comes to soothing the savage breast. I resisted the urge to help myself.

"Now, what did you say your name was?" she asked as she came bustling back into the room.

"Leah Nash. I just ran into your mailbox." I upped my voice volume a touch to accommodate her hearing loss.

"Oh dear. That's the second time in the last six weeks." A frown creased her forehead and she absentmindedly dislodged her headband as she moved her hand through springy silver curls.

"I'm really sorry. Of course I'll pay for a new one and whatever it costs to get it put back in."

She handed me a plate with several cookies. "Milk?"

"Yes, please."

I couldn't wait and took a bite—just the right temperature, warm enough so the chips were gooey, cool enough so the cookie was crisping around the edges. She smiled at my evident enjoyment.

"Whenever I make a batch, I always do a workout to sort of even things out."

"These are great." I was feeling calmer by the minute.

"Thank you, dear. Now, about the mailbox—did you get the post too?"

"Yes ma'am. Sorry."

"Well, that will set you back about $125 for both. Don't worry about the labor. My grandson Mickey will take care of it."

I got my checkbook out of my purse and realized I hadn't asked her name.

"It's Aurelia. Aurelia Wright."

I wrote out the check, pausing between lines for another bite. After I swallowed I said, "If you give these to everyone who takes out your mailbox, no wonder it happens so often."

"Well, not everyone stops. Last time it was just the mailbox, not the post, but still he should have stopped. Really surprised me. Jamie is such a nice boy. Of course when I found out it was the night his father killed himself, well, I just let it go. A mailbox didn't seem that important."

I nodded, still lost in the bliss of the cookie. Then I processed what she had said.

"Jamie Whiting drove by your house the night Garrett died?"

"Yes, it was late. Early morning, really. I was in bed but my dog Flash—" she pointed to a corner of the kitchen near the stove. I saw that what I'd taken for a rug was actually an extremely relaxed sandy-colored dog.

"He's a sweetheart. A cocker spaniel and poodle mix. No trouble at all, except that night he ate something that didn't agree with him. He woke me up to take him out at 3:15. I know because I looked at the clock and told him no more people food."

"Are you sure it was Jamie? It would have been too dark to see the driver, wouldn't it?"

She nodded. "Well yes, but I know that Mini Cooper of his. My daughter has one. Ridiculous things with the kind of winters we have. Still, they are cute. I've seen Jamie drive up and down this road a thousand times. I know that car. I'm sure it was him."

"Was he driving away from the Whiting house, or toward it?"

"Oh he was driving away from it. He had to be on the right side of the road in order to hit the mailbox. That's where it is."

"So at 3:15, he was driving from the Whiting's house toward town. And it was definitely the night Garrett Whiting died?"

"That's why I remember so well. Are you a friend of Jamie's?"

"No, I've never met him. I know his sister Isabel."

"I used to babysit for both the kids when they were younger. Jamie was such a sweetheart. I felt so bad when Isabel told me he was having a problem with drugs a few years ago. So sad."

My brain was racing.

"Were you surprised Dr. Whiting killed himself?"

"Well, I have to admit he didn't seem the type. He liked himself pretty well, that one." She gave little gasp and put her hand to her mouth. "Oh! I shouldn't have said that. He was always perfectly polite to me. Just sometimes was a little, snooty, maybe. Wasn't one to neighbor much."

"You said Jamie was a sweet kid. How about Isabel, what was she like?"

"She was a clever little girl. And very, very pretty. Always took special care of her little brother, too. Jamie could get into some mischief, but Isabel always tried to help him out of it. I used to love brushing that long blonde hair of hers."

My phone chimed and I saw a text had come in from Coop. I clicked it off to read later.

I stood up and put my jacket back on and grabbed my purse. "Thank you so much for the cookies and milk. And I really am sorry about your mailbox."

"That's all right. Gives me a chance to change up the color. I've had red the last two times; maybe I'll try blue and see if I have better luck. Nice meeting you, dear."

After I got in my car and buckled up, I opened Coop's text.

> *Charlie Ross is messing with you. Talk to me about Whiting before you do anything.*

Too bad I didn't get that about four hours earlier. It might have saved me from making a fool of myself for Ross. Though now, after talking to Aurelia, I was having the tiniest of second thoughts.

What had Jamie been doing driving toward town at 3:15 a.m., when according to him he was still partying and didn't tumble into bed half-conscious until 4 a.m.? If he'd really been home much earlier than that, as Aurelia Wright insisted, then his alibi for his father's death wouldn't cut it. Garrett had died between 11 and 3, the medical examiner said. I drove slowly, as much because I wanted time to think as because of the snow-covered roads. When I pulled into the Himmel Police Department parking lot, darkness was already setting in.

I pushed through the double doors and into the scruffy waiting area, with its scuffed linoleum and orange plastic chairs. Melanie Olson, the HPD secretary, sat behind the pass through counter that separated the offices from the reception area. Her eyes were glued to the computer screen, and she didn't look up.

"Hey, Melanie, is Coop in?"

She didn't answer, instead clicked her fingers rapidly across her keyboard. When she finally acknowledged me with a barely perceptible raising of her eyes, I noticed that her wiry hair was swept into an improbable updo with a cascade of curls coming down on her forehead, something like a 1940s pin-up girl.

"Your hair looks amazing." Which was true, though not in the way I hoped she'd take it.

She raised her hand and cocked a thumb in the direction of Coop's office.

"I'll just run on back then."

She lowered her head back to her screen as I raised the pass through and went down the hall. Coop was on the phone, so I hovered in the doorway until he waved me in.

I flopped into the chair in front of his desk.

"How bad was it?"

"Bad."

"I figured. Darmody talked to Charlie Ross today, that's when I texted you, but too late, I guess."

Darmody is Dale Darmody, not the brightest guy in the Himmel Police Department, nor the most discreet. Which often works to my advantage. Not this time though.

"What did he tell you?"

"That Ross said it was about time you took a tumble off that high horse of yours and found out you weren't the genius you think you are. His words, not mine," he added at the look on my face.

"He's such an ass. I had to admit he was right, and he loved it."

"That was a pretty jerk move of his."

"I appreciate the solidarity. You tried to tell me not to play Rescue Ranger with Isabel. But I did, and I got burned." I told him about Garrett's Parkinson's and about the insurance.

"Parkinson's would be a good reason for a guy like Garrett Whiting to kill himself. Could be he wanted to be in control of how things would end for him. And a million dollars is a pretty good incentive for Isabel to want his death to be anything but suicide."

"I know. Except—"

"Except what? Whiting had a good motive to kill himself, and Isabel and her brother don't get any money if their father's death was suicide."

"Well, but look at it another way. The insurance policy is also a reason why Garrett Whiting wouldn't kill himself. He took out a policy to protect his children. He only had six months to go. Why wouldn't he tough it out to ensure financial security for his kids?

"And I didn't tell you this part. The Whiting's neighbor said she saw Jamie driving away from the house toward Himmel around 3:15 that morning. But he told police he got home around 4 a.m., went straight upstairs to bed, and more or less passed out until Isabel woke him in the morning to say their father was dead. He's got a buddy who corroborated his story, but he wouldn't be the first person to get a friend to lie for him."

"How reliable is the neighbor?"

"I don't know, she seemed pretty certain. She said he hit her mailbox with his Mini Cooper. She saw him because she was letting her dog out, and she had just looked at her clock."

"He can't be the only person with a Mini Cooper."

"That's true, but she saw it coming from the direction of the Whiting's house."

"Would it do me any good to point out that you just got burned by Isabel? And that you just got punked by Charlie Ross?"

"I know, I know. You're right. But it's just kind of bugging me."

"Is it bugging you because you don't want to admit your instincts were wrong, or because there's actually something there?"

"I think there's actually something there. Even if Ross did do his job. For once. Trouble is, the guy doesn't have any imagination."

"Some might say you have too much."

"Oh, some might, might they? C'mon, Coop. Besides a Mini Cooper driving away from the direction of the Whiting house when Jamie was allegedly passed out—which by the way Ross did *not* investigate very well—there's the fact that Garrett asked Isabel to come home, because he was worried about Jamie. Why would he decide a few minutes later, screw Jamie and too bad if Isabel finds me dead in my chair? And forget about providing for them. I can't wait even six months to take myself out. I'll just shoot myself now. And the cheese. Don't forget he left a pound of Hook's on the counter."

He smiled a little, as I had intended him to do. Then he got serious again.

"Those are odd things. But do they add up to murder? Maybe that call to his daughter was as close as he could come to saying goodbye— asking her to take care of her brother. Maybe Isabel heard things the way she wanted, or needed to hear them." He paused to see if his words had any impact. "Are you even listening to me?"

"I hear you, but I'm not listening."

"You're impossible, you know that?"

"Thank you."

"All right. I give up. Moving on. Anything else you want to tell me?"

I was genuinely mystified. "No, nothing else going at the moment. Unless you want to talk about the startling developments in the case of Melanie's new hair."

"Oh. I thought you might want to mention that your ex is in town."

"How did—OK, Miguel, right?"

"He's an excitable boy. I saw him downtown this afternoon. He was pretty shook up that a piece of your past stopped by to say hello last night. What's goin' on?"

"Nothing, seriously. Nick was there when Miguel dropped me off and I didn't have time to explain things to him. Actually, I didn't know what was going on. But, you know Nick."

"Not really. I only met him a few times. You didn't exactly have a long marriage."

"Thanks for pointing that out. He's in Wisconsin, teaching at Robley. He's been coming down to teach a night class at Himmel Tech, but he said he had to work up the courage to talk to me. Now why would that be? Nice, approachable, open-hearted me?"

"So what did he want?"

"Forgiveness."

"Huh. Did you give it to him?"

"Yeah, I guess. Hey, you want to come for dinner? Mom's cooking. Mac and cheese, then we're gonna watch an old movie. Cowboy flick. *The Big Country*. Fun times."

"I'd like to, but I've got plans."

"You had plans the other night, too."

"What? A man's not allowed to have plans?"

"Sure. You're just being kind of mysterious about yours lately."

"Not really."

"Yes, you are, but whatever. I better get going. I'll talk to you later."

I waved to Melanie as I left, but she didn't notice. On the way home I tried to think what might be making Coop so reluctant to divulge his "plans." And what could be a bigger attraction than my mother's cooking? The only thing I could come up with was that he was doing some kind of police operation he didn't want me to know about. He wasn't very trusting when it came to my ability to keep the lid on a story.

And with good reason. I couldn't guarantee anything. The worst thing a reporter can do is get too cozy with the cops. When you start identifying with sources, you can't do your job. We'd had a couple of tussles stemming from that before—him doing his job, me doing mine. It didn't always mesh. He might be thinking it was easier just to avoid me, unless and until he could tell me what was going on. But it was my job not to be spoon-fed information by the police, not even when they were my very good friends. I'd have to do some digging soon.

CHAPTER 11

TRUE TO HER PROMISE my mother had my favorite meal, four-cheese macaroni and cheese, waiting on the table when I got home, along with a big salad and apple crisp for dessert. Over dinner I told her about Isabel's grievous omissions.

"So you're dropping this?"

"That was my plan."

"But I can see why Isabel left those key points out. She was afraid you'd react like you did."

"Wait a minute. Weren't you the one who told me be careful, don't get caught up in this, consider my motivations, remember it's Isabel's fight, not mine?"

"Hmm. I do give good advice, don't I? But I'm just saying I can understand why she wasn't completely upfront with you."

"I don't remember you having this relaxed approach to the truth when I was younger. And I'm mad as hell that Isabel wasn't straight with me."

"But?"

"But nothing. That's all."

She waited.

"OK. I've got a gut feeling that something isn't right. And maybe it wouldn't hurt to take another run at this." I looked at her out of the corner of my eye to see how she was taking it. She started to speak, then cut herself off.

I stood up and started loading the dishwasher. She gathered up our leftovers and packaged them for the refrigerator. As she reached around me to grab a plastic container from the cupboard, she stopped and instead put a hand on my arm and turned me around to face her.

"I don't want to tell you what to do."

"That would be a first."

She made a face, then got serious. "It's kind of hard to know the right thing to do, isn't it? You feel sympathy for Isabel. I do too. Then again, you don't need to get tangled up in something right now. You've got the page proofs for your book sitting on the coffee table. Aren't they supposed to be going back? I thought I heard you tell your agent two days ago that you were all over it."

"I am. I'm just about done," I said, with the same amount of righteous indignation I used to use when she accused me of not doing my math homework. And the same amount of truth. I'd actually have to pull an all nighter soon to get the page proofs back to the publisher by the promised date.

She looked at me skeptically but didn't say anything.

"I just can't let it go, Mom. Not yet. Something's off; I just don't know what."

A half hour later we were both in our pajamas, sock-clad feet propped up on the coffee table, afghans in place and a bowl of popcorn in each of our laps. We were ready to watch *The Big Country* for the hundredth time. Nobody rocks a Friday night like the Nashes.

Truthfully, I enjoy the occasional early night at home, and there is worse company than my mother and Gregory Peck. The opening credits were running when Miguel knocked on the door. I paused the DVD player and called to him.

"Come on in, it's open."

"Chica, nice jammies. Where are your fuzzy slippers?"

I had my usual winter sleep uniform on: a tan oversized long-sleeved T, slightly ragged on the sleeves, and a pair of blue flannel pajama bottoms with sheep on them.

"Shut up." I threw a piece of popcorn at him. "What's your look called?"

He wore a plaid flannel shirt unbuttoned over an olive green T-shirt, dark wash jeans, and hiking boots. Quite a change-up from his typical style.

"Lumbersexual," he said with a grin.

"What is that?" my mother asked.

I answered for him. "It's for hot hipsters who want to walk on the rough side and dress like a lumberjack. I see you had to draw the line at a beard."

"I think you look very nice, Miguel," my mother said.

"And you look *muy linda*, very pretty, Carol, as always."

"You are such a suck-up," I said.

"Gracias, Miguel. For that you can grab yourself a bowl and have some popcorn. Do you want to watch a movie with us?"

"No thanks. I'm meeting my amigos. We're going to the Caliente Club in Milwaukee tonight. I just stopped to tell Leah what I found out today."

"Anything good?"

"No-no-no. You get nothing. Nada. Not 'til you tell me about your *husband!*" He'd contained himself remarkably well up to that point, but now he squeezed onto the couch beside me and took both my hands in his.

"I never even knew you were *married!* How could you keep that from me? What is he doing here? When did you get married? Married, chica. I can't believe it. He's *muy guapo*. Very hot. *Dígame*. Tell me everything."

"Nothing to tell. We were married for half a minute when I lived in Grand Rapids. It didn't work out. We got divorced and I haven't seen him for six years."

"You never even mention him to me? Carol, you tell me. What's the real story?" he asked, dropping my hands and leaning around to get a good line of sight with my mother.

I answered before my mother could. Lord knew what she'd say.

"I told you the real story, Miguel."

"Maybe, but not all of it."

"OK. His name is Nick Gallagher. I met him when I worked in Michigan. He was a temporary faculty member in the Psych Department at Grand Valley State University. We got married. He didn't get the 'forsaking all others part.' We got divorced. It wasn't fun for either of us. We both had some growing up to do. He stopped by to ask me to forgive him. I did. End of story."

His dark eyes were dancing with excitement. "No, no, chica. That sounds like the beginning of the story." I knew that his imagination was concocting a Lifetime movie scenario.

"No. Stop right there. We are not star-crossed lovers. He did not ask me to take him back. I did not say 'I've always loved you.' He said he was sorry. I said it's OK. And that's that. Now, I met my part of the deal. Tell me what you found out."

He wanted to talk more about Nick, I knew, but I set my face in an expression that said *no way*. He put his curiosity aside for another day.

"It wasn't very busy at the salon today. I listened to lots of bad husband stories. But no Garrett Whiting."

"That's all right. I—"

"No, wait. You are so *impaciente*. It was quiet, until I did the shampoo and conditioner for Mrs. Caldwell."

"Traitor. You gave a Miguel special to that nasty woman who tried to get me fired?" Georgia Caldwell is the ex-wife of Miller Caldwell, the lawyer Isabel had identified as one of Garrett's oldest friends. He's nice. She isn't.

"Commerce, chica. Got to keep the customer satisfied. I had to massage her head. But it didn't mean anything. I thought about you the whole time. Don't you want to hear what she said?"

"Yes, you know I do."

"I just did a little chatting about Garrett Whiting, how sad the suicide was, and she took over from there." He nodded, pleased with himself, as he put a handful of popcorn into his mouth.

"C'mon, c'mon, tell me already."

He finished chewing and said, "She didn't like Dr. Whiting."

"So she didn't like him. So what? She doesn't like anybody."

"She likes me," he said with a slightly smug smile.

"Don't make me question her judgment. What did she tell you about Garrett?"

"He was handsome, and he chased women."

"Anyone in particular?"

"She said, and this was not so nice, 'garden variety sluts.' And the worst one was Francesca Saxon."

"Frankie Saxon? I know her. She's a counselor at the high school. I like her," my mother said.

"I know the name, too," I said. "Isabel told me she helped get her brother Jamie into rehab. She didn't say her dad dated her."

"Maybe she didn't know," my mother said. "In my experience, children often find it hard to believe their parents aren't past all passion."

"Oh, that's your experience, is it? Miguel, was this a recent relationship?"

"I didn't get a chance to ask. She just said that Frankie was an Italian witch who got what she deserved."

I was pretty sure that Georgia Caldwell had not said "witch." But Miguel is very circumspect with his language, which I admire but find hard to emulate.

"What did she mean by that?"

"*No sé.* I don't know. Some scandal? Georgia's stylist came and got her, so I didn't get any more."

"I don't remember the details. There was some kind of drama there years ago, but I didn't pay much attention. You don't have to dredge up some malicious old scandal, do you?"

"Mom. I work for the *Himmel Times,* not *Gawker.* There will be no scandal writing. But it's interesting. Well done, Miguel. Thanks."

"*De nada.* It was nothing. I'm happy when you are, chica." He grinned, getting up to leave. Then he turned back, "You're coming to my Christmas party, aren't you? Both of you?"

"After your Cinco de Mayo soiree, I'm not sure I should."

"Chica, you have to. Anything can happen."

"That's what I'm afraid of."

"You and Paul are coming aren't you, Carol? It's gonna be fabuloso!"

"No doubt, Miguel. But that's the night Paul and I are going to La Folie in Madison. He's been planning it for weeks."

"*Muy elegante.* Very fancy! Come by after."

"We'll try."

"Now you, chica. Promise. Two weeks from tomorrow. You can bring a friend. Maybe an old boyfriend? An old husband? Whatever you like. The theme is holiday sparkle."

"You're not selling me on it." His face fell and I felt bad. Don't rain on Miguel's party parade.

"Just kidding, Miguel. I'll be there. I'm just not sure what I'll wear. Sparkle isn't a big part of my wardrobe."

"It's not what you wear, it's who you're with. I can hardly wait.

Now, I have to go. The Caliente Club waits for no man."

"So, I didn't know you and Paul were going to La Folie. That's pretty swank. What's the occasion?"

"Nothing special. Paul's been wanting to go ever since it opened. It's really hard to get reservations, and he's really looking forward to it, so I can't say no. I'd rather go to Miguel's, actually."

"Soft music, candle light—sounds pretty romantic. Maybe I better ask him what his intentions are. He might be planning a marriage proposal."

"Don't even say that. That's not what's happening."

I looked up from rearranging my blanket and putting my popcorn within easy reach, surprised at the vehemence in her voice.

"OK, OK. Just kidding."

"Well don't. Now are we going to watch this movie or not?"

"Yeah, sure." And we did, but I kept stealing glances at my mother, trying to figure out why a little light teasing had irritated her so much.

CHAPTER 12

I RARELY SLEEP IN, even on a day off, unless I'm sick. So I was already showered, dressed, and eating Honey Nut Cheerios when my phone rang at 8:30 Saturday morning. Given the way I'd left things with her, I was surprised to see Isabel's name pop up.

"This is Leah."

"Hi. Don't hang up, please. Let me say this first. I am really sorry I didn't tell you everything. I know I can't expect you to help me when you can't even trust me. It's just that you were the only person who would even listen to me. I didn't want you to brush me off, too. I'm not making excuses, I'm just saying that's why. But it was wrong, and I totally understand why you're so angry at me."

She sounded resigned and really, really sad. And I wasn't angry anymore. That's one benefit of a quick temper—it doesn't last long.

"Isabel, I can see why you did it. I'm sorry I blew up at you. But you've gotta know that your father's illness adds a whole lot of credibility to the suicide verdict—and it was already on pretty solid ground."

"I know that's how it seems, but you didn't hear my dad that night. He wasn't a man about to commit suicide. He wasn't, and I don't care what you or anybody else believes. He wasn't!"

"Take it easy. Actually, I did come across something after I left that's making me rethink things."

"You did? What?" I winced at the hope in her voice, because I was pretty sure the thing that made me change my mind wasn't going to go down very well with her.

"Isabel, how sure are you that Jamie's story for that night is solid?"

"Jamie's story? He didn't have much of one. You don't when you're as messed up as he was. He just came home, passed out, and woke up to find dad was dead."

No point in dancing around. I came straight to it.

"Someone saw Jamie driving toward town around 3:15 a.m."

"That can't be right."

"Maybe it isn't, but your neighbor Mrs. Wright believes she saw Jamie's car, when Jamie says he was passed out at home."

"She's wrong, that's all. She's very scattered. If she saw a car it wasn't Jamie's."

"You do understand that I'm going to have to talk to Jamie."

She rallied. "Yes, sure. Of course. You'll see, when you meet him. Jamie isn't the violent type. He and my father didn't always see eye to eye, but he would never, ever hurt him."

"There's another thing. You mentioned Francesca Saxon. You didn't say she and your father were lovers."

"That old gossip? My father was a single, good-looking doctor. A lot of women threw themselves at him. Maybe he and Frankie were involved once, but if so, it was a long time ago. If it's true, I don't think it was any big romance. He was pretty old for that." I remembered my mother's comment about children and their parents' love lives.

"Doesn't matter. But I'll be checking it out. Maybe she knows more about your father than you thought."

"I don't care who you talk to, as long as you keep asking questions. I know Jamie had nothing to do with it, and I doubt Frankie did either. But the more you ask, the more you'll see I'm right. I know we can prove my father didn't kill himself."

"OK. But you need to understand something."

"What?"

"This isn't about you and me against the world. This is about a reporter chasing down leads and following them wherever they go. It might end up that the police were right, or it could be that your father was murdered—but this investigation has a life of its own now. I won't be checking with you to see if you're cool with it. And I'm going to follow it through until there's no more for me to find out."

Big words that I'd have a tough time following up on if Rebecca decided to block my way. I could do it without her support, even with her opposition, but it can get pretty tiring running against the wind all the time. I had to bring her in on it, now that I'd committed the full force of her paper's senior reporter to the story.

"I get it. I'm not worried. Find out the truth. I trust you."

"OK then. I'll talk to you soon."

"So you want to pursue a theory you have that Garrett Whiting was murdered, based on what again? Your instincts?" Rebecca's eyes still focused on the spreadsheets she had continued to study while I updated her on Isabel. She often spends Saturday morning at the paper doing important Rebecca things in her office.

"That's right." I struggled to keep my voice level. What I wanted to say was, *"Yeah, instincts. Reporter's instincts. Something a paper pusher like you wouldn't know anything about."*

"But my instincts are based on the facts I just gave you."

"Are they really facts, Leah?" She finally looked up and pulled off her glasses, the better to impale me with her icicle stare. "You've outlined an alternative theory of how Garrett was killed and you've pointed out holes in the son's story, but you also discovered a major motive for suicide and a reason for the children to push a murder agenda. They do not pass GO, do not collect $1 million, if daddy killed himself."

"I know, you're right. But sometimes it isn't one or two major reveals, it's a whole bunch of little inconsistencies that tip you to the real story. I know you're worried about upsetting advertisers and getting the sheriff's undies in a bunch—" Oops. Wrong tack to take.

"You really do enjoy your self-righteous role as the last real reporter in captivity, don't you? Yes, I have to think about advertisers and subscribers and budgets. That doesn't mean I don't care about journalistic integrity and the truth. So don't patronize me talking about your 'instinct' and your ability to go where no journalist has gone before. Bottom line, you do your job and I'll do mine. You turn up something more substantial than 'inconsistencies' and gut feelings. If you don't, the story is dead. Understood?"

"Yeah, OK. Understood."

"Anything else?" She had put her glasses back on and her eyes were once more cast down, looking at the lines of numbers.

"No. No, that's it." I left without saying goodbye, and Rebecca didn't seem to notice. I had gotten what I wanted, the go-ahead to pursue the story without active obstruction from Rebecca. But somehow it felt like I had lost.

"Won't you come in?"

It was nearly five o'clock that afternoon when I followed Francesca Saxon into the living room of her house on Pine Street. It was the room of a reader, with stacks of books and several magazines on end tables. In front of me on the coffee table, a book was turned face-down with a pair of glasses and a half-full wine glass beside it.

"Thanks for seeing me on such short notice, Mrs. Saxon."

"Just Frankie. Please, sit down." She pointed to one end of a green sofa.

The name was tomboyish, conjuring up freckles, skinny legs, and short, ginger-colored hair. This Frankie had dark brown tresses caught up with a clip, a few tendrils escaping and curling softly at her neck and in front of her ears. A light fringe of bangs drifted across her forehead, and she had the beginnings of fine laugh lines fanning from the corners of her brown eyes. She wore leggings with flats and a tunic-length ivory sweater. So this was the woman Garrett had dumped. She couldn't be much older than me. She was beautiful.

"Would you like a glass of wine?"

I almost said no, but caught myself. Sharing a glass is a way to get the conversation, and sometimes the truth, flowing.

"Yes, thank you. Pinot Grigio if you have it, but any white is fine with me."

She left the room and returned in a minute carrying a nearly full bottle and a glass into which she poured a generous amount. She went to the sideboard and topped her own glass off from a bottle of red wine. Then she sat down next to me, one leg tucked under her. She leaned back a little against the throw pillows in the corner of the couch.

"So you're writing a story about Garrett Whiting's life?"

"Actually, I'm looking into his death."

"His death? I don't understand."

"The family isn't completely satisfied with the suicide verdict. Some of the questions they have made me curious enough to see if there was more to the story."

"The family? Isabel and Jamie?" She seemed taken aback.

"Yes. That surprises you?"

"Not that they don't want to believe their father killed himself. But surely you don't—Jamie and Isabel—don't think their father's death was an accident? I don't understand how you could accidentally shoot yourself in the head."

"No, not an accident. Murder." I said the last word with a little dramatic spin, like a television attorney trying to jolt an incriminating statement from a complacent witness. It didn't work.

"Murder?"

"It's possible."

"No, I don't believe that," she said, shaking her head so vehemently she spilled a few drops of red wine on her pale sweater.

"According to Isabel, Garrett wasn't the kind of person to commit suicide."

"What 'kind of person' is that? Suicide isn't restricted to a type." Her voice was sharp.

"You're right. I didn't phrase that very well." I backed off a little. "I'm just trying to get a handle on what motivated Dr. Whiting, what pressures he may have been dealing with, what his relationships were like. That's all."

"I really wouldn't know anything about that," she said, taking a sip from her glass—because she was thirsty, or to buy some time?

"I know you helped him get his son into a drug rehabilitation program a couple of years ago."

"Yes, I did. But that was in a professional capacity. I'm a counselor at the high school, and Jamie was a troubled student. I helped his father like I would have helped any parent."

"I see. But you knew Dr. Whiting before that, didn't you?"

Another drink before she answered. "I've known him for a long time, yes."

A flush crept up her flawless olive skin, though that could have been the wine. I went in another direction to keep her off-kilter.

"I guess it must have been pretty upsetting when Jamie relapsed, after all the work you and Dr. Whiting put in helping him."

"Relapsed?"

"Yes. Didn't you know? Isabel said he started using again a month or so before Dr. Whiting died."

I couldn't read the look on her face—surprise, disbelief?

"I didn't hear anything about that."

"Dr. Whiting didn't ask for your advice? That's odd. So you hadn't talked to him in quite awhile?"

"We weren't social friends. We weren't in regular contact."

I nodded. "So you wouldn't have any way of knowing if Dr. Whiting was suffering from depression. You probably didn't know that he was seriously ill?"

"Ill?" Either she was very good, or this really was news to her.

"Yeah. Parkinson's. He was diagnosed not long before he died."

"I had no idea."

"It must feel weird not knowing what was going on with someone you used to be so close to. I mean years ago, way before Jamie's problems."

A cornered look came into her eyes. It's what I'd been looking for. But I didn't feel very good about it.

"I already said I knew Garrett for years." She fussed with her wine glass, setting it on the table, then picking it back up.

I put my own glass down and half-turned on the sofa so that I was facing her directly. In a quiet voice I said, "You more than 'knew' him, didn't you, Frankie? You and Dr. Whiting were lovers once. What happened?"

She downed the rest of her wine. Got up, went to the sideboard again, and poured another. Came back, sat down, and stared into it, as though looking for the answer there. I waited. Then she blew out a long sigh before looking up.

"It's not exactly a secret. More of a forgotten scandal. At least I hoped it was forgotten. What happened is that 10 years ago we fell in love. Or rather I did."

"Were you still married?"

She nodded. "He wasn't. But I was. Jerry and I were high school sweethearts. He was the only boy I'd ever dated. Marissa was born seven months after we were married. She was a beautiful baby. We did all right at first. Jerry had a good job at a factory, he had his bowling, his buddies, his beer. But I didn't want to let go of my dreams. I was only 19. I thought I'd be the first person in my family to earn a college degree. I wanted my parents to be proud of me, not disappointed in me."

The words were tumbling out now, as though she couldn't stop them.

"When I started college, Jerry hated it. I agreed to have another baby, my son Caleb, because I thought it would make Jerry feel more secure, less resentful. But then I graduated and got a teaching job, and he hated it even more. He didn't like my new friends, he didn't like my new interests, he didn't like that he and the kids weren't 'enough.' His words, not mine. We fought all the time. It was exhausting. Then I met Garrett."

"Was it serious, your relationship with Garrett?"

"I thought it was. He said he loved me. He was intelligent, witty, charming. He was much older. I couldn't believe a man so sophisticated could fall in love with me. He made me feel like we were soul mates. It turned out he specialized in making women feel that way." She gave a humorless laugh.

"What happened?"

"He'd already broken it off with me when my husband found out. Jerry went crazy. Went to the country club one night, when Garrett was receiving a civic award. He made a huge scene, threw a punch, had to be escorted out. Half the town saw it, and the other half heard about it." She closed her eyes as through reliving the humiliation.

"Then he filed divorce papers on me at work. Right in my classroom. Tried to keep me from sharing joint custody because of my relationship with Garrett. Told everyone I abandoned him, neglected the children, flaunted my lover. I nearly lost my job when one of the school board members wanted to invoke the 'moral turpitude' clause in our contract. If it weren't for Father Lindstrom, I would have. He intervened with a couple of the board members, and they changed their minds. It was the worst time in my life. And my kids. My poor, sweet kids. They were too young to really understand, but they knew something was very wrong."

"I'm sorry. I'm sure it was hard on everyone."

"Yes. It was. You make your choices, and you have to accept the consequences. But not your kids. Your kids shouldn't suffer for something you did. You're not going to write about this, are you?"

"I'm not planning to write about an affair that happened a decade ago, no. I'm sorry if I upset you." And I was. But it didn't stop me from pressing on.

"Were you surprised when you heard that Garrett had committed suicide? Did that jibe with the man that you knew?"

"I was stunned. Garrett was exciting, brilliant, self-centered, egotistical. When I knew him, I never once saw self-doubt, or depression, or anything but absolute self-satisfaction."

"How did you find out about it?"

She paused before answering. "I think I got a text from a friend that Monday, the day after. Yes, I'm sure that's how I heard about it. I ran in a 10K in Lake Neshaunoc on Saturday. I try to do that one every year."

I nodded, and her voice picked up speed as she went into greater detail, twisting a strand of hair as she spoke. "It's a pretty trail, really spectacular when the colors are changing. I decided to make a long weekend of it. I took a personal day on the following Monday so I could stay up there, relax, visit some antique shops. I really enjoy antiquing, but I didn't find anything this time. But the weather was beautiful. And I did some shopping. My mother's birthday is coming up, and I drove out to look at some quilts at a really nice little place outside of Lake Neshaunoc. She's looking for a wedding ring pattern in a particular shade of green. So that's why I wasn't here when I got the news. It was such a shock."

My antennae had gone up slightly. People not used to lying often offer up too much information. They get nervous and start rambling, as though piling on details will make their story sound more credible. All it does is give them more ways to trip themselves up. But before I could follow-up, she stood and set her wine glass on the edge of the table, where it teetered precariously for a second.

"You'll have to excuse me. I just remembered I have to pick up my daughter. I'm sorry I wasn't able to help you. I really do have to go."

With that she lifted my half-full glass out of my hand, plunked it down on the table, reached for my jacket, which she had laid across a chair earlier, and hustled me to the foyer. I was at the front door, still wriggling my arm in my sleeve, as I said, "Of course, all right. Thank you for—"

"You're very welcome. But I've really told you everything I know, and it's all too upsetting to talk about again. And I would appreciate your discretion about my relationship with Garrett." And the door was closed.

CHAPTER 13

As I started to pull my car out of the driveway, a tall dark-haired girl came down the sidewalk. I waited for her to pass before backing up. Instead, she turned and walked up the path to Frankie's house. On impulse I turned off the car and got out.

"Hi. I'm Leah Nash. I'm a reporter with the *Himmel Times*. I was just talking to your mother for a story I'm doing."

"I'm Marissa. Marissa Saxon. You're a reporter? That's cool. Are you doing a story on my mother?" She was puzzled, but interested.

"No, about Garrett Whiting. You probably know his kids, Jamie and Isabel?"

"I know who Isabel is, but we never hung out or anything. I know Jamie though. He's a pretty cool guy."

"He had some problems though, right?"

"Yeah, that's true. He was into drugs for awhile, but my mom helped him get into a program. He seems fine now. I mean, as far as the drug stuff, of course not about his dad." The wind blew a strand of long dark hair across her eyes, and she pushed it out of the way.

"So you knowing Jamie, his dad's death, that must have been pretty upsetting to you, too."

"Totally. I came home early that Monday to check on Mom. She was just sitting in bed crying. It really freaked me out. She told me Dr. Whiting was dead. That he shot himself. It was surreal."

"You had to check on your mother? Why was that?"

"She got really sick at this big race she runs in. She came home Sunday night; we were already in bed. But when I got up in the morning she told me she thought she had food poisoning or the flu. She looked so bad that I wanted to stay home with her. But she said the worst was over; she just wanted to sleep. I came home at lunch to see how she was doing. I'm glad I did because she just got the text about Dr. Whiting, and she was really upset."

Before I could ask anything else, the front door opened. Busted.

Marissa looked up. "Hi Mom, I—"

"Honey, come on in, I need you to help me with something." She spoke to her daughter, but she was looking at me.

"Right. Well, good to meet you, Marissa."

"Yeah, you, too." She was a nice kid.

"Thanks again, Frankie," I called. She didn't answer, just stood there waiting for her daughter. As soon as Marissa crossed the threshold, the door closed.

So, Frankie was home Sunday night, the night Garrett died. And she lied about it. And she hadn't needed to pick up her daughter today, and she definitely didn't want me talking to Marissa. Too late.

On Monday I had a couple of interviews in the morning and then a lunch meeting of the Himmel Holidays Committee to cover. Feeling pretty virtuous about my productivity, I decided to use part of the afternoon to make a visit to the Whitings, in hopes of catching Jamie at home. But first I stopped by the paper to pick up a camera. I try not to go anywhere without one. A wild art shot of a cute squirrel or a kid walking his dog has rescued more than one *Himmel Times* front page when a planned-for story fell through.

When I walked in, Miguel was leaning over the front counter chatting and laughing with Courtnee. Both of them sprang apart and stared at me.

"What? What are you guys looking at?"

"Chica, it's what *you'll* be looking at."

"It's on your desk. Go look on your desk!" I hadn't seen Courtnee this animated since Taylor Swift's last album came out.

"Why?" Suspicion was heavy in my voice. A few months ago, after I wrote a story someone didn't like, I'd received a box of still-steaming dog poop. I was not up for such high jinks today.

"Come on, andalé, just go!" Miguel grabbed my hand and pulled me into the newsroom, Courtnee hard on our heels. There, in the middle of my desk, sat a big bouquet of red roses.

Oblivious to the look on my face, Courtnee was bouncing up and down with the wonder and amazement of it all. "Leah! You got flowers! Roses! Who would ever, ever, ever think someone would send you flowers?"

"All right, Courtnee, that's one too many 'evers' there. I've gotten flowers a time or two."

She gave me the kind of look the prom queen might bestow on the head of the clean-up committee.

"What? I have."

"I know you have, chica, but who are these from? And so many!"

I had an inkling, and I surreptitiously slipped the card tucked into the flowers into my jacket pocket. But not stealthily enough.

"Read it, Leah, read the card!" Courtnee commanded.

I opened it and read aloud, "'Super story on Grandma's shot glass collection. Thanks, the Chumley Family.'"

"That's not what it says."

"Yes it is, and very nice of the Chumleys it was," I said as I collected the camera for a quick getaway.

"No." She put a hand on my arm to stop me. Closing her eyes halfway to aid her powers of recall she said, "The card says, 'Leah, your forgiveness means everything, Nick.'" Her voice went up in a little squeal.

"Courtnee, you read my card? You opened my personal mail?"

"I had to. I mean, like, the delivery guy said they were for you, but I was pretty sure that couldn't be right. So I had to look at the card. I was being proactive. Isn't that what you're always telling me to do?" Her tone was self-righteous and long-suffering at the same time. "Besides it wasn't the mail. I mean it didn't come from the Post Office. It was more like a note. Like a post-it note, really."

"A post-it note inside an envelope marked 'Leah.' "

She pouted. "You're always yelling at me. 'Think, Courtnee, think!' Like I'm stupid or something. Then I try to like, do what you want, and you're still all up in my grill."

"You violated my privacy."

Miguel could contain himself no longer. "Yes, yes, you're right, chica. Courtnee, you shouldn't have done that. But Nick. Your ex-husband sent you flowers!"

"Ex-husband? Leah was married?" Apparently Miguel had saved that tidbit for the big reveal.

"Yes!" He leaned in to give her the lowdown, and as she cross-examined him excitedly, I managed to slide out from under their gaze and dash to my car.

Flowers from Nick. He was always a fan of the over-the-top gesture, and roses are his favorite. Tulips are mine.

It was after 1 p.m. when I reached the Whiting house a few miles outside of Himmel. Jamie's Mini Cooper was in the driveway. I rang the doorbell, but instead of Isabel or her brother, a middle-aged woman wearing jeans and a long-sleeved T-shirt, her hands encased in thin plastic, opened it.

"Yeah?"

"Hi. I'm Leah Nash. I was hoping to see Jamie or Isabel?"

"Which one do you want?" Her voice was nasal and slightly twangy.

"Uh, well, Jamie, I guess. Is he here?"

"Sleeping. Most days he's not up before 2."

"Is Isabel up and around?"

"Her? She was gone when I got here." Her hand shifted slightly on the door as she got ready to close it.

"Oh. Well, it's almost 1:15. Would you mind just checking to see if Jamie's awake and could talk to me?"

She sighed in annoyance, then motioned me in. "I guess. Follow me."

She led me past the living room where I had talked with Isabel. I saw that the furniture was moved, cushions were piled high, and the air was redolent with the smell of furniture polish. A large vacuum sat in the middle of the floor.

"I'm cleanin' in there," she said unnecessarily.

She led me down a hallway to a room that I immediately recognized as Garrett's study. Not exactly the receiving room I would've chosen for guests, but then the housekeeper bore a closer resemblance to Mrs. Danvers than to Mrs. Potts. The room showed no evidence of its grim recent past. Various sized boxes sat on the floor, partially filled with books. One armchair was gone. The other had a box on it. The wall had obviously been repainted.

She rolled the padded leather executive chair out from behind the desk and put it in the middle of the floor. "You can sit there."

"Thanks, Mrs. ...?" I knew who she was from reading the police report, but I was trying to get a little conversation going.

"Godfrey. Evelyn Godfrey. I'm the Whiting's housekeeper."

"Looks like you've got your hands full today."

"Isabel, she finished goin' through her dad's stuff and it set there for weeks. Then all of a sudden she decides stuff has to get moved today. She left me a note this morning."

"You've got to move all these boxes? Today?"

"Well, no," she admitted grudgingly. "She's not done yet. But she wants me to take this one here." She pointed to a large box on the edge of the desk. "She wants it dropped off to Dr. Whiting's office manager. Way across town. It's my regular day to clean the living room and the kitchen, plus I gotta make something for supper. I don't know how I'm going to get that to that office today. And I'm not supposed to lift anything real heavy." Her voice was aggrieved, and the lines that bracketed her mouth deepened as she pressed thin lips together.

"I'm going to town after I talk to Jamie. If it's just the one, I can drop it off. Would that help?" It wasn't just the latent Girl Scout in me that prompted my offer. The office manager, Elaine Quellman, was one of the people Isabel had suggested I talk to.

"I guess maybe it would," she said, unwilling to give up a grievance so easily.

"No problem then. Where's the office?"

"It goes to Elaine Quellman." She gave me the address and then reached into another box and brought out a roll of packing tape. "Here, you can seal it up with this."

"OK. Will do." She stood, waiting for me to apply the tape. For someone who had such a tight schedule she didn't have time to drop off a box, Mrs. Godfrey seemed reluctant to leave. I wanted to get a look inside before sealing it shut.

"OK then, Mrs. Godfrey. You know what, I wouldn't mind a cup of coffee if you've got it." I began pulling off a length of tape as though ready to seal the box and laid it across the top.

"I'd have to make it." She spoke in the same overwhelmed tone I might use if asked to produce Thanksgiving dinner.

"That's fine," I said, my voice as chipper and cheery as I could make it. "I don't mind the wait. And that will give you time to let Jamie know I'm here."

Any goodwill my volunteer delivery service had engendered vanished.

"It's gonna be awhile."

"No problem."

As soon as she left the room, I lifted the tape up and pawed through the box. It was wide but not very deep. I pulled out a bubble-wrapped pen and holder—the Montblanc I'd seen in the crime scene photos. Then the silver-framed photo that had sat on the desk, also swaddled in bubble-wrap. What kind of a narcissist kept a photo of himself on his desk? At the bottom of the box was a leather portfolio that I opened without much hope. Another bust. Just a pad of pristine paper. And that was the sum total of the box. No patient files, no secret diary, no second set of books.

I was putting everything back in place to seal the box when a voice behind me made me jump.

CHAPTER 14

"Finding everything all right?"

As I finished rewrapping the photo and putting it back in the box, I tried to assume a casual tone. "Jamie. Hi. Leah Nash, we haven't met officially." I held out my hand. "Mrs. Godfrey asked if I'd drop this box off at your dad's office. I was just admiring his Montblanc pen. Really beautiful."

"Yeah. I know who you are." He took my hand with a firm grip, but let it go quickly. He ran his fingers through thick, slightly curly blondish-brown hair, ruffling it up a little. He and Isabel had the same slim build, and they were about the same height. He was good-looking in an ethereal, hot vampire kind of way–slender, with long-lashed blue eyes under straight brown eyebrows, and a thin, sensitive mouth. "So. You wanted to see me. Here I am."

"Would it be easier to talk in a different room?"

"You mean because my old man died here? I don't believe in ghosts."

OK, then.

"Isabel has some concerns about your father's death." I sat down on the chair Mrs. Godfrey had dragged out for me, while he moved a box off the armchair and took a seat.

"Yeah, I know." He slouched down in the chair, stretching out his legs and sticking his hands into the pockets of his jeans. He wore a tan v-neck sweater over a white T-shirt. His long feet were bare. He definitely looked like he'd just woken up, but his eyes were steady and clear.

"I realize this is hard, Jamie. I—"

"It's not hard. It's just bullshit. My father was an asshole. He wasn't Izzy's favorite when he was alive, either. The truth is, he didn't care about either of us. Especially not me. That wasn't a picture of us on his desk, was it? Just him, the way he liked it. He would've been happier if we were never born. Talking about him isn't hard. It's just pointless."

"You don't care that he's dead?"

He shrugged and sat up a little, taking his hands out of his pockets and rubbing one thumb over the other. "I learned to stop caring after he never went to a parent-teacher conference, never showed up for a school play, never watched me run cross country. Was never there, period. Except to criticize everything I did and tell me what a disappointment I was. I've been clean and sober for over two years. But he never once said he was proud of me. What can I tell you? We weren't close. He didn't even bother to tell me he had Parkinson's. I found out from Isabel after he died. What does that say about our 'relationship'?"

"That he wanted to protect you?"

I've never actually seen a sneer, but the look he gave me seemed to fit the bill. "Right. Because he was such a great father. He wasn't trying to protect me; it just never occurred to him to include me in anything in his life. Most of the time he didn't even remember I existed."

"Is that why you got into drugs? To get your father's attention?"

"You've been watching too much Dr. Phil. Thanks, but I don't need pseudo-analyzing. I did drugs because I liked how they made me feel." His tone was belligerent, but I tried again.

"OK. Can we talk about how your father died? Your sister—"

"Yeah, I know. Isabel's convinced herself it wasn't suicide. That Garrett wouldn't do that to us. She's delusional."

"That's pretty harsh."

"Look at the way he died. A nice blurry mix of rum and Coke with some Kpin to take the edge off, then a single bullet to the head. Clean, calculated, in control. Just like he was."

"He hurt you a lot, didn't he?"

"I got over it." His words were dismissive, but anger and pain were evident in his eyes. He must have realized that, because he lowered them as he shifted position, crossing an ankle over his knee. He began picking at a loose thread on the hem of his jeans.

"You say your dad didn't care about you. But he had a life insurance policy that would pay you and Isabel $1 million when he died. That seems to say 'I care' in a big way."

"Yeah well, excuse me if I don't get all teary eyed about his generosity. Especially since he'd already stolen $100,000 from me. And he made sure neither Isabel nor I would ever collect on his insurance."

"What do you mean your father stole $100,000 from you?"

"My mother left me the money when she died, and my father was trustee until I turned 21. Which I will next month. Then a few weeks before he kills himself, he tells me that he made some 'unfortunate' investments, trying to 'strengthen' my portfolio, and it's all gone. It wasn't enough for him to lose his own money; he had to take mine too."

"What about Isabel, did he lose her inheritance too?"

He looked confused for a minute, then embarrassed. "She didn't have one. Not from our mother."

"It wasn't my idea," he added defensively. "She was always—distant to Isabel. She got heavy into prescription drugs when we were young—runs in the family," he said, with a self-mocking aside. "When she left, she never looked back. I was shocked that she left me anything. Doesn't really matter now though, does it? Garrett evened things out. Right down to zero. Killed himself just six months short of us collecting. Typical dick move of his."

"You seriously think your father timed his death so you couldn't collect the insurance? Wouldn't it have been a lot easier to cancel the policy?"

"Do you think you're funny? Because you aren't. You don't know the first thing about my father. But this time the joke's on him. I don't care about the money, and I'm happy he's gone."

"I talked to Frankie Saxon today. She made it sound like your dad came through for you when it really counted, when you had your drug problem a couple of years ago."

For the first time he gave a genuine smile. "Frankie's a good person. A really good person."

"She and your dad were pretty close at one time."

He stopped picking at the hem of his jeans and looked up. "Are you talking about the 'affair' they had?" He shook his head. "That's old news."

"You don't think it might have started up again?"

"No way. She'd never be with my dad again. Frankie's way too smart for that."

"It's not about how smart you are. You can't always choose who you love." A little voice in the back of my mind snorted—I have a very obnoxious inner voice—*Who are you trying to convince, yourself or Jamie?* I squelched it by veering in a new direction.

"You told the police you got wasted the night your father died. Why did you? After all that time sober, I mean?"

"No reason. I have to choose to be sober every morning. And every night, and every time someone offers me something to get high. I made a bad choice that night, that's all."

"Was there anything that happened that day? A fight with a girlfriend, an argument with your dad, something that triggered your fall off the wagon?"

"I told you no. Just stupid, just testing the limit. I just felt like it. Why is this any of your business?"

"Why does my asking make you so mad?"

"I'm not mad. I just don't see the point."

"I want to make sure that I've got things straight, that's all. The police report says you went to a party, got pretty messed up, and left with a friend after a neighbor threatened to call the cops. You got home around 4 a.m. Is that right?"

"Yeah, I guess. Like I told the cops, my memory of the night isn't very clear."

"You must've really been out of it. You didn't notice a light on in here?"

"I came in the back and went up to my room. I thought you said you read the report." His irritation was growing. I pretended not to notice.

"I'm just trying to figure out what your father's frame of mind was. If you take yourself back in your mind, you might remember something now that didn't seem important at the time."

"I didn't see anything. I didn't notice anything. I hadn't even been home for three days before he killed himself."

"So you were at the family cabin Eau Claire for the weekend. By yourself? Wasn't that kind of lonely?"

"I like to be alone up there. It's peaceful. I do some writing, some hiking in the woods. I wasn't coming home until Monday, but I forgot my charger and my phone went dead. So I came home Sunday instead. I was almost here, but I needed gas. When I stopped to fill up, I ran into Keegan. He asked if I wanted to party, and I said yes."

"So you have this Thoreau weekend and get all one with nature and all, then you come home and party your brains out?" My voice was heavy with skepticism. I switched to a more understanding tone, trying to play both bad cop and good cop myself. "You know, Jamie, even if you had a fight with your dad before you left, you don't need to feel guilty. Your fight didn't make him die."

"Nothing happened. I don't feel guilty," his voice had risen to an angry shout as he jumped to his feet. "Stop pretending you care about me, or Isabel, or my father's suicide. You're just after a story. And the bigger, the messier, the dirtier it is, the better!" He towered over me, clenching his fists so hard I knew he wanted to take a swing at me. I stood up and moved in close, into his space. Time for bad cop to return in a big way.

"What is it you don't want me to find out? You might as well tell me, Jamie, because one way or another, I will find out." The problem with that approach was that I wasn't a cop, and he wasn't scared of me. But he sure was mad.

He grabbed me by the shoulders and shoved me aside as he left the room. I lost my footing and slipped, hitting the edge of a small table as I fell. He didn't even look back. By the time I got to my feet, Mrs. Godfrey was standing in the doorway. She held out a cup to me.

"You want that coffee now?"

CHAPTER 15

OUT IN THE DRIVEWAY I loaded the box into my car and cast a quick glance up at the windows. No sign of curtains twitching or Jamie glowering down from the third floor.

I walked over to his yellow Mini Cooper, found a hand sanitizer in my purse, and squirted some on the grime-encrusted passenger's door, then wiped it off with a wad of Kleenex. Squatting down, I looked it over carefully for signs of a run-in with Mrs. Wright's mailbox. I rubbed my fingertips lightly over the midsection of the door. There it was. A slight indentation, a small concave spot that should have been smooth. I peered closer. Just to the left was a long, light surface scratch and what could be a speck of red paint. The decapitated mailbox had been red.

Conclusive? No. It could have been the aftermath of a close encounter with a car door in a parking lot. But it was suggestive. As was Jamie's out of control behavior at the end of our interview.

I got into my car and drove toward town. Why had Jamie gotten so angry at me? What had happened the night Garrett died? Had he seen something—or done something?

He hadn't looked like he was in the throes of a relapse—though a person can fake sobriety. Then again, he can fake being drunk or high, too. What if Jamie wasn't out of it at all that night? If Garrett was the sadistic son-of-a-bitch that Jamie described, if he'd been undermining his son's confidence his whole life, and then actually stole $100,000 from him, maybe Jamie decided he'd had enough.

Maybe he spent the weekend thinking about his dad and how he'd never been good enough. And what he could have done with the money his mother left him. Maybe he got angrier and angrier. I was a witness to his temper. There was a lot of fury inside that kid. Maybe he came home earlier—and far less drunk—from the party than he said and decided to do something about it. I let the scene form in my mind's eye.

He gets home from his party well before 4 a.m., and he's not near as wasted as he pretends later. And he's got a plan. He sees the light on in his father's study as he drives up. He comes in through the kitchen like always, only this time he slips a pair of the housekeeper's plastic gloves into his pocket. He takes out some of the Klonipin he's bought or stolen and grinds it up, then stirs it into a rum and Coke. He grabs a bottle of water for himself. Then he heads for the study. He apologizes to his father for disappointing him. He offers his dad the drink and says he's sticking to water, proving what a clean and sober son he is. Maybe Garrett responds the way Jamie feels he always has, with criticism and sarcasm, removing any doubt from Jamie's mind about what he's going to do.

When Garrett starts to nod off, Jamie puts on the gloves, takes the gun out of the drawer, wraps dear old dad's hand around it, and pulls the trigger. Then off to bed it is, maybe after a fortifying beer or two for verisimilitude to bolster his alibi. And he's finally free. And, he thinks, he'll be half a million richer when the insurance money comes through—that can make up for a lot of adolescent angst. What a crushing blow when he finds out about the suicide exclusion. No wonder he's so pissed off at the world.

But wait a minute—what about the Mini Cooper that Mrs. Wright had seen that night? What did that have to do with anything?

I didn't realize the light had turned green until a horn honked behind me. I took my foot off the brake. Instead of going straight to the office, I turned and headed toward the Himmel Police Department. I needed Coop to help me think this through. But when I stopped by the front desk, Melanie said he had the afternoon off.

"Is he at home, do you know?"

"Couldn't tell you," she said, patting the odd poof of curls that was apparently now a part of her standard hairdo. The phone rang and she turned away to answer it.

I tried his cell as I stood there, but it went straight to voicemail. I didn't bother to leave a message. When I got to the parking lot, an involuntary groan escaped me. Dale Darmody was warming his backside against my car, chowing down on a burger in the sunlight of an unseasonably warm day.

"Hey, Leah. Long time, no see." As he spoke, a bit of burger tumbled out of his mouth, bounced off his jacket and hit the pavement.

"Hi, Darmody."

"Old Charlie Ross hit you with a sucker punch on that Whiting file, didn't he?" Darmody started laughing, and then he started choking. It's no testament to my character that I hesitated for a second before I slammed him on the back, and he dislodged the piece of bun that was impeding his airway.

"Yeah. It was hilarious. Thanks for rubbing it in."

"Aww now, hey, don't be like that. I'm not the one that did it. Fact of the matter is, I told the lieutenant as soon as Charlie told me what he was up to." He coughed a little, and his blue eyes watered from the effort. He had taken his hat off and set it on the roof of my car, as he used the hood for a picnic table. A light breeze ruffled the rapidly-diminishing strands of gray on his head. The sun in his face highlighted fine hairs sprouting randomly from his ears and nose. Somehow that was a little endearing. Darmody is like a beat cop in a 1940s movie. Jovial, friendly, just not all that smart. Still, he loves his job, and he loved his town, and I've known him since I was 12 years old.

"Never mind, it's all right, Darmody."

He smiled then, and I did, too. "Haven't seen you around much lately."

"I've been around. It's Coop who's MIA. What's up? Is he working on some big undercover operation or what?"

He laughed, a little nervously I thought.

"What? Is he? Come on, you can trust me."

"Well, I prob'ly shouldn't say anything. I mean the lieutenant—"

"Dale!" From across the parking lot came a voice that could peel paint. Darmody snapped to attention in a way I was sure he never did for a senior officer.

"Hi, hon. I was just keepin' Leah company while she ate her lunch." He quickly shoved the bag he was holding into my hand and shot me a pleading look.

"Dale, the doctor said you are not supposed to eat red meat. Your cholesterol is sky high." By this time Angela Darmody had reached us. She stretched her tiny five-foot frame to the max and pulled Darmody's head down to her level, sniffed, pushed him back, and said "Hamburger!" She turned a fierce gaze on me that I tried to avoid.

"Don't look away, Leah Nash. You are aiding and abetting Dale right into a heart attack."

"Sorry, Angela. Won't happen again. I asked Dar—Dale to share lunch with me. He just did it to be polite."

"Hmph!" She wasn't buying it, and I wasn't about to stand around waiting for my turn while Darmody got reamed out.

"Good to see you, but I've got to go." With that I handed Darmody his hat from the roof of my car, tossed the burger bag into the nearest bin, opened my door and scooted onto the seat, all before Angela finished reading him out. I'd have to wait another day to find out what Coop was up to—or ask him myself. Though if I were the sensitive type, I might think he was avoiding me.

I was heading toward the paper when I remembered the box in the back seat of my car and my promise to Mrs. Godfrey. I made a U-turn and drove toward Hickam Avenue. A sort of mini-medical row had built up in the last 10 years in the blocks surrounding Caldwell Memorial Hospital. Several medical practices had offices there, a few dentists, an optometrist. A couple of buildings housed specialists like dermatologists, oncologists, nephrologists, and others who practiced at larger hospitals in Madison or Milwaukee, but kept office hours once every week or two in Himmel. The surgical practice of Garrett Whiting, M.D. was located there.

The waiting room had that smell peculiar to a doctor's office, a combination of antiseptic and anxiety. I approached the sliding glass window, lugging the box with me. I set it down and tapped gently on the glass to get the attention of the receptionist. She was frowning as she stared at her computer screen. She opened the window without looking up and said, "Sign in please, include the time. Fill out this form, and we'll call you in a few minutes." She slid a clipboard and a pen toward me and closed the window. I tapped again. This time she looked up with the pained expression of someone who has heard one too many stupid questions that day.

"Yes? Do you need help with the form?"

I used the clipboard to block the window so she couldn't shut me out again if she were displeased with my answer.

"I'm not a patient. I'm delivering a box for Dr. Whiting's family. His daughter Isabel asked me to drop it off for his office manager, Elaine Quellman."

"She's not here. But you can take it through that door." She pointed to her right. "Janelle is working in her office, and she can help you." She moved the clipboard and shut the window before I could bother her again.

Hefting the box, I walked through the door, and as she had indicated, there was an office immediately to the left. I tapped on the half-open door and walked in.

"Hi, I'm delivering a box from Dr. Whiting's daughter, for Elaine Quellman. Where should I put it?"

The woman sitting on the floor surrounded by file folders and banker boxes was young, maybe early 20s. She had gone a little heavy on the liner and eye shadow, but she was very pretty with long red hair tucked behind her ears and a dusting of freckles on her short, straight nose.

"Miss Quellman isn't here. I guess you can put it over there in the corner." She pointed to one of the few empty spaces on the carpet. I dumped the box unceremoniously, then dropped down beside her and held out my hand. "I'm Leah Nash. I'm a reporter with the *Himmel Times.*"

"Janelle Bigelow." She gave my hand a limp squeeze.

"Will Miss Quellman be back tomorrow?"

"I doubt it. She's all emotional, because of Dr. Whiting and all."

"She's still not coping?"

"I know, right? It was like a hundred years ago."

"Actually, more like six weeks ago."

"Well, still. Get over it. So she came back to the office and everything, but then when we had to start transferring patients and closing out Dr. Whiting's files, she flipped out. She's been off forever, and I'm the one stuck doing everything."

"So. She and Dr. Whiting were close? Were they…" I let my voice trail off, waiting to see if Janelle would fill in with details of a long-standing office romance. To my surprise, she burst out laughing.

"Doctor and Miss Quellman? Not hardly. She's got to be like 100. She was like his hover mother. Always all over us about his special coffee, and his special pen, and his special paper, and his special self. My grandma is kinda like that with my dad. Drives my mom crazy. So what's in the box? More junk for me to take care of, I suppose."

"No, just some things from Dr. Whiting's desk at home. I think his daughter wanted Miss Quellman to have them as keepsakes."

"Someone will have to take them to her house. Probably me. No one else ever does anything around here. She only lives over on Newton Street, but it's totally the opposite direction from my place. The newspaper office is over by there, isn't it?" She looked hopefully at me.

I ignored her subtle suggestion that I be the one to deliver the box.

"Is his associate Dr. Bergman going to keep the office open?"

"I hope so. He's seeing patients and stuff, but we've been transferring a lot of Dr. Whiting's patient records, so I don't know. And there was, well, that thing."

She stopped, but her eyes begged me to ask more. I recognized the look, having received it from Courtnee many times before. There was gossip to be had.

I leaned in and lowered my voice to show her I knew how this was done. "What aren't you saying, Janelle?"

She met my lean with an incline of her own, so that our heads were nearly touching and she spoke in a lowered voice, as though we were in a crowd of people, instead of the only occupants of a small room. "I heard Dr. Whiting yelling at Dr. Bergman. 'You have f'd up for the last time. But I'm damned if my reputation is going to be f'd up with you!' Only he didn't say 'f'd,' he just dropped the whole f-bomb."

"What did he mean?"

"I don't know. I only overheard them because I ran back in to get my coat. The office was just closed. But that old bag-head Miss Quellman was standing at the back door like, 'Hurry up, Janelle. You don't have business in there after hours.' Like she's the big sheriff of the office. Well, she is kind of, I guess. They were still going at it, but I had to leave," she said, her regret evident.

"When was this?"

"I'm not sure exactly. But not very long before Dr. Whiting killed himself."

"Did you tell anybody else?"

"Just a couple of the girls, but then Miss Quellman heard me, and said she'd fire me if I didn't stop gossiping. It wasn't gossip. It was true," she said virtuously. I was beginning to think that I had found Courtnee's spiritual doppleganger in Janelle.

"What did you think of Dr. Whiting?"

She didn't hesitate. "Bossy old bastard. Not like Dr. B."

"And what's Dr. Bergman like?"

"Hot. I mean the car, the clothes, he flies his own plane. He's super sexy."

"But you don't know if he's planning on buying the practice for himself?"

She shook her head. "I'd be the last one to know. Nobody tells me anything."

"OK, then. Well, I'd better let you get back to work. Sorry I interrupted you," I said, standing up.

"It's OK. I needed the break."

Judging from the half-hearted way she'd been moving files around, I doubted it.

"Yeah, I'll bet. You know what? Let me take that box over to Miss Quellman for you. That's one less thing you have to take care of."

"Her house is right next to the Presbyterian Church on Newton. It's gray with white shutters," she said as I lifted the box again. "Here, let me get the door for you."

CHAPTER 16

As I REACHED MY CAR, a shiny black Mercedes pulled into the parking lot. I watched a man who defined the term "metrosexual" get out. He had a bronzed face, despite Himmel's seasonal lack of sunshine, and subtle highlights in his layered dark brown hair. A luxurious camel hair coat covered his tall, lean frame. As he pressed the lock button on his key fob, I tossed the box into my car and called out, "Dr. Bergman!"

He paused, and I hurried up to him. He seemed vaguely familiar. As I got closer, I realized he looked a lot like the movie star Johnny Depp—without the facial hair and glasses.

"Dr. Bergman, hi, I'm Leah Nash, a reporter with the *Himmel Times*. I'm working on a story about Dr. Whiting's death—" His expression, which had been merely curious, now looked wary.

"Garrett's suicide? Why would you be doing a story on that now? It happened weeks ago."

"I know, yes, but his family is concerned the death was investigated too quickly. They—"

"I don't understand why that would be."

"There are some unanswered questions."

"Not that I'm aware of. If you'll excuse me please, Liz, is it?"

"Leah. Leah Nash."

"Right. Sorry. But I do have to go." He turned toward the building. As he did, I put my hand on his arm. He gave me a withering look. If we were in elementary school, he would have accused me of having cooties at that point.

"I'm sorry. I'm sure it's hard to talk about losing a friend."

"We weren't friends. Dr. Whiting owned the practice. He was a mentor and a very good surgeon. I'm sorry he's dead, but it wasn't a personal loss. Again, please excuse me." He was getting away. Time to bring out the big guns. I spoke to his retreating back, and what I said made him stop and turn around.

"I heard he could be pretty rough on you. Someone said you guys had some harsh words not long before he died. Must be tough, one of your last memories of him being a shout down."

"I don't know what you're talking about." His voice was as cold as the winter wind off the Himmel River, but I had his attention now.

"He didn't say, 'You have f'd up for the last time. But I'm damned if my reputation is going to be f'd up with you!'?"

"Who told you that?"

"Is it true?"

Now it was his turn to grab my arm. "If I ever hear that you've repeated that lie I will sue you and your paper for everything you have. If you ever come on this property again, I will have you arrested for harassment, trespassing, and slander." For emphasis he gave my arm a hard twist, then he flung it away and walked quickly into the building.

Well, well, well, now we were getting somewhere. Dr. Hal Bergman just joined Jamie Whiting and Frankie Saxon on the persons of interest list. And, mostly just because I didn't like the smug bastard, I put him right at the top.

"Elaine Quellman?"

"Yes, that's right. You are?" The woman who opened the door wore a white turtleneck and navy trousers. Her salt and pepper hair was cut in a bob with straight bangs that grazed her eyebrows and focused attention on her amazing aquamarine eyes. Though clearly well into middle age, she was far from the "old bag head" Janelle had described.

"I'm Leah Nash, a friend of Isabel Whiting's. I have a package for you from her," I said, shifting the box slightly. It wasn't that heavy, but it was a little unwieldy to hold.

"Oh! Really? She didn't mention it. Well, please come in." She waved me into her living room. "You can put the package on the coffee table, if you would."

As I did, she went to a desk in the corner and retrieved a letter opener. I watched as she used it to slice open the box. She hadn't asked me to sit, but then again she hadn't asked me to leave. So I waited, noting the room's cool gray walls hung with modern art reprints, the light oak floors, and the uncomfortable-looking low sofa and chairs. She pulled out and unwrapped the pen and the photograph. When she came to the portfolio, she gave a little cry and looked up at me.

"What a lovely, thoughtful thing for Isabel to do. I gave this to Garrett years ago." She ran her fingers lightly over the embossed initials on the cover, like a blind person reading a message in braille.

"It's beautiful."

"He always carried it with him. He refused to use the computer for notes and correspondence. Always a Montblanc pen and a sheet of lined paper. That's why I bought this portfolio for him. To hold his pads of paper."

"He didn't use email?" That hardly seemed possible.

"It's not as though he didn't know how to use email. He preferred not to. He had beautiful handwriting, very precise." Her voice had taken on a distinct chill at the perceived criticism of her boss.

I tried to warm her up a little.

"You and he worked together really well, I guess."

"We did. For over 20 years. We were often at the office together on Sunday mornings. We both enjoyed the quiet time to catch up. The last time I saw him was at the office, the day he died." Her voice had softened.

"What was he doing? What kind of mood was he in?"

"Well, he wasn't suicidal, if that's what you're asking. I certainly would have done something if he were," she said, her voice tinged with annoyance again.

"No, of course. I'm sure you would have. I've been talking with Isabel, his daughter, and she's been trying to piece together his last day. I just thought maybe I could tell her how he spent that morning."

"It was just the same as always. He made calls, did some correspondence. We had coffee together. I noticed he'd used the last page of his pad of paper on a letter he'd written, so I brought him a new one. He thanked me. I picked up the mail to take to the Post Office, and we walked out together. He told me to have a good day. Just ordinary, just like a hundred times before. I had no idea it was the last time I'd ever see him." Her eyes glistened.

"I'm sorry," I said.

"Yes. Well." She flicked a tear away, assumed a brisk tone, and said, "Thank you for bringing these to me. I was about to have coffee. Can I offer you some? Leah Nash, you said your name was?"

"Yes, that's right. Thanks, that would be nice."

"Of course." As she turned to get it, I followed. If she were disconcerted to have me at her heels like an imprinted duckling, she had the good manners not to show it. I hoped that if we were seated together at the kitchen table, the intimacy of the setting would help her open up a little.

She pulled cups from the cupboard, then poured coffee from an already brewed pot.

"Don't I know your name? Aren't you the reporter who exposed the chicanery at DeMoss Academy?" She sat down across from me as she asked.

"Yes. I'm a friend of Isabel's, but I also work for the *Himmel Times*. I'm actually investigating the death of her father. Isabel doesn't believe he killed himself."

"I don't either."

I hadn't expected flat-out agreement.

"You don't? Why?"

"He wouldn't have left without saying anything." She gave a small, sad smile.

"You mean you don't think he killed himself, because he didn't leave a note?"

She didn't answer my question directly. "I loved him. Oh, not like some of those nitwits at the office think. I'm aware they called me his office wife, laughed behind my back, thought I was a deluded old maid. It wasn't like that."

"What was it like?"

"I didn't harbor any romantic dreams about him. I wasn't 'in love' with him. I loved his skill, his confidence. He was arrogant, and he could be cold and even cruel sometimes, but he was brilliant. People like Garrett are rare. They demand the best of themselves and of others. They deserve special care and attention. It was my pleasure to give it to him."

"So you think he couldn't have suffered the self-doubt or depression that could lead ordinary people to suicide?"

"That's not what I said. I realize he was subject to human frailties. But I don't believe he would end his life without making a statement. It wasn't in his nature. He would have written a suicide note."

"You knew about his financial losses?"

"Of course. He trusted me with everything."

"Then you knew he had Parkinson's, too?"

"What? No. He didn't."

"Yes, he did."

"That can't be right. Garrett would have told me. He wouldn't keep that from me. From everyone else, perhaps, but not from me." Her voice faltered as she processed the information and its implications. The man she idolized and trusted had not trusted her with his secret.

"I was his right hand. He always said, 'Elaine, you're the glue that holds this place together.' I know he trusted me. He did!" She said it with defiance.

"I'm sure he did, but the diagnosis must have been devastating to him. He probably didn't want to tell you until he'd come to terms with it. He wouldn't want you to suffer along with him." I highly doubted that, from what I'd been learning about Garrett Whiting, but I wanted to offer her a little comfort.

"Yes. Yes, you're right." She rallied, taking a breath and composing herself. "I know he would have told me. I wasn't just his office manager. I was his trusted confidant." She said it with pride, but it struck me as sad that she had settled for what seemed to me so little.

"Is it possible that his financial losses, combined with his illness, might have driven Dr. Whiting to take his own life?"

"Not the money. No. It was never about the money. It was always the work. And I don't believe the Parkinson's would have either. Garrett was a strong man, a brave man. He wouldn't give up, not without a fight." Her voice had risen and I wondered if she were trying to convince me or herself.

"Did the sheriff's department talk to you?" I didn't recall seeing a statement from her.

"They didn't come to me after he died. But I finally called them. I felt I had to tell them about Dr. Bergman, but they weren't interested."

"What about Dr. Bergman?"

"He was stealing prescription pads and sample drugs. Quite possibly he still is. Either for himself or to sell. Perhaps both."

"Did Dr. Whiting tell you that?"

"I told him. Drugs were missing from our sample closet. And our prescription pad counts and order numbers didn't match."

"Why did you suspect Dr. Bergman? Did you confront him?"

"Only three people had unrestricted access to the locked cabinet where they were kept and the authority to order them. It wasn't Garrett. It wasn't me. That left Dr. Bergman. I didn't approach him about it. Garrett told me to let him handle it. He didn't want me involved."

"So Dr. Whiting confronted Dr. Bergman. That's why he said Dr. Bergman was f'd, and he wasn't going down with him, or words to that effect."

"I see you've spoken with Janelle. Garrett didn't want the practice dragged into Dr. Bergman's mess. And Dr. Bergman begged Garrett to give him an opportunity to put his affairs in some kind of order, perhaps a chance to make some kind of deal with the authorities."

"And Dr. Whiting agreed?"

She nodded. "I didn't think it was wise. But Garrett wanted to handle it as quietly as possible, without tainting the practice. That Sunday before he died, he told me not to worry, that everything was taken care of as far as Dr. Bergman was concerned. I took that to mean that Dr. Bergman was going to the police. Or that Garrett was."

"But Dr. Bergman didn't confess and go the authorities, did he? And Dr. Whiting didn't either. He died. Do you think Dr. Bergman had something to do with his death?"

She stopped short of that. "I don't know. But after Garrett died, I called the sheriff's department. I talked to the detective on the case and told him what I knew about the prescription drugs."

"And?"

"He wasn't much interested in what I had to say. He told me that Garrett's death was a suicide, period. He thanked me for the information on Dr. Bergman and said they would follow up. He also advised me not to discuss it with anyone. He said if I did, it could impede their investigation into Dr. Bergman. I could see the wisdom of that, so I haven't. But that was weeks ago and nothing's been done."

My mind was teeming with possible directions to go here. OK, even that moron Ross would've had to check out the prescription drug story, or he would've turned the lead over to the Himmel Police Department. Unless he didn't need to, because they already knew. Maybe that's what Coop was up to. He was part of a multi-agency task force cracking down on prescription drug rings. Ross was sure Whiting's death was a suicide. He was in no hurry to act on Miss

Quellman's tip because he knew the task force already had Bergman in their sights. I pulled my thoughts back to the present.

"So why are you talking to me now?"

"Because Dr. Bergman is still in practice and that isn't right. A brilliant man is dead. Dr. Bergman can't be allowed to continue as though nothing happened. He can't be allowed to get away with no punishment. I respect what you did for your sister. I believe you'll make something happen here, too."

Oh, I was going to make things happen. I just wasn't sure what things and to whom.

"I'm certainly going to try. If you think of anything else, please call me, any hour. Trust me, I will be following up on this." I handed her my card and as she took it, her hand shook a little.

She hadn't told me to call her Elaine, so I didn't, but I said, "I'm very sorry for your loss, Miss Quellman."

"Thank you," she said, accepting the condolence as her due. And after 20 years of faithful service to a man few seemed to miss, maybe it was.

"Those are beautiful flowers."

I had hoped my mother would be in her room, or doing laundry or something, so I could slip them into my bedroom without being noticed. No such luck.

"Yeah."

"Where did you get them? From your guilty expression, it looks like you stole someone's funeral arrangement."

"Funny. They're from Nick. I only brought them home to stem the tide of Miguel and Courtnee's endless speculation."

"Nick? Why?"

"I don't know. A gesture of thanks, I guess, for not taking his head off. Let it go. It's been a really long day." To distract her I launched into a recap of my adventures.

"Rebecca's not very impressed, but at least she didn't tell me to stop. I wanted to talk to Coop about things, but he was out again. I saw Darmody and he started to tell me that Coop's doing something secret. I think it might be something with the Drug Enforcement Agency. There's a rumor that there's a task force operating in the area. I could've gotten it out of Darmody, but Angela came by and started in on him before he could finish. I guess he's got high cholesterol. No surprise really. Though he's so scared of Angela, I can't believe he won't toe the line." My rambling did not distract her.

When on the scent, my mother has the tenacity of a bloodhound. "Those are very expensive flowers. Are you sure Nick is thanking you, not courting you?"

"'Courting' me? Yes, he is Ma. And I hope you and Pa will let us sit in the front parlor and spoon when he comes to call. No. He's not 'courting' me."

"You know, sarcasm is not attractive. Is he trying to get back together with you?"

"I don't think so. Remember, Nick always favors the excessive gesture. And apparently he's forgotten that I hate getting things like that at the office. Miguel and Courtnee haven't given me a minute's peace. That's why I brought them home. Out of sight, out of mind. Except no, now you've got to start in."

She didn't say anything for a minute, but I could see the wheels turning behind her dark blue eyes, calculating just how far she could take this. When she spoke, it surprised me.

"I'm sorry. Whatever is going on —" She held up her hand to stop me as I started to interrupt, "No, let me finish. Whatever Nick's intentions are, they're none of my business. You're right. I just don't want to see you hurt again, but that's all I'm going to say about it." I doubted it, but decided not to say so. She was the one who changed the subject.

"Thanksgiving is Thursday, you know. Paul and Miguel and Father Lindstrom are coming. Is Coop?"

"No, I thought I told you. He's going to his sister's, but he said he might stop by later to watch the game."

"OK. There's some leftover roast beef in the fridge if you want to make a sandwich for dinner. We're running low on just about everything. I'm going to the store and then stopping at Paul's for a minute. Do you want anything?"

"We're out of Honey Nut Cheerios. Otherwise, no, I'm good. I'll probably be in bed when you get back. I'm beat."

And so it was. At 9 p.m. on Monday night I was tucked in my bed and in my jammies when I got a text from Isabel.

Jamie is really mad. What happened?

I'm not sure. He just went off. Saw Dr. Bergman today. Interesting.

Meaning?

Bad blood between him and your dad. Could be something there.

What?

I'll talk to you later this week.

She sent another text, but I was done. I understood why she wanted to know all the details, but I couldn't do my job if I had to report back to her every step of the way. I'd have to remind her of that. My glance fell on the giant bouquet sitting on my chest of drawers. I really should thank Nick, but I wasn't up for another conversation with him. I texted instead. He texted back right away.

Thanks for the flowers. Very pretty.

Glad you like them. I should have done more of that when we were married.

No, just less of a few other things.

Ouch. Moving on. Getting anywhere with Dr. Whiting story?

Maybe. Talked to someone today. Definitely had the means. Whiting's partner. Maybe the motive too.

121

Want to meet for drinks Thursday or for dinner?

It's Thanksgiving.

I forgot. No plans.

This I knew was my cue to say *"Why don't you come to dinner?"* But for several reasons I didn't. First, my mother would kill me. Second, the new Nick was an improvement over the old, but I was leery of his let's-be-friends schtick. Third, my mother would kill me.

OK. Got to go. Later.

Maybe dinner Saturday?

I didn't answer. But since I was in the texting mood, I shot one off to Coop.

WTF? Why are you never around?

He answered right away.

Can't talk. In the middle of something.

Later this week?

I'll see you Thursday, when I get back from Tracy's. Bye.

That definitely felt like a brush off, and very not like Coop. It made me think that I was probably right. He was working on a DEA task force. Rural areas are prime locations for under-the-radar drug rings, because of the isolation and the limited law enforcement budgets and manpower to combat them. So the DEA sometimes sets up a task force that uses their personnel with local cops to pool resources and expertise. If Coop was assigned to work on one, that would explain why he'd hardly been around lately. And why he wasn't giving me any answers.

CHAPTER 17

FATHER LINDSTROM looked a bit nonplussed when he pressed the buzzer on our front door and *All About That Bass* boomed out, but he took it in stride.

"Sorry, Father, Mom changed up her doorbell tunes, but she left the volume a little high. Happy Thanksgiving. At least she didn't start dancing it out with you."

"Very catchy song, Leah," he said with a distinct twinkle in his eyes.

My mother gave him a quick hug and led him into the living room where Paul and Miguel were already sitting. She handed him a glass of the wine Miguel had brought, and they all sat back to watch the endless pre-football programming while I helped Mom finish up in the kitchen.

Thanksgiving dinner was predictably epic. My mother is a great cook, and Paul knows his way around a green bean casserole.

"Wonderful meal, Carol," Father Lindstrom said. "I'm afraid I may have flirted with the second deadly sin today. Gluttony," he added, for those of us not well-versed in the Baltimore Catechism.

"I'm sure God will forgive you," I said. "Jesus himself would have a hard time resisting Mom's turkey stuffing."

"Great job, sweetheart." Paul leaned over and kissed my mother on the cheek.

"*Tan bueno.* So, good. Thank you, Carol."

My mother stood and took a small bow. "Thank you. I'm just glad so many of my favorite people could be here. Who's ready for pie?"

A collective groan went up.

"How about later, when we're watching the game? We need some time for this to digest," I suggested.

As everyone was nodding in agreement, Paul, Miguel, and Father Lindstrom started clearing the table. My phone rang. Isabel. I'd forgotten to get back to her like I had texted I would on Monday. I just had so much work to cram in at the paper because of our early holiday deadline.

"Hey, Isabel."

"Hi, Leah. I'm sorry, I know it's Thanksgiving, but this will just take a minute. When we texted earlier this week, you were going to call and talk to me about Jamie. He's been in a terrible mood ever since you questioned him, and he's barely talking to me about anything. And then today he just took off. I'm worried about him. I just thought if there was any more you could tell me, maybe I'd know what to say to him. And—you know what? This is stupid. You're with your family, it's a holiday. Forget it. We can talk tomorrow."

Her voice was both wistful and apologetic. I felt a stab of guilt that I hadn't called her, or even spared a thought for what this first family holiday without her father might be like.

"No, no, that's okay. I'm sorry I didn't get back to you. It was crazy busy at work, but how about if I run out to see you now?"

"Oh, no. You don't have to do that. Not on Thanksgiving. It was stupid to call."

"No. It wasn't. I'm practically on my way. See you shortly." I hung up and realized that my mother had been listening.

"You're leaving?"

"Just for a little while. I feel like a jerk. Isabel is all alone in that house. I never even thought about her. I'll be back before Coop gets here to watch the game."

"Why don't you take her a plate of food and some pie?"

"Yeah, I guess I could. She might like that."

"Good. I'll make enough for both her and her brother. And I'll make one for Vesta too. You can drop it off on the way."

"Whoa. Wait a minute. I told you I was out of the delivery game as far as Vesta is concerned, after last time."

Vesta Brenneman is an elderly eccentric who lives in a tumbledown house on the outskirts of town. She spends her days riding her bicycle all over the county with her little dog Barnacle in the front basket. Even winter doesn't deter her, as long as the roads are plowed. She hardly ever speaks, and when she does, it's mostly to quote Bible verses. She should probably be in an assisted living home, but she'd fight for her independence tooth and nail. And she'd never, ever give up her dog. My mom and some of the other women from St. Stephen's look out for her with gifts of food and clothing, and someone makes sure she always has her heat on.

"She chased me right out the door last time. And she's way on the other side of town from the Whitings."

"Oh stop it. It will take an extra 15 minutes, just run it in. Think what a nice treat it will be for her."

"Chica, I'll go with you. I'm parked behind you anyway. It'll be fun. I'd like to meet Vesta."

Ten minutes later I was in the car with Miguel. Mom's Thanksgiving boxes of goodies for Vesta, Jamie and Isabel sat in the back seat. Rain had fallen off and on during the morning and early afternoon, but the temperature had dropped, and now it was turning into a light, silvery sleet.

As we came to a stop sign Miguel's car fishtailed a little, and the Thanksgiving bounty slid and shifted on the back seat.

"Hey, take it easy, unless you want to accessorize your outfit with a slice of pumpkin pie on your shoulder."

"Sorry, chica. Black ice. Which way to the famous Vesta's house?"

"She lives on Birch Street, the last block, the only house left standing." We were both too full of turkey and trimmings to talk much as we neared the southern edge of town. As we turned onto Vesta's street, out of the corner of my eye, I saw her pedaling toward us on her bike. I started to unroll the window to hail her down, just as her bike wobbled and leaned precariously over. She managed to keep it upright, but her dog Barnacle bounced out of the basket, staggered, then ran yipping across the road right in front of us.

"Miguel!"

He slammed on the brakes. The wheels locked and the car spun out on the slippery street as he lost control of the steering wheel. A blue pickup coming in from a side street blared its horn and tried to swerve out of our path, but too late. As Miguel's Toyota caromed off the side, the airbags deployed, hitting us both in the face. Then we were bouncing across a vacant lot strewn with broken concrete, old tires, and potholes, each more jarring than the last. Finally, blessedly, the car came to a stop. We both took a second to get our bearings, coughing and choking on the chemical dust that shot into the air along with the airbags.

"Are you OK?" I managed to croak, undoing my seatbelt and turning to look at Miguel.

He nodded.

"Let's get out of here. Can you move?"

"Yes, yes, chica, I'm fine." He smiled, but his grin looked as shaky as I felt. When Miguel tried to open his door it was jammed shut. By now the truck driver had run over to us, and he yanked my door open so fast I almost fell out.

"You guys all right?"

"Yeah, yeah. Fine. The driver's door is jammed shut though. Miguel, can you slide over, get out on my side?"

It wasn't easy with his long frame, but he managed to wrestle with the deflated airbag, scoot across the console, and squeeze out the passenger door.

"I already called 911," the truck driver said. He was a big man in a Carhart coat that hung open over his well-stuffed flannel shirt. "I'm Gus Lundquist. You're sure you're all right now, the both of you?"

"Leah Nash, Gus. This is my friend Miguel Santos." We extended our hands and Gus shook each of them in his bear-size paw. It was then I noticed Vesta hovering behind him, Barnacle shivering in her arms.

"Are you all right, Vesta?"

"'O thou afflicted, tossed with tempests,'" she said. Then surprisingly, she scurried forward and took my hand, pulling me in the direction of her house.

"Now hold on there, ma'am." Gus turned to her. "We got the police and the ambulance comin.' These folks need to be checked out."

"'Out of the South cometh the whirlwind, and cold out of the North.'" She continued to tug on my arm.

"Let's all go with her," Miguel said. "It's freezing out here." His teeth chattered in testament to the fact.

"Vesta's house is right across the street," I said.

"You go ahead then. I'll wait in my truck for the cops; it's plenty warm for me. I'm gonna call back and say that's a negative on the ambulance, though, unless you two feel worse than you look."

"I'm fine," I said.

"Me, too."

"All right then. You go with the lady there."

So there we were, Vesta in the lead, holding Barnacle in one arm, tugging me with the other, while I grabbed onto Miguel's hand to reassure myself that he really was all right.

Once inside the oddly furnished little house, Vesta flipped a switch. Two bare lightbulbs hanging overhead came to life and threw faint light into the gloomy space. She gestured for me to sit on her iron-framed bed, made up with a faded and frayed pink chenille bedspread. She gently set Barnacle down in a basket on the floor, near an ancient wall-mounted gas furnace that sent welcome hot air into the room. She moved to the small stove and turned the burner on under the teakettle, then set out two cups and retrieved a withered teabag from a saucer on her small counter.

Next, she turned her attention to Miguel. She pulled him to the sink and turned on the porcelain handle of the hot water faucet. She reached for a slightly grimy washcloth that she lathered with a yellowed and cracked bar of soap. She moved it gently over his forehead.

"Ouch!" He jerked back a little, and I saw that Vesta's ministrations had uncovered a quarter-sized abrasion on his forehead. She stopped, a stricken look in her eyes. Miguel saw he had alarmed her.

"No, it's fine, Vesta. Thank you. Gracias. It feels much better, thank you," he said in a soothing voice and smiled. She smiled back.

"You saved Barnacle," she said, in the most coherent sentence I'd ever heard her utter. At the sound of his name, the little dog leaped from his basket and ran to her feet. She picked him up and cradled him in her arms. As she stood there in her baggy, raggedy pants at least a size too big, her grubby fisherman's knit sweater hanging down on her skinny thighs, still wearing her hooded yellow slicker, a tear ran down her weathered cheek. She nuzzled her face in Barnacle's fur and looked very small and very vulnerable. I reached out to touch her arm in a gesture of reassurance and kindness. It was not reciprocated.

"'You are strangely troublesome,'" she said, turning an accusatory glare on me. The quote came from *Henry VIII*. I know my Shakespeare better than I do my Bible. Apparently she couldn't find a verse there to sufficiently express her irritation with me. She may have made room in her heart for Miguel, but clearly there was no vacancy where I was concerned.

"We almost got killed because of you and your dog, and I'm the troublesome one?"

Her only response was to hug Barnacle closer and edge a little nearer to Miguel, who appeared oblivious to the combined odor of sweat and menthol Vesta was exuding as she warmed up. As she smiled at him again, the teakettle whistled. She put Barnacle down, turned it off, and poured hot water into each of the cups she'd set out. I watched as she dipped the used teabag back and forth into the water in the two cups. Miguel and I exchanged a glance, but knew there was nothing to do but accept Vesta's version of a tea party. Satisfied that the brew had reached maximum potential, she squeezed the bag with her fingers over each cup, then put it back on its saucer and handed us each a mug.

"*Salud!*" Miguel said, as he clinked his cup with mine. I closed my eyes and swallowed, trying to focus on the warmth not the flavor, which was reminiscent of dirty dishwater and essence of Vesta.

"What is all this, Vesta?" Miguel asked. He gestured toward the feather and stone-filled plastic bags on the windowsill; the naked, bald plastic baby dolls piled in a jumble on the top of a tall dresser; and a woven basket on the floor that held tightly crunched shiny balls of aluminum foil in varying sizes.

"My collections." She preened a little as he complimented her on her specimens. "She doesn't have collections," she said with a disdainful nod in my direction. "Do you, boy?"

I saved Miguel from disillusioning his new friend by announcing that the police had arrived, and we should go outside.

He nodded agreement, then turned to Vesta. "Gracias so much for taking care of us."

But before she let him leave, Vesta carefully applied a Cookie Monster bandaid to Miguel's forehead. Me, she ignored. Which actually was an improvement over chasing me out the door.

CHAPTER 18

WHEN WE GOT TO THE CAR, our truck driver friend Gus was already talking to the cops.

"You go ahead, Miguel. You and Gus need to exchange insurance information. I'm going to call Isabel and tell her what happened. I'll be over in a minute."

Isabel picked up on the first ring, and I explained the situation.

"Yeah, we're OK, but Miguel's car is in pretty bad shape. He's definitely not going to be driving away from this one. Hold on just a second." I gestured to the cop, who was looking my way, to indicate that I was wrapping things up.

"OK, sorry. I better go."

"I'll come get you and take you home."

"Hey no, you don't need to do that. I'll just call my mother; we only live a few miles away."

"Too late, I'm pulling out of my driveway. This wouldn't have happened if I hadn't called you. The least I can do is give you a ride. What's the address?"

It was still sleeting, my hair was getting wet, my hands were freezing, and I didn't feel like arguing. I gave her Vesta's address.

"Be there in a few minutes."

I walked over to talk to the officer and added what I could to Miguel's account. He was pretty nice and let him off without a ticket. It may have been because it was Thanksgiving, or maybe because of the extremely sad expression on Miguel's face as he watched the wrecker come and load up his car. Gus, our pickup-driving friend, had stayed around to the end.

He clapped Miguel on the shoulder as the tow truck pulled away. "Looks totaled to me, amigo," he said. "Still, you walked away; that's gotta be a good feeling."

"Sí. That's true," Miguel said, as he tried to rally from his loss. "Thanks, Gus, for being so cool. I'm so sorry I hit your truck."

The big man shook his head. "Couldn't be helped. Glad you didn't hit the old lady's dog. You take 'er easy now, buddy." He climbed back into his pick up and gave a beep on his horn as he pulled away. Just then a green Escalade came driving up the street.

"Who's that?" Miguel asked as he watched the car pull up and park in Vesta's driveway.

"Isabel is giving us a ride back to mom's."

She parked and stepped out of the SUV. Vesta came barreling out of her house as we walked toward Isabel and planted herself in front of her.

"'When the enemy shall come in like a flood, the Spirit of the Lord shall lift up a standard against him.'"

Isabel took a half-step back.

Miguel went for Vesta as I came up behind Isabel.

"Thanks for coming. Don't be alarmed, Vesta doesn't like strangers."

"I can see that," she said, her nose wrinkling slightly as *eau de Vesta* wafted her way.

"Vesta, *cálmate*. Calm down. It's fine. This is Isabel. She's not here for you. She's taking us home. But first let me take you inside. It's too cold out here for you." He whisked her back into the house before she could protest.

"Now there's an odd couple. What is Miguel doing with her?"

"We were just dropping off some Thanksgiving dinner my mother sent her. It went the same way yours did, all over the car. Sorry."

When Miguel came back out, Isabel gave him a hug.

"Miguel! It's been a long time. Since high school I think. It's nice to see you."

"Hi, Isabel." His greeting was more subdued than usual. "I'm sorry about your papá," he added.

"Thank you. Well. Why don't you both get in the car? The heater's on high, and you look like you need it."

As we approached my house I saw Coop's car parked out front.

"You can park in the driveway, Isabel. Where Miguel's car would have been. He won't be needing the space anymore."

He emitted a sound between a whimper and groan. "Chica, you have no heart."

"Too soon?"

"No, I shouldn't come in," Isabel said. "You've got company, you've just been in a car wreck—"

"Please, come in. I know my mom would like to meet you."

The predictable pandemonium broke out as we entered and my mother got a good look at us. Somehow, between introducing herself to Isabel, demanding to know what had happened, plying Miguel with a big fluffy towel to dry his hair, and handing us both a shot of Bailey's in a cup of coffee, she managed to put together a plate of food for Isabel and sit her down at the kitchen table. I slipped off at the height of the activity to stand in a hot shower for five minutes. When I emerged Coop was talking to Isabel at the table, and Father Lindstrom was offering Miguel a ride home.

"Gracias, padre. But I don't want you to miss the game."

He waved off Miguel's polite resistance. "I'm taping it, and I should be getting home any way. Early day tomorrow. You might find an early night and a hot shower of benefit as well."

"He's right, Miguel. If not for yourself, do it for your hair." His usually perfectly styled hair was hanging down in his eyes, and he looked fried.

"What are you going to do about your car?" Coop asked.

"I don't know. My Aunt Lydia and Uncle Craig only have the one car. I can't borrow theirs, because what if my uncle got the call for a kidney? *Ándale*, they'd have to go. I can't be 30 miles away with their car. I have to check with my insurance. I don't know." He sounded uncharacteristically down as the full implications of being without a car hit him.

"Don't stress Miguel, we'll figure it out. Get your hair back to normal and everything will look better in the morning."

He gave me a half-hearted grin, and then he and Father Lindstrom took off.

"I should go too," Isabel said.

"Oh, have a piece of pie, won't you? It came out pretty well if I do say so myself."

"Well… "

"I'm going to take off too," Coop said, pushing back from the table. "Good meeting you, Isabel."

"Hey, don't go, Coop. I've hardly seen you in weeks. I want to tell you—" I stopped because part of what I wanted to tell him and ask him and debate with him were the various leads in the Whiting story. And I wasn't ready to share all those with Isabel yet.

"I know. I want to talk to you, too. It just didn't work out today. How about Saturday? We could grab some lunch?"

"Saturday? OK, yeah, that would be good. Meet you at the Elite at noon?"

"Yep, that works."

I walked him out.

"I know that you're involved with some big secret investigation. How about some details?"

"Not going to work, Leah. I told you, we'll talk Saturday. Sounds like we both have information to share. Until then, you'll just have to wait."

"Then you are working on something big, aren't you? Something with the DEA? Just tell me. I bet you have a cool windbreaker with

DEA stenciled on the back. Are you wearing a DEA super agent T-shirt under that sweater?" I made as if to lift it up, and he laughed and pushed my hand away.

"Saturday. OK?"

"Got it. OK. But there better be a big reveal to make all this waiting worthwhile."

He gave me look I couldn't quite read and said, "There will be."

Bemused, I wandered back into the kitchen where Isabel was telling my mother and Paul about meeting Vesta.

"Those crazy eyes and that hair and that outfit. She looked like something from a horror movie." Her graceful hands fluttered as she talked, and her voice ascended into a passable impression of Vesta squawking out a Bible quote. She was a good mimic, but after witnessing Vesta's vulnerability this afternoon, I didn't feel like laughing. I could see my mother didn't think it was so funny, either.

"Vesta was a college professor years ago. When her sister was diagnosed with Huntington's, she took care of her. It's a terrible, terrible illness. After Dora died, Vesta had a complete breakdown. She never really recovered. Just became more and more eccentric and alone. It's a sad story."

Isabel looked abashed. "That's awful. I'm sorry. I didn't mean anything by what I said. I didn't know."

"Well, how would you?" my mother relented. "Can I get you another piece of pie?"

"No, it was delicious. Everything was. But I should get going. I just wanted to talk to Leah for a minute."

"Sure. Paul, let's see how the game is coming." The two of them returned to the living room, and I sat down next to Isabel.

"Jamie's pretty mad at me for getting you involved in this."

"I got that impression when we talked. He and your dad—Jamie seems to hate him."

"He doesn't mean it, not really. My father wasn't the warm, fuzzy type. But he loved us. I know he did." She said the last part emphatically, though whether to convince me or herself, I wasn't sure.

"Isabel, you didn't mention that your mother left money to Jamie, but none to you. Why didn't she leave you anything?"

"She never thought of me as her 'real' daughter, even though she adopted me. I was used to it. And it's not like I ever expected anything from her."

"And your father lost Jamie's inheritance?"

"Not all of it. He used part of it for Jamie's rehab. Private boarding schools are very expensive."

"You should have told me that."

"I didn't think it mattered."

"Isabel, everything matters. You can't be the one who decides what counts and what doesn't, not if you want me to find out the truth. It seems to me Jamie has some pretty good reasons to be angry with your father."

She waved it off as though it weren't worth talking about and changed topics.

"Mrs. Godfrey told me you took the box of my father's things over for Miss Quellman. Thank you for that. Did you find out anything from her? Or when you talked to Frankie?"

She seemed desperate for anything that would take the spotlight off Jamie.

"The more I dig, the more odd things I'm turning up. Let's just say I'm very curious about Dr. Bergman. And I caught Frankie in a lie, but I don't know what that means yet."

"What? What did you find?"

"I'm not getting into specifics right now. And I'd appreciate it if you don't share with anyone—especially Frankie and Dr. Bergman—what I've said." I was regretting my information share, scant though it was, already.

"I wouldn't say anything! But you really think Frankie is lying about something?"

"I know she is. But the question is why. She struck me as one of those women who just can't get it right when it comes to men." *Unlike you who has such a stellar track record,* said that snide, inconvenient internal voice. I hate that voice.

"But does that mean you don't think Jamie had anything to do with it? Because he didn't, I'm sure."

"Isabel," I said with a touch of exasperation, "that's why it's probably best if I don't give you any details. You're too close to things, and you're going to worry and imagine and try to second guess, when I don't even know where things are going yet."

"I'm not pushing you. Even though it probably sounds like it. I do appreciate that you're helping me. I really do."

She stood. "I should go." She raised her voice so my mother could hear her. "Thanks so much for the dinner, Mrs. Nash."

"You're very welcome, Isabel." I noticed she didn't tell Isabel to call her Carol. She must still be a little miffed about Isabel's Vesta mimicry. My mother doesn't forgive and forget as easily as I do.

CHAPTER 19

NEXT MORNING I went to the office early to do some checking on Frankie's story about her weekend race. The weather was weird. Yesterday's freezing drizzle had turned into dense fog and a light rain, but the temperature was a balmy (for winter Wisconsin) 45. I left without even a jacket, despite my mother's protests. The *Times* wasn't officially open. We always take a long holiday weekend at Thanksgiving, but I half-expected Rebecca to be there. She wasn't. I parked out front and went through the big double doors. The reception desk, as expected, was Courtnee-free. I had the blissful silence of an empty office to myself.

Of course if anything came in on the scanner, given Miguel's car situation, I'd have to roll. But if it didn't, I could really get some work done on the Garrett Whiting story, which I hadn't touched since earlier in the week.

The first thing I did was bring up the *Lake Neshaunoc News* online. It's a weekly with an even smaller circulation than the *Himmel Times* and an even smaller staff. Which was good for my purposes, because it meant that the paper printed just about everything handed to them by the community. That should include a very thorough description of the Fall Fun 10K Run. If Frankie Saxon had been there, I should be able to find her name in a story.

I dug into the online archives. The results included the names of all the entrants, listed in order by their times for finishing the race. I checked it forward and backward. Twice. No Frankie Saxon, no Francesca Saxon, no F. Saxon. No Saxon at all.

The write-up also included the name of the race organizer and a phone number. He answered on the first ring.

"This is Gil Teed."

"Gil, hi, this is Leah Nash at the *Himmel Times*. I was wondering if you could give me some information about the 10K run you organized a couple of months ago."

"What kind of information?"

"Do the runners all have to enter beforehand?"

"We try to enforce that. We have prizes and gift bags donated by local merchants, so we need a good count. Once in awhile someone just shows up though, and we usually let them run."

"Do you have a lot of no-shows?"

"Hardly any. They pay the fee in advance, so they lose it if they don't come."

"You know, I know someone who was telling me she really enjoys your event. Tries to run every year."

"Really? Who's that?"

"Frankie Saxon."

"Oh, sure. I know Frankie. Real nice gal. I was sorry she didn't make it this year. She signed up, but she was one of the no-shows."

"Yeah, she was ill, I think. Well thanks, Gil, this has been really helpful."

Frankie didn't come home that Sunday night because she was ill. She never even went to the race. She could have been in town the whole weekend. Which meant she had no alibi for Garret's death. And her elaborate lie about what she had done that weekend was an indicator that she might have needed one.

I was just getting ready to put in a call to Garrett's friend Miller Caldwell when I heard someone tapping on the glass doors of the front entrance. I went out, hoping it wasn't Betty Meier, lost again.

Instead, Isabel stood there holding two steaming paper cups in her hands. She smiled when I opened the door and waved her in.

"I stopped by your house. Your mother said you were here. I thought you might like a coffee break. Chai latte is your favorite, isn't it?"

"Yeah, sure. C'mon back." I noticed then that in addition to holding the refreshments, she was clutching a hoodie under her arm. She saw my glance and said, "Your mom asked me to bring you this. She said you left without a jacket."

"She's cold, so *I* need a hoodie." I took it from her.

"Well, it's getting colder out there; you might be glad to have it. But, oh, it's sure warm in here."

"Yeah, the furnace has two settings: Arctic Circle and Hell." She handed me my chai, then shrugged out of her hoodie, which was identical to mine. I took it and laid both of ours on Miguel's clean desktop.

"It's not what I thought a newspaper office would be like," she said, looking at the sparsely furnished, slightly dingy newsroom, with its two beat-up desks, plastic visitor chairs, and dinged-up beige filing cabinets.

"Not exactly the *New York Times*, right? But you did catch us on an off day. We're actually closed. I'm just here taking advantage of the peace and quiet."

She pulled up a plastic chair and sat beside my desk. She took a sip of her coffee, then said, "I'm sorry to bother you again, but I didn't want to say anything with everyone around last night. I have to tell someone. I'm pretty sure Jamie's using again."

"Why do you think so?"

"Well, that would explain why he got so mad at you. That's not like him. Not like the real Jamie anyway. He's quiet and kind of shy. Really sweet. And he's been taking off, won't tell me where he's going. He's dropped all his classes at UW."

"Could be that's just how he's coping with his loss. He seemed pretty clear-eyed to me. Pretty mad, but he definitely wasn't high."

"Maybe. I hope so. You already know he didn't feel the same way about Dad that I did. Dad was always tough on Jamie. I think to make up for the way our mother treated me—like I didn't exist. But Dad loved Jamie. I don't think Jamie ever believed that. Anyway, I don't want you to get the wrong idea about him."

"What idea is that?"

"Well, you know. You said Mrs. Wright saw Jamie's car driving away from the house the night Dad died. And he got so mad at you, and he told me he sort of shoved you and everything. I don't want you to think that he was mad because he had something to hide."

She was obviously used to being the protective older sister. A role with which I was very familiar.

"I'm not coming after Jamie, Isabel. True, I'd like to know why his car—or what looked like his car," I amended as she started to protest, "was seen driving away from the direction of the house that night at the time that he says he was at a party in town. But there are lots of other things I want to know too, involving other people."

"You mean like Frankie and Dr. Bergman?"

I put my hands up in the time-out sign. "Isabel, I've already told you all I'm going to say about my research for right now. Please stop trying to wheedle it out of me."

"Sorry."

I lightened up a little.

"It's all right. Let's not talk about it anymore. This chai is really good, thanks."

We made small talk for a few minutes, and when we had finished our drinks she said, "I'll let you get back to work. No, don't bother." She waved her hand as I started to get up. "I can find the way out." She grabbed her hoodie and then turned back as she reached the door. "I won't call you. You call me, OK?"

"Deal," I said. "As soon as I have something to tell you."

I had no luck reaching Miller Caldwell, but left messages at his office and on his home phone. I didn't have a cell number for him, and his secretary wasn't inclined to give it to me. I wasn't quite ready to call

Frankie yet and confront her with what I'd found out. Besides, that would be better done in person. Instead, I stepped away from the Garrett Whiting story for awhile and tackled something that might actually earn me a brownie point or two with Rebecca: filling out my mileage and expense reports before the end of the month.

As I emailed the forms to Courtnee, I felt extremely pleased with myself. In celebration of my mastery over paperwork, I decided to call it a day and check in on Miguel. I stood and started to pull my hoodie on, then realized something wasn't quite right. Besides smelling faintly of Isabel's perfume, the zippered sweatshirt was extremely soft inside, with the fluffy quality of a new, never-washed hoodie. And it was at least a size too big. I like mine roomy, but the sleeves on this one came well past my wrists.

Isabel must have taken mine by mistake when she left. I'd have to call and arrange for an exchange later. I walked down the hall and pushed open the door. As it slammed behind me, a chilly gust made me thrust my hands in my pockets and admit that my mother might have been right. I jogged to my car, head down against the wind.

When I pulled out my hand to open the door, I also pulled out a piece of paper that fluttered to the ground. I picked it up and smoothed it out. An ATM receipt for a $500 withdrawal. I looked closer at it. The time stamp was Oct. 13, 3:30 a.m. The day Garrett died. And the ATM location was JT's Party store, a straight shot down the road from the Whiting house. What was it doing in Isabel's jacket, when she told me she didn't arrive home until 8:30 a.m.?

CHAPTER 20

MY PHONE RANG before I had time to process the thought.

"Leah, hi, this Isabel. I just realized I must have grabbed your hoodie when I left. Can I come down and switch it with you? The thing is, it's really Jamie's. He isn't even awake yet, so I'll get it back before he gets up. He hates it when I borrow his things without asking."

Jamie's hoodie. Not Isabel's.

"Leah? Hello? Is it all right if I come down now?"

"Uh, yeah, sure. I'll see you in a few."

Back at my desk, I laid the ATM slip out and stared at it. Jamie's jacket. Jamie's ATM slip. Jamie, who told police he was at a party until 4 a.m., so wasted he didn't remember anything. Had he instead used the party and the drunken, hazy memory of a friend as his alibi? Had he gone home much earlier and killed his father, set up the suicide, and then taken a quick and cold-blooded trip to the nearest ATM?

"Isabel, can you explain why this was in Jamie's pocket?" I shoved the ATM withdrawal slip over to her. "Look at it. It's date-stamped just 15 minutes after Mrs. Wright saw Jamie's car driving away from your house. When Jamie said he was at a party in town."

"I don't understand. He *was* at a party. Keegan was with him. Ask him. He'll tell you. They didn't leave until 4 a.m. He couldn't have been at an ATM at 3:30. Besides, this says it was a $500 withdrawal. Jamie doesn't have $50 in his account, let alone $500."

"But I'm sure your father did. I bet if you look at his account, you just might find a $500 withdrawal from it. Made when he was already dead. That's quite a trick."

"What are you saying? That Jamie killed our father for $500? That's crazy. Anyway, how would he even know Dad's pin number?"

"Your father kept a list of his passwords and pin numbers taped to the bottom of his keyboard. I'll bet you and Jamie both knew that." She didn't deny it.

"But Jamie was with Keegan. They left the party at the same time. He couldn't have been at the ATM at 3:30."

"If your best witness is a guy who was drunk off his ass, that's not very reliable."

"But the police believed him."

"And the police believe your dad committed suicide. So they're totally wrong about that, but infallible when it comes to assessing a witness? And there's the Mini Cooper driving away from your house."

"Mrs. Wright is an old lady who can't hear and probably can't see either. It was dark, it was late, who knows what kind of car she saw. If she even saw a car."

"Jamie pretty much told me he hated your father. He described him as manipulative, verbally abusive, neglectful, incapable of loving his own son. And Jamie was very angry that your father took the one thing that he got from his mother, his inheritance, and pissed it away on bad investments. Your brother might have felt he had some pretty good reasons to kill his father that had nothing to do with $500. That may just have been a bonus."

"No. My father loved Jamie. It wasn't his fault he got taken in by an investment scam. A lot of people did. And besides, I told you, Jamie's rehab was really expensive, and Dad was having cash flow problems then. He had to use the money. But he took out the insurance so we'd have something to fall back on." She was twisting her hands in her lap, her voice tight with anxiety.

"Maybe so, but Jamie didn't know that, did he?"

"Jamie didn't hate our father. He didn't kill him. I want you to stop saying that. I want you to stop it right now." She reached out and grabbed me by the shoulders, thrusting her face close to mine. "Do you hear me? Stop saying that. Stop, stop, stop. And stop investigating."

She released me and began to sob. After a minute I handed her a Kleenex, and she blew her nose noisily. When she looked up, the only evidence of her crying jag was a little dampness around her large brown eyes and a slight hiccup to her breathing. In similar circumstances I would have presented with an ugly red nose, swollen eyelids, and a thread of snot running down my chin.

"Leah, please. Promise me you won't go to the sheriff. It's already done, right? They said it was suicide. I was just crazy to think it wasn't. This other stuff, you're just guessing. You don't know anything. It doesn't matter."

"Yeah, it does. I can't just stop cold because you don't like where it's going."

"Well, at least will you talk to Keegan before you go to the sheriff? He was with Jamie. He'll prove Jamie couldn't have done it. And maybe the ATM slip wasn't even for my father's account. We don't know that for sure. I bet when I check his bank statements there won't be any withdrawal. Like I said, maybe Jamie found that slip and picked it up, you know, just stuck it in his pocket. Couldn't that have happened? Don't go to the sheriff. Please, talk to Keegan at least."

I hesitated for a minute, but in the end it wasn't that hard to agree. Not so much because of my tender heart, but because I was walking a fine line here. I thought the information I had dug up: Jamie's car on the road, his attitude about his father, his probable lie about where he was and what mental/physical state he was in. It all added up to something I knew I should take to the sheriff's department. But if I did, would it just get tossed aside, especially after the funny "joke" Ross had pulled on me? I didn't have a lot of credibility there.

If I took a little more time, I might be able to get the real story from Jamie's friend Keegan, or even better, I might be able to get security video of Jamie using the ATM.

"All right. I'll talk to Keegan. But you do something for me. Check your father's bank statement, see if there was a withdrawal of $500 the night he died. And don't talk to Jamie. Not yet. Agreed?"

"Agreed."

"I'm serious."

She gave a solemn nod. And then we both went on our way.

I called Coop at his office.

"Sorry, Leah, Coop has the day off today. Do ya want to leave a message?"

"No, that's OK, Melanie. I'll try his cell."

I had no luck. It went straight to voicemail. I didn't bother to leave a message. Instead I texted him.

Hey, any chance we can connect today? Things are getting interesting on the Whiting story.

I tried Miguel next.

Hey, I need you to help me think. I'm at the paper.

No luck there, either. I considered my next move. I didn't want to text or talk to Rebecca, but I probably should. I was leaning toward not contacting her, when in a surprise takeover, the keep-your-job part of my brain won. I texted Rebecca. I hoped Coop would respond first, because I'd like to get his take on things before I took on Rebecca.

I was three for three with no answers. I focused again on the ATM slip. Time for a trip to JT's Party Store.

JT's rundown building near the railroad tracks still has the same dented yellow aluminum siding it had when I was a kid. The faded red awning over the door is still positioned so that rain, snow, or sleet slide merrily off it and right onto the heads—or down the necks—of entering customers. When I was a kid, JT himself, a big bald man with a belly that rested comfortably on the low counter, kept a watchful eye on the grubby-handed kids who lusted after his stock of sugar-laden treats. The store had since changed hands, but the new owner kept the name. The emphasis now was on more adult-friendly treats—lottery tickets, liquor, cigarettes, and, I heard, fairly decent coffee. I hadn't been there in years. When I pushed through the heavy glass door, the scent of overcooked hot dogs rotating slowly on a glass-encased rotisserie hit me. But it was the sight of the person behind the counter that stopped me in my tracks. Cole Granger. Part-time drug dealer, part-time con man, full-time asshat.

CHAPTER 21

HE LOOKED UP as the bell over the door rang, then gave an insolent grin.

"Well now, if it ain't Miss Hot Shit reporter. I hear you got you a big book deal. Gonna be real famous ain't you? Did you come here to get some quotes from me? Gonna tell everybody how grateful you are for me helpin' you get the real story on that little sis of yours?" He looked pretty much the same as the last time I'd seen him a year ago—slicked-back mud-brown hair, yellow-flecked green eyes, thin-lipped mouth always on the verge of a cocky grin. His dragon tattoo, which I knew stretched up one arm, was covered by the long-sleeved T-shirt he wore. It stretched tautly across his thick-muscled chest and over the beginnings of a belly that would rival the original JT's one day.

"I thought you left town."

"I'm real touched at you keepin' tabs on me, but you're a little behind the times. I did leave town for a while. Had me some business opportunities. Unfortunately, they didn't work out. So here I am. Just another cog in the wheel of commerce." Cole and his then-girlfriend Delite had given me vital information about the death of my sister Lacey, in exchange for every dollar I had, and a few Miguel contributed too.

"Cole, just cut the crap. I'm working on a story. I'd like to talk to the owner about his ATM machine."

He ran his thumb and forefinger down either side of his chin before he answered.

"That would be my Uncle Chaz. He ain't here right now. Fact is, he won't be back 'til spring. He and Aunt Florinda, they got a nice little condo in Alabama for the winter. You could say I'm in charge." Cole didn't speak with the typical middle Wisconsin accent—a combination of brusque Germanic tones oddly laced with a light Scandinavian lilt. Instead, he retained the drawling cadence of the Kentucky hills his family came from and used a vocabulary that showed he wasn't as dumb as he looked.

"You're in charge? Why do I find that hard to believe?" He had a history of petty theft, small time drug dealing, and general bad behavior. I doubted even an uncle blinded by family feeling would leave him in charge of a business where money changed hands regularly.

"I'd just have to say that's because of your judgmental nature, Leah. Now why, I wonder, do you want to know about our time machine?"

Anyone not from Wisconsin might be taken aback with Cole's reference to something that seemed to belong in *Dr. Who* or an episode from a *Rocky & Bullwinkle* cartoon. But here in the land of milk and cheese, when ATMs were first introduced they were promoted as Take Your Money Everywhere (TYME) machines. The name stuck with some people, even as the acronym faded. So it's not unheard of for someone to refer you to the "time machine" in the lobby. Though it might be a letdown to discover that you're only making a cash transaction, not booking a trip to another dimension.

"I told you, it's for a story. What kind of security camera do you have on it? How long do you keep the recordings?"

"It's a fine piece of equipment. Real safe and secure for our customers. 'Course it don't exactly have a security camera on it. This is what you call a gently used older model. Doesn't have all the bells and whistles. Little cheaper that way, and Uncle Chaz is very economy-minded. But like he says, we keep a real sharp eye on it, so our customers got no problems with it."

"You don't have any video?" My heart sank. I'd been sure that if I could get security footage from the ATM, it would show Jamie there in the early morning hours after his father died.

"Hold on there. I didn't say we got no video. Just we don't have video on the ATM. Happens we got a real deluxe video surveillance system right here in the store. Look up there, see? That camera right behind me? And that one over there by the machine?"

"So you do have video? Would you have it from October 13th, early morning? How long do you keep it?"

"I'm not sure I should be tellin' you all our security measures. Might give the wrong element an idea about how to take advantage of things. I don't think Uncle Chaz would like that."

"I really need to see that video."

He assumed a baffled expression, tilting his head to one side and raising an eyebrow. "Now, what's that got to do with a story about ATMs?"

"The video. Please." It took all I had to plead, but he had the advantage. And I'm willing to grovel, if it gets me the information I need.

"Sorry. Don't have anything to show you."

"But you said you have store surveillance video."

"Now, see, that's why you ain't in the big time anymore, Leah. You just don't listen. I said, we got a video surveillance camera, but I never said we had the video. This here system records on SD cards. Like I told you, Uncle Chaz, he's real economy-minded. We only keep 'em awhile, maybe a few weeks, and then I reformat and we reuse 'em. That video from, what did you say, six weeks ago? I'm pretty sure that one's long gone."

"Pretty sure? But maybe it isn't? Could you look?"

"Well, I'm awful busy right now, as you can see."

He stopped, and I stepped aside as a woman came up carrying a six-pack. I waited with mounting impatience while he checked her ID and rang her out.

When she left, he leaned forward, his hands on the counter.

"Now, what were you sayin'?"

"Couldn't you check, see if you might still have the SD card for the early morning of Oct. 13th?"

"October 13th, huh? My mama's birthday was October 12th. Had a real nice party for her. But I had to leave early. Had to work at 11 that night."

"Come on Cole, give me a break. Just look and see if you still have the card."

"Well now, I don't see as how it's worth my while. I'd have to go into the office, get down the box we file 'em in. Look all through it. Put it in the computer. I mean, you're askin' a lot, Leah, on such a busy day, too. I just can't see how there's any percentage in that for me."

I knew what he was getting at, but even if I had the cash, I couldn't use it for this story. I'd wiped out my bank account to find what he knew about Lacey, but that was personal. It wasn't for a story. I couldn't pay a source for information. Not and have it be worth anything.

"I don't have any money, and if I did, I wouldn't pay you for it."

He gave a fake wince. "Now you're hurtin' my feelin's, sweetheart. I don't believe I said anything about money. I just said I'm awful busy, and I don't think I have what you need. Leastwise not in the technology department. I'm sure I could meet your needs in other ways." I glared at him and he laughed.

The door opened again, and two college-age boys came in, followed by a group of teenagers laughing and shoving each other.

"Now, as you can see I got some customers need my attention. Can I help you find anything, or are you all set?"

"Thanks. For nothing." Defeated, I turned to go. He gave a nod and a smirk.

He was messing with me. I'd tipped my hand and let him know how much I wanted it, so he took pleasure in toying with me. I had to find some leverage, something that would make him let me see the footage for that night. What, I didn't know at the moment.

Back in the car I pulled out my phone. 2:45. I was bursting to talk to Coop or Miguel about what had turned up, but neither had answered my text. Not even Rebecca, who I really didn't want to talk to but probably should, had responded. I drummed my fingers on the steering wheel while I thought, then went back to the paper to track down an address for Jamie's friend Keegan.

CHAPTER 22

THE COLLEGE-AGE KID WHO OPENED the door was big. I mean line backer big, with a thick neck, heavily muscled arms, and a really large head. His belly was big too, pushing out between the bottom of his Milwaukee Brewers T-shirt and the top of the drawstring sweatpants he wore. His blue eyes had suspiciously large pupils. As he struggled to focus, he blinked and gave a shake of his head, like a befuddled buffalo.

"Yeah?"

"Keegan Monroe? Hi. I'm Leah Nash. I'm a reporter with the *Times*. Can I come in for a minute?" I spoke briskly, and already had a foot in the door before he had time to say no. He stepped back a little, and I squeezed through the opening and into a studio apartment that looked even smaller because of his massive size.

The single room with a tiny kitchen in one corner was littered with pizza boxes and empty beer cans. A tangle of sheets and blankets lay on the open hide-a-bed sofa in the middle of the floor. A trail of tiny styrofoam pellets leaked from a vinyl beanbag chair. The only other seat, which he gestured for me to take, was a wooden chair with two spindles missing from the back.

He dropped down on the edge of his unmade bed, making it jump up from the floor on the other side. A faint sweet odor lingered in the apartment, and I noticed an ashtray holding the stubs of several joints. Keegan rubbed his fingers lightly over the stubble on his jaw and nodded slowly at me, as though he didn't dare execute a rapid head movement.

"I'm hoping you can help me, Keegan. I'm doing a story on Garrett Whiting, and I'm trying to put together his last day."

His expression remained befuddled. He got up and lumbered to the refrigerator for a Coke, then grabbed a bag of chips off the counter. He chugged down the drink, followed it with a loud burp, reached into the bag of chips, and tried talking around the mouthful he had shoved in.

"Sorry. I didn't really know Dr. Whiting."

"But his son Jamie is a friend of yours, right? I talked to him the other day, and I know you were with him the night his father died." I compressed several bits of information together and hoped that he would assume Jamie had given me that information, not the police report.

"Yeah. Yeah. We were at a party." He spoke slowly, as though measuring each word. I couldn't tell if that was his natural speech pattern or the result of the weed he'd just smoked.

"It's almost unreal, isn't it? I mean you and Jamie, out having a good time at a party, and right across town, there was his dad so depressed he took his own life. Makes you think, doesn't it?"

Clearly, not very much could make Keegan think right at the moment, but he gave it a try, drawing his thick eyebrows down and tilting his head slightly. "Yeah. Absolutely. Want some chips?" He extended the bag toward me, his latent sense of hospitality apparently having awakened.

I shook my head. "No, but thanks. You go ahead. You and Jamie have been friends for a long time?"

He knew this answer without any thinking at all. "Yeah. Since kindergarten."

"It must have been rough, watching him go through all that happened these last few years. His mom dying, I mean, then the drug issues, and now his dad commits suicide. Unbelievable."

"Yeah. Heavy stuff." He frowned at the Coke can he was holding in his thick, meaty fingers. I'd been worried that he'd be wary of talking to me, intent on protecting Jamie's alibi, but whether it was the relaxing embrace of a marijuana high, or a naturally non-inquisitive nature, he didn't seem to have any problem with my questions.

"Jamie doesn't really remember much about that night. Maybe it's a good thing. If he weren't so out of it, he might have been the one to find his dad's body. What time was it that you guys left the party?"

"The party?" He looked around as though a group of fellow stoners previously unnoticed might be found lounging in the corners.

"The party you and Jamie went to that night? Remember, he ran into you at the gas station, you invited him to go with you to somebody's place. Got kind of loud and everybody was pretty wasted?"

"Ohhh. Yeah, the gas station. Jamie always takes it to the max. Wait a minute, I mean the min, right? His gas tank, I mean. He was runnin' on empty or I wouldna seen him that night. 'Cause he was getting gas."

"Right. Yes. But about the party you went to?"

"Yeah. The party. Wow. That was a party." He paused and grew silent, perhaps reliving the happy event. I prodded again.

"So you were there with your friends, having a good time. Now what time was that?"

"Jamie was really out of it." He laughed. "Me, too. I had such a good time, I don't even remember most of it. If Isabel didn't remind me about it, I probably wouldn't remember anything."

"Isabel?"

"Yeah, she called to tell me about Dr. Whiting. Said Jamie was really messed up. She was kind of mad at me. But hey, I didn't make him come. I mean, I just asked, but it was like, his choice. Do you think it's, like, my fault Jamie got wasted?"

"No, I don't. Keegan, are you saying you didn't actually remember when you and Jamie left the party until you talked to Isabel?"

He shifted a little and looked slightly abashed. "No. Yeah, kinda, I guess. I was kinda hazy, but it came back. Isabel, she like, refreshed my memory."

"How could she 'refresh' your memory if she wasn't there? She wasn't, was she?"

He laughed. "Not her thing. But she said we musta got back really late, because Jamie was still pretty out of it when she got home. She said the cops were gonna make a hassle for him if he couldn't remember when. So, like we talked about the party for awhile, and that kinda helped bring it back. Besides, 2 in the morning, 4 in the morning? What's the difference anyway?"

"So you told the police you left at 4, but you didn't really remember it?"

"Yeah. Sure. I mean, I didn't tell them I didn't remember. Like, I did remember, after Isabel reminded me, just not at first. What's it matter? Jamie's my bro. I got his back. Who cares what time we left? Jamie and me, we were both pretty turnt up. He couldn'ta stopped his dad anyway, no matter what time he got home."

It was clear Keegan wasn't the brightest star in the Monroe family firmament. And that it hadn't occurred to him he had been pushed by Isabel to give Jamie an alibi for murder, regardless of the fact that he had no real memory of how the evening played out. Why she did it was obvious.

Isabel arrived home, found her father dead and her brother in bed. She didn't believe her dad had committed suicide, but if it were murder, she wanted to be sure Jamie wasn't a suspect. When she woke him up, and he said he couldn't remember anything, she believed him. But she knew the police might want more than his word. Enter Keegan, a willing stooge, ready to stand by Jamie. She got the two of them on the same page, and it worked. She pushed me to Keegan because she thought it would work again. Maybe it would have, if he hadn't been high, and I didn't already have serious suspicions about Jamie.

The silence between us had stretched on for some seconds as I processed this, but Keegan was unperturbed by the quiet. He dug lustily in his bag of chips, then polished it off by tipping the open bag over his mouth and shaking the last crumbs down his gullet. He got up and came back with a bag of M&Ms, and attacked them with the gusto of someone in the grip of major munchies. He did politely hold the bag out to me. This time I accepted a few.

"I don't suppose you remember who was at the party?"

"Dude, I don't even remember where the party was. Some guy's house, somewhere around here. Had to be kinda close, 'cause I walked home. It was just, you know, organic. Some guys are hangin' out, and then somebody texts somebody else, and then somebody else, and before you know it, you got a whole lotta people, and a whole lotta party. It's not like we had sign-in sheets." And then he started laughing at his own joke, probably picturing a party of drunk kids smoking weed, wearing nametags, and exchanging business cards.

One last question came to mind. "So do you and Jamie still get your stuff from Cole Granger?"

He gave me a knowing smile, like we were all stoners together. "Might be worth checkin' out. He's got like, what you call it? A small client base. Works out of a party store in town. JT's. But you gotta have an in, or he won't deal. Tell him Keegan sent you."

I may just have gotten that leverage I was looking for.

"Thanks Keegan, you've been great!" I said with such enthusiasm that he blinked.

"No problem, man." The smile on his good-natured face made me smile in spite of the situation.

It was almost four o'clock, and I started for home, then decided to swing by the paper on the off chance that Rebecca or Miguel had stopped in. I was anxious to talk to somebody, and I really did think I'd gathered enough to get even Rebecca a little excited about the story.

As I drove into the parking lot, I didn't see either of their cars. I did see one that brought me up short. Jamie Whiting's Mini Cooper. His door opened even before I pulled into a spot. By the time I got out, he was standing in front of me, so close I could feel his breath on my cheek. He had me backed up against the car, and I didn't like the feeling. I put my hands up and pushed, not hard, but the surprise move threw him off balance and gave me time to move away from the car and reestablish my personal space.

"What can I do for you, Jamie?"

"You can quit telling my sister that I killed our father." His voice shook and his fists were clenched at his side.

So, Isabel had told him. It was probably too much to expect that she wouldn't. I doubted I would keep something like that to myself either. Not if my brother were at risk.

"I didn't say you killed your father. I'll ask you what I asked her. Why did you have an ATM receipt in the pocket of your hoodie? Date and time stamped when you and your friend Keegan told police you were at a party?"

"I don't know what you're talking about. And I don't owe you an explanation." His eyebrows were drawn down in a ferocious frown. "You're taking advantage of Isabel. She's all messed up about Garrett. You need to stop."

We were out in the open on a reasonably busy street, so although I wasn't very comfortable facing down an angry Jamie, I was pretty sure he wasn't going to do me bodily harm.

"Isabel came to me; I didn't approach her. But now that I've started, I'm going to finish. You don't have to answer my questions, that's true. But there are too many of them for me not to go to the police. And they'll ask more questions, not just to you, but your friends, your sister, your school, your neighbors. The truth will come out. All of it."

"I'm telling you the truth. I didn't kill my father. I don't know why you think I did. But if you don't leave this alone, people are going to get hurt." With that he turned on his heel and walked toward his car.

"Wait, Jamie. What people? Who's going to get hurt? Why?" My questions were drowned out in the roar of his engine as he peeled out of the parking lot and down the street.

CHAPTER 23

MY PHONE HAD PINGED a couple of times with text messages as I drove home, and I checked them as I walked into the kitchen.

Sorry. Can't get away. See you at Elite tomorrow.

Well, that was one confidante down. The next text didn't have any better news.

Chica, out with friends tonight. Details tomorrow.

Miguel was out of reach as well. I started to give a shout to my mother, who I assumed was in her room, when I noticed the note on the bar.

Leah, Paul and I went to Omico shopping, and then we're going to see a movie. Plenty of leftovers in fridge.

Great. My entire support system was AWOL. Even Rebecca had ignored me. I briefly thought about buzzing over to Father Lindstrom's, but decided to wallow in aggrieved self-pity instead. I piled a plate high with yesterday's bounty and sat down at the table to enjoy it. When I finished, I cut myself a piece of pumpkin pie, buried it in whipped cream, and slowly savored it.

My mother makes a pumpkin pie that is as close to a religious experience as I am ever likely to come. The cool sweetness of the whipped cream contrasted with the spiciness of the pie filling and the crisp crunch of flaky pie crust—pure bliss. By the time I finished I felt somewhat less alone in the world. I was also so full that it was time for either yoga pants or pajamas. I chose pajamas, even though it wasn't even five o'clock yet. Then I sat down with my laptop to review what I knew.

Things that say suicide
- Garrett's fingerprints on gun
1. Absence of struggle
- Absence of other fingerprints
- Health problems
- Financial problems
- Klonipin and alcohol in his blood, easy for doctor to get the drug

Things that could say murder
- Isabel's phone call with her father the night he died
- Garrett's book order, why would a suicide order a book the night he plans to die?
- No history of depression
- No note

Knowledge that if he killed himself, Isabel & Jamie would be SOL for the insurance
- Possible for someone else to administer Klonipin/alcohol mix, then pull the trigger

People who had reason to kill him
- Frankie—past affair, woman scorned?
- Dr. Bergman—drug use/fraud/sales—fear of exposure
- Jamie—suppressed rage over years of emotional abuse; anger over loss of inheritance
- Other??

Case against Frankie
- She lied about where she was that weekend. Why?
- Weak—she could be lying because she's having an affair, she's hiding a secret for someone else?

Case against Bergman
- He denied fight with Garrett, but was furious when I pressed, threatened lawsuit/arrest

160

- Miss Quellman's belief he was abusing/selling drugs
- So-so—need more information on drug situation
Case against Jamie
- His car or its twin seen driving away from house at 3:15 a.m.
- ATM slip stamped 3:30 a.m., crumpled up in Jamie's hoodie
1.   Keegan's inability to corroborate Jamie's story
- Jamie's violent reaction to my first interview with him
- His $100,000 inheritance, lost by his father
- An insurance policy that would give him financial freedom
- Question: did Jamie know about suicide clause?

I got up and grabbed my notebook. Riffled through the pages and found the notes I'd taken when I'd called Charlie Ross to eat crow. I always take notes when I'm talking to a source, even on background, unless it spooks them too bad. Sometimes I even take notes when I'm talking to a friend or to my dentist's office. I feel more comfortable communicating with a pen in my hand.

While Ross was gloating and rubbing it in about the insurance policy, he'd given me the name: Security Mutual Life. I knew Marty Angstrom was the agent; he was our insurance guy as well. I looked at my watch—4:55 on a Friday. What were the chances? Still, I made the call.

"Marty, hi! It's Leah Nash. I'm surprised I caught you."

"What can I do you for real quick, Leah?" I always like talking to Marty, because he's got that "up north" Wisconsin accent, which is stubbornly resistant to the homogenizing influence of television and a wired world.

"I'm hearing that Garrett Whiting had a life insurance policy with you that won't pay out for his kids, because it had a suicide clause. Is that true?"

"That's pretty confidential stuff there, ya know?"

"But your client is dead, Marty, and I got the information from Charlie Ross. Are you saying he got it wrong?"

He mulled that over for a second. "No, no. Charlie's right. But it's a standard clause, ya know? I don't want you puttin' anything in the paper, makin' the company look bad."

"This isn't for print, Marty." I moved on quickly before he thought to ask exactly what it was for. "Did Jamie and Isabel know about the suicide clause?"

My phone flashed a text message coming in. I ignored it.

"That was bad. Real bad. Real tough visit to make."

"So you had to tell Isabel and Jamie? They didn't already know about the clause?"

"Yah. Yah, I did. They said no. Jamie, he just kinda laughed. He's a strange sort of young fella. That suicide clause, when it kicks in, that's a tough one. Ya gotta think a guy was real far gone in his thinkin' to do that. Real hard on the families when they think they got some financial security, then find out they don't. Only had to break the news a coupla other times."

"But Garrett, he definitely understood about the clause?"

"He sure shoulda. I explained it all real clear when I wrote it up. If he had any questions, he coulda called me any time. I had a long talk with him a few months ago about changin' up his house insurance. He had some real good questions, but he never mentioned the life insurance. And I never talked to him again. Is that it Leah, or no? Only I got to stop by the store real quick, pick up some brats for dinner, is all."

"Yeah. That's it, Marty, thanks."

Things weren't looking any better for Jamie. If he'd known about the insurance, but not the suicide clause, and set up his father's "suicide," no wonder he was freaking out over Isabel pushing for a murder investigation. OK, so he didn't get the money he expected, but at least he was going to get away with murder, unless Isabel didn't give up.

I clicked on the text that had come in. Not from Coop with a change of plans, as I'd hoped. From Clinton, my agent, with a pointed question about whether or not I would have the page proofs of my book done by Sunday, as I'd promised. And a reminder that I was a new author who couldn't afford to clog up the production schedule.

He was right. And I pride myself on meeting deadlines. I sighed, then put everything else away and grabbed the page proofs sitting on top of the bookshelf. I worked steadily until I finished, sometime after midnight.

My mother was still sleeping when I left the house Saturday morning around 10. Coop and I weren't supposed to meet until noon, but I couldn't wait any longer. I drove over to his house, prepared to roust him out of bed. Enough of this elusive bullshit. I needed some face time with him.

I pulled in the driveway behind his car, which struck me as odd, because he always parks it in the garage. Unless he's building a new piece of furniture. His detached double garage serves as housing for both his car and workshop. He's really pretty good, and sometimes his projects get pretty ambitious.

I went through the breezeway to the side door, gave a quick knock, and walked on in like I usually do. But what I saw inside the kitchen as I stepped in wasn't usual at all.

Rebecca was standing at the counter, wearing one of Coop's blue work shirts and, it appeared, nothing else. Coop was sitting at the table in a white T-shirt and jeans. All three of us stared at each other for a minute, frozen in position like action figures abandoned in the middle of play.

Rebecca was the first to reanimate.

"Good morning, Leah. Care to join us?" She held out the coffee pot she was about to pour from.

"Uh, no. No, that's all right. Actually, I should go, I just—"

I glanced at Coop, who seemed to think that was a fine idea.

"Don't be ridiculous. Have a seat while I go get my day clothes on." She set the pot down on the counter and left the room.

Coop still hadn't said anything, and I burst out with the first thought that came to mind. Not a good idea.

"Rebecca?" I hissed. "Are you freaking kidding me? Is that the big secret stuff that's been going on? You've been seeing Rebecca?" My words ended on something between a squawk and an outraged yelp that seemed to jolt Coop into a response.

"Settle down, Leah. Yeah, Rebecca and I have been seeing each other for a while."

"So listening to me tell you how impossible she is, how controlling, how micromanaging, how she's always on my back—that makes you think, 'Wow, that sounds hot. I'd really like to date the woman who's making Leah miserable?'"

He stood up and walked over to where I was rooted to the floor.

"I know you and Rebecca don't see eye-to-eye at the paper. And I respect your feelings. That's why I didn't tell you before. I really like Rebecca. I wanted to tell you, but I wanted to do it the right way. I've been having a hard time trying to figure out what that was. You and I just see her differently."

"I'll say."

Rebecca returned then, wearing a sweater that clung to her lean frame tightly enough to make clear it was hers, and not Coop's, over a pair of skinny jeans. Her blonde hair was pulled back and she'd slipped on her glasses.

"I'm sorry you found out like this. David and I talked about how to tell you, and we really didn't want it to be awkward, but, well, here it is. Awkward."

"Don't worry about it."

David and I? Nobody but his mother had called Coop "David" since we were in seventh grade. *David and I talked?* I hated that she and Coop had talked about me and had jointly decided what to tell, or not tell, me. I hated that they discussed me like I was some kind of external problem. I was his best friend, not some awkward situation.

"It's probably a good thing you're both here. I wanted to talk to you both about Garrett Whiting." True enough, though my choice was

Coop first, to help me filter and reframe the facts for Rebecca's consumption. That wasn't going to happen. I plunged in and went over what I'd found out, wrapping up with the lists I'd put together last night.

"I have to give you credit. You've made a reasonable case for murder instead of suicide. I take it your money is on the son, Jamie?" Rebecca asked.

"At this point, yes."

"What are your chances of getting cooperation from this Cole Granger? The one you think might have access to video of Jamie using the ATM?" Before I could answer, Coop interrupted.

"Don't count on anything there. Cole's a conman from way back. He's just stringing Leah along, trying to see what he can get from her. Or even just to jerk her chain."

"I know the type," Rebecca said. And suddenly my story was the focus of a conversation that excluded me.

Stung, I interjected, "Excuse me. I think I know when a source is stringing me along. Cole knows something. I just may have an incentive that will make him talk."

"Now what does that mean? Don't do something stupid. He's a garden variety lowlife, but he can still be trouble." Coop was frowning at me, and his gray eyes held a warning.

"I don't need you to tell me how to do my job."

"No, that's my job," Rebecca said. "I agree with David. You need be careful with this Cole character."

"You're planning on sharing all this with Charlie Ross, aren't you?" Coop interfered in the conversation again.

"Yes, Coop, of course I am. Though that isn't exactly your call," I said testily. Before I could get any further unnecessary input from either of them, I made my exit.

"Well, I think we can skip the lunch date. It looks like we've both shared our news already, so I'll get going. See you guys later." I was moving toward the door as I talked and was already through it as I heard Coop say, "Leah, wait—"

I was in my car when he came barefooted onto the driveway. He looked so forlorn there, his naked feet on the freezing concrete, his arms waving to stop me, that I had to smile at the sight in my rearview mirror. It wasn't until I was several blocks away that I realized my eyes were watering. Damn allergies.

CHAPTER 24

"WHY DID IT HAVE TO BE such a big deal secret? That's what I don't get."

"Don't you, Leah?" Father Lindstrom sat across from me at the Elite, which was empty except for us in the late morning lull before lunch. I'd called him after my meet-up with Coop went bust, because I wanted to talk my feelings through but couldn't deal at the moment with Miguel's exuberant curiosity or my mother's probing questions.

"No. I don't. You don't lie to people you care about. He said he wanted to tell me 'the right way.' That was just an excuse to not tell the truth."

"Oh?" He gave me a quizzical look. "People keep things hidden for many reasons, not all of them bad. And not sharing private information isn't the same as lying."

I understood what he was saying. I just wasn't having any of it.

"This is different," I said stubbornly.

"All right." He took a sip of his tea, then set the cup down and finished off the apple strudel he'd ordered.

"So we're done talking about it? You don't think Coop was wrong?"

"I think that it's not my place to judge Coop."

"Or mine either?"

He didn't answer. This was not going the way I'd planned.

"You're a priest. It's kind of your job to make moral judgments, isn't it?"

"No wonder you left the Church, Leah, if that's what you think the role of a priest is. I'm sorry if I disappointed you. I believe you'll figure this out on your own, in time. I would only urge you to remember there are things you can change and things you cannot. And now, I must go. I've got a wedding this afternoon." With that, he pushed his chair away and reached for his wallet.

"No, no way. I invited you. My treat. Sorry if I was a little snippy. Whoa, and I'm sorry I just used 'snippy' in a sentence. When did I become my Aunt Nancy?"

He touched my hand as he left and said, "Thank you, Leah. You weren't snippy, maybe just a little frustrated." His smile held so much warmth that I felt better than I had since I'd opened Coop's kitchen door.

Dinner offer is still open, any takers?

Yes. What time?

Really? I'll pick you up at 6.

Not at the house. I'll be at the paper.

Some people might say I'd changed my mind about dinner with Nick because I was pissed at Coop. Which of course would be an absolutely stupid reason to go out with my ex. And which of course was absolutely true. But despite being born of petty anger and self-pity, it turned into a pretty good evening. I had Nick pick me up at the *Times* to avoid the gimlet-eyed stare of my mother, and he took me to McClain's. Sherry sashayed over to check out the new talent and impart what she thought was a bombshell of information.

"Hi, I'm Sherry. I'll be serving you tonight. What's your pleasure?" she said, batting her admittedly long and lustrous lashes at Nick, while ignoring me.

"I think I'll have a Sam Adams and the lady—well, what will the lady have, Leah?"

"Jameson on the rocks."

"Coming right up." She smiled at Nick and then leaned in toward me for the kill.

"So, guess who came in for lunch today, and they were very cozy."

"Kim and Kanye."

"Coop and your boss Rebecca! What does he see in that blonde bitchsicle?"

Nick was watching our exchange, and I took care to keep my expression neutral. "To each his own."

"Well, I just thought you should know."

"I already knew, Sherry. I had coffee with them this morning." Not strictly true, but close enough. And it pleased me to see the deflated look on her face. She recovered quickly though, flashed a smile at Nick, and said, "Be right back with your drinks."

"What was that about?"

"Sherry's had a crush on Coop since high school. She's upset because he's dating the ice queen. My boss, Rebecca Hartfield."

"She seemed to think it would bother you."

"It doesn't."

"Hmm."

"Hmm, what?"

"Nothing. Just the way you always talked about him. Why didn't you get together with him when you came back?"

"We're together. As friends. You know, men and women can be friends, Nick. I realize that's a foreign concept to you, but trust me it can be done."

"Ow! I think you drew blood with that one." We were both quiet then, until he said, "I've got an idea. Let's have a moratorium on the verbal jabs. We'll pretend we just met." He held out his hand. "Hi, I'm Nick Gallagher."

I hesitated for a second, then shook it. "Nice to meet you. I'm Leah Nash."

It was silly and kind of stupid, but kind of fun too. We proceeded to ask each other about our jobs and our lives and listened with the care and curiosity you accord interesting new acquaintances. Nick was witty and charming and on his absolute best behavior. No matter how flirty Sherry was whenever she came to our table—and she came way more often than she needed to—he treated her with absolute politeness and nothing more. I refrained from making any snarky comments.

He told me stories about work and his colleagues and the research he was doing. I brought him up-to-date with my own career trials and tribulations. He asked me about the book that was coming out soon, and if he could read it before publication. We stayed very carefully away from recounting memories of our past life together, good or bad. And some were really very good. We sat talking long after we'd finished eating, and when I looked at my watch I saw that it was after nine.

"I probably should get going."

"Oh, not yet. Let's go over to that little park you took me to once. I'll push you on the swings."

"Riverview Park?"

"Yeah, that's the one."

Dinner had been fun, and it felt like I hadn't had a relaxing evening in a long time. I wasn't anxious for it to end.

"All right, let's do it."

The park was deserted under a clear night sky with a few stars beginning to appear. We followed the sidewalk that ran through the park, walking into pools of light cast by the old-fashioned lampposts, then out again into the shadows, all the way to the swings. Only to discover they weren't there, apparently unhung and stored for the winter.

"Too bad. I guess we'll have to go down the slide instead." He pointed to a tall stand-alone slide with metal steps and hand rails all the way up and a small platform at the top from which to launch yourself. It was the one relic of a less safety-conscious era that hadn't been replaced since I was a child.

"You're kidding."

"Why not? We're both dressed for it." He was wearing jeans, like me, and we both had on winter jackets.

"All right, let's do it. I'll race you there." I got there first, probably because I'd taken off before he realized we were in competition, and clambered up the ladder. The sharp cold of the metal bit into my gloveless hands. I sped up and reached the top, then swung myself onto the steel slide, its smooth and slippery surface hurtling me down until I shot off the end into the soft wood chips at the base. Nick was right behind me. Before I could get up from the half-crouch I'd landed in, he careened into me and we both wound up on the ground entangled and laughing. His face was so close to mine I could feel his breath on my cheek, and suddenly we both stopped laughing. He bent toward me and kissed me softly on the lips. I kissed him back for a second.

Then I pulled back quickly and jumped up, brushing bits of damp wood chips from my clothes and chattering nervously.

"Well, that was quite a ride. Not quite as high as I remembered it from the last time I went down the slide, but still high enough. That metal was really cold, wasn't it? I wonder if you can get frostbite in under 30 seconds? You know, we used to take pieces of waxed paper and rub down the slide to make it more slippery, so we could go faster. Sometimes we'd sit on a square of it too. We'd really fly off the ends then! My fingers are freezing. How about you? Are your hands cold?"

He had stood up too and was silent until I finally wound down.

"I'm not going to apologize, because I'm not sorry. But I won't do it again. You'll have to make the next move, Leah, if you want to."

"Nick. It's been a really nice night, but I—"

"But you don't trust me. I understand. I can wait."

I didn't want to let him think there was even a slight chance I'd reopen that door.

"Nick, it's not going to happen. I really had fun tonight. And I can see that you're trying hard, and maybe you've changed. But so have I. I'm not willing to be that vulnerable to anyone, ever again. But, we can

171

be friends. Real friends. After all, we already know the worst about each other, right?"

I put my hand on his and looked up, hoping the doubt and confusion I felt didn't show in my eyes. I knew that getting back with Nick would be a very bad idea. But right at the moment I was having trouble remembering why.

I was a little disappointed when he didn't protest. Instead he turned his hand over so it clasped mine and gave a firm shake. "OK. Friends it is. Hey! Your hands are like ice!"

"Yours aren't much better."

"Let's stop at the party store across the way. It might feel good to wrap our hands around a warm cup of coffee. Then I'll take you back to your car."

"That, my friend, is a great idea."

CHAPTER 25

INSIDE JT'S there was a bit of a rush. Several teenagers were attempting to convince the clerk that they had forgotten the IDs required to purchase the case of beer they'd hauled up to the counter. A whiskery-faced old man wearing a battered John Deere hat waited for his turn at the register, holding a pint of Jim Beam and a bag of peanuts. At the coffee station we stood behind two women in scrubs who were pouring coffee into large containers, doubtless fortifying themselves for a long shift ahead at the hospital. Out of the corner of my eye, I saw a familiar figure at the back door give a quick glance right and left before stepping out. That was odd. Why would Cole take a break in the middle of a rush, and why was he so furtive about it?

"Oh, Nick, I left my phone in the car. I'll just run out and get it. Can't be a reporter without being in constant contact, right?"

Before he could answer I was out the front door. With luck, I would catch Cole doing something illegal, like selling a bag of weed or something worse to one of the "special" clients Keegan had mentioned. Maybe I could even get video of it. Anything that would give me leverage enough to get him to give up the video of the night Garrett died. I circled around to the back, coming up behind a dense thicket of evergreen bushes that gave me some cover. I crept up as close as I dared, stooping down low in the poky shrubbery to stay unseen. About 20 yards away were two men. One of them was Cole Granger. The other was Dr. Hal Bergman.

They kept their voices low, so I could only make out a word here and there, but their posture and gestures made it clear they were arguing. I waited a couple of minutes, holding very still to avoid their attention. Then I tried to move just a little farther forward to catch at least some of their conversation. A vicious branch nearly poked my eye out. I pushed it away. The branches and dried leaves around me crackled and rustled. Both men turned in my direction. I flattened myself down as low as I could go. I lay absolutely still, unless you counted the way my heart was jumping around in my chest. My eyes were at ground level, so I could only see a pair of feet coming my way. I calculated how quickly I could escape the tangle of shrubbery and run toward the light and safety of the parking lot out front. He was only steps away. I'd never make it. I steeled myself to stand up and avoid the indignity of being hauled from the bushes. And I prepared to yell really loud. Just then the blaring of a car alarm rent the air with repeated whoops of ear-shattering sound.

The feet stopped. Cole muttered something. I heard the thud of a car door and the smooth start-up of a luxury engine. The alarm continued. Cole's footsteps retreated. I waited a second, then backed my way out like a crawling baby in reverse. I hightailed it to the bright lights of the front parking area.

Nick was standing beside his car, fumbling with a key fob, as several people shouted advice on how to shut down the alarm. He saw me coming, and suddenly the horn stopped.

"There, got it. Sorry for the nuisance, everyone."

I hopped into the SUV and he did the same. As we pulled out, I said, "Nicky, you just saved my butt. Thank God you hit the panic button by accident." The nickname I had used in happier days slipped out of its own volition. I hoped he wouldn't notice.

"Freud says there are no accidents."

I stared at him. "Are you saying you did that on purpose?"

"I do know you, Leah. I saw you watching the clerk who left out the side door. And then all of the sudden you needed your phone? When you didn't come back by the time I paid for the coffee, and neither did he, I put the cups in the car. Then I walked to the back edge of the building and looked around the corner. I saw him and another man arguing, but no you. I heard a noise and saw the bushes shaking. One of the men started walking toward the thicket, and I thought a diversion might be in order. So I hit the panic button."

I was speechless. For a second or two. "Were you this smart when we were married?"

He smiled. "And I brought you coffee then, too. Now, can you tell me why that butt of yours needed saving?"

As we drove to my car, I filled him in. When I finished, Nick let out a low whistle.

"So you think the son Jamie killed his father?"

"I did. I'm not sure now. I never expected to see Bergman there. Now I'm wondering if Cole and Bergman are partnered up. Bergman could be part of a much bigger drug distribution operation. That would explain his connection to Cole. But Jamie's kind of a wild card. He was probably one of Cole's customers in the past—and maybe still is. If Cole and Bergman are connected, then there's a link to Jamie, too.

"You think both Jamie and this Bergman are linked to Garrett Whiting's death?" He sounded doubtful. That was OK, I was pretty unsure myself.

"I don't know. All of the leads were pointing in one direction: Jamie. But Bergman had a strong motive to want Garrett dead, and Jamie did too. Maybe they worked out something together."

"Leah, if I were you, I'd just hand it over to the police."

"That's because you don't know Ross. This will go nowhere if I don't give it to him tied up with a big bow. And I owe it to Isabel to get it right."

"That's what it's really about, isn't it? You know you're a fraud, don't you? Underneath that tough reporter act, you're a softie, an easy mark for anyone in distress."

"I'm not. I just want to do the job right. And yeah, OK, I'd like things to work out for Isabel. I want to help her. Is that such a bad thing?"

"Helping is different from rescuing. You're putting yourself at risk when you get so emotionally involved. You did what you told Isabel you'd do. Now you can let it go to the police."

"But that's just it. I didn't do what I promised. I said I'd follow it through to the end. It's not the end yet."

He sighed. "I can see there's no point in arguing with you. But at least be careful. I might not be there to save you next time."

And because I owed him, I let it pass.

But I didn't make any promises, either.

"OK then. Thanks, Nick. For everything. You were great."

True to his word, he made no move to swoop in for a goodnight kiss, for which I was very glad. Or so I told myself.

"Leah? Is that you?" My mother's sleepy voice called down the hallway. No matter how quiet I was, she could always hear me coming in.

"No, Mom. It's a psychotic killer."

"Don't be such a smartass. Good night," she said sleepily.

I went straight to bed and fell immediately asleep. Until, that is, I sat up with a start at 2 a.m., fully awake, with the knowledge that I had dropped my phone in the bushes behind JT's. Clearly, at some level, my mind had registered that when I scrambled out of the thicket, my phone wasn't in my jacket pocket, bumping against my hip as I walked. But my subconscious has always preferred to wake me up out of a sound sleep, rather than alert me at the time the crisis happens. I couldn't leave it lying in the bushes. I groaned, got up, put on my clothes, and crept silently out of the house. I didn't worry about waking my mother when I started the car, because once she believes I'm safely moored at home, she sinks into a sleep that a hibernating bear would envy.

I didn't pull into the lot at JT's. Instead, I drove a little way down the street to avoid attention, parked, and got my flashlight out of the glove compartment. Then I jogged up the sidewalk until I got to the outer edge of the party store's property. The lone light in the back cast a glow that faded long before it reached the shrubbery. I walked quickly over, then crouched down and turned on the flashlight as I entered the bushes.

I soon realized I'd have to do this search on my hands and knees. I didn't relish rooting around in the dead vegetation and debris, but I wouldn't find my phone otherwise. I held the flashlight in my mouth and crept forward, my hands stretched out in front of me feeling the ground. I made one forward pass with no luck, then stood up and moved over a little to try another crawl heading from front to back. My hands were cold and wet and encountered old beer cans, candy wrappers, discarded cups and straws and a couple of slimy things I didn't want to think about. The earth smelled dank and loamy, and the wet ground was penetrating the knees of my jeans.

I couldn't give up. It had to be here. My light grew dimmer as the batteries in the flashlight weakened. I shook it impatiently as though that would re-energize them. It must have worked, because all at once I could see better. Then a voice I knew well spoke, and I realized the light source wasn't from the flashlight I was holding.

"Whyn't you come on out of there, Leah?"

There was nothing to do but back ungracefully out of the bushes. I turned and faced Cole, who was holding a Maglite flash in one hand. In the other he jiggled my iPhone on his palm.

I reached out to grab it, but he snatched it away.

"Not so fast. Ain't there some kind of a reward? This is a valuable piece of equipment. And how do I know it's yours?"

"Yes, how do you know it's mine?"

"Well, outside of you crawlin' around in the bushes lookin' for it like a pig rootin' out grubs, there's the fact that I saw you lurkin' in this very thicket earlier tonight. And when I come back out after you left, there it was."

"Give me that!" I said, grabbing for it again. But his grip was tight and I wasn't about to engage in hand-to-hand combat with him. I took a breath. "All right, Cole, what is it you want?"

"I want to know what you heard when you were sneakin' around eavesdroppin' on private conversations tonight."

"I didn't hear anything. You were talking too low."

"And what did you see?"

"Just you talking to some guy. I couldn't tell who it was."

"Hmm. Now I wonder why I don't think you're tellin' me the truth?"

"Because you have a suspicious nature."

"You are right. I surely do. It comes from a sad life of hard livin.' But that isn't why I'm doubt'n' you, Leah. I think you don't have confidence in my goodwill and changed ways. I think you don't trust me enough to tell the truth, and that makes me feel real bad."

"Right. Look, it's 2:30 in the morning. You have my phone. Either give it to me, or don't, but I'm not standing here arguing with you anymore."

"Oh, I'm gonna give it to you, Leah. And I'm gonna throw in a free piece of advice, too. You best forget you saw anything at all tonight."

"Is that a threat?"

"It pains me to hear you say that. I am not threatnin' you. I am suggestin' that there are things that are none of your business. There are forces at work you know nothin' about. Sometimes it's a good thing when the right hand don't know what the left hand is doin.' And sometimes we think we know, and we don't. There are people in this world not as committed to nonviolence as I am. And they will not take kindly to your interference."

He flipped the phone to me then, and I caught it with both hands. Before he left I played my only card, the only thing I could think of that might make him give me the SD card.

"What do you suppose Coop will say when I tell him you're still dealing?"

"Now why would you go sayin' somethin' like that?"

"Well, I just hear things, you know."

"Yeah?"

"I understand you're the man to see for weed, pills, a full range of high quality products. Is that really wise? It would be a shame if you got arrested again. That new circuit judge is really tough, especially on repeat offenders."

"What's this about, Leah? Are you still tryin' to get hold of that SD card? I wonder what's on it that could make you want it so bad you're tryin' to extort an old friend like me?" He shook his head. "That makes me right sad. 'Specially when you think about how I saved your ass not three hours ago. That nameless gentleman is not someone you want to cross."

It almost sounded like he really *was* trying to warn me.

"Cole, I think there's something on that SD card that ties Jamie Whiting to his father's death."

"You think Jamie killed his old man?"

"I'm not saying that. I'm not saying anything except quit playing with me. This isn't a game. I really need to see that video."

"Now, I told you—"

"You told me you didn't have it, but I don't believe you. And now I have something to make it worth your while to find it."

"You got nothin.' So what if you tell the cops you heard I was dealin'? Hearin' don't make it so."

"With your record, I suspect the cops will definitely take some extra interest in you. Stop by unexpectedly and frequently. Coffee's good here. Maybe JT's is about to become Cop Central, the place to be for a late night cup of joe and a chat with the friendly staff."

He squinted, and I could tell he was running the odds in his mind. What did I really know? How much trouble could I cause him? What would Bergman do to him if JT's really did became Cop Central? After a few seconds he said, "Like I said, I don't believe we still have that particular SD card you want, but I'll go take a look."

"That's really nice of you," I said, following him in and to the office in the rear of the store. He didn't ask, but I took a seat behind the desk on which sat a laptop computer. I waited while he got a step stool, reached to the top shelf of a wall cupboard, and pulled out several small plastic storage cases. He set them down on the desk and opened the first one. I saw it contained multiple SD cards.

"I thought you didn't keep the cards longer than a couple of weeks."

He didn't answer, just flipped through the box, closed it and reached for another, searching until he found the card he was looking for. He slipped it into the computer and said "There. Anythin' else I can get you?"

"Some popcorn would be nice."

The bell on the door rang as he shook his head and went to the front of the store. I turned my attention to the video. I fast forwarded, stopping whenever anyone approached the ATM. In the early part of the evening there was a mother with tired eyes who held a toddler on her hip; an older man who weaved back and forth and took multiple tries to steady his hand enough to put in his card; then later a shift worker in a hurry, holding a cup of coffee in one hand and punching in her numbers with the other.

And then nothing, nothing, nothing, nothing. Until a figure in a hoodie suddenly appeared on camera, head lowered and hood pulled forward so his features weren't visible. He walked quickly to the machine, slid in a card and hesitated a second (trying to remember his father's code?) before punching in the numbers. Even though his face was hidden, I was sure I was looking at footage of Jamie Whiting. The hoodie, identical to my own, the height, the build, the furtive air to avoid being recognized. It was him. And here was the link to the ATM slip.

I stopped the video and ejected the SD card. As Cole came in, I was putting it into my purse.

"I take it you found what you were looking for."

"Yes, I did. I'll make a copy and get it back to you."

"That there belongs to my Uncle Chaz. You can't just take it."

"I'll get it back to you. Look, I really need this."

"Sometimes we don't know what we need—or what we got. It's a real complex world we live in. Full of surprises, 'specially if we don't keep our eyes open. You think on that."

"Whatever. I'll make a copy and get this back to you." I was in motion the whole time I was talking, closing my purse, standing up, turning from the desk, and before he could stop me I was out of the office and at the front of the store.

I pushed out the door and held it for a cop who was coming in.

"Hey, Officer Kline," I said to the young cop who'd given me a speeding ticket the month before. Cole looked at me as though I had assumed magical powers and conjured up a friendly policeman just when I needed him.

If my happy greeting surprised the patrolman, I didn't stick around to find out. I ran to my car, my brain going faster than my feet. Jamie had the ATM slip in his pocket, and I had the video to put him at JT's at 3:30 a.m. He had lied to Isabel, to the cops, to me. I couldn't think of a single plausible explanation for the fact, other than that he killed his father and cared so little that he stole the man's ATM card and slipped out to get some quick cash. But was there anything to a Bergman-Cole-Jamie connection? Was that what Cole meant about the right hand not knowing what the left was doing? Was I missing something?

The first thing I did when I got home was go straight to my room and make a copy of the SD card on my computer. Then I took the card, put it in a plastic baggie, and put it in my purse along with the ATM slip. In the morning I'd take them to the sheriff's department. I pulled on my pajamas, brushed my teeth, and was just pulling back the covers when my phone chimed. Who would be texting me at 4 in the morning? I grabbed the phone off my nightstand. I had to read the text twice to take it in. And even then it didn't make sense.

Jamie is dead.

CHAPTER 26

WHEN I DROVE UP, Ross was coming out the Whiting's front door, his head down and his phone to his ear. I noticed Jamie's car in the driveway. Had Isabel found him here? But if that were true the area would be full of police and crime scene technicians. There was only Ross's car next to Jamie's. I parked my Focus off to one side of the wide driveway and scrambled out as he ended his call.

"I heard Jamie's dead. Is he inside? What happened?"

He looked up in surprise. I realized he hadn't even noticed me until I spoke. When he answered, he sounded more tired than hostile, and he gave me the information straight, no gratuitous insult thrown in.

"Nah. His car's outta gas. He took the dad's SUV to the county park. Two 12-year-old kids found his body around midnight. Sneaked into the park on some damn dare after the gates closed for the night. Ridin' their trail bikes. Stupid, dangerous. Those trails got tree roots, rocks; they coulda broke their necks."

"Is that what happened to Jamie? Did he fall on one of the trails?"

"His head was pretty well stove in on the right side. We found a rock tossed off the trail. Could be the weapon. M.E. won't commit 'til after the autopsy, but it looks like somebody whacked him a good one."

"Did the medical examiner give you a time?"

"Won't go closer than late afternoon to 10 p.m. Rigor's set in, but bein' cold like it is, doesn't mean much."

"Ross, who would want to kill Jamie?"

"I thought you might have something to say about that, Nash."

I didn't trust him; I didn't believe that he was capable of untangling this case. He was even less capable of admitting that he'd screwed it up in the first place. I didn't want to give him anything. But I knew I should. After all, he was the investigating officer, he had more resources than I did, and it was his job. Still, I hesitated. Then I looked into his eyes. Yes, they were piggy with a trace of truculence, but despite their appearance and rude manners, pigs do have a reputation as intelligent animals.

"Yeah. Yeah, I do."

He motioned toward his car.

"All right then. Get in there. I want to hear everything you've been doing, everyone you've been talkin' to, everything you think you know."

He turned the car on, and the heater enveloped us in a rush of warm air and an odd sense of intimacy. He pushed his seat all the way back to accommodate his size and half-turned, so he could look at me while I spoke. I went over the facts that led me to believe Garrett didn't kill himself and why I had suspected Jamie. I didn't mention that I'd seen Cole and Bergman together earlier in the evening. I didn't say anything about Frankie, either. Although this was as close as Ross and I would probably ever come to a kumbaya moment, I wanted to see how he responded to what I'd said before I gave him everything.

He sat very still as I spoke. Not surprising, maybe. After all, the facts I'd laid out were a litany of his incompetence. He must be beating himself up over the way he'd mishandled things. Even after all the history between us, I felt a little sorry for him.

"Goddammit, Nash. You went around double-checkin' everything we did? You just gotta be the smartest person in the room, don't ya?"

OK. Detente officially over.

"Not hard when the only other person there is you. Look, I'm not saying I had everything right. I really thought Jamie had killed his father. But maybe he's dead because he knew something that made him a danger to someone."

"You ever consider that kid is dead because you had to be the big detective, the superstar reporter? You should've come to me with this information a long time ago. When are you gonna get you got no business mixing in an official investigation and withholding evidence?"

That was so grossly unfair it took my breath away. Though I still managed to eke out a few words. "Oh, no. No. Don't even try to go there. There was no 'official investigation.' You had already written Garrett Whiting off as a suicide. You didn't believe me about Garrett; you sure as hell weren't going to listen to me about Jamie. Don't you try to put this on me. You missed one murder completely. Then when I started investigating, started doing the job you couldn't be bothered to do right, all you did was make me the butt of your stupid joke.

"Your ego is so big you couldn't admit that you might have been wrong. Again." I was shaking and it wasn't from the cold. Why hadn't I followed my instincts? There was no way Ross was going to take any theory I had seriously. Not unless I could provide very specific, very solid, very irrefutable proof. Ross was so committed to believing I was out to get him that he wouldn't accept a winning lottery ticket from me, let alone a crime theory that ran counter to his.

"You're holding possible evidence. You get me that ATM slip and that video, and you better be ready to make a signed statement at the department first thing in the morning. And you stay the hell away from this investigation, or—"

"Or what? Here's the ATM slip." I unzipped a pocket in my purse and pulled out the clear plastic bag I'd slipped it into. "And here's the SD card." I handed it to him before he could demand it. "I'll be there to make a statement tomorrow. Right now I'm going to see Isabel. Her brother just died. Remember?"

He was still talking as I stepped out of the car. He leaned over to the passenger side and looked up at me before I could slam the door shut. "You do anything to mess up this investigation and you're gonna regret it."

"The only thing I regret is having to read you in."

Isabel opened the door and all but collapsed in my arms. She seemed to have all the weight of a dry leaf, and I had the odd sensation as I walked her to the kitchen that if I didn't hold tight, she'd blow away. Once there, I sat her at the table, rummaged in the cupboards for cups and tea, then put the kettle on.

All the while she sat without moving, staring into space, not crying exactly, but with tears streaming down her cheeks from a seemingly endless well of grief. The expression in her eyes was something I'd seen in the mirror once, a long, long time ago. When the water boiled, I poured it over the teabags and set the cups on the table, taking the seat across from her. She looked at me then and for the first time she spoke.

"Leah, why is this happening?"

I covered her hand with mine. "I am so sorry, Isabel."

"It's my fault. If I had never called you, this wouldn't have happened. If I had just let things go. Now Jamie's dead, and my father's dead and I'm all alone. Jamie and I had a fight Friday and then a really bad one yesterday. The last time I ever saw him, and I ended up screaming at him."

"What were you fighting about?"

"On Friday I did what you said. I looked at dad's bank statement. There was a withdrawal. I confronted Jamie. I told him what you said. I'm sorry, but I had to ask him. I had to hear what he said. I knew he had to have an explanation for it."

"Did he?"

"He said he didn't know what I was talking about. He said you'd say or do anything, hurt anybody just because you wanted a big story. I begged him to tell me how the slip got there, but he just left. He didn't come home until really late. When I went to bed at 1:30, he still wasn't here. But on Saturday, yesterday, morning he was in the kitchen when I came down around 11. He'd made coffee for us both, and he asked me to sit down with him and talk. I was so happy. He said he was sorry we'd been fighting so much. He said. He said. He said." She kept repeating the words, her voice stuttering, unable to go on. She stopped herself and took a deep breath, then tried again.

"He said we only had each other. We shouldn't be arguing. He said again that he didn't know where the ATM slip came from. He begged me to believe him. He said that you were driving a wedge between us. I told him no, that we had to know what really happened to Dad. He got mad again then, got right in my face and started yelling.

"And I got mad right back. I said some terrible things. I told him he never cared about anything or anyone except himself, that he messed up his own life with drugs, and that he was probably using again. I said, 'Why do you want Leah to stop so bad? Maybe she's right. Maybe you did have something to do with it.' He didn't say a word. He just turned and walked out. That's the last time I saw him. That's the last thing he ever heard me say. And I didn't even mean it."

"When was this?"

"Around noon or so. After he left I couldn't stop pacing, couldn't calm down. I couldn't believe I'd said such awful things to him. He was right, there was only us left. And I was driving him away. I had to get out of the house, had to calm down, had to think. I decided to go for a hike on Patmore's Ridge and then try to talk to him when he came back. I left a note for him. I told him nothing was worth losing him. I told him I was done trying to find out what really happened with Dad. I said I would get you to stop. I said I was sorry."

"Do you have any idea what Jamie was doing at the county park?"

She nodded miserably.

"It was me. He came to find me. My note—I just said, 'going for a hike.' I didn't say where. I do usually hike at the county park, but yesterday I felt like climbing. And it was beautiful, the air was cold, but so clear. You know you can see for miles from the top of the ridge. Everything seems so much less important up there, you know? I just felt like we'd be able to get through this. I thought maybe we would just sell the house and get away. Maybe go somewhere together, for a while anyway, just to start living again." She stumbled over the last words and started crying. I handed her a tissue and waited.

"I just feel like, if I hadn't left that note, he wouldn't have come after me. He wouldn't have been in the park. He wouldn't be dead."

"Isabel, stop. Don't do that. You don't even know for sure that Jamie came back home and saw your note. Listen to me, please, this is not your fault."

Ignoring my reassurances she asked, "What's going to happen now?"

"Well, the sheriff's department will investigate, there'll be an autopsy to determine official cause of death. And they'll look for potential witnesses, talk to you, to his friends, try to figure out who had a motive for killing Jamie."

She gave a bitter laugh. "So, now I've got what I wanted. A full-fledged police investigation. But I never thought it would be into Jamie's death. And you. You thought Jamie killed our father, are you happy now that he's dead?" Her voice had risen and had a slightly hysterical edge.

"No, of course I'm not. I want to find out what happened and why as much as you do. Jamie's death could be connected to your father's. Or maybe to his drug use. And the investigation could lead them to reinvestigate your dad's death. That's what you wanted, isn't it?"

"But not this way. What does it matter now?"

"Look, why don't you come home with me for the rest of the night? In fact you could stay with us for a few days, even. As long as you like. You shouldn't be here alone."

She shook her head. "I'm sorry, but I just don't want to be around a happy family right now. It would be harder for me at your house. You go on. Get some sleep. I'll be fine." She stood up and I could see she wanted me to go.

"All right. But call me if you need anything. I mean it. Any time."

CHAPTER 27

I DIDN'T SLEEP MUCH after I got home. Around 6 I got up and showered and dressed. My mother came into the kitchen as I was finishing coffee.

"You're up early for a Sunday. Planning to go to Mass with me?"

"Hardly. But it wouldn't hurt to say a prayer for Isabel Whiting."

"What happened?" She stopped in mid-pour of her own cup of coffee.

"Her brother was killed yesterday. Now she's got no one." I filled her in on some, though not all, of the details. "I tried to get her to come home with me, but she said it would be too hard."

She nodded. "I understand that. You know, after Annie died and your father—well, when it was just the three of us, you and me and Lacey, it seemed like everywhere I looked there were happy families living the life that I was supposed to have. Everyone was kind, but I felt so isolated and angry. And, I'm not proud to say, jealous. I couldn't stand to be around people who got to be happy and carefree when my life was shattered. It took a long time before I could let go of the self-pity and resentment and accept that it was just my turn. And someday it would be someone else's, while I carried on with my own happy life."

"I didn't know you felt like that."

She sat down across from me and smiled. "Thank you, hon, that's the best thing you could have said to me. I didn't want you to know. Lacey was so young; she didn't realize what we'd lost. But you did. I didn't want you to see me struggling, too. Luckily you had Coop to keep you out of trouble—more or less. He was such a good kid. He was a good influence on you." She said the last part in a teasing tone to lighten the conversation and get a rise out of me. She did, but it wasn't what she expected.

"Too bad I don't have more influence on him. He's making a big mistake."

"Really, what?"

"Not what, *who*. Rebecca." It pained me to say it, but I'd better get used to it. "They're in love or in lust or whatever. I wouldn't know, because Coop didn't even tell me until I stumbled on them myself. Apparently it had to be some big secret until Coop could tell me 'the right way.' Seriously, what's the right way to tell your best friend you're dating the person who's making her life miserable?"

A visitor might have been surprised when my mother burst into song at that point, but I took it in stride. She has a great voice and a vast catalog of song lyrics that she's prone to belting out as musical examples of her point. This time it was "When a Man Loves a Woman." I waited 'til she got past the part about the guy being willing to turn on his best friend if he disses his woman.

"OK, OK, I get it. I know. It's not my call, and I have to accept Coop's choice."

"Exactly. Besides, maybe you're wrong about her." She held up her hand as I started to object. "I know she's hard to work for, but frankly, honey, she doesn't seem that bad to me. She must have something good about her if Coop is attracted to her, right?"

"Well, yeah, sure. She's attractive if Elsa is your fantasy girl." My mother gave me an exasperated look, and I grudgingly admitted that Miguel liked her, too. "Apparently she told him some sad story about her miserable childhood—her mother committed suicide when she was a kid, she lived in foster homes, physical abuse, no family—she's a regular Dickens poster child. Miguel is convinced there's marshmallow creme under her tough cookie coating. Father Lindstrom said kind of the same thing. But then, he likes everybody."

"They may be right. And maybe you two don't get along because you're too much alike." I was too shocked at the comparison to retort before she went on. "You'll just have to wait and see what happens. If she's not what he thinks she is, Coop will come to his senses. Just like you did with Nick."

An uncomfortable silence followed.

"Yeah. About that." It seemed as good a time as any to own up to my dinner with Nick, which seemed way longer ago than the night before.

It did not shock me that her sage 'live and let live' advice went right out the window when it came to telling me what to do.

"Leah Marie, why would you do that? What possible good can come from it? You know how hard it was for you to recover when he cheated on you. You were a basket case."

I squirmed uncomfortably. I don't enjoy reminders that I'm not as emotionally invulnerable as I like people to believe. And my mother knows exactly where the chinks in my armor are. Fortunately I had enough presence of mind not to fall into her trap and offer any defense. I really wasn't up to being on the witness stand in Carol's Court, at which she sustains all her own objections and overrules mine.

"Thanks, Mom. I appreciate your concern, but I've got this," I said, as I put my cup in the dishwasher and grabbed my coat off the hook. "I'm going to the paper. I have to call Rebecca and update her, get in touch with Miguel, check on Isabel, and I have to stop by the sheriff's department and make a statement. I'll catch you later."

And I left her in a position that my mother truly hates: having a whole lot to say and no one to say it to. I suspected a call to Paul was in the offing.

I stopped at the sheriff's department. Ross wasn't in, so another detective took my statement. I still didn't mention the meeting I'd witnessed between Cole and Bergman. I didn't feel like giving any more leads away—or like being ridiculed for thinking it was a lead. When I was finished, he told me that Sheriff Dillingham wanted to see me. The door to his office was half-shut, but when I tapped lightly, he called for me to come in.

I pushed the door all the way open and saw that he was on the phone, though it appeared he was just wrapping up his conversation.

"Yeah, that's right. I'll see what I can do on this end, but I just thought you should know. You might be better equipped to handle the situation. Real good, then. Bye." He hung up the phone and turned his attention to me.

"What situation needs handling, Sheriff?"

He ignored my question. "Appreciate you coming in to make your statement so prompt, Leah. Sorry Charlie wasn't here to take it."

"That makes one of us. What can I do for you?"

He nodded his head a couple of times and then gave me a smile that looked more like a grimace of pain. I smiled back and waited. He shifted his weight, bringing his chair upright so he could lean forward, his arms resting on the desk in front of him.

"Leah, you know I like you. I don't hold it at all against you, what you did on your sister's case. Though I'll be the first to say you are a royal pain in my backside sometimes. If you'da come to us, we maybe coulda moved things along a little faster and less dangerous for you." He paused and smiled again, to show there were no hard feelings. As my contribution to our friendly chat, I refrained from pointing out that his department had, far from helping me, tried to arrest me. And that we'd had a very similar conversation just a few weeks ago when I'd picked up the Whiting file.

"I feel the same way about Charlie Ross. Really like the guy, but I'll be the first to admit, he can be a pain. But what I don't understand is why the two of you are always crossways with each other." He shook his head slowly, to emphasize his bewilderment over the fact that Ross and I weren't best friends. "But I'm tellin' you for your own good, you need to stop it. You got to trust him. I understand you did some follow-up on your own with that ATM slip you found." I started to interrupt, but he made a tamping down gesture with his hands and continued.

"No, now let me finish. You know Cole Granger is a pretty lowlife character. You don't want to have dealings with him. You let us take care of things. If you don't, you just might get hold of the wrong end of the stick here. Could be there's more to this case than you think. And it's got nothing to do with us makin' a mistake on Garrett Whiting's death, because we didn't."

"Well, tell me what's going on, then."

"It's need to know, and right now, you aren't one of the people who need to know. There's things going on, and I don't want you getting in the way." The pseudo-affability was gone now, and his irritation with me was clear.

"Sheriff, I'm not trying to make Ross look bad, or make your job harder, but two people in one family are dead now, and I think there's a connection. If you're honest, I think you'll admit that, too."

He shook his head in frustration. "You are one stubborn girl. Don't make me call your boss. I told you, when there's something to know, I'll tell you. Is that so hard?"

"Sorry, Sheriff. It doesn't work like that."

Back at the office I did a little copy editing while I waited for it to be late enough on a Sunday to call Rebecca or text Miguel. And I did a lot of thinking about who had picked up a rock and bashed Jamie Whiting in the head. And why.

How would Jamie's killer know he was going to the park? He wouldn't. Unless either he or Jamie had set up the meeting. The more I thought, the less I believed Jamie going to the county park had anything to do with misunderstanding Isabel's note. No. Jamie was there to meet someone. I could think of three possibilities. One, Jamie did kill his father and the person he met was blackmailing him, and something had gone wrong at the meet up. Two, Jamie didn't kill his father, but he knew who had, and he was trying some blackmail of his own that worked out badly. Three, Jamie's death had nothing to do with Garrett's. He had a history of drug abuse; he could've been involved somehow with Bergman and his prescription drug theft. Maybe Cole was involved too.

Which brought me back to my suspicion that Coop was involved in a rural DEA task force. Bergman and Cole could be part of something larger than a small-time local drug operation. And Coop, as well as someone from the sheriff's department, could be part of a DEA task force trying to bring down a much bigger network. That could be why Sheriff Dillingham warned me away, and why Coop was so insistent on me steering clear of Cole Granger.

Jamie's history with drugs could have brought him into contact with Cole and possibly Bergman. If Garrett found out there was a link between Bergman and Jamie, then all bets were off. Wouldn't he go straight to the cops, regardless of his concerns about the reputation of his practice? And if Bergman was connected to a bigger drug operation, he had more to worry about from Garrett than career loss and jail time. Bergman's drug bosses would kill him to prevent exposure of their operation. Bergman couldn't let them know that was a risk. So he could've killed Garrett for the most elemental of motives—to save his own skin. Or, he might have played on Jamie's anger toward his father and manipulated him into doing it. Then Jamie got cold feet, and Bergman had to take him out, too. I didn't have that many suspects, but there were a hell of a lot of motives.

"Gaarrgghhh! Why can't I figure this out?!" I shouted out loud and hit the top of my desk with the palm of my hand, sending my phone clattering to the floor just as it started ringing. I grabbed it and said a slightly breathless hello.

"Leah? Miller Caldwell. I have a note here from my secretary, Patty. She said that you've been trying to reach me. How can I help you?"

"Hey, Miller. Thanks for calling back. I really need to talk to you, but I'd rather do it in person. Could I stop by your house later today?"

"You can come by my office right now if you want. I'm going through a stack of things Patty left me. I just got back last night."

"That'd be great."

"The front door is unlocked, just come straight through to my office."

Miller Caldwell is a big, handsome man who resembles Robert Redford in his prime. His brown hair has grown a lot grayer in the past year, and there's a look of wariness in his blue eyes that wasn't there before, but he still has the easy manner of a natural politician. Which he almost was a year or so ago. That's when he upended his run for state senate by announcing that in addition to being a Catholic, married father of two teenagers, and president of the Bank of Himmel, he was also gay.

Confession may be good for the soul, but it had taken a toll on his professional and personal life. He was forced to step down from the bank, and he withdrew from his political activities. His wife divorced him and his children were just coming to terms with the new reality of their father's life. About six months ago he reopened his law practice, and I knew he did consulting on business deals for a small group of clients. He wasn't hurting financially—his family had major money—but losing your professional identity, your political ambitions, and your family life in one fell swoop had to be pretty hard to take.

He stood as I came into the office carrying two cups of coffee and two rugelachs from the Elite.

He smiled as he took them from me and cleared a space on his paper-strewn desk.

"You're a lifesaver. Jet lag just sneaked up on me about 10 minutes ago, and I've got a lot of paperwork to go through before I call it a day. Mrs. Schimelman's coffee will get me through."

"So you were what? In China? Every time I called, your secretary said you were unreachable. She made it sound like the President personally sent you on a trade mission and that me asking to talk to you was both untoward and impossible."

"Patty tends to overstate my importance. I think it's to convince herself that I'm worthy of her. Which I absolutely am not. Best secretary ever. Anyway, my contact with the State Department was very routine, had to do with a Wisconsin company that an old friend of mine owns. He's going to expand its operation to several sites in China, and he asked me to consult in a few areas. I jumped at the chance, and it was the trip of a lifetime."

"When did you leave?"

"About six weeks ago. We took advantage of some time to travel in the rural areas of the country before we had to settle down to business."

"So you were gone when Garrett Whiting died?"

"Yes. Actually I left the night he died. I didn't know that then, of course. Why are you asking about Garrett?"

"I'm sure you know his death was ruled suicide, but it's looking like that might not be true. Especially in light of what happened yesterday. Jamie Whiting's body was found in the county park."

"Jamie! He's just a boy. What happened?"

"It's not official yet, but I got it from the investigating officer. Jamie was killed. It looks like murder."

"Murdered? But why? By whom?"

"I don't know, but I was hoping you could help me figure part of it out. You and Garrett were friends, right? You were his lawyer?"

"We've known—we knew—each other for a long time. Georgia and I and Garrett and his wife Joan used to socialize years ago. My daughter Charlotte and his daughter Isabel played on the tennis team together in high school. But I haven't been his lawyer for years, not since I took over at the bank. And I can't say we were close friends. I don't know that he had any, really. He was good company, witty and amusing, though his humor could be a bit cutting. I saw him now and then, and we had the odd drink together over the years. That's about it."

"So you didn't know he had Parkinson's?"

"No, I had no idea. When I heard he committed suicide, it surprised me, but if he had Parkinson's… His work meant everything to him. I can see why he might take his own life. But you don't think he did?"

I explained in general terms about the things that didn't fit. "I thought Jamie might have something to do with his father's death. He was evasive and angry when I talked to him, and when I checked it out, his story about where he was the night Garrett died didn't hold up. But now that he's been killed, I don't know if it was because he was somehow involved in his father's death, or if there's another reason."

Miller didn't respond, and he had a somewhat dazed look on his face.

"I'm sorry, I know this is a lot to take in. I just really want to get some answers for Isabel as soon as I can, and I don't have much faith in Detective Ross's ability to do it."

"No, no, I understand. It's just—" He shook his head the way you do when you you're trying to clear out the cobwebs. "If I'd had any idea there was any question—I thought I was just respecting their privacy." His last few words trailed off into a half-whisper.

"Miller, what is it? Whose privacy?"

He sat up straight and put his coffee cup down on his desk. He leaned forward as he spoke.

"The night Garrett died, I drove by his house on my way to Chicago. I had an early morning international flight to catch. I meant to get away sooner, but I got caught up in some things here and didn't leave home until after 11. Garrett had offered me his noise canceling headset for the flight. I decided if there was a light on at his house, I'd stop, even though it was late. When I was almost to his driveway, I saw a car parked there, and the inside light came on as the door opened. I recognized the person who got out." He stopped. If it were me talking, the pause might have been for dramatic effect. In Miller's case, I was pretty sure he was still debating whether or not to tell me who he'd seen.

"Who? Who was in the car?"

"It was Frankie. Francesca Saxon."

CHAPTER 28

"FRANKIE WAS AT GARRETT'S HOUSE? Why didn't you tell anyone that you saw her there?"

"I was on my way to China, remember?" He said it in a much calmer tone than I'd used. "I didn't hear Garrett had died until a week or so later, and I was told it was suicide. It didn't occur to me that it might be important."

"Oh, it's important all right. It means Frankie was at the scene that night. She could be the killer. I know she wasn't where she said she was, and I can't think of too many reasons she'd be at Garrett's the night he died."

"Maybe for the reason I assumed. That she and Garrett were in a relationship again. Why would she kill him?"

"Jealousy, revenge, I don't know. But the thing is, she lied to me. She told me she was out of town when Garrett died. And now I know exactly where she really was. You need to talk to Ross. No, wait, make it the sheriff. He won't be happy, but I don't think he'd try to cover anything up. I think they've got the wrong angle on this, and you could help set them right."

Miller was quiet as I rattled through the list of instructions I had for him. He was so quiet that I eventually wound down. Belatedly, it occurred to me that I actually had no authority to tell him to do anything, that he was used to being the "bosser," not the "bossee," and that he might not like me switching it up.

But when he spoke, it was without any sign of irritation.

"I can't believe Frankie had anything to do with Garrett's death. She's a very warm person, and she was extremely kind to our son Sebastian when Georgia and I divorced. Charlotte was away at school, so she was out of the fray, but Sebastian really struggled. It was Frankie who helped us get our relationship back on track."

"Hey, I think she's a nice person too. I'm not saying she killed Garrett." Although his lifted eyebrow reminded me that I had, in fact, pretty much said that a few minutes ago. "I know, but I was just thinking out loud. It's a possibility. I'm not saying she did it. The thing is, she was there that night. And she lied. At the very least, she's hiding something that might help solve two murders."

"It could be as simple as the fact that Frankie didn't want anyone to know she was involved with Garrett. Maybe she was just there for a few minutes, and he killed himself hours after she left."

"It's possible. 11 p.m. to 3 a.m. is the time of death window. But Frankie still might have seen something or heard something that should be brought out. Protecting her secrets doesn't trump finding out what really happened to Garrett. And Jamie."

"I agree, and I'll call the sheriff. I just hate to see all that old gossip revive. Small towns can be vicious." He spoke from firsthand knowledge, I knew.

"I understand that, but I think it's too late for Frankie to preserve her privacy. She might have some important answers. I know there are some questions I'm going to be asking her."

"Shouldn't you leave that to the sheriff's investigators?"

"Let's just say I'm performing a fail-safe function. Because if they don't find out what Frankie knows, I will."

"*Híjole*, chica! I can't believe it!" I'd finally connected with Miguel. We were in the newsroom eating a fast food lunch following my conversation with Miller.

"Which part? Coop and Rebecca? Me and Nick? Jamie's death? Frankie at Garrett's the night he died?"

"All of the above. Coop and Rebecca. So that's why she started taking those long lunches, yes? A little afternoon delight."

I shuddered. "Don't go there."

"Why not? I think it's nice."

"Nice? You think it's nice that Coop is hooking up with the ice queen?"

"Sí. I do. Rebecca is OK. She just doesn't warm up to people very fast. But Coop, he must know how to get her temperature rising." He said it with a lift of his eyebrows that was more Groucho Marx than Latin lover. I couldn't help laughing.

"Shut up. It wouldn't have been so bad if Coop had told me. I felt so stupid running right into their big fat secret. And Rebecca was so condescending. 'David and I,' and 'We didn't want this to be awkward.' My ass."

"Hey, if he's happy and she's happy, then you better get happy. Don't make Coop choose."

"You sound like my mother. I wanted him to find someone better for him. He deserves it."

"*Qué será será.*"

"Thank you, Doris Day."

"Don't be so *enojona*, chica. Being salty gives you wrinkles. Now what about you? Nothing like a night chasing bad guys to bring a chico and chica together."

"Nick and I weren't 'chasing' bad guys. He just helped me out of a tight spot with Cole and Bergman. We're just, I don't know. Friends, I guess."

He nodded in a knowing way that I found more than a little annoying. I made an abrupt return to the real news.

"So, anyway, I left a voicemail for Frankie. If she doesn't call me back, I'm just going to drop in on her. I'd like to talk to her before Ross does."

"What do you need me to do?"

"Well, you could stop by and see Isabel. She may not be very receptive, but I think she needs the company. I texted her awhile ago, but she didn't answer."

"Sure, I can do that, but I mean reporting, investigating, that's what we do, right?"

"I don't suppose you want to meet with Rebecca instead of me? She'll be here in an hour or so."

"No thanks, chica. That one's for you."

"Kidding. Sort of. You know, you could check out Miller's story for me. See when his flight was, chat up his secretary Patty, see if you can corroborate the timeline he gave."

"You don't believe Miller?"

"Yeah, I do. I just don't want to get sandbagged by something unexpected. Just in case Ross decides to do some actual detecting. I want to be sure I'm moving ahead on solid ground. You know the reporter's code, Miguel. 'If your mother says she loves you—'"

"Check it out," he finished for me.

"Also, see if you can find out anything about Cole Granger selling prescription drugs, maybe hooked up with a local doctor. Bergman is who I'm thinking."

People sometimes dismiss Miguel as a lightweight because he's so upbeat and funny. That's their mistake. You don't grow up in a neighborhood full of gangs in Milwaukee and not learn a lot about the darker side of life.

"OK. *Lo tengo.* I've got it. I'm gonna bounce before Rebecca gets here. Good luck!"

"I'm not sure you understand the editor/reporter dynamic, Leah. You don't make decisions about what and how we cover things, I do."

The light glinted off her lenses, so I couldn't read the expression in her eyes. I didn't need to. Rebecca's frosty voice conveyed her displeasure pretty clearly.

"I know that. That's why I just brought you up to speed, that's why I gave you an update yesterday morning, remember?"

"But it wasn't a very complete update yesterday morning, was it? You said you believed Jamie Whiting had killed his father. You didn't say you were following up on a lead with Miller Caldwell, you didn't even tell me that you suspected a connection between Dr. Bergman and Cole Granger. And now Jamie is dead, and you've got more theories than a conspiracy website. Maybe it's Bergman, maybe Bergman and Cole are working together, maybe Jamie's death was about drugs and had nothing to do with his father, maybe Jamie knew something about his father's death and that's why he was killed. Maybe Francesca Saxon is involved."

She took off her glasses and stared at me. Looking in her eyes was like looking into a glacier crevasse, just as cold, blue, and forbidding.

"Maybe, Leah, it's time for you to step back and report on what the police find, not try to prove you're smarter than they are. You're too emotionally involved in this."

"Come on, Rebecca, that's not fair. I told you what I knew for sure yesterday. A lot happened between the time we talked and this morning. Sure, I'm fired up about the story, but I'm not attached to how it comes out. I can be objective. Things pointed to Jamie Whiting, but there were always other possibilities. I've got no stake in which one pans out."

"Can you honestly say you're not hoping to make Detective Ross look like an idiot? And let's not forget you've got a book coming out in a couple of months. Maybe you're a little too distracted for your news judgment to be reliable. Can you admit that's possible?"

"Seriously? I've barely thought about my book the last few weeks. Just ask my agent. As for having it in for Ross, the answer is no. I can't help it if I keep stumbling over his incompetence. I'm not out to get him. But I'm not going to watch from the sidelines while he screws things up."

"And I'm not paying you to conduct a personal vendetta on the paper's dime. No. The *Times* is going to pull back from this story. We'll wait and see what the investigation into Jamie's death turns up, but there are plenty of other things to work on. We're a community paper, not a supermarket tabloid. Miguel can handle it from here."

I was stunned. I tried to salvage things.

"Wait a second. You don't have to do that. Ross may be a little pissy with me, but I can still get the story. Don't take me off this, please."

"Leah, I've had a call from the sheriff. He's unhappy with the way you've been interfering with his investigative team, and he can make it hard for us to get the basic information on the things our readers want to see every week. The B&Es, the accident reports, the drunk driving arrests. When the sheriff's ready, he'll give us the results of their investigation. I have to ask, are you fighting me so hard on this because you feel like I've already taken something important away from you?"

I didn't like where this was heading.

"I know you're not happy that David and I are in a relationship. You have to learn to separate the personal from the professional. I've made up my mind. I'm pulling you off this story. Any future developments, Miguel will cover."

"I can't separate the personal and the professional? Why are you even bringing Coop up? Your relationship with him is your business and his. And what kind of an editor waits to be handed information? We're supposed to be watch dogs, not lap dogs."

"I understand you're upset, but you're dangerously close to the line. One more word and you'll be over it."

"Then you'd better get out of the way, because I'm about to take a running leap. You're terrible at your job, and I shouldn't have stayed here this long. No need to fire me. I quit."

CHAPTER 29

"SO YOU REALLY QUIT YOUR JOB."

"Yes, Mom. I quit my job. Why do you keep repeating that?" She was sitting in the living room when I came storming in from the office, and had listened to my story while I got out glasses, ice, and poured each of us a generous measure of Jameson. Now we sat across from each other in the living room, she on the couch, me on the wingback chair. I took a large sip from my glass, closed my eyes and sighed as the icy burn went down my throat.

"I'm just trying to get used to the idea. What are you going to do?"

"I don't know."

"That sounds like a good plan."

"How about a little support? Something like 'I can't believe you lasted so long with that incompetent woman. You're twice the reporter she could ever think of being.' That would be nice." I took another sip, smaller this time.

"Sorry. How about 'I'm sure when your book comes out in a few months, you'll be rolling in money and fame, and Rebecca will be holding a sign on a street corner, begging for food.' Is that supportive enough?"

"Look, I had to quit or kill myself. I've been sweating blood over this story, and because it developed faster than I expected and she didn't have minute-by-minute bulletins from me, she decides to pull me off it and give it to Miguel."

"You're sure she wasn't on to something when she said you were bent out of shape over her relationship with Coop?"

"With 'David' you mean? No. Absolutely not. Yeah, I wish he were with someone else, but whatever, it's his life. I can deal with it. Taking me off the story doesn't make any kind of sense. I know it inside out. So she doesn't like me, so what? I don't like her either, but she's not stupid. She has to see that I'm on to something. And she knows Miguel is good, but he doesn't have the experience."

"Maybe it just doesn't matter that much to her. Why does it to you?"

I stared at her, the answer so self-evident I couldn't believe she was asking. "Because, Mom, I'm a reporter. There's a story. I need to find out what's going on."

She retreated a little in the face of my intensity. "Fine, Nellie Bly. So what are you going to do now?"

"I'm going to get the story. I already talked to my friend Lisa at the *Milwaukee Journal*. You remember her, don't you? She was at the *Green Bay Press* the same time I was."

"You're working for the *Milwaukee Journal*? That was a quick job hunt."

"Not working. Lisa said she'd look at it on spec."

"Oh. On spec." She paused and took a sip from her own glass. "So that means you're going to investigate it and write it, but you don't have any real commitment that they'll print it or pay for it, right? You might wind up writing it and get nothing for it, right?"

"Well, yeah, basically. What else can I do?"

"Let it go? Call your agent, tell him you're ready to roll on whatever promotion things he thinks you should be doing. Start thinking about another book?"

"Maybe this story will be the second book in my new life as Leah Nash, true crime writer. Have a little faith. I'm on to something, and I'm going to run it down."

The phone rang and I looked at it, prepared to send it to voicemail. I'd already ignored multiple texts from Miguel and a call from Coop. But when I saw the caller ID, I picked up.

"Leah, this is Frankie Saxon. Is it true? Is Jamie Whiting dead?"

"Yeah, it is. His body was found in the county park last night."

She gasped and then started breathing rapidly.

"Frankie? Are you all right?"

She took in a big breath and held it before she answered. "Yes. I'm all right. But I need to talk to you. Can you meet me at the EAT tonight?"

"Yes, sure. When?"

"I'll be there at 9."

The EAT HEARTY restaurant, known locally as the EAT, is a Himmel institution that's been on the decline since it opened 30 years ago. The only explanation for it still hanging on is that, though the food is terrible, it's cheap. And a certain number of Himmel residents will tolerate a hot mess of beige on a plate if the price is right. It's a good place to meet if you don't want to be seen, because there never seems to be anybody there. The coffee isn't bad though, and I had already downed a cup when Frankie pushed open the heavy glass door. The collar of her trench coat was pulled up like a spy's in a bad movie, and her dark eyes behind tortoise shell glasses darted back and forth looking for me. I lifted my hand and she nodded, then hurried toward me and slid gracefully into the booth.

"What happened to Jamie? People are saying he was murdered." Her knuckles were white as she gripped the tabletop.

"People are right. Someone hit him in the head with a rock. Or that's how it looks right now."

"But why?"

"I thought maybe you could tell me, Frankie."

The surprise in her eyes seemed real. "Me? How would I know?"

"Come on. We both know you've been hiding things. You didn't run at Lake Neshaunoc the weekend Garrett was killed. In fact, you were in Himmel, at his house, the night he died. If I can find that out, so will the police. You lied to me about being involved with Garrett again. Oh, I get it. You didn't want to start all the gossip again, maybe you didn't want your ex-husband to know, so you decided to keep it on the down low. What happened?

"Was Garrett true to form? Did he have someone else on the side? Did he make a lot of promises and break them again? I can see why you'd be angry. Jealous, even. From what I've gathered, Garrett wasn't a very nice man. Did he push you too far this time, Frankie? Did you feel like a fool falling for him again? Did you decide you'd had enough? Did you decide to kill him, Frankie? Did you go to his house that night? Offer to make him a drink? Slip in a little Klonopin that you confiscated from one of your students? Did he get really woozy and out of it? It wasn't hard after that, was it? Just slip on the gloves, pull out the gun, and one quick shot, you're good to go."

She was staring at me, not as I'd hoped, dumbstruck by my awesome reconstruction of the crime, but as though I had lost my mind.

"I wasn't having an affair with Garrett."

"Come on. Miller Caldwell saw you at his house at 11 p.m. the night Garrett died."

She shook her head. "No. Not Garrett. It was Jamie. I was in love with Jamie."

If she'd said she was having an affair with Father Lindstrom, I couldn't have been more surprised.

"Jamie? But—"

"But he was 17 years younger than me? But I'd had an affair with his father years ago? Yes, I know, it sounds like a bad plot from a romance novel. But it wasn't like you think."

"Oh? What is it that I think?" The disapproval was plain in my voice and probably my expression. But come on, she was the kid's teacher. His counselor, really, which made it even worse.

"That it was tawdry and exploitative and maybe even illegal. It wasn't any of those things."

"OK. Tell me how it was."

"Ohhh," she expelled a long sigh. She pulled off her glasses and set them on top of her head, then rubbed the bridge of her nose with long, graceful fingers. She fidgeted, started to speak, then stopped herself. Finally she began rubbing the fingers of one hand across the palm of the other, and that seemed to soothe her enough to talk. She started off slowly, with information I already had.

"When Jamie got into trouble with drugs, I helped Garrett find a program for him. It was strictly professional—as though Garrett and I had never been intimate. That was fine with me. He listened to my advice. Jamie did his senior year at a residential school for kids with drug issues. And he did really well. I sent him a card when he graduated to congratulate him and tell him I was proud of what he'd accomplished, and that was that."

"Well, obviously not."

"No, but I didn't see him again until this past summer. He stopped by one day when he saw me working in the yard, just to say hello. He told me he'd finished at Himmel Tech, and he was transferring to UW in the fall. It was really nice to know he'd kept himself straight. While we talked he just started bagging up the grass I'd raked, and then he kept working alongside me. I invited him in for an iced tea. After that he started dropping by a few times a week. He was funny and smart, and I enjoyed his company. And I needed the help. The kids were at their dad's for the summer, and there was a lot to do in the yard."

"He wasn't bad looking either, was he? Now let me think, how old was Jamie, 20?" I shook my head. "And what about his relapse? It didn't bother you that he was using again?"

She flushed, and I felt a little bad for shaming her.

"He wasn't using drugs. I don't know why Garrett would say that. And don't make our relationship sound like something it wasn't. Jamie wasn't my student, and he wasn't a child. He was a young man. We worked together, and we had fun together. We laughed and we talked about books and music and movies. And we fell in love. Maybe it was clichéd, and maybe it wasn't realistic. But it wasn't tawdry. It was real. For both of us."

I saw the pain in her eyes. Maybe she really had loved him.

"OK. What happened?"

"Garrett found out."

"How?"

"I don't know. But he called me about a week before he died. He was furious. He said I was taking advantage of Jamie, that I would ruin his life, that I was ridiculous. But I really think he was angry that Jamie was happy. I can understand a little now, since you told me he had Parkinson's. His life, as he wanted to live it, was over. And Garrett was never what you'd call an unselfish man. I think he was jealous that Jamie had his whole life in front of him."

"Nice dad."

"But surely you've learned that's how he was. He said if I didn't break it off with Jamie that he'd ruin me. Everyone in town would be talking about the cougar teacher who took her student as a lover. My kids would find out. The school board would find out. My ex-husband might take my son, Caleb. I couldn't go through that again. And I knew that he was probably right. Deep down, I knew all along it couldn't last."

"So you broke it off?"

She nodded. "The weekend I told you I was at the fun run, Jamie and I had gone to his family's cabin. I didn't tell Garrett I was taking that last two days with Jamie. It was the only time that we actually spent time away together. I waited until Sunday evening to tell him. It was so hard."

"Did you tell him why?"

"No. It was part of the deal with Garrett. Besides, I didn't want to damage his relationship with his father any further. I told him that he was too young, and we didn't have enough in common. I told him I was bored with him. That was the worst lie I ever told in my life. He just, he just stared at me in such utter bewilderment it broke my heart." Tears had welled up in her eyes and were spilling down her cheeks, but she didn't move to wipe them away.

"He got angry then, asked me if any of it was true, if I'd ever cared about him. I said yes, of course, but that it was time to move on. I needed someone older, more mature. He called me terrible names, and I let him, because I deserved it. I loved him, but I knew it could never work in the real world. I indulged myself, and I hurt him so much." She started actually crying then with quiet sobs. I reached for the napkin dispenser and pulled out a handful to hand to her.

"Frankie, what were you doing at Garrett's that night?"

"I had to tell him I'd done it. That I'd broken things off with Jamie. I had to be sure he knew, had to be sure he wouldn't tell my ex-husband or my kids."

"And what did he say?"

"He didn't answer when I rang the bell, but the light was on in his study. The front door wasn't locked, so I went in and called out to him. I went to his study. He was at his desk writing something. He actually jumped when I spoke. He put down his pen, and he said, 'Did you do it?' I told him I had and begged him to keep his word.

"He said, 'Don't worry, no one will hear about it from me. Goodbye, Frankie.' I stood there for a minute. I'd expected more anger, or more recriminations, more warnings to stay away from Jamie. But he was so calm and so distant. I just said, 'OK,' and I left."

I wanted to believe her, but she had a big fat motive to kill him. He could destroy her life. And Garrett wasn't exactly a trustworthy man. He'd set her up for a fall before, and she had to wonder if he'd do it again, despite what he'd said.

"You said he was writing. What? A letter, a list, a report?"

"I don't know. I couldn't really see. Later I assumed it was his suicide note. Then I started worrying that maybe he'd written about me and Jamie as a cruel last trick. But when nothing came out, I knew he hadn't."

"Nothing came out, Frankie, because there wasn't any note. Are you absolutely sure you saw him writing something?"

"I—well, I—," she faltered. "I think so. Yes, I'm sure." But her voice was tentative.

"You know you need to go to the police."

A panic-stricken look came into her eyes. "I can't. I can't have all this come out. What good would that do now?"

"Miller Caldwell saw you. He's probably already talked to them. And they're going to come to you."

"But I didn't do anything! I don't know anything! Please, you have to believe me."

"It's the police who have to believe you." It was a little cold, but I was irritated by her weakness, her poor judgment, her failure to see the consequences of her actions. She was too soft. And she kept making the same mistake. Choosing the wrong man, over and over. And maybe I was more than a little irritated that if Garrett really had been writing something, I might be the one who had been making a big mistake.

"I'm sorry, Frankie, but you'd better get ready to answer some pretty tough questions."

CHAPTER 30

As I DROVE THROUGH TOWN my thoughts careened off each other like bumper cars.

What if Isabel and I were wrong all along? Garrett is determined to take control of his illness before it takes control of him. He decides to kill himself, and he's so angry about Jamie and Frankie that he doesn't care if suicide means both Jamie and Isabel will lose the insurance money. Not very fair to Isabel, but nothing new in that family. Only Garrett can't let go completely. He uses his suicide note for one last attempt at control by destroying Frankie's life, by further tormenting Jamie, by ensuring that Bergman is caught at whatever he's doing? Maybe all three. If Jamie found it, taking it away would protect Frankie. It could also give him information to blackmail Bergman.

But Frankie could be mistaken about a note. She had an emotional personality and that night her feelings would have been at fever pitch—fear, resentment, guilt, and grief. Was she really seeing and remembering things accurately? Even if she were, maybe Garrett was writing up case notes or a reminder to himself about a meeting or something he had to do, and then filed the note away. Or was he writing something incriminating that his murderer took with him?

Then again, was Frankie flat out lying? There never was a note. She made the whole thing up to make it seem as though Garrett killed himself, once she knew that someone saw her and she needed to explain away her presence at the Whiting house. But if that were true, that would mean Frankie wasn't the vulnerable, emotion-wracked woman she seemed, but a much stronger, more calculating thinker.

When I pulled in the driveway, I reached for my phone to call Coop. As soon as my fingers wrapped around it, I dropped it back in my purse. Not a good idea. We'd been on the outs before; in a 20-year friendship it happens. But this time it was a complete break in understanding. He had lied to me. The firm ground of our relationship had shifted. And there was no doubt about it. Reasonable or not, it hurt.

I turned my thoughts back to the problem at hand. Was there a note, or wasn't there? How could I find out?

My phone rang, and I was actually glad when the caller ID said Nick.

"Hey."

"Hi. Just thought I'd check in and see how you're doing."

"Well, you missed a big day in the little town of Himmel. Jamie Whiting was murdered, I joined the ranks of the unemployed, and my Garrett Whiting murder theory is on life support." I spilled out to him what I would normally have told Coop.

"I can understand why you quit. Rebecca sounds pretty vicious."

"Thanks for the solidarity. She's probably not as bad as I'm making her sound. But pretty close."

"I don't doubt it. A colleague and I did a study in a corporate setting last year. We were looking at saboteurs in the workplace. Psychopaths really. They're not always violent, you know. Sometimes they get their thrills destroying other people's lives—and careers. We're presenting our findings at a conference next March."

He said the last with a clear note of pride in his voice.

"That's great," I said, and it was, but at the moment my interest was forced. I really wanted to pick Nick's brain about Frankie.

"What are the odds that Frankie is remembering what she saw that night accurately?"

He switched gears with me, and I made a mental note to ask him all about his conference as soon as things settled down. He really was being very nice.

"Well, memory isn't a digital recorder. It doesn't take in unfiltered data and play it back when you press the right button. Eyewitness accounts are notoriously unreliable, because our minds fill in the gaps between what we actually see and what we think we should be seeing."

"Say again?"

"Frankie sees Garrett that night. She's in a highly stressed state. Later, she's told he committed suicide. Her mind reconstructs the memory, but it's based not only on what she saw, but on her expectations. She expects that the arrogant, controlling Garrett she knows wouldn't commit suicide without leaving a note. So she 'remembers' he was writing something at his desk."

"Then she's making it up."

"Not what I said. Our minds interpret what we see and hear. Sometimes the interpretation and the actual event matches, but sometimes it doesn't. That's why a victim can swear that she recognizes her rapist and believes it, but years later DNA evidence proves it couldn't be him."

"You're not helping me."

"Sorry. I live to serve, but there isn't a black and white answer. Is it better if Frankie's right or if she's wrong?"

"Could be better for her if she's right. But it could be good for me, too. If Garrett was writing a suicide note, then Frankie would be off the hook. On the other hand, if he was writing a note that incriminates his killer, that would sure make things easy for me. My problem now is there's no way to know if a note existed, let alone what it might have said… " My voice trailed off and I fell silent.

I was thinking about Elaine Quellman, Garrett's office manager, running her hand over his leather portfolio like a blind person reading braille. Only not braille. Indented writing. I wasn't aware I'd said the words out loud until Nick repeated them.

"Indented writing?"

"Garrett used a lined pad of paper in a leather portfolio to write down lists, notes on patients, personal correspondence."

"And so?"

"So, she—Elaine Quellman—the office manager has the portfolio. Isabel gave it to her as a keepsake. And she said she'd put a new pad of paper in it for him at the office. The morning he died."

"OK. I'm still not following this."

"Indented writing! Remember Jane Barstow? She was a forensic document examiner for the Michigan State Police Crime Lab? She opened her own practice in Grand Rapids, and I did a feature story on her?"

"Vaguely."

"She told me that it's possible to get handwriting from the impressions made in the paper below the one you're actually writing on. In fact, you can get impressions off as far down as four pages, maybe even more. She uses an ESDA machine—an Electrostatic Detection Apparatus. She demo'ed it for me. It was pretty amazing."

I explained how Jane had taken a piece of paper that looked totally blank to me. I couldn't see dents from heavy pressure of a pen, nothing like that. She put the paper on the platen of her machine and covered it with a clear film, sort of like plastic wrap. Then she turned on a vacuum in the machine, and it basically sucked the film onto the paper so the two were melded together.

"Then abracadabra, she waved an electrified wand over it. I'm not sure, but I think she chanted a spell, too. The wand leaves a heavy static charge in the indented areas of the document. When she sprinkled a little pixie dust over the whole thing—actually, she said it was more like toner—it settled into the impressions in the paper. The 'invisible' writing on the paper showed up, and I could read what I couldn't even see before."

"You mean like on TV, when someone rubs a pencil over a blank piece of paper and brings up the killer's address."

"That doesn't work in the real world, or all forensic document examiners would need is a supply of number two pencils. It just ruins the paper so the tests that do work can't be used. Jane's ESDA is magical."

"So you're saying—"

"Yes! If Garrett wrote the suicide note Frankie says she saw, he would have written it on his portfolio pad. Elaine Quellman has the portfolio. I can get the pad from her and ask Jane to do her forensic magic. Then I can read whatever Garrett wrote."

"Including something that might tell you who the killer is, or at least point you in the right direction."

"Exactly."

"It sounds like a Hail Mary play, but I hope it works for you. How about meeting me for coffee after I teach on Thursday night? You can tell me how it comes out."

I was already scrolling through my phone, focused on finding Jane Barstow's number.

"Maybe. Text me later."

The only number I had for Jane was her business phone, so I left a voicemail and asked her to call me back in the morning. I wanted to head over to Elaine Quellman's house to borrow the portfolio, but when I looked at my watch I saw it was 11 p.m. I might have a better chance of persuading her if I didn't roust her out in her pajamas. It could wait until morning.

At home, my mother was already in bed. My phone had been chiming with text messages from Miguel with increasing frequency, so I finally sat down and called him. I had to hold the phone away from my ear when he answered.

"*Díos Mío*! You quit? Why? What's wrong?"

"What did Rebecca say?"

"She said I should ask you."

"Typical. I quit because she accused me of being unprofessional, because she killed the Whiting story, and because she's terrible at her job."

"But Leah, I don't want to work there without you." He almost never called me Leah, always chica. He sounded so sad.

"I'm sorry, Miguel. I planned to leave anyway, just not this soon. You'll be fine. Rebecca will find someone to take my place and then you can be the bossy senior reporter. And I'm not gone out of your life, just out of your newsroom. Maybe she'll promote Courtnee." Fortunately his naturally sunny temperament responded to my feeble attempt at humor, and he gave a small laugh.

"I know. But it won't be the same."

"Nothing ever is."

"What are you going to do?"

"I'm still working on the Whiting story. I'm going to do it on spec for a friend at the *Milwaukee Journal*."

"Oh, I almost forgot. Word is your amigo Cole Granger has been selling prescription drugs out of JT's. Not a lot, just as a favor to some old customers. I don't know who he's getting them from."

"It's got to be Bergman. Why else would he and Bergman even be talking to each other?" I filled him in on Miller and Frankie and what she'd told me about Jamie. And about Frankie seeing Garrett writing something before he died, and my plans for the portfolio.

"You know, I'm starting to rethink Frankie Saxon as a suspect."

"*Recuérdate*, remember, you only know what she told you. What if Dr. Whiting forced Jamie to break up with her, not the other way around? She killed the papá for revenge, and Jamie found out. He was gonna tell, so she had to kill him. Or what if she did tell Jamie that his papá wanted them to split up? Maybe she pushed him to get rid of his father. But then he got scared, and she was afraid he'd confess, and they'd both be arrested, so she has to kill him, too."

"Listen to you, being all grown up with your theories. It could have happened. What you're saying could be true, but the more I think about Frankie, the less I think so. Nothing in her life says she's capable of masterminding that kind of crime. She's too impulsive, I think, and she doesn't have the killer instinct. When her husband verbally abused her, she tried to appease him by having another baby. When Garrett dropped her, she slunk quietly away until her husband kicked up a public ruckus. When Garrett ordered her to drop Jamie, she did it without any pushback. I think even if it were reversed, and Jamie dumped her, she'd go into hiding to lick her wounds, not plot a revenge killing. No, Miguel, there's something I'm not seeing, something that ties this whole thing together, but I can't get hold of it. Yet."

CHAPTER 31

I WOKE TO THE SOUND OF VOICES in the kitchen and jumped up with a start. My clock said 8 a.m. I was going to be late for work. Wait a minute. I didn't have "work" anymore. I wasn't late for anything. But I was curious about who my mother was talking to, so I brushed my teeth, pulled my hair up into a clip and walked to the kitchen. When I saw Coop sitting at the table, I almost walked back out.

"Coop said he's had trouble getting hold of you. I told him you'd be up in a few minutes and here you are. You want some eggs and toast?" She sounded a little nervous, as well she should after setting up an ambush for me.

"No, thanks, that's OK." I turned to Coop. "I did get your calls and your texts. And I wanted to call you back, but now why didn't I? Oh, yeah. I was waiting to call you back the right way, seeing how I know you're very particular about doing things 'the right way.'"

"I think I'll go put in a load of laundry. Good seeing you, Coop. Don't be such a stranger." My mother scurried off, her part in the set-up over.

"Leah, sit down. Please."

I dropped into the chair across from him, folded my arms across my chest, and said, "Well?"

"Look, I'm sorry for the way it came out about me and Rebecca."

"You lied to me. By omission if not outright. You told Darmody? But you didn't tell me? How do you think that makes me feel?"

"I didn't say anything to Darmody. Why would I tell him?"

"Well, he knew. The real question is, why wouldn't you tell me? Don't give me that 'I thought you'd be upset' excuse either."

"But you are upset. Rebecca and I thought it would be better if we waited to see if our relationship was going anywhere. She knows you don't like her, and she knows how important you are to me. She didn't want you upset for nothing, if things between us didn't work out. And I wanted to tell you the right way, at the right time."

"Yeah, you said that already. So, I take it that things are 'working out' then?"

He nodded with a stupid grin on his face.

"I'm glad you're so happy. But things aren't going so well for me. Your girlfriend fired me yesterday."

"That's not exactly how I heard it. She said you quit."

"I had to. She may slay you, but she was killing me. She's a piss poor editor, who wouldn't admit I had a great story if the Pulitzer Committee handed me the prize."

He ignored the trash talk about his girlfriend and tried to lighten the mood with a little teasing. "Oh, think this Whiting story is going to be a Pulitzer, do you?"

"Maybe. I'm still going to write it, you know. Only I'm going to sell it to the *Milwaukee Journal*. Probably be top of the fold." I cringed inwardly at the desperate-sounding bluster of my words.

"Hey, that'd be great." His voice held the same condescending note of pity that my teacher's had, when I told her my dad was on a secret mission for the CIA and that's why he couldn't come to Dads and Daughters Day at school. I hated it coming from Mrs. Bole then. I hated it especially coming from Coop now.

"Yeah, I've got a line on a tie-in with a prescription drug ring in the area. I think I know who two of the players are. And one of them is linked to Garrett Whiting. But you probably know something about that already?" I was baiting him, trying to get a reaction other than complacent patience. Because that's the kind of immature asshat I am.

"What do you know about the investigation?" He wasn't complacent anymore, and though I was going in blind, I was pretty sure I'd hit the mark.

"You mean the DEA Task Force you've been working on?"

"Darmody told you," he said in disgust.

"No. I asked, but he didn't give you up. He just stammered and stopped talking. No wonder. You were a busy boy, hooking up with Rebecca and working a major drug case. Poor Darmody wasn't sure which secret life I was asking about. You and Rebecca or you and the DEA. No worries, I'm an investigative reporter, right? I found out both."

"Darmody didn't know about Rebecca. I didn't tell anyone and neither did she." I felt a tiny bit of forgiveness slip into my soul. At least he hadn't confided in Darmody.

"But what about the DEA? He knew about that, didn't he? But you didn't even give me a hint. You know I can protect a source."

"Not my call. I can't be your source on this. I'm just one guy on the task force, and we're all under strict orders to keep the lid on tight. We're closing in on a big one. Any leak could ruin months of work."

"So who local is involved in the task force? You and a couple of guys from HPD? Someone from the sheriff's department? How close are you to cracking it?"

He didn't answer.

"Coop, come on, I'm just asking for a general heads up. How about this, I'll give you a name and you blink your eyes if I'm right. Is Dr. Hal Bergman involved?"

"Leah, when there's something to tell, you'll be the first reporter I call. That's all I can give you."

The first reporter. But not the first person. That would be Rebecca. This was it, the moment when our friendship was redefined. I remembered something Father Lindstrom had said a few days ago. There are things you can change and things you can't. This looked like one of things I couldn't change. And if I didn't stop trying, I might lose what I wanted most, Coop's friendship.

"All right. I understand."

"Do you?"

OK, now that was uncalled for. There I was prepared to take the high road and there he was pushing me right back on the low road.

"Yes. I understand that you aren't going to help me on this. I understand that you want me to back off. Now you better understand, I'm going to do whatever I have to do to get the story. Thanks for stopping by. I've really enjoyed the update on your personal and professional life. I've got to get a shower now. You can let yourself out."

When I got out of the shower my mother was gone. Coward. I checked my phone and saw a voicemail had come in from Jane Barstow.

"Leah, just listened to my office messages. I'm in the airport, on my way to a family reunion cruise. Won't be in the office until Dec. 11th. But I'd be glad to take a look at the pad you mentioned when I get back to Michigan. Just package it carefully and send it registered mail. Oh, and if you have samples of the victim's handwriting—business or personal letters would be good—include them. If I'm able to bring up anything on the portfolio pad, then I can compare the writing and authenticate it as being written by him. Got to go. Bye."

Well, good news and bad. Good Jane would look at it, bad I'd have to wait 10 days or so. I called Elaine Quellman and explained what I needed. She wasn't happy to give up custody of the portfolio, but I assured her it would be returned in perfect condition. By the end of the conversation she had volunteered several letters she had from Garrett, handwritten as per his eccentric preference, too. While I was talking to her, a text came in from Rebecca, instructing me to turn in my keys and pick up my things, which I had neglected to do while making my grand exit.

Courtnee was munching on Junior Mints when I walked through the front door.

"I was looking for the Donniker anniversary photo in your desk. I found these." She held the box out to me, and I shook my head. "You shouldn't leave them in the drawer. The mint part gets all hard instead of creamy if you leave them too long," she said, displaying no guilt about searching my drawers or being caught with contraband candy.

"Mrs. Donniker was all, like, up in my business, but I told her you probably lost it. But she just kept, like, talking about how she needed it back."

"I put the Donniker picture in your in basket three weeks ago, after I scanned it. It's your job to mail photos back, not mine."

"Well, I have a lot of jobs around here, especially now that you got fired." She tilted her head and cast her slightly protuberant blue eyes upward, a signal that she was thinking, or at least as close as she ever came to it. "Maybe it got filed in the Missing drawer." I briefly considered asking why she kept a drawer labeled "Missing," but decided that way madness lay.

"I think it was really mean of Rebecca to fire you. Especially after she stole your boyfriend."

"She didn't fire me. I quit. And Coop wasn't my boyfriend."

"Ohhh. I get it." She nodded. "That's what my Aunt Darlene said after her boss let her go for stalking her ex-fiancé from her work computer. We're not supposed to talk about it. It's still in court."

"Courtnee, Coop wasn't—never mind. I'm just going back to pick up my stuff. Is Rebecca in?"

"No. She went to an early 'lunch' with Coop." She made air quotes with her fingers, which I ignored. I went into the newsroom to pack up my things, but Courtnee followed me.

"Are you still going to Miguel's Christmas party? I am. My outfit is super cute. I've got a picture on my phone, do you want to see it?"

"No." I found a box and started taking things off my desk, my back to her, but she was undeterred.

"You should go to Miguel's with Nick. I mean, since Coop is Rebecca's bae, you should have somebody. But don't get all thirsty with him, Leah. Guys don't like girls who are desperate."

"I'll keep that in mind."

"Guess what?" She didn't wait for my response. "I saw Louis C.K. going into the Sunny Side Market yesterday."

"No, you didn't."

"Yes, I did." Ever since Courtnee and her father had spotted Brett Favre on a trip to Himmel to visit his cousin, she's been convinced that a continuous stream of celebrities is making incognito visits to town.

"Did anyone else see him?" I didn't know why I was even having the conversation, but Courtnee has a way of luring me in.

"Well, no. He was, like, in disguise. But I could recognize him. He has that dad body, and he was wearing a black T-shirt."

"OK." Sometimes you just have to know when to walk away. "Well that's it, I guess." I turned as I hoisted my box and held my keys out to her with one hand. "I'll see you around."

To my surprise she leapt toward me, knocking my small carton of personal items to the floor as she gave me a hug. I was taken aback, but I returned it gingerly.

"I'm sorry you screwed up and got fired. I'll try to find the picture you lost. And I'll tell Mrs. Donniker you got fired, too, so that'll make her feel better. On account of you had consequences for losing her anniversary photo."

"Thanks, Courtnee. I guess." As she turned to leave, I could have sworn her eyes were damp. I actually felt a little verklempt myself.

Without the structure of a daily job with deadlines, I felt a little lost. I picked up the portfolio from Elaine Quellman, packaged it, and sent it from the Post Office. I stopped by St. Stephen's where my mother worked several days a week in the parish office and had an unsatisfying discussion of her role in ambushing me that morning. She didn't argue with me, just shook her head and said, "Oh, Leah. I'm sorry you're hurting." Which made me feel bad for yelling at her and worse that she didn't understand this wasn't about hurt feelings, it was about honesty and loyalty.

I called Isabel to see how she was, but she didn't answer, so I just texted that I was thinking about her. I ran into the Elite and bought five rugelachs and a coffee, then drove to Riverview Park and ate them all while I thought about the time Coop saved me from an oncoming train, and what an ass he was now. Finally when my stomach was so full I could hardly breathe, I went back home. I laid down on the couch, exhausted as though I'd actually done something that day. Self-pity takes a lot out of you.

Finally I got up and made dinner as a peace offering to my mother. Then while it was in the oven, I started pacing up and down the hallway, talking out loud to myself. Which I do when I've alienated everyone else and I need to get my thinking in order.

"All right. Coop's in the Rebecca zone now, so get over it. He'll see what she's like, or he won't, but I can't do anything about it. I can, however, move forward on this story. I need to review my notes, make a plan, and get going." Sufficiently buoyed by my self-generated pep talk, I went to my room and pulled out my notebooks, but within minutes my mother got home, the timer dinged, and I got caught up in serving large helpings of twice-baked potatoes, green beans, meatloaf, and apologies.

"I'm sorry I got so mad at you. It's not your fault Coop is being so stupid, and you're right."

"Wait a second, could you say that again? I'm not sure I heard you."

I made a face, but I was way happier to be talking to her normally than to be angry at her. "You heard me. You're right. Coop's girlfriend is Coop's business, and it will only make things worse if I keep criticizing her. I'm done. Pretty much."

"I think that's wise. You've got enough on your plate with your book and this story on spec you're trying to do. How's that coming?"

"I feel like all the threads running through this thing—Garrett's death, Jamie's murder, the sheriff warning me off, Dr. Bergman and his connection to Cole Granger, Jamie's visit to the ATM at JT's—are somehow connected, but I can't quite knit them all together."

"Interesting metaphor, given your aversion to the homemaking arts, but I get your drift. So you don't think Frankie Saxon is involved?"

"Not really. I hate to say it again in such a short span of time, but I think you were right. I don't think she has it in her, at least not to kill Garrett so dispassionately. And I believe she really loved Jamie."

There was a knock at the kitchen door and Miguel came in, stamping his feet from the cold.

"Mmmm, it smells good in here."

"Leah made dinner; pull up a chair."

"Really, chica? I didn't know you could cook."

"There are lots of things you don't know about me." I stood up and got him a plate of food and handed it and silverware to him.

"*Qué tal?* How are you doing?"

"Not that great."

"Me either. Ohhh, this is so good! I might ask you to marry me."

"I might say yes. Why is your day not so good?"

"We are *muy ocupado*, very busy, at the paper. Rebecca had Courtnee shoot pictures at the Middle School today so I could run cops. She took video instead of photos. I can put a clip on the website, but I have to go in and grab a still for the paper. And I so don't have time. And my insurance called. My car—a moment of *silencio*, please—is totaled."

"Oh, no. I'm sorry, Miguel. I feel responsible. If I hadn't asked you to take dinner to Vesta, it might not have happened."

"That's true, Mom. It is kind of your fault."

"No, no, no, Carol. Don't let her tease you. It just happened. No one's fault, but I don't know what I'm going to do. I still owe on my car, and now I have to get a new one."

"You can borrow Mom's car for awhile, since it's really her fault. She and I can make do with mine. Now that we're both not working."

"Yes, Miguel, please."

"No, no, don't worry. *Está bien.* It's fine. I have the rental car for another week. I'll figure something out. So, chica, your turn. Why is your day so bad?"

"It really isn't I guess. I'm just having trouble figuring out what to do next. I was going to take a look at the security video from Cole again, want to see it?"

"You two go ahead, I'll clean up here."

"Sí, sure."

I took him to my room, where my laptop was set up with the SD card already inserted. I skipped ahead to the part where Jamie approached the machine.

"See, it's him. He's wearing the hoodie." We watched as he entered the pin number. The lighting was terrible, the angle was bad, and the video quality was poor. But it was Jamie. It was proof he was there, but what good did that do now?

"I don't know, chica, you can't really see his face. Lots of people wear Badger hoodies." As someone who would never make a hoodie a staple of his wardrobe, he shuddered slightly. "Couldn't someone else have taken Garrett's ATM card before he was killed? You know, maybe he lost it, or left it in a machine and somebody picked it up, then tried to use it?"

"But I found the ATM slip in Jamie's pocket. The time stamp matches the time here on the video."

"But why would he go the ATM in the middle of the night?"

"Add that to the pile of things I don't know."

"Oh, I have something for you. Jennifer at the sheriff's department told me they brought Frankie Saxon in for questioning today, but they let her go."

"They brought her in, or Frankie came in on her own?"

He paused and looked abashed. "I'm not sure. When Jennifer told me they were questioning Frankie, I didn't ask. Not very good reporting."

"It doesn't really matter, I was just hoping Frankie would go in herself. It might help a little if she took the initiative. But maybe not. Her affair with Jamie is going to look like a big fat motive to Ross. I hope she had a lawyer with her."

He sighed and changed the subject. "Are you still coming to my party?"

"I don't know, I—"

"Chica, you have to! My car is ruined. My finances are ruined. Don't ruin my party. Here, let me look in your closet and find you something fabulous to wear." He pulled open the door, flipped through the clothes hanging there, then said, "Never mind. We'll go shopping tomorrow. You can't hide from Rebecca like a scared little bunny."

"I'm not hiding."

"Then prove it. Promise you'll be there."

"Fine. I'll be there. But—" Miguel's phone rang and I waited while he took the call. I couldn't get much from his side of the conversation, but from the way his face lit up, I knew it was good news. He hung up and turned to me with a wide smile.

"That was my Aunt Lydia! There's a kidney for Uncle Craig. We have to go now!"

"Go, go on, get out. Good luck. Keep in touch!" He was gone before I finished. And I smiled because he was so happy, and because now Rebecca had no one but Courtnee to help her get the paper out, and deadline was only two days away. Oh, that was too bad.

CHAPTER 32

I TRIED ISABEL AGAIN on Tuesday morning and this time she picked up.

"I just wondered how you're doing, if there's anything you need?"

"I'm all right. But Leah, something really strange happened yesterday. Detective Ross came to see me. He asked me about Frankie Saxon and Dad. I told him I was just a kid then. I knew there was kind of a scandal because Frankie was married, but it didn't really have any impact on us. But then he started talking about Jamie and Frankie and if I thought they were close. And I told him Jamie really liked her, and I did, too, because she's the one who really made Dad get involved and help Jamie get straight. But he made it seem like he thought they were having an affair! Why would he ask me that?"

"Because they were, I guess. At least according to Frankie. I wasn't going to tell you yet; I thought you had enough to deal with just now."

There was silence for a few seconds.

"But does that mean they think Frankie had something to do with Jamie's death?"

"I'm not exactly in the loop, but I imagine so."

"She was his teacher, his counselor! She slept with our father and then she slept with Jamie? That's sick! Did she kill Jamie? And my father, too?"

"Hold it, hold it, hold it. We don't know anything yet. Ross is just asking questions. That's his job."

"But he must suspect something. Why would he even be asking if he didn't have some evidence? You know, don't you? Please, tell me what's going on."

"All right, but this may not mean anything. Miller Caldwell saw Frankie in the driveway of your house the night your father died."

"Frankie? Frankie killed him?"

"No, Isabel, not necessarily. Frankie admitted she was there, but she said your father was alive when she left. And I think I believe her."

"Why? You could believe that Jamie killed his own father, but you can't believe that Frankie killed someone?"

"She could have, but it just doesn't fit with her temperament. Anyway, I'm still checking some things out."

"What?"

"I'll tell you if they work out. In the meantime, try not to think about this too much." I realized how ridiculous that sounded as soon as I said it. How could she not think about it?

What she said next, and the way she said it, almost broke my heart.

"Detective Ross told me something else. He said." She stopped and tried again. "He said they're going to release Jamie's body today."

"Oh, Isabel. I know how hard that's going to be. I could go with you to make arrangements. You shouldn't do that alone."

"No, it's all right. I've already talked to Mrs. Delaney at the funeral home. There won't be any service. Jamie wasn't religious and neither am I. We don't have any extended family to speak of. No, I'm having him cremated. And then, I don't know, maybe later I'll scatter his ashes at our cabin. He was really happy there."

"Are you really sure? You've had a tremendous loss. A service might help you—"

"Help me what? Get 'closure'? Nothing is going to help me get past this, nothing will bring me closure. I just—oh, never mind. I know you're trying to help. But there isn't any help."

"No, you're right. I'm sorry. That was stupid. But will you call me, please? I'd like to do something, anything."

"Yes. I will."

But I knew she wouldn't. There are some things so terrible, some grief so searing that no one can help.

It's how I felt when Annie died, and when my father left. It's how Isabel must feel now.

I was just starting to highlight and organize some of my notes, in search of that elusive connecting thread, when my phone rang. It was my agent, Clinton Barnes. I'd almost forgotten I was writing a book.

"Leah, the final pages look great. Wonderful job. The story is really compelling. We're all set for launch: interviews, book signings, podcasts. You'll be a busy girl for awhile. Do you have a stylist?"

"A stylist?"

"You know, a person to help you get your look right. Clothes, accessories. You want to project a certain image."

"Um, sort of," I said, thinking of Miguel, but not at all liking the thought of my "image" and how I needed to look. I hadn't considered the promotion part of book publishing much.

"You need to get working on that. I have someone if you don't. Let me know. And we need to talk about your author photo for the back cover."

"I sent you the photos two weeks ago. Didn't you get them? You can choose either one you want. I trust you."

"The thing is, I think we want to go a little more awesome with them. Maybe you standing on the cliff where Sister Mattea went over. I see you maybe staring out at the horizon, looking kind of pensive but determined. You know, a Katniss Everdeen vibe going."

"You're kidding."

"I'm not. It goes with the narrative. You know, sister protecting sister, strong, confident."

"I am not posing like the heroine of a young adult novel."

"It's very in now. Very on fleek."

"'On fleek?' Clinton, I hate it when you talk millennial to me. English, please."

"Well, don't worry about it. We have time. We'll talk again. We want everything to be right. *True Crime: Unholy Alliances* could be a blockbuster."

"Really?" Clinton's words made my current unemployed state a little easier to take.

"Absolutely. I know you were a little disappointed with the advance, but we got you a great contract. This could be a very good deal for all of us, Endres Press, you, me. In fact, we need to talk about your next book. We want to capitalize on the momentum. Any ideas?"

"Well, what about the Mandy Cleveland murder?" That was the original story I'd queried Clinton—and a thousand other agents—about a few years ago. He'd taken me on but hadn't been able to sell it. "I thought you said that we could try that again."

"We will, we will. Not yet. It's a good story, but maybe a little too complex, a little too nuanced at this stage of your career. We want to follow *Unholy Alliances* with another fast mover. It's what your readers will be looking for."

"I don't have any readers."

"You will. What about this murder you're working on now? Could that be your next book?"

"I guess, maybe. Depends how it plays out. I don't have any idea how this ends, yet."

"Get me an outline as soon as you can, and I'll start pitching it. Well, got a meeting, got to go. Let me know about reshooting the author photo."

"I already let you know, I said—" But I realized I was speaking to dead air; he'd already hung up. I'd only met Clinton face-to-face once; everything else was text, phone, or Skype, and it was always twice as fast as any normal human being communicated. He was in constant motion. But I really liked him, and I appreciated his faith in me. There would be no posing on a cliff, but I might give some thought to the Garrett Whiting story as a book. If I could ever figure out the ending.

I went back to my notebooks again, and when nothing struck me, I pulled out the case file I'd gotten from the sheriff's department. This time I read the phone records more carefully than I had the first time. I looked at all of the calls for the preceding week, thinking maybe I'd see Frankie's number, or one that could be Bergman's. But aside from a few 800-number marketing-type calls, there was only one other local number listed. It looked vaguely familiar, but as I started to punch in the numbers to see who answered, a text came in from my friend Jennifer at the sheriff's department.

Frankie Saxon was arrested.

I knew I wouldn't get anything walking into the sheriff's department. In addition to being *persona non grata* to both Sheriff Dillingham and Ross, I didn't even have the quasi-official status of a newspaper affiliation. I texted Jennifer back.

Can you take a break and meet me in the Court House parking lot? 10 minutes?

Yes

I had just pulled into an out-of-the-way spot next to the trash dumpster when Jennifer opened the passenger door and slid in.

"I can't stay. I'll be in big trouble if the sheriff or Ross know I'm talking to you."

"What's going on?"

"They arrested Frankie this afternoon."

"You already texted me that. What's the evidence?"

"Frankie didn't have a lawyer yesterday when they interviewed her. She talked too much. She said she was there at the Whiting house that night. She admitted Garrett had found out about her and Jamie and that he told her to break it off."

"But they let her go yesterday."

"That was part of the plan. Get her shook up, then let her go home and think she's off the hook, then reel her in again. She's got a lawyer now, but it's Jim 'let's-make-a-deal' Gilroy." She rolled her eyes, and I knew why. Jim Gilroy is a not-very-ambitious lawyer who never met a client he didn't want to plead out.

"So what happened today? Why'd they arrest her?"

"They've got phone records that show a call from Jamie's cell to Frankie's home phone on Saturday. They think either Jamie actually helped her kill his dad, or he knew that she had. Either way, he got a bad case of nerves, and he told her he was going to the police. She set up a meeting in the park, told him they'd talk about it, maybe even go in together. Instead, she killed him."

"That's not good."

"No kidding."

"Jen, I don't think she did it."

"Well good luck with that. They're all doing a victory lap around the office right now. They wrapped up a murder case in three days. The only thing keeping Ross from kissing himself all over is he has to admit Garrett Whiting didn't commit suicide. But he's so fired up over catching a double murderer I think he's gonna be okay with that."

"This is moving too fast. They're totally ignoring any other suspects."

"You got someone in mind?"

"As a matter of fact, yes I do. What do you know about the DEA Task Force?"

"And that's my cue to leave," she said, reaching for the door handle and sliding out.

"Wait a second."

"Nope. Sorry." Jennifer didn't mind giving me the inside track on Frankie; she knew most of it would be released in a back-patting press conference soon, or I'd get it from Frankie herself. But she'd never give up details on something as hush-hush as a drug operation, regardless of how much time we spent together in the kindergarten time-out corner. Nevertheless I tried, giving her my most compelling stare, one eyebrow raised.

"Quit trying to pressure me with 'the look.' I'm not telling you. Why don't you ask Coop?"

"Not gonna happen. We'll do lunch, I'll tell you all about it. C'mon. Just give me a crumb."

"Well, there is one way you might get some information."

"Yeah?" I leaned in toward her a little closer.

"The sheriff's still looking for a date for the Elks Club Christmas dance. If your mom's not busy?"

"Goodbye, Jennifer."

"You should run it by her at least. Lester's been trying out a new after-shave. It's pretty intense. Could be sparks would fly. Maybe some intel, too. Who knows, you could get the information and a new stepfather too." She was still laughing as she shut the door. Not funny. Well, OK, a little funny, but I wasn't in a laughing mood.

CHAPTER 33

ON IMPULSE, I drove out to the Whiting house. If Isabel didn't know already, she'd soon hear the news. I didn't think she should be alone.

"Leah, it's over. The police arrested Frankie. Detective Ross just called me." She sounded different. Jubilant, almost. Looked different, too. Her eyes had lost their dullness and were a clear, warm brown again. I followed her into the living room. As we sat down she said, "Thank you, for all you did, and for sticking by me. I know I didn't make it easy."

"You seem a lot better."

"I didn't think anything would make a difference. But it does. Knowing who killed Jamie and my father, well, it's as though something shifted inside me. I don't know how to explain it. It's like, there's an ending. It won't go on and on and on, with me never knowing why. And I know now that Jamie wasn't at the park because of my note. It wasn't my fault. He went there to meet Frankie."

"Isabel—" I started to tell her maybe it wasn't over. That Bergman had a strong motive and was much more likely than Frankie to commit a calculated crime like Garrett's murder. I stopped myself, because I didn't want to take away whatever comfort she was finding at the moment.

"What?"

"Nothing. I, uh, I'm just. I'm glad you feel better about things." But she was too perceptive not to hear the hesitation in my voice.

"You don't think Frankie did it, do you? You still think Dr. Bergman had something to do with it? Isn't that what you said the other day?"

"I just don't see Frankie having the temperament for a cold-blooded killing like your father's."

She didn't answer right away, and I thought she might be angry at me.

"Leah, you've done so much for me. Not just investigating when no one else would, but you really cared. I'll never forget that. But maybe you cared too much. Maybe it's just hard for you to realize it's over. Frankie killed them both, I know she did." She reached out and touched me on the arm. "But I don't want to argue with you. Can we just not talk about this for awhile?"

"All right, sure." I nodded agreement. What was the point of trying to convince her? She felt a little better and I didn't have any hard evidence, so couldn't I just back off for once? Yes, I could. Coop would be proud of me. As if that mattered.

"Good. I want to ask you about something else," Isabel said.

"What's that?"

"Do you think Miguel would want Jamie's car? I know his was pretty wrecked the night you guys were coming to my house."

"The Mini Cooper? He'd love it, but he couldn't afford it."

"I wasn't planning on asking much. I have three cars now. Mine, my dad's, and Jamie's. I need to get rid of two of them. And I don't like seeing the Mini in the driveway. It just reminds me of Jamie. Do you think he could afford $500?"

"I think so, yeah, but that's a ridiculously low price."

"It isn't really. It has a lot of miles on it—it was mine before it was Jamie's. Actually it still is mine; we never transferred the title. The other thing is, it's pretty bad inside. Jamie wasn't exactly a neat freak. And the police went through it too. It's beyond messy. But I can't make myself clean it out. So Miguel would have to take the car as-is."

"Isabel, if you're sure you want to do this, that wouldn't be a problem." In my mind I saw Miguel sitting in the yellow convertible. He'd be ecstatic. "If you're serious, text him and see what he says."

"I will. Thanks."

I stuck around for awhile longer, hating to leave her in that big house alone, but she insisted she was fine. On the way home I got a call from Marissa Saxon, Frankie's daughter.

"Leah, they arrested my mother!"

"I know, I heard. I'm sorry."

"But she didn't do it!"

"Marissa, I can't imagine what you're feeling."

"No, that's right. You can't. It's your fault."

"My fault?"

"You tricked me into telling you she was home the night Dr. Whiting died. You made me break her alibi."

"No, Marissa. That's not why she was arrested. Someone saw her at Dr. Whiting's the night he died."

"I know all about that," she interrupted. "And I know about Mom and Jamie. She told me after you talked to her that day I met you. She got scared I'd find out. She wanted me to hear it from her. We had a huge fight. It was so totally gross. She and Jamie. But it was Jamie's fault, too. It's not like she came on to him."

I was touched that she was defending her mother for something that must seem to her pretty indefensible. It's hard for a kid to admit her mother has a sex life. Finding out that she's been having it with someone a lot closer to your age than hers would be even worse.

"And she didn't kill him, either. She wasn't even in Himmel on Saturday. She was at the mall in Madison all afternoon. She didn't get home until dinner, and we were together all evening. Someone must be trying to set her up."

"Marissa, there's a record of a phone call between her and Jamie on Saturday."

"I know, but it wasn't her. I'm the one who took the call."

"What?"

"Mom was gone. The phone rang, and I saw it was Jamie. He needed to leave her alone. I picked up the phone, but he didn't wait past hello. He started saying 'Frankie, I have to talk to you. You're not picking up your cell. I need you—.' I didn't let him finish. I told him to leave her alone, and not to call her ever again. And I hung up. But I never told Mom he called. Don't you get it? I didn't tell her. She didn't make any plan to go meet him at the park, because she couldn't have known he was there."

"Did you tell that to Detective Ross?"

"I tried to. He didn't believe me. He thinks I'm lying to help my mother."

"What about her cell phone? If tracking was on, it would show where she was."

"She's got this new app that really drains the battery, and she didn't realize her phone was dead until she got home. Jamie said she wasn't picking up her cell. That's because it wasn't ringing! Don't you get it? She never talked to him, didn't even know he was trying to call. And because the battery was dead, the GPS tracking doesn't work. She can't prove where she was."

"Marissa, your mother was at the Whiting house the night Garrett died," I repeated.

"I know that." Her voice was hard, angry. And scared. "But that doesn't mean anything. He was alive when she left. She told me! She didn't kill him, and she didn't kill Jamie! What's going to happen to her? Mom can't be in jail all alone. They won't even let me see her." Her anger crumbled and she started to cry.

"Listen, she hasn't been arraigned yet. That will probably happen tomorrow or Thursday. She may get bail, and then she'll be able to come home while she waits for trial. You're not alone, are you?"

"No. But grandma's just saying the rosary and crying her head off. I'd rather be here alone. It's because of you. If you left it alone, my mother wouldn't be in jail for something she didn't do. And we won't be able to afford bail. They're not going to just let her go. This is your fault, and I hate you for it!" She hung up before I could say anything. And really, what would I say?

It was 4:30 when I got home. My mother was sitting in the living room, a glass of wine beside her and a pensive expression on her face. There was no sign of anything happening meal-wise in the kitchen.

"Hey. Want to order a pizza for dinner?"

She didn't answer. "Earth to Mom, earth to Mom. Hey, are you hungry? Because I'm starving. I haven't eaten since breakfast."

"What? Oh, no, not really." Her tone was distracted, and it was most unusual for her not to ask for details of my day. I tried a small test.

"I thought I might call Nick and see if he wants to come over tonight to watch a movie." When she didn't immediately start telling me why that was a bad idea, I knew something was up.

"OK, what's going on? Why are you acting so weird?"

"I'm not. What did you say about pizza?"

"I said let's order one. But I'm gonna need something first. Like I said I'm starving. And this has been a terrible, horrible, no good, very bad day." I put together a plate of cheese and crackers as I spoke. I poured myself a healthy shot of Jameson and carried both into the living room. I needed something to blur the edges.

Her cell phone was sitting on the end table next to her chair, and it pinged with a text message just as I passed it. I reached to hand it to her, but she leaped up and snatched it out of my grasp.

She walked into the kitchen to read it, and I could her furiously tapping something in response as I gave myself over to contemplating the delicious smoked Gouda on my cracker. Say what you will about Wisconsin, but we've got some mighty fine cheese.

I vaguely heard some additional frenzied typing and then she walked back into the living room.

"What was all that mad texting about? Updating your *Plenty of Fish* dating profile again?" She didn't even smile at the small joke.

"I was just texting with Louise. She asked me again at the last minute to make a sheet cake for a funeral dinner. I told her no. I'm tired of it, that's all." Her voice had risen slightly, and she looked way more tense than the situation seemed to warrant.

"Mom, I have to tell you, you seem a little over the edge. It was just a cake, right?"

"Do I? Well, I'm sorry if I'm not reacting the way you think I should. It's nothing you need to worry about. I have to go check my email." She turned and went to her room.

OK, this was seriously strange. I wondered if she'd had a fight with Paul. Maybe the text was from him? I took a long sip of my drink and felt it send its warmth through my entire body. At least some things were reliable. Then because the cheese and crackers had barely penetrated my hunger wall, I phoned in my pizza order. While I waited for delivery, I got a call from Miguel.

"Uncle Craig is doing great!"

"Oh, Miguel, that's so good. I'm so happy for you guys."

"And also, Isabel texted me. She wants me to buy Jamie's car. For $500!"

"Yeah, I know, she told me. That would be perfect for you. I can just see you buzzing around town with the top down on your little Mini Cooper."

"Yaaasss! But..." Hesitation had crept into his voice. "I don't think it's totally fair. The car is worth way more dinero than that."

"Hey, you're not cheating her. The car has a lot of miles on it, and she wants to get rid of it. She told you it reminds her of Jamie, right? And that's hard for her."

"Sí, she did."

"So take it already!"

"I will!"

"When are you coming back?"

"My grandma is here and my mamá and some of my cousins. Aunt Lydia needs us. So I told Rebecca I couldn't come back until Friday. She wasn't so happy."

"Don't worry about it. You're the only reporter she's got right now, so she's not going to fire you." She was, however, going to have a few more tough days without him. So sad.

"How are you doing?"

I told him about Frankie's arrest and Marissa's phone call.

"Chica, you can't fix everything. Frankie, it's not your fault."

"I know, but I feel for the kid. And I believe her, about Jamie's phone call."

"What are you going to do?"

"Look into where Bergman was the night Garrett died. Find out what he was doing on Saturday when Jamie was killed."

"I don't know, chica. Coop said—"

"Coop told me to stay away from his task force. I will. I'm just trying to see how Bergman fits into the Whiting murders. If he even does. C'mon, Miguel, I can't let Frankie go on trial for something she didn't do."

"*Comprendo*, but still. Just wait until I get back, let me help."

"No, you don't need to get tangled up in this."

"Chica, why don't you let me help more? I'm your amigo. I told you before, there's no Thelma without Louise, no Butch without Sundance, no Ben without Jerry, no—"

"Hey, did you just call me butch? No, I know, I get it. Let's see where I am when you get here Friday. For now you go need to focus on your aunt and your uncle and your grandma and your mom and your million cousins. I'll see you soon. Bye." I hung up before he could extract any promises of nonaction from me.

CHAPTER 34

I KNOCKED ON MY MOTHER'S DOOR after the pizza arrived, but she said she had a headache and wasn't hungry. She clearly wasn't in the mood to talk, either, so I left her alone.

As I ate my pizza, I thought about Marissa's description of Jamie's phone call to Frankie. It didn't sound to me like Jamie was accusing Frankie or threatening her. It sounded more like he was asking for her advice or her help. Had Jamie made arrangements to meet Bergman at the park to accuse or blackmail him even, but he got scared? Had he wanted Frankie to know where he was, so he could tell Bergman that someone knew who he was meeting and would know who to blame if anything happened to him?

This was getting me nowhere. And meanwhile, Frankie was sitting in jail and her daughter was enduring probably the worst night of her young life. I sighed. And maybe it was the extra-large Jameson affecting my judgment, but I decided to call Coop.

"I'm surprised to hear from you." His tone was cool.

I felt for the first time that the fissure in our friendship could grow into an unbridgeable chasm. And it scared me. I gritted my teeth and said words I didn't really believe, but I knew I had to speak.

"I wanted to apologize for the way I reacted to you and Rebecca. And how I was this morning. And I'm sorry I was so mad at you about the task force. We don't see things the same way, but that doesn't make you wrong or me right. It just means we have different perspectives." God, it was painful to say that. Because of course he was wrong, but he sure wasn't ready to hear it yet.

"It's all right. I'm sorry, too, that things came out the way they did."

"I suppose you know Frankie Saxon was arrested."

"I heard."

"Coop, I don't want us to fight again, and before you say it, I don't want to do anything to hurt your investigation, but could we just talk for a minute about Frankie?"

Silence.

"I just want to run something by you."

"Leah, c'mon. I'm not involved in that."

"I understand. But just listen, just for a minute. Let's say that Frankie didn't kill Jamie. Or Garrett either. Her daughter Marissa says *she* took the phone call from Jamie, on Saturday, not Frankie. That Frankie was shopping in Madison all afternoon and into the evening. If that's true, then how would she know where Jamie was?"

"That's 'if,' Leah. Marissa wouldn't be the first person to lie to protect someone she loves." An impatient note had crept into his voice, a note I wasn't familiar with. He got frustrated with me sometimes, and angry sometimes, but he'd never before sounded like he was tired of talking to me.

"Yes, I know. But Frankie's history, her pattern of dealing with issues, isn't confrontation, it's running away or caving in. She's emotional; she's high-strung. She doesn't have the kind of cool thinking it would take to kill Garrett, or the cold-blooded self-preservation she'd need to kill someone she really loved like Jamie."

"Frankie had a strong motive for both murders. She killed Garrett because he was splitting her and Jamie up. Then Jamie found out what she'd done, and he turned against her. She had to kill him. Self-preservation is a pretty strong instinct."

"But listen, Coop, Bergman was stealing drugs and prescription pads, and Garrett gave him an ultimatum. I think the threat of jail, financial ruin, and the end of his professional life are pretty strong motives to kill the person threatening you. That's definitely self-preservation. I know you won't say, but I'm pretty sure Bergman is connected to the drug ring you're looking at."

"No, stop there. I'll tell you this much. Bergman's on our radar. But he didn't kill Garrett Whiting. We know he was out of town at a medical conference the weekend Garrett died."

"Well, but he could've left the conference, driven back here, killed Garrett and driven back."

"No, he couldn't. It was in Sioux Falls, South Dakota. That's six hours away, maybe even a little more. He was an after dinner speaker at the closing banquet Saturday night. He didn't leave the dais until 9:30. If he drove like hell, he might've made it to Whitings by 3:30 a.m. but that's outside the window the ME gave. Besides, he was in Sioux Falls Monday morning at 8 a.m. for a consultation with another surgeon. The timing just doesn't work."

I'm not so good with the story problem time tables, so I dropped that for the moment.

"What about Jamie then? Where was Bergman this past Saturday?"

"Leah, I don't owe you any more information. I'm just telling you, it wasn't Bergman. You need to trust the sheriff's department got it right. Frankie's the logical killer."

"I disagree," I said, careful to keep the anger and frustration I was feeling out of my voice.

"Understood. But that doesn't change things. I've told you more than I should. Now stay away from Bergman. I don't want him to catch wind of the fact that we're looking at him because you're poking around. I want to get him for the crimes he's actually committed, not lose him because you're chasing him for ones he didn't." I heard someone in the background talking to him, but I didn't catch what was said. Probably Rebecca.

"I have to go. I'll talk to you later."

247

"Yeah. Sure. Bye."

The perfect ending to a perfect day.

In the morning my mother announced she was going to visit my Aunt Nancy in Michigan for a few days.

"That's a little sudden, isn't it? Is Aunt Nancy all right?" My Aunt Nancy likes to have everything planned out at least 10 years in advance. A spontaneous visit wouldn't normally be on her list of happy surprises. In fact to her, surprise and happy are two words that don't go together.

"She's fine. I've just been thinking about her, and I haven't seen her in a while. So I thought I'd just get in the car and go."

"OK, well, when are you leaving?"

"This morning. I'm already packed; I was just waiting for you to get up to say goodbye. It's one of the benefits of being unemployed. I can go where I want, when I want." I was surprised when she didn't burst into the Mama's and the Papa's "Go Where You Wanna Go." One of her favorites.

"Well, have fun, I guess. Tell Aunt Nancy hi. And make sure she knows this wasn't my idea." I gave her a hug, and there was something in the way she held on just a second longer than usual that made me pull back and ask, "Mom, are you OK? Not still upset about the sheet cake wars, are you?"

"What? No, of course not. I just feel like seeing Nancy, that's all. I'll be back probably late next week. I'll call you when I get there."

I walked to the door with her and stood waving goodbye until her car turned the corner and disappeared.

I couldn't stop thinking about Frankie. Or Marissa. Isabel was at peace now, but Marissa was in her own special hell and so was Frankie. But I couldn't figure out a way around Coop's confident assertion that Bergman was in the clear for Garrett's death. When I couldn't stand going in circles anymore, I put on my coat and went for a walk.

The air was cold and a brisk wind made it even colder. I turned up my collar, curled my fingers up inside my mittens, and half-trotted down the street. The faster I moved, the warmer I got, and after a few blocks, I began to enjoy the clear sky and the bright sunshine. In a half hour or so I felt better and turned homeward.

As I reached the front door, the roar of a low-flying single engine plane was so loud I looked up to see if it was about to land on the street. It wasn't. But when I looked away, I had an idea. Inside the house I got the box of things I'd taken home when I cleaned out my desk. I flipped through the pages in one of the notebooks and reread the notes I'd taken at the Board of Supervisors meeting weeks ago—the one Grady O'Donnell had appeared at to defend his private airfield against noise complaints from his neighbors. Then I looked at the notes I'd written up after talking to Janelle at Bergman's office.

When I got to Grady's house, his wife told me I'd find him in the hangar working on a plane. She pointed me down a private dirt road that ran from the back of Grady's barn for about a quarter of a mile before jogging to the east for another quarter mile. It ended at an airfield with two large hangars. I could hear banging and other mechanical sounds coming from the nearest building as I got out of my car.

The door was open and I called out.

"Hey, Grady, how you doing?"

He was standing on a short ladder, bent over the open engine compartment of a plane. He straightened and looked up at the sound of my voice.

"Real good, Leah," he said, pulling his cap off his head, revealing a bald head damp with sweat. He rubbed his forehead with the sleeve of his blue work shirt before replacing his hat. "What can I do for you?"

"Well, I was just going over my notes from that Board of Supervisors meeting last month. I thought maybe I'd do a follow-up on your operation here." Mostly true.

"I gotta tell you, I'm not real anxious for more publicity. The board just kinda talked around things, and I'm hopin' to keep a low profile and see if things don't just fade away. Vi and Harvey Schmidt, that's the ones who complained, they got some new four-wheelers that make a lot of racket. I'm thinkin' we might be able to strike a deal between us—we don't bellyache about their machines runnin' all through the countryside, and they don't fuss about a few planes takin' off and landing. Besides, one of my renters who flies the most, he's takin' himself a long vacation, so things should be pretty quiet the next few months."

"Oh? Who's that?"

"Doc Bergman. This here's his Beechcraft. Real sweet plane. Me and Doc took it out for a spin one day, got up to 200 mph. Don't tell Beverly that. I still can't get her reconciled with me flyin', and it's been near 30 years."

"I know Dr. Bergman. He flies a lot, does he?"

"Oh yeah, most every weekend."

"Just up and around local, or does he like to fly long distances?"

"You wouldn't have a plane like this if you weren't doin' some serious flying. Couldn't tell you where all he goes. The pilots keep their own logs and all. I just furnish the airfield and the hangars."

"So you don't have to, I don't know, sign them in and out, or run a radio tower or whatever for air traffic control?"

He laughed. "This isn't exactly O'Hare, Leah. Basically, alls I do is keep the landing strip in good shape, plow it in the winter, make sure the runway lights are good, and keep the hangar clean and secure."

"So you don't necessarily know when they're using their planes and when they're not?"

"That's right."

"And you said you have lights on the runway, so that means they fly in at night, too, right?"

"Oh sure, yeah. That's what got old Harvey all shook up. Sometimes they come in kinda late at night. Bev and I both sleep like the dead, so we didn't notice. But Harvey said the missus sleeps real light, so the planes wake her up. Hard work and a clear conscience, that's how you get a good night's sleep. I sleep good every night," he said with a grin.

"I'll bet you do."

So Bergman's plane could fly 200 mph. He could come and go from Grady's airfield without any attention being paid. He could make a 500 mile trip in three hours easy. Coop was wrong. Bergman would have had plenty of time to fly back to Himmel, kill Garrett, and fly back to Sioux Falls.

"So, anyway like I said, I'd appreciate if we could just kind of let sleeping dogs lie. Not do that follow-up piece."

"Sure, I understand, Grady. No problem."

The sound of a well-tuned car engine caught my ear, and both of us looked out to see a black Mercedes coming down the road. When it parked, Hal Bergman got out and walked toward the hangar.

"Hey Doc, we were just talkin' about you." Grady seemed not to notice the scowl on Bergman's face when he saw me.

"I can't imagine why."

"Not really about you, Dr. Bergman. More about your plane. Grady was telling me it can travel 200 mph. Amazing. You know, I really hate long car rides. A plane like this would be great. I mean, instead of driving five or six hours from Himmel to Sioux Falls, I could be there in three hours, right? Heck, I could go there and back in less time than it takes to drive one way."

Something flickered behind his eyes. I wasn't sure if it was fear or anger or just distaste. He turned from me without commenting and addressed Grady.

"Were you able to get that part?"

"No problem, Doc, it's all set. Everything else checked and she's good to go any time. When you takin' off?"

"Not quite sure, Grady. So, I'd like to settle my account today."

"I'm not worried about that, Doc. I know you're good for it."

"You know, I might have to look into a plane one of these days. It sure makes coming and going easy, doesn't it, Dr. Bergman? Yep, I'm definitely gonna do that. Get a plane when my ship comes in."

Bergman stared at me but didn't say anything.

Grady finally picked up on the tension between us and laughed uneasily. "That's a good one, Leah. Get a plane when your ship comes in."

"I assume you're here bothering Grady and harassing me because you don't have anything else to do. I understand you were fired from your job, and I can see why."

Grady's face showed surprise and a little confusion, but he stayed out of it.

"I'm still working, Dr. Bergman. Just not at the *Himmel Times*. I'm on a big story right now. You remember, I'm sure. Garrett Whiting's death."

"I know that the high school teacher was arrested for his murder. I would assume the story is over."

"Oh, twists and turns, Doctor, twists and turns. You never know how things will come out in the end. Stay tuned. You might find it interesting."

I turned then and left before I edged any closer to the boundaries Coop had laid down about Bergman.

CHAPTER 35

ALL RIGHT. Now I knew Bergman could have made it back to kill Garrett. But what about Jamie? Had Bergman killed him because of something to do with his drug activities, or because Jamie knew Bergman had murdered Garrett? How could I get more on Bergman without screwing up the DEA investigation? There was no way I could talk to Coop about it. Or anything else. I needed to do something different for a while and let my subconscious turn things over, because my conscious brain was drawing a blank. And I knew just what would take my mind off it. I called Isabel.

"Hey, I talked to Miguel yesterday. Did he get back with you?"

"He did. He's going to buy the car for $500."

"Well, I've got a thought, if it's all right with you." I explained that I'd like to surprise Miguel by cleaning the car, so it was all ready for him when he got back on Friday. That way he could just take possession, get his insurance, and drive his happy little self around town.

"Would that be OK?"

"Yes, sure, that's a great idea. Is tomorrow soon enough? It's an easy switch. He already electronically deposited the money with me. I'll sign the registration and bring it to you with the car."

"So you doing all right?"

"Yeah, I'm OK. I'm just more sure every day that I need to get things straightened out here, and then I need to get away. I'm thinking about graduate school out east maybe."

"Yeah? That could be really good for you." I wondered if she ever thought about connecting with her birth family. Maybe her biological mother would welcome contact with her. Then again, what if her birth family didn't want to hear from her? What if they were worse than her adopted family? Though that hardly seemed possible. But it definitely wasn't the time to even mention it. But maybe something else would help.

"Isabel, my mother's out of town, and you're on your own—how about getting some dinner tonight?"

She hesitated.

"Come on. It'll be good for both of us."

And it was. We didn't talk about anything that mattered. She teared up a few times, but that was all right. You just have to let each wave of grief wash over you. It recedes and you have a little space where it doesn't hurt so much. If you're lucky, over time, the spaces between get bigger. At the end of the night, I think she felt a little better. At least she seemed to.

Isabel and her housekeeper dropped Jamie's car off in the morning. As I started working on the clean up, I thought again how much fun Miguel was going to have with this car. If ever a boy was made for a bright yellow convertible, it was him.

The inside was as bad as Isabel had said. Fast food wrappers and bags were crumpled and tossed in the back, empty soda cans, a stack of books, a magazine, flashlight, jumper cables, unopened mail. I tossed everything in a sack to go through later and determine what should go back to Isabel. Then I got seriously busy dusting, wiping down, cleaning the chrome and leather. I was major head sweating by the time I got to the vacuuming.

I pushed the driver's seat all the way back to give me full access to the floor and found an envelope wedged underneath. Had that kid ever cleaned this car? I tossed it into the bag as my cell phone rang. I pulled it out and saw the call was from Paul, my mother's boyfriend.

"Leah, can I talk to you?"

"Sure. Aren't we doing that right now?"

"No, I'd like to see you in person. It's important." That alarmed me a little.

"Paul, what's it about? Have you heard from Mom?" I'd spoken to my mother the day before when she arrived at Aunt Nancy's and she'd sounded fine.

"No, that's not it. Well, that is it, but not exactly." Curiouser and curiouser. Paul was not the stammering, stuttering type, but he was having a hard time getting his words out.

"OK, sure. When?"

"I had a cancellation. A root canal, so I've got an hour to spare right now. Can you meet me at the Elite in 10 minutes?"

"All right." I put the vacuum away, shoved the bag in the corner of the garage and went inside to do something with my hair. My head sweating had caused it to hang limply, and pieces of it were plastered to my skull. Not a great look. A hair clip was the only remedy in the time allotted, so I changed my shirt, slammed in the clip, and ran out the door.

Paul was already sitting at a table when I got there, his normally cheerful face fixed in a worried frown. He pushed a chai latte over to me as I pulled up a chair. He already had coffee, but it didn't look as though he'd drunk any.

"What's up?"

He ran his hand through his curly brown hair before he answered.

"I think your mother is having an affair."

Now, of all the things that had run through my mind since he called, that was definitely not one of them.

"You're kidding, right?"

"Do I look like I'm kidding?" And no, he did not. His brown eyes, which were usually alight with laughter, were serious and there were dark circles under them.

"Why would you say that? Mom thinks the world of you. And even if she didn't, she'd never do anything like that. She wouldn't hurt you that way."

"I'm crazy about her, Leah. You must know that. Heck, everybody must know that. I thought she felt the same way. But these last few weeks, she's been, I don't know, different. Sort of distant, and when I bring it up, she says I'm imagining things. And she always seems to be busy when I suggest we do something, like she's avoiding me."

"Even if that's so, it's a big leap to an affair, Paul. How would she hide something like that, not just from you, but from me, too? I haven't noticed any hang-up phone calls or late night rendezvous." Though I, too, had noticed my mother behaving a little oddly, like the night we were watching a movie and she practically snapped my head off when I teased her about Paul's "intentions." Then there was the text that upset her so much a few nights ago. The one she said was from Louise about a funeral cake.

"She called me this morning from Michigan. She didn't even tell me she was going. Said she was sorry, but she wouldn't be able to go to La Folie on Saturday. Leah, I made reservations weeks ago. I was going to ask her to marry me. Now I can't even get her to tell me why she doesn't want to see me."

"She didn't say that, did she?"

"No," he admitted. "But I asked her when she was coming back. She said she wasn't sure, maybe a week or so. I asked her why she went, and she was vague and said something about just feeling like a getaway. That's not like Carol. I got a little angry at her, and I asked her what was going on. She said nothing. I told her I didn't like where we were in our relationship. And she said she was sorry, but maybe we should take a break. I said yeah, maybe we should. But I don't want to, Leah. I just want Carol to tell me straight out. If she doesn't love me, if she has someone else, I just need her to tell me."

"Paul, Mom doesn't have anyone else. I'm sure of that. She is not having an affair. But as for the rest of it, I don't know. That's something you two are going to have to figure out."

"But couldn't you talk to her, maybe find out—"

"No," I said without hesitation. "I can't get in the middle of this." He looked so dejected I put my hand over his and said more gently, "I want this to work for you both, I do. But you have to figure it out for yourselves. I don't know what else to tell you."

I almost called my mother after I left, despite what I'd said to Paul about being Switzerland and staying out of it. But I didn't, because I knew that my mother, despite her predilection for diving feet first into my life, was very feisty about keeping her own private. Still, it worried me. I knew she wasn't having an affair, but what on earth was going on? A chill went through me. What if she was ill? What if something was seriously wrong, and she was pulling away from Paul because she didn't want to burden him? Maybe she went to see Aunt Nancy to tell her and get advice? I pushed the thought away. I refused to believe that whatever guiding force there is in the universe could take away the last part of my family that I had left. No. That wasn't it. But what was it?

I spent most of the afternoon putting the finishing touches on Miguel's new car. While I worked, I pushed thoughts of my mother and Paul out of my mind and focused instead on how I could find out where Hal Bergman was the day Jamie was killed. If Coop's super-duper DEA team could miss the fact that he had a private plane that could have allowed him to get to Himmel, kill Garrett, and get back to his conference, then who knows what they'd missed or assumed about his movements on Saturday. I didn't have to prove Bergman committed either crime, but if I could kick up enough reasonable doubt for Frankie's attorney to work with, maybe she wouldn't spend the rest of her life in jail.

By late afternoon the Mini Cooper was pristine inside and out, and I'd even found a cleaning product that left the interior smelling like a new car. He was going to be so happy. And that made me happy. And I had generated so much good karma with my cleaning frenzy on Miguel's behalf that I actually came up with a way to find out more about Bergman.

I'd go to Cole. If things were starting to heat up for Bergman, Cole might be ready to cut his ties and bail. On his way out, he just might toss me a bone and give me something I could use against Bergman. Of course that would put me in his debt; not a great place to be, but I was willing if I could get something useful from him.

I was tired and sore and dirty, and I decided that what I needed even more than answers was a hot shower, a bowl of Honey Nut Cheerios, and a night spent listening to '80s power ballads.

CHAPTER 36

FRIDAY MORNING I texted Miguel and asked him to stop by my house before he went home, once he got back into town. He answered right away to say he was already on the road and he'd be here by 10. "*Mucho* to do for the party tomorrow. And I have a surprise for you!"

That could mean anything from a match he'd found for me on craigslist personals, to a gift certificate for a make over at Making Waves. Or anything in between.

I buzzed over to JT's party store on the off-chance that Cole was working the day shift. He was not. I had no idea where he was living, probably with one of the many women he seemed to be able to charm into supporting him. Though charm wasn't exactly the right word. Maybe mesmerize, the way a cobra hypnotizes his prey.

Nadine, or so her name tag read, was running the register. She was young but had a hard edge. Her eyes were heavy with liner and her lashes spiky with mascara; her blonde hair showed dark at the roots. She tapped aqua-tinted fingernails on the counter to signal her impatience with me.

"Do you know when Cole will be in again?"

"I don't make the schedule."

"Do you have his phone number?"

"What do you want it for?"

"I just need to talk to him."

She looked at me suspiciously, perhaps gauging whether I was a rival for Cole's affection, or maybe one of his "special" customers.

"Can't give out his number. It's against store policy." I highly doubted that JT's had anything close to a "policy," but I could see I wasn't going to get anywhere with Nadine.

"All right. But could you get in touch with him for me? Just ask him to call Leah? Please, it's important." I handed her my card, which she took reluctantly.

"Just get it to him, please. Tell him I've got something he needs." It was really the other way around, but I hoped he'd be curious enough to call.

"Yeah?" She looked me up and down. "I doubt it."

I got home in time to check over the car and rub out any stray smears. Just as I finished, I heard Miguel's rental car in the driveway. I ran out to meet him and as he got out I commanded, "Close your eyes until I tell you to open them." I led him through the side door of the garage. The Mini Cooper sat in the center of the floor, directly under the overhead light.

"OK, open them!"

There was a sharp intake of breath as he took in the shiny yellow car, and he promptly burst into tears.

"Oh! She's so *hermosa!* So beautiful."

"Get in, get in, let me take a picture."

I took several shots with his phone, so he could text them to his mother and grandmother, and then he wanted to drive around town. With the top down, of course.

"Miguel, it's 25 degrees out!"

"C'mon, chica. Just ride with me to get the plates and insurance. Then I'll put the top up until spring. I just have to do this one time. Quick, before Rebecca knows I'm back in town," he added with a grin.

"All right, all right. Let me get my jacket. And hat. And scarf. And mittens. And blanket."

After a very cold, but very fun, drive through town to the DMV to register the car in Miguel's name, we clambered back in and drove to the A+ Independent Insurance Agency. As we walked up, I noticed the lettering on the glass door had been redone in a modern font. The extra-large phone number caught my eye and reminded me that I'd forgotten all about tracking down the local number I'd seen on Garrett's phone record. I didn't need to now, because it was right in my face. Marty Angstrom's office number was the local phone number I'd seen in Garrett's phone records. But when I'd called him about Garrett's life insurance, Marty said he hadn't talked to Garrett for months before he died. In fact he made a point of telling me that. Marty was holding something back. What? I felt a little thrill of excitement run through me. Sometimes breaks in an investigation come from the most unexpected places. Maybe I was going to get one. Finally.

"So, you got a fancy new car. Hope you take better care of it than you did your Toyota." Ivah Rollins, Marty's secretary, waggled her head in disapproval at Miguel as we walked through the door. Her large bun of steel gray hair didn't budge. She'd anchored it with a pair of chopsticks, from which dangled a fishing lure. At least that's what it looked like. Ivah has her own sense of style.

"I couldn't help it. But the Mini Cooper, she's not just a fancy car. She's my passion. I will let nothing bad happen to her, ever!" Miguel said, with a dramatic sweep of his hand to his heart.

Ivah raised her eyebrows and looked stern, but I saw a grin tugging at the corners of her mouth.

"C'mon, Ivah, don't scold Miguel. The accident wasn't his fault; he was trying to save a little dog. And he didn't get a ticket, remember. Hey, is Marty in? I need to ask him something." Maybe face-to-face he'd be more forthcoming—or truthful—than he had been on the phone with me.

"No, he's over to his in-laws in Oshkosh. He won't be back until Monday." My disappointment must have shown on my face, because she continued. "Don't worry, I can take care of anything you need."

"Thanks, Ivah, but I don't think so. I really need to see Marty."

Her tone shifted from helpful to slightly affronted. "I know everything that goes on here. Marty might be the agent of record, but I know everything he does about insurance."

"Oh, I know you do. But it's not about insurance. I just wanted to ask him about a phone call he made to Garrett Whiting the week before he died. Afraid you can't help me."

"Well, you're wrong there. Marty's the one can't help you. I called the doc. Marty wasn't even in the office. He was out with the shingles for better than two weeks."

The little thrill of excitement I'd felt a few minutes before disappeared. Still, I didn't give up completely. Marty couldn't tell me anything more about Garrett, but maybe Ivah could.

"Did you call about his life insurance policy? Did Garrett want to change it? Did he ask about the suicide clause or anything?"

"No, nothin' like that. That little girl of his got herself in a pickle with a fender bender she had up to Eau Claire last 4th of July. She tried to take care of it under the table, because she already had one claim from a deer accident over to Michigan last winter. Then Mr. Shyster that she hit changes his mind, starts talkin' whiplash and disability, and I got nothin' on the accident. I must've called her five times. Never returned a message. Finally, I calls the doc. He was pretty unhappy, I can tell you that. And Lady Isabel, she wasn't too pleased either that I called her dad. Came in not long after her dad died, cancelled her insurance, took her business elsewhere. Suit yourself, I told her."

So that's all it was. A stupid parking lot accident and a guy who tried to take advantage of Isabel's fear of rising insurance rates. Sometimes a cigar is just a cigar, and a phone call is just a phone call. One of the hard lessons of investigative journalism.

At least Ivah had been working all the time she was talking, and now she pushed some papers over to Miguel to sign. "Well, there you go Mr. Mini Cooper. Here's your proof of insurance. Put that in your fancy car. And you drive safe this time, or I'll have to get in there and give you a lesson one day."

"*Gracias*, Ivah. You can give teach me any time. You'll look *muy bonita* riding in my convertible with a yellow scarf to match my yellow car."

"Cheeky!" Ivah said, but she flushed with pleasure. "I could teach you a thing or two, I can tell you that."

"Do you like it, chica?"

I held a very sparkly, and what I suspected would be rather clingy, gold top in my hands, which I'd lifted from the beribboned box Miguel handed me as we sat on the couch at my house.

"Um. Wow. It's really, really shiny. And pretty. Yes. So pretty." I felt now exactly as my mother must have felt when I presented her with a birthday gift of the world's biggest, shiniest fake diamond earrings and matching necklace. Torn between horror at the gaudiness of the gift and a rush of intense affection for the giver who was so excited to present it.

"It's for my party tomorrow night. Remember, it's all about the sparkle. When I looked in your closet, chica, no, not happening. So I bought you this. You can wear your Amish black pants with it, so you won't feel so nervous. But you will look so hot! You love it, yes?"

"I love you for giving it to me, Miguel. It's amazing. I don't have words."

"You don't have to be nice. I know it's outside your 'comfort zone.' But you're way too comfortable there. You got to break free. You got to move, move, move. You got to groove, groove, groove." He grabbed my hand, pulled me off the couch, and started doing exaggerated dance moves with me around the room. Until finally we were out of breath from dancing—and laughing.

"Oh chico, you got the wrong Nash here!" I said, as we flopped down on the couch.

"No, you just have to learn to let it go."

"No, don't even—" But it was too late. He had already launched into a spirited rendition of Elsa's theme song.

Which I have to admit I joined in. Despite my voice deficiencies, I got the music in me—and my mother's propensity for bursting into song at a moment's notice.

"All right, all right. I'm going to your party. I'm wearing this very outside-the-box sparkly top. Are you happy now?"

"Well, if you promise to find a nice pair of gold high-heeled sandals, put a little makeup on those fantastic hazel *ojos*, don't pull your hair back in the clip like that, and come to my party happy, I will be *ecstático*."

"I give up. All right. I'll dress up like your life-size Barbie doll, but only because I'm so happy everything went so well for your uncle and aunt, and because I'm really glad you're back," I said, giving him a hug. And it was true. I felt more light-hearted than I had in weeks. Miguel has that effect on me.

"Me too, chica. But I better bounce. Need to check in at the office, and then I've got lots of things to do for my party tomorrow. Now, *recúerdate*! Remember what you promised."

CHAPTER 37

I RANG THE DOORBELL shivering slightly in my skimpy gold top, black pants, and gold high-heeled sandals, purloined from my mother's closet. My hair had been cut and styled at Making Waves. It hung in a silky, shiny, coppery-brown curtain that swung out like a shampoo commercial when I tossed my head. Too bad there wouldn't be many reasons to whip my head from side to side at the party. I'd taken extra pains that night to do Miguel's faith in me justice, and I was pretty happy with the results. I'd never be a cute little curvy thing like Sherry, or a willowy, icy blonde like Rebecca, but for a sturdy upper Midwestern chick, I looked pretty good.

"Chica!" Miguel threw open the door and pulled me inside, taking my coat from me and hanging it in the closet with one fluid motion. He wore black trousers and a black and white striped shirt with silver cufflinks that had a glittery stone in the center. His dark hair was artfully messy, and his eyes shone with the excitement of one of his favorite things—hosting a party for a million people.

"You look amazing. But you're a touch subtle on the sparkle," I said.

"You know me, chica, I'm all about the subtle. *Además*, it's not good manners to outshine my guests." He gave me a smile with plenty of dazzle. "But you have just the right amount of shiny. You are on fleek! *Perfecto*." The doorbell rang again, and he touched me lightly on the arm as I drifted into the house.

A Christmas tree twinkling with white lights stood in Miguel's living room. Candles in glittery glass holders flickered on tables and window ledges, and the fireplace mantle was festooned with gold and silver garlands that shone and winked in the light. A long table laden with food held wine bottles that had been liberally rolled in glitter. The house shimmered with light and hummed with laughter and conversation. As always at a Miguel soiree there was an eclectic mix of young and old from all strata of Himmel society. Miller Caldwell stood in a corner holding a glass of punch and talking to Courtnee—with an understandably bemused expression on his face. Miguel's current boyfriend Adam was sitting at the piano next to Mary Beth Delaney, who with her husband Roger owned the funeral home.

Sherry had broken completely with her McClain's waitress uniform of tight white shirt and black pants and had draped herself on the arm of a chair to show off her charms in a tight red-sequined dress. Insurance agent Marty Angstrom appeared delighted with the effect, but from the way his wife Noreen was bearing down on them, it looked like Marty's enchanted evening would be short-lived. There were lots of other people I recognized, and some I knew by sight only, and many whom I had no idea who they were. Miguel has never met a man, woman, or child he didn't want to get to know better, and it appeared he'd invited all of them within a 50-mile radius tonight.

I said hello to various friends and acquaintances as I made my way to the kitchen in search of the Jameson that Miguel keeps in his cupboard for me. I felt I needed to be fortified with something stronger than punch before I ran into the two people I dreaded seeing, but who were sure to be there. Fortunately, I had a drink in my hand when I felt the presence of someone tall looming over my shoulder.

I turned with a forced smile to say a civil hello to Coop and Rebecca. Instead, I felt a genuine grin spread across my face. "Nick! I didn't know you were coming!" I'd never been happier to see him, and if he was taken aback by the quick hug I gave him, he didn't hesitate to return it.

"I almost didn't. Miguel invited me a couple of weeks ago, but I've got an exam to finish writing for the class I'm doing at Himmel Tech and final papers to grade for my regular classes at Robley. But there are only so many freshman term papers you can read before your red pen starts to drip blood."

"Grab a drink and a plate of something. I'll find someplace for us to sit. Looks like there's a vacancy coming up on the corner of the couch and the chair next to it." Suddenly the night looked a little more fun, and I was actually enjoying the jazzy version of "Walkin' in A Winter Wonderland" Adam was playing on the piano. And really, who knew Mary Beth had such a strong alto?

But my happy Christmas glow was short-lived. The smell of Chanel Allure wafted toward me, and my worst fears were realized. Rebecca was just steps away. I looked a little wildly for Nick, but he was at the buffet loading up plates.

"Leah. How are you?" Rebecca was wearing a short ice blue dress with a shimmery shawl covering her bare shoulders. I stood up quickly, taking a slight lurch in my unaccustomed strappy sandals.

"Fine. You?"

"Busy. We're a little short-handed at the *Times*."

I looked for, but didn't detect, any sarcasm in her voice.

"I understand you're writing a piece on spec for the *Milwaukee Journal*."

"Yes."

We stared at each other for a few seconds, neither having anything to say, and neither willing to cede any ground. Then Coop walked up behind Rebecca and put an arm around her shoulder. She looked up at him, but not without smiling the victor's smile at me first.

"Leah, hi. You look nice."

"Thanks. New do. You look pretty good yourself." Coop had made no concessions to 'the sparkle.' He wore a dark gray herringbone blazer that had Rebecca's fashion advice all over it, but his tie was one I gave him for Christmas a few years ago, so score one for me. Though I wasn't sure exactly what game she and I were playing.

I smiled with relief as Miguel came up and said "Rebecca! C'mon, you have to meet Chloe. She's the new marketing director at the hospital. You look *fabuloso!*" He hustled her away before she, or Coop, could say anything. But not before he winked in my direction.

"So, you here alone?"

"Nick is here. Somewhere." Of course I hadn't come with Nick; I was just noting that he was there. Coop could infer whatever he liked. I looked around then, realizing Nick was taking an awfully long time to get a plate of food, then spotted him trapped in a doorway by Courtnee. From the confused look on his face as she rattled on, I assumed she was detailing her latest incognito celebrity sighting.

"Oh. Nice." He nodded and I smiled. I took a drink of my Jameson and wished it were a little stronger. This was agony. I wanted to talk normally to him, tell him what I'd found out about Bergman's plane from Grady, how I'd had to drive around town with Miguel in the freezing cold so he could show off his new convertible, discuss my mother's odd mood, and Paul's bizarre suspicion about why. All the regular things I'd say if things were like they had been. But they weren't. So I didn't. Out of the corner of my eye I saw Nick break away from Courtnee and make his way over. Thank God.

"Nick, you remember Coop, don't you?"

"Absolutely. How are you?" he said, handing me the high-piled plate of food he'd carried over, then shaking Coop's hand.

"Good. I hear you're teaching at Himmel Tech this term."

"Almost done. Filling in for a friend. My day job is teaching psychology at Robley College."

"Good school." Coop nodded.

"Yes, I'm really enjoying it. Not as exciting as your job, but it has its moments."

"Well, you know. What's the saying? Police work is hours of boredom interrupted by moments of sheer terror."

"That sounds like academia, if you substitute complete despair for sheer terror." He smiled to show he was joking, and Coop chuckled to show he was polite.

Rebecca reappeared at that moment, and I introduced her to Nick. The four of us chatted in a stilted way for a few minutes. Then Nick and Rebecca discovered they had mutual friends at Grand Valley University, where Nick had taught before moving to Wisconsin.

"Yes, Ingrid and Erik Solberg are old friends. Ingrid and I met years ago in a fitness boxing class." *Of course they did*, I thought. Rebecca likes fitness training almost as much as she likes destroying newspapers, and I had to admit that her long, lean, strong body showed it. How could such a physically perfect human being have such a corroded soul? Somewhere there had to be a Dorian Gray-style portrait of her shriveling its way to monstrous deformity.

She was droning on about visiting her friends in Michigan every year and yada yada, and I tried to catch Coop's eye for a subtle raised eyebrow, then caught myself and remembered that he saw her very differently than I did. In fact, he seemed to find her inane conversation fascinating. I did not. I was getting ready to break free with a trip to the secret Jameson cupboard for a refill when she touched Coop's arm and said, "I really hate to do this, but I'm getting a massive headache. I need to get home and get my medication before it turns into a full blown migraine."

He jumped up, and they were on their way with a quick goodbye.

"Nick, what's your professional opinion? Is Rebecca a narcissistic sociopath?"

He laughed. "It's a little hard to make a diagnosis after five minutes of party conversation. Although after 30 seconds with Courtnee, my professional opinion is that she's deranged. She was telling me some story about seeing Johnny Depp at the county park."

I shrugged. "Courtnee's hobby is seeing celebrities who aren't there. I'm pretty sure she's certifiable, but mostly we just ignore it. So, Rebecca was on her best behavior tonight, very charming to you, very civil to me. You fell under her spell, right?"

"How about we stop trying to analyze your former boss, and let's go over to the piano and see if Adam knows 'Last Christmas.'"

"Hey, you remembered. My favorite holiday guilty listening pleasure." We circulated for the next couple of hours. Nick met a lot of the people I knew, and sat in Miguel's new car, and took over the piano from Adam, and was very engaging and a lot of fun.

"Chica, he's pretty good for second prize," Miguel whispered in my ear as Nick played "All I Want for Christmas is You."

"Who's first?"

"You know. But Coop, he's got it bad for Rebecca."

"For the millionth time, I don't want Coop for my boyfriend. I just want him back for my friend."

"Then go after Nick. Make him your own. Again."

"It's complicated."

"No. It's easy. You're complicated."

Around midnight people started leaving. I asked Nick if he'd like to come to the house for a cup of coffee.

"I'm not sure I'm up for Carol's disapproving glare."

"She won't be there. She's in Michigan visiting Aunt Nancy."

I could tell by his expression he was trying to determine if this was just a friendly invitation to coffee talk, or something more. I wasn't sure enough myself to help him with the answer.

Just as he started to say yes, I heard the familiar chirp of a text.

Got some information for you. Meet me at ice rink warming house.12:30.

A phone number I didn't recognize. But the message I was waiting for. Cole. It had to be. Nadine must have come through after all.

"I'm sorry. That was Isabel. She really needs to talk. I have to go see her."

"So late?"

"She's in a really bad place right now. Rain check?"

He looked disappointed but said, "Sure, no problem. Hey, there's a faculty end-of-term party next Friday night. Want to go?"

"Yeah, maybe. Look, I better get going; I'll text you later."

CHAPTER 38

I FELT A LITTLE BAD about lying to Nick, but he might have wanted to come, which just wouldn't fly with Cole, I knew. I didn't have time to go home and change, so I headed straight to the park.

The ice rink in Founders Park hadn't opened for the season yet. But I knew the warming house was good to go. A few weeks earlier I shot pictures of the city crew moving park benches inside to serve as winter seating and stacking up the firewood for the large open fireplace.

Once we had multiple consecutive days below freezing, the rink would be ready for future figure skaters and hockey stars who would be on the ice every weekend. When their toes were frozen and their fingers numb, they'd head for a break inside the old wooden building, jostling for a place nearest the warmth of the fireplace. The concrete floor would ring with the sound of ice skate blades, and the big room would smell of wet mittens, sweat, hot chocolate, and coffee—the sound and smell of many a childhood weekend for me.

Tonight, however, the park was deserted and the warming house, contrary to its name, was freezing and dark. I checked my watch and saw I had another 10 minutes to wait. I paced around in front of the building, but the icy gusts of wind penetrated even my heavy wool coat, and I was losing feeling in my feet. I cursed Miguel for talking me into the flimsy, fanciful gold party shoes. I tried the heavy wooden door of the building, expecting it to be locked, but it swung inward noiselessly.

I lit the way to a bench near the fireplace with the flashlight on my phone. I turned off the light to avoid draining the battery. Then I sat down, brought my legs up on the bench and pulled my coat down over them. I wrapped my arms around my knees, then rested my chin on them in a futile attempt to encase the little body heat I had left.

I hoped what Cole had to share would be worth it. Had he decided Bergman and his "associates" were too dangerous to deal with? Was he getting out? Did he know something about Garrett's murder—or Jamie's? Could he place Bergman at the scene for either one? What would he want in exchange for telling me? There always had to be something in it for Cole. Unless there was an altruistic side to his nature that had never surfaced before. Then again, he hadn't outed me to Bergman in the parking lot, and he'd warned me about him. Sort of.

The wind had picked up speed outside, and overhead the bare branches of trees scraped the metal roof of the building. I thought I heard a car door slam. I got up and opened the door, peering into the darkness, ready to call to him that I was inside. There was only blackness and the wail of the wind.

I walked back to my bench and huddled up again. I looked at my watch. 12:35. I hoped Cole wasn't going to stand me up. I leaned against the wooden slats of the bench and closed my eyes. It was so cold. My eyelids fluttered. I tried to keep them open, but it was as if a gentle hand was pressing them shut. I nodded off, until my chin dropped and I woke with a start. I shook myself, changed position, and looked at my watch. 12:45. Five more minutes and I was out of there. I yawned. My eyelids drooped.

Pain from a sharp blow on my upper arm jolted me awake. My head jerked up and my eyes flew open.

"Mind your own business, bitch!" The raspy whisper from behind a ski mask was hard to understand, but the bat the dark figure held aloft made the message perfectly clear.

I rolled to the right and scrambled under the bench. The bat hit the wooden slats with a cracking sound. I curled into a fetal position under the bench. The bat came down again and slammed in frustration the wooden seat I'd just vacated.

Before he could turn the bench over, I kicked out as hard as I could with my left leg, the sharp spike of my heel making contact with bone and flesh. I felt the heel of my shoe give way. The bat dropped to the floor as my assailant groaned and stumbled back. Still under the bench, I rolled onto my back, pressed both hands palm side up on the slats and pushed as hard as I could. The bench tipped on its side and I scooted out from underneath. I kicked off both shoes and ran to the door without looking behind me, focused on getting through the door and away. I pounded down the concrete sidewalk in my bare feet, my coat swinging out behind me.

I ran flat out, and I could hear footsteps close behind me. I did then what Satchel Paige counseled so wisely against. I looked back and saw the dark figure right at my heels. I tripped over my own terror as much as over the uneven sidewalk beneath me. I desperately tried to stay upright, but I'd lost my equilibrium. I felt a thump on my mid back as the tip of the bat made contact. It wasn't a hard blow, but enough to throw me completely off-balance. I hit the ground and curled into a ball, covered my head with my hands, and yelled as loud as I could. I braced for the next blow. Instead I heard a voice.

"Hey! What's goin' on there? You! Stop right there!"

The bat clattered to the ground and landed several yards from me as my attacker sprinted away, shin injury notwithstanding.

"Stop, police!"

Sweeter words were never shouted. I tried to sit up, but the pain in my left arm was so intense I settled for rolling onto my back to get my bearings.

"Stop! Oh, shoot."

Wait a minute. Shouldn't that be "Stop, or I'll shoot"? Not "Stop, oh shoot"?

I gritted my teeth as I struggled to a sitting position. My rescuer rushed to my side and slipped an arm around my waist to help me stand. I leaned for support into his very round, but surprisingly firm, belly. When I was fully upright, I looked into the eyes of my guardian angel. Dale Darmody.

"Holy smokes, Leah. Who was that?"

I managed to persuade him not to call my mother, but he insisted on taking me to the hospital despite my protests that I would be fine. There I was subjected to poking, prodding, and a few admiring whistles—not at me, but at the size, swelling, and deep red hue of the bruise that was engulfing my left bicep. After my doctor, a sharp-featured man with bright black eyes, looked at my x-rays, he pronounced me free of broken bones.

"You've got a severe contusion of the bicep. A pretty impressive one, but that's all. Your thick wool coat probably saved you from worse. You're a very lucky woman. Ice your arm and rest it at least 48 hours. Expect it to be pretty sore. You can take some ibuprofen for the pain. See your family doctor if it doesn't start to feel better in a few days."

Darmody was in the waiting area when I came padding out in a pair of thick hospital socks with rubber grippers on the bottom. My shoes—my mother's shoes, that is—were back at the park.

"What are you still doing here? I thought we finished my statement?"

"Well ya can't go home alone. I called the Father and I'm just waitin' 'til he gets here."

"What? You woke him up in the middle of the night? Darmody, come on. I told you I was fine."

"You told me not to call your mother, and I didn't, but you shouldn't go home alone tonight. I know half the town was at Miguel's party and are probably three sheets to the wind. So I called the padre. He'll be here in five minutes."

I pulled my "sparkle" top as high up as the low neckline would go.

"It's too late to argue then, I guess. Maybe he'll run me to the park to get my car."

"Nope. The doc said you're supposed to rest. We'll get it back to you tomorrow."

"Just because you're my hero doesn't mean you can boss me around," I said. "You know, you really did save me tonight. Now, tell me how you happened to be there just when I needed you."

"It's my prostrate. I tried that pill that's supposed to make you not have to pee all the time, but it's not workin' for me. I was patrolling the road around the park. It was quiet tonight and I was just heading out, when bang. I hadda go. You know it just hits a man and you can't wait. It's a terrible feelin,' I'm tellin' you Leah—"

"No, that's OK. You don't have to tell me that part. Just what happened after."

"Well, I parked the car and I found a place to pee, an' I was just zippin' when I heard you—well, I didn't know it was you—but I heard hollering over by the warming house. I takes off and I see this guy standin' over somebody on the ground, gettin' ready to swing a bat or a pipe or somethin.' I shouted, and he dropped it and took off. I knew I wouldn't catch him, and I hadda see how you were. I shoulda got him, though."

"Darmody, you did great." Words I never expected to hear myself utter. But there'd been a lot of unexpected things happening lately.

"I wish I woulda at least seen his face, but it was dark and he was all in black, and he never turned around. Just ran. I'm gonna hear from the lieutenant about this. Maybe I should sign up for that fitness class Angela wants us to take."

"I can't describe him either, and I was a lot closer than you were. He had a ski mask covering his face, just eyeholes and a mouth. And his hoodie pulled down over his head. I told you, I'm pretty sure it was someone Bergman sent. I went because I thought it was Cole, but this kind of thing, that's not him. Lying, stealing, scamming, conning, yes. Violence, no. Besides, Cole's got a thicker, squattier body. This person was lean, trim. With a really good swing."

Out of the corner of my eye I caught sight of Father Lindstrom, his fluff of white hair more tousled than usual, hurrying toward us.

"Leah! Are you all right?"

"Yes, Father. I'm so sorry you got called out in the middle of the night. I'm fine."

"Nonsense." He turned to Darmody. "Dale, thank you for calling me. What a fine, brave thing you did tonight. Leah is blessed that you were there."

Darmody's grin was priceless.

"Awww, Father. Just doin' my job. Protect and serve. It was a pretty dangerous situation there though. I had to use all of my trainin' and—" He launched into a retelling of the night's events, this time with a few more flourishes. I sensed that a legend was being born. Darmody would repeat the story many times, but however he might exaggerate and embellish, there was a core truth I wouldn't forget. Darmody had been there when I needed him.

Father Lindstrom listened, nodding and expressing appropriate levels of admiration, all the while skillfully helping me maneuver into my coat and gently moving Darmody toward the door. When we reached the parking lot, I thanked him again and gratefully got into Father Lindstrom's car.

CHAPTER 39

"LEAH, THIS IS VERY DISTURBING. Who would do this to you?" Once inside the house, I shuffled off to my room to put on my pajamas, robe, and a pair of fuzzy slippers to warm up my freezing feet. I stopped in the bathroom to wipe the remains of my party self off my face. When I got to the living room, Father Lindstrom had made me a cup of tea and one for himself. As I took a sip, I realized he'd laced it with whiskey and honey. I love him.

"I think it was someone Hal Bergman sicced onto me, because he's afraid I'm going to prove he had something to do with Jamie Whiting's death. And Garrett's too."

"Dr. Bergman?"

I liked so much how he asked me with normal surprise, instead of with the kind of patronizing disbelief I'd been getting from everyone else. I gave him a brief summary of why I suspected Bergman. I didn't say anything about Coop and his DEA task force.

"Despite what Miller saw, I don't think Frankie Saxon killed Garrett or Jamie. I think both deaths are connected to Bergman, and both probably have to do with his drug activities. And I kind of let him know that when I saw him the other day. And he wasn't very happy. By the way, you know I'm not working at the paper any more, right?"

"Yes, I heard that from your mother. But Leah, I'm very concerned. If you're correct, you've crossed a very dangerous man. And even if your theory about Dr. Bergman is wrong, you've alarmed someone who is intent on inflicting serious harm on you. Or worse."

"No, see, Father, that goon who came after me tonight wasn't supposed to kill me. He was supposed to scare me. Mission accomplished, by the way. But if he'd really wanted to do me in, he could have. He had a bat, I had nothing. But I got away with a sore— really sore—arm. Bergman wants me to back off. Which proves I'm on to something."

He was shaking his head. "Leah, I understand and applaud your desire to help Frankie. I believe in her innocence, too. But she wouldn't want you to sacrifice yourself to clear her name."

"No, that's just it. I don't have to. Bergman isn't as smart as he thinks he is. By trying to scare me off, he just brought the kind of attention he doesn't want from the Himmel Police Department. They're going to investigate, and they're going to find a connection to him. And then they're going to ask why he wanted to hurt me."

He still looked worried.

"I'm fine. And I'm sure Darmody will drive by here a few times before his shift ends. Nothing more is going to happen. Definitely not tonight. Now please, promise that you won't call Mom. She'll just freak out and come home, and frankly I'm not sure I'm ready to deal with that drama right now. Something's going on with her and Paul and I think she could use the breather—without worrying about me. She'll be home next week, and I'll tell all then. Right now, I could use about 10 hours of sleep. And you've got early Mass in just a few hours."

For added leverage, I made a quick sign of the cross and said, "Bless me, Father, for I have sinned. You just heard my confession, so you can't say anything."

"That's isn't exactly how it works, Leah, as I know you're aware. But all right. I'll leave you to get to bed. And I'll promise not to call your mother, if you promise to call Coop and get his advice on this."

"Yeah, OK, I'll call him. Tomorrow."

I crawled into bed, pulled up the comforter, and didn't move until almost noon. When I did, my arm was seriously hurting, so I took some ibuprofen, took a shower, left my hair to dry on its own, and sat down with coffee and toast.

I put off calling Coop despite my promise, because I was sure he'd have heard by now and would be calling or stopping by to check up on me. But the day stretched on, and there was no call or text.

My arm hurt. Bad. Coop must know what happened. He'd have seen the reports, and Darmody definitely would have told him. Apparently, he didn't care if my arm had to be amputated, which at the moment, that's what it felt like it was telling me. *"Leah, arm speaking here. I'm too far gone. Can't make it. Cut your losses. Goodbye."*

I got up and put some ice in a baggie and dutifully applied it to my bruise, which by the size and color really did deserve the name "contusion," instead of plain old bruise.

I got my phone and called JT's on the off-chance Cole might be there. He wasn't. I got Nadine instead. "I told you, I don't know when he's comin' back to work. I put your message on the desk. If he wants to call ya, he will."

I texted Miguel, and he didn't answer. I texted Nick.

Want to come over?

Sorry, papers to grade. Tomorrow?

Sure.

I'll bring pizza.

I didn't relish telling Nick that I'd lied to him about the text I'd received at the party, but it seemed that would be better coming in person. I did the ice thing again. At least when my arm was frozen it wasn't throbbing. The color had changed from angry red to a rather pretty deep indigo shade. I flexed it experimentally, then stopped. Too soon.

Why didn't Coop call? Or come over? Or text me? Or why didn't Miguel? Maybe he was still cleaning up from the party. Maybe Coop and Rebecca and Miguel were off having brunch together while I was alone and crippled with pain, a possible target of a drug lord. I texted Miguel. No answer.

I turned on the television and landed in the middle of a rerun of *Pirates of the Caribbean*, watched 'til there was a run of commercials, then turned it off. Finally I went to my room and pulled out my notebook and worked on my Bergman theory.

Garrett's murder

Motive—selling drugs, exposure, bosses higher up want Garrett shut up

Means—easy for him to get Klonopin, easy to arrange meeting with Garrett

Opportunity—he could use his plane to get back and forth to Himmel in plenty of time

Jamie's murder

Motive—Jamie knew about his prescription business and was trying to blackmail him, or

Jamie had discovered that Bergman killed his father and wanted to blackmail him, or Jamie

killed his father in partnership w/Bergman, then got cold feet

Means—crude but effective, a rock to the head. No weapon to dispose of, nothing special required

Opportunity—that was still a question

I knew he was in town; I saw him at JT's that night. But Jamie was dead by then. Where had Bergman been in the afternoon? Was that what Cole and Bergman were arguing about? Had Bergman told Cole he'd had to get rid of Jamie? Was that why Cole warned me off?

I had to find Cole. He knew what Bergman had been up to. Maybe that's why he was making himself scarce. He was hiding out. Or something had happened to him. I texted Coop again. No response. I almost called Rebecca, but I couldn't quite bring myself to do that.

I wished Nick had been able to come. Maybe I should have told him about my close encounter with a baseball bat last night. Then the doorbell rang. "Who are You?" was the current tune my mother had set up. I opened it and Isabel immediately stepped inside and wrapped me in a hug that left me howling with pain. She was a deceptively strong girl.

"Owww!"

"Oh, I'm so sorry. How stupid of me. I just heard about what happened."

The jungle drums were beating then. "From who?"

"I stopped for coffee at JT's, and a couple of people were talking about you."

"Who?"

"I don't know, I just overhead 'Leah Nash' and 'beating.' What happened?"

"Bergman happened. Come on, we don't have to stand in the doorway. Would you like tea or coffee?"

"Let me make it. You sit down and tell me everything."

When I finished, she was sitting across from me, her eyes wide and troubled, her own coffee untouched.

"You think Dr. Bergman beat you up with a baseball bat?"

"Not Bergman himself. The person wasn't tall enough, and besides, he wouldn't run the risk himself. He's warning me to back off. Nothing else makes sense."

"I don't know, Leah. The police have evidence against Frankie. No one even brought Dr. Bergman's name up, except you."

"All right, then listen to my evidence." I outlined how and why Bergman could have killed her father.

"I guess it's maybe possible. And if he was in town like you said, I suppose he *could* have killed Jamie as well. But Miller Caldwell actually saw Frankie at the house the night my father died. And Detective Ross said that Jamie called Frankie, from the park the afternoon he was killed. There isn't any witness to what you say Dr. Bergman did, nothing that really links him."

"Then why did he have me attacked last night? No, Isabel, I know I'm right. I—wait a minute." I grabbed my phone and punched in Courtnee's number.

"Leah! I heard you were in a coma. Everybody's saying you got airlifted to the hospital in Milwaukee. My mom said Marge Leary saw you at the E.R. and you were barely conscious. Are you calling from Milwaukee?"

"Yes, Courtnee. I was in a coma, and the first person I wanted to talk to when I woke up was you."

"Really?"

"No, Courtnee. I wasn't in a coma; I got hit on the arm by some thug with a baseball bat, but I'm all right. I'm at home. Courtnee, Nick said he talked to you at the party last night—"

"He's pretty hot, Leah. I think you should try to get him back. I told him how Ben dumped you and then Rebecca stole Coop and really, you'd probably be a lot nicer if you had a boyfriend. My mom says—"

"Courtnee, did you tell Nick you saw Johnny Depp at the county park last Saturday?"

"Why are you asking? So you can tell me how I didn't? He was driving a black Mercedes. Isn't that the kind of car a movie star drives? Yes, it is."

"Did you see him actually in the park?"

"Almost."

God help me, please.

"What do you mean almost?"

"Well, I was driving by on my way to my friend Shawna's. She lives out on River Road. And anyway, I looked over and I saw Johnny Depp, just sitting in his Mercedes on the side of the road, talking on his phone! If I didn't have to get to Shawna's with her emergency hair color kit—she always wants to be blonde like me, but I tell her 'Shawna, mine is natural. You have to pay big money to get this, you can't just do it yourself.' But no, she never listens and this time, her hair turned kind of green. I mean not cute-on-purpose green, I mean hair-falling-out-pea-green. So obvs, I had to get there to help. She's just kind of basic, but she is my bestie, so you know—"

I had tried to interrupt the flow several times to no avail. Finally I shouted, "What time was this?"

"I don't know. Like, 3:30, maybe. Or maybe earlier. Or later."

"OK. Bye Courtnee."

"But—" whatever she wanted to say was lost in the ether.

Isabel was looking very confused, as well she might. "Johnny Depp?"

"Courtnee is the Haley Joel Osment of celebrity sightings. She sees famous people, all the time. Only they're always just regular people, who may or may not bear a resemblance to the actor or singer or TV star she's sure they are."

"And so?"

"So who does Bergman look like? Johnny Depp. I noticed it the first time I met him. Courtnee didn't see Johnny Depp by the side of the road; she saw Dr. Bergman. And that puts him at the park at the same time Jamie was."

She put her hands up on either side of her face and held her head with her eyes closed for a second. "Leah, I don't know. I just can't handle this. I want it to be over. And that's not much to go on. I don't think that will convince anyone."

I was about to say that maybe the DEA task force had Bergman under surveillance because of the drug operation. If so, that might put him at the park. I stopped myself in time.

"I know Courtnee's not a good witness, but it's a start. Maybe I can dig up someone else, or probe into that scary brain of hers and get something more. I could start looking for people who saw shiny black cars at the county park. I'm not sure what I'm going to do. I have to think some more."

After Isabel left, I did sit down for some serious brain exercise.

Realistically, unless our relationship took an upturn, Coop probably wouldn't be sharing anything about Bergman's whereabouts with me. If he even could. Maybe I could go to Frankie's lawyer, Jim Gilroy. He didn't have to prove she wasn't guilty; he just had to prove there was reasonable doubt. And putting Bergman in the mix could give him something to go on. Though he'd still probably advise Frankie to plead out instead of go to trial. Maybe I could convince Frankie to get a different lawyer.

I started feeling tired, even though I'd done basically nothing all day. I laid down on the couch and promptly fell asleep. When I woke up the house was in darkness. I was disoriented, unsure if it was night or day, uncertain even where I was. As I rolled over on my left side to get up, the sharp pang in my arm brought it all back to me. What time was it? I stumbled over to the lamp and turned it on, then looked at my watch. 7:30 p.m. Now that was an epic nap. I downed two ibuprofen, then my phone rang. I was tempted to let it go to voicemail, but knew I'd have to deal with it sooner or later.

"Hi, Mom."

"Leah, are you OK? I just heard—"

"Yes, I'm fine. No serious damage."

"No damage? You're beaten up in an alley by a gang of thugs, and you expect me to believe there's no damage?"

"That's not what happened, Mom."

"Well, I wouldn't know that, would I? Because I had to hear about it from Courtnee's mother. What is going on?"

"It's fine. Just listen." I ran through an abbreviated version of what had happened, and why I didn't think anything else would be forthcoming from Bergman. She wasn't totally convinced, but I sensed she was wavering.

"What does Coop say?"

"I haven't actually had a chance to talk to him about it yet."

"He hasn't been over to see how you're doing?"

"He's all wrapped up in something at work. I'm sure Darmody filled him in and he knows I'm fine." I hoped that was true, but it bothered me a lot that he hadn't answered my texts. But I didn't want to hear my mother tell me I brought it on myself by not falling all over his new girlfriend, so I changed the subject.

"So, I talked to Paul a couple of days ago. Mom, he thinks you're having an affair."

"What?" She sounded completely mystified.

"Yeah. He's worried. Says you've been avoiding him, making up reasons to not go out with him, and then when you took off this week, he was really upset."

"I don't want to talk about this right now, and Paul shouldn't have involved you."

"Mom, you're not sick or something, are you?"

"Leah, why are you asking me that?"

"Well, I know you'd never have an affair. But I know something's been on your mind and I—"

"And so you thought I had some deadly illness and was trying to spare you? No. I'm perfectly healthy. Don't worry about it. I'll talk to Paul when I get back. But please, don't get involved."

"I'm not planning to."

We chatted a little about Aunt Nancy and some of the cousins, and I reassured her a few more times, and then I wound things down. "OK, Mom, see you soon. Have fun. I love you."

"I love you, too."

It's a good thing, I thought sourly. Because apparently no one else did. No word from Miguel, nothing from Coop. Nick was too busy. Fine. I was perfectly capable of taking care of myself. I cued up the "sad bastard" playlist on my iPod, so-named by Miguel because it's a set of mostly melancholy tunes. Then I sat back with a bag of potato chips. After an hour or so, and multiple checks to make sure I hadn't somehow not heard the phone ring or a text come in, I tottered off to bed with an icepack to soothe my throbbing arm and an aggrieved sense of self-pity.

CHAPTER 40

IN MY DREAM someone was leaning in very close to me. All I could see was a mouth that kept saying "Who? Who? Who?" in a sharp staccato demand. It was a minute before I realized that the front door bell was being hit repeatedly, resulting in an extremely jerky rendition of the ringtone of the week, "Who Are You?", which had invaded my sleep.

As soon as I opened the door, Miguel burst in.

"What time is it?"

"Chica! You'll never guess! *Qué emocionante*! Amazing! Everything, all over. The big papers, the television news, radio, everything! A big drug bust!"

Belatedly he took in my bedraggled appearance, the soggy icepack that in my stupor I'd clutched in my hand, and the incomprehension on my sleep-drugged face.

"Oh, your arm! Come on, come on, let's go sit down." He gently steered me to the kitchen where he put on coffee and put the loaf of bread he'd been carrying on the counter.

"Chica, oh, *lo siento*. I am so sorry. I didn't forget you, but Rebecca, she was on fire yesterday. We were running like crazy all day. And Darmody, he told me you were OK, just had to rest. Oh, *perdóname*. I brought you ciabatta bread from Argento's. Your favorite. I'll slice some and make you toast. Forgive me?" The stricken look on his face as he handed me coffee was comic.

"Hey, I'm all right. I'm not so needy I can't go without daily contact. I figured you must be busy, I just didn't know on what. Sounds like a killer day. Put the knife down, don't bother with the toast. I'm not awake enough to be hungry yet." I smiled, even as I felt guilty for my doubts about Coop and Miguel. No wonder I hadn't heard from either one of them.

He still looked unsure.

"It's OK. Really. I'm fine. But could you tell me at less than warp speed exactly what's been going on?"

Reassured, he immediately jumped back up from the table—apparently to ensure he had sufficient scope to wave his arms and bounce around the room as he told his story. His expressive eyes shone with excitement.

"Imagine, chica. A DEA Task Force, with Coop, sheriff deputies, *policía* from other counties, federal agents! They took down a big prescription drug ring. Huge. *Enorme!*" He spread his arms to indicate the humongous size of the operation.

"It started early yesterday. Raids on houses, pharmacies, even people in church. At the same time, bam, bam, bam, people getting scooped up in Milwaukee too."

"So is that where the drug ring was headquartered?"

"*Sí*. The big drug *jefe* was there. He had all these *chicos malos*, bad guys, selling all over in the rural counties. They can make, like, $50,000 on one prescription pad, a DEA agent told me."

"So were they selling the drugs or just the prescriptions?"

"Both. Some recruit people to fill the fake prescriptions so they can get the product to sell. Some sell the prescription sheets or the pads. It was a big enterprise, chica, lots of layers and lots of players. All over south central Wisconsin and east to Milwaukee."

"Wow, that's a big story for the *Times* to get a piece of."

"*En serio*. I know! Everybody rolling out, bringing in suspects, booking, interviewing. So exciting. I was running around trying to get the pictures, the interviews, send tweets for the paper, it was intense." I could see that he'd loved it. Any reporter would.

"So there was a lot of press there?"

"Oh, *sí*, yes. It was so big. But I was the primero. The first! But there was the TV and online and the radio, and a reporter from Omico and Hailwell. Oh, also, Dr. Bergman, he was arrested!"

"Maybe now that he's in custody, and I've had the crap beaten out of me, Coop will take what I've found seriously."

"Chica, you said you were fine. Did you get more hurt than your arm?" He looked at me with such concern I felt bad.

"OK, well, not exactly the crap beat out of me. But look—" I pushed up the sleeve of my shirt and showed him the quite spectacular blue and green bruise covering my bicep.

"*Ay mierde!*"

"Yes. But it's getting better." Which, I realized, was true. "Hey, what about Cole Granger, did he get rounded up too?"

"No, he didn't."

"He must've skipped town before everything went down, then."

"So chica, I'm sorry. I have to get in to work. I already posted some video on the web, but Rebecca, she—"

"I know. Go. Go! I'll see you tomorrow."

"You're sure you're fine? When is Carol coming home?"

"Not until later this week. Honestly, I'm fine. Coop will probably stop by later, and Nick's bringing pizza for dinner."

Only Coop didn't come over later. Father Lindstrom did, and brought me a chai latte and told me Frankie Saxon hadn't been able to make bail. It was set really high because of the charges. My mother called while he was there, and I put him on the phone to reassure her, which worked and so that was one good thing. But then he left, and Coop still hadn't called or come over. I tried his cell, and he didn't answer. I called HPD and Melanie said he was in his office, but he couldn't be disturbed. I understood, sort of. A bust that big brings paperwork even bigger. But I really, really wanted to talk to him about Bergman.

Around 5 the doorbell rang. Nick with the pizza. I was so ready. I was in the laundry room doing a one-armed wrestle with the washing machine, so I stuck my head out and yelled, "Come on in, door's open. Get that pizza in here, please. I'm starving."

But when I walked down the hall to the kitchen, it was Coop I saw, not Nick.

"Hey! Congratulations on the drug bust. That's really great. I called a couple of times, but I guess you were pretty hung up with... " My voice gradually wound down as I finally registered the look on his face. It did not read *"So glad you're OK, sorry I wasn't here sooner."*

"What's the matter? Come on, let's sit in the living room."

He shook his head. "No thanks. I won't be here long. Leah, why did you tell Darmody you thought Bergman was behind whoever took a swing at you in the park?"

"Because he was. Because he had to be. He knew I was on to him, that I knew he was a murderer."

"And how would he know that?" He didn't give me a chance to answer. "He'd only know that's what you thought if you disregarded everything I asked you not to do."

"Coop, I didn't try to talk to Bergman after you told me not to. I can't help it if I ran into him at Grady's. I went there to talk to Grady, to find out about planes. And Coop, that's the thing. Bergman could have gotten back and forth from his convention in plenty of time to kill Garrett, because of his plane. I know the drug ring is a big deal. I know it's important. But Bergman killed two people, and Frankie Saxon is under arrest for crimes she didn't commit. Isn't that important too?"

He ignored what I'd said.

"I didn't come or call until now, because I was so angry I knew I couldn't be in the same room with you. Do you realize we had to pull the trigger before we were ready, because of you and your obsession with Bergman? You jeopardized an investigation that took us months to put together. Do you have any idea of the man hours, the expense, the danger that involved? For our team? For our CI's? Do you care how many kids have gotten hooked because of this drug ring? How many lives ruined? How many families shattered? You're damn lucky we were so close to shutting it down. Once I heard from Darmody, I knew we had to move or we'd lose Bergman, and maybe a lot more."

"Yes, of course I care! I told you, I didn't go after Bergman, he just showed up where I was. And you're not listening to me. He used his plane to get back and forth from the medical conference. His alibi is no good."

"Listen to me carefully." He spoke slowly, enunciating each syllable. "Bergman did not kill Garrett Whiting. Yes, he could have flown back and forth in his plane. But we know he didn't."

For the first time my confidence in Bergman's guilt wavered. "But Coop, Grady said pilots come and go day and night out there. Bergman's plane goes 200 mph. He could easily have flown to a private airport near Sioux Falls and flown back again the night he killed Garrett. I haven't checked it all out yet, I'll probably have to drive to Sioux Falls myself to talk to somebody—"

"Don't bother. Bergman didn't fly his plane anywhere. He was with a woman that night. Another doctor at the conference. Her husband was having her followed by a private investigator. Suspected she was cheating on him. She was. With Bergman. We've got time and date-stamped pictures of the two of them together. Plus the PI's testimony. There's no way Bergman killed Garrett."

My throat had gone dry, and I was finding it a little hard to breathe. "Then maybe he got Jamie to do it. Bergman needed Garrett to be quiet about the prescription drugs. Jamie hated his father, and he could've been connected to Bergman through the drug ring. Then the guilt got too much, he wanted to confess, and Bergman killed him. It's possible. I think Cole Granger knows something. You need to find him—"

"Cole is one of our confidential informants. He's been feeding us information on Bergman for months. That video you thought was so important, the one you kept badgering him about? I told him to give it to you. I hoped that would keep you busy and away from Bergman. But then Jamie died, and you were right back tramping all over our operation."

"Cole was your CI? But you said he was a conman, a liar, a—"

"What do you think a confidential informant is? Cole's ex-girlfriend worked in Bergman's office. Stole a pad. Bergman caught her. Instead of firing her, he wanted in. He and Cole were small timing it at first, just the two of them with Cole recruiting people to get the scrips filled and selling the product. Then Bergman wanted more. Cole hooked him up with a big operation out of Milwaukee. Then things got a little too big, a little too physical for Cole. He wanted out, but knew they wouldn't let him just walk away. He came to us. He gave us Bergman and a lot more.

"But because you always know everything, you're always right, you had to push ahead. He probably *was* behind your beat-down at the warming house. Maybe because he wanted to scare you into backing off, but more likely because you pissed him off. He's a bad guy, and he's a mean guy. He knew any poking around that you did could be trouble for him, especially if his bosses got wind of it. So he decided to cut his losses and run. We picked him up at Grady's airfield yesterday morning. He almost got away."

"But that doesn't mean he didn't kill Jamie, or use Jamie to get to Garrett."

"Look, we got Bergman, we got his boss, we got dozens of his associates. The bad guys are in jail and now it's up to Ross and the sheriff and Cliff Timmins to decide what happens to Frankie Saxon and their investigation. It's not my business, and it sure isn't yours."

"So you're OK with Frankie being charged with a crime I know she didn't commit."

"Oh, how do you 'know'? That famous 'reporter's instinct'? That sixth sense that makes you so infallible? Funny, it looks to me like you've chalked up a lot of mistakes on this investigation." His voice was scathing, and it evoked an equal measure of anger in me.

"Don't you dare talk to me like that. You've been so wrapped up in this DEA thing you couldn't see anything else. And to prove you're so smart, and I'm so stupid, you're not going to lift a finger to help Frankie." He started to say something, but I rolled right over him.

"No, you listen to me for a minute. Maybe I did get some things wrong about Bergman, but I know that Frankie had nothing to do with Garrett's or Jamie's death. If it wasn't Bergman, I'm going to find out who it was. Don't be surprised if it turns out that he's in the mix somehow."

"You've always been bull-headed, but you are way beyond that now. Darmody said you got hit in the arm, not the head. I have to wonder. I'm sorry that you got hurt by one of Bergman's guys. And we'll do our best to get him for that. But Rebecca's right, you put your own damn self in his sights. You're all in for Frankie like you've been all in for Isabel all along. Why? Because you ran some Leah litmus test and decided she's telling the truth?"

"Rebecca's right?" I choked out the words.

"No, my turn."

I was so incensed I could hardly speak anyway, so I waited for him to finish.

"You won't admit that Isabel is using you to get what she wants, which is a murder verdict on her father, so she can collect the insurance. Rebecca saw it before I did. Isabel is always lying to you. She lied to you about her dad's illness, the insurance, Jamie's alibi, and who knows what else. She's a user, and you can't see it. OK, fine. That's your business. But you can't give me the same respect I'm giving you. I'm involved with someone you don't like, and it's always your way or no way. Not this time. Rebecca matters to me. If you can't accept that..."

"*Isabel's* a liar? At least she was trying to get justice for her father. What's your excuse for lying to me? Because Rebecca told you it wasn't time for me to know about your relationship? You wouldn't tell me jack about the DEA investigation. If you'd been honest, told me what you really had on Bergman instead of 'mansplaining' to me how stupid I was, and how I needed to just trust your superior judgment, maybe the takedown would have unfolded the way you planned. And if you would give half the credence to what I say that you give to your precious Rebecca, maybe an innocent woman wouldn't be charged with murder. You're willing to toss me into the trash can because Rebecca tells you to."

"Rebecca has never once told me what to do, or how to do it, or said anything mean or undermining about you. Unlike the way you talk about her. She's gone out of her way to take your feelings into consideration, she—"

"Please, you're making me physically ill. You are so besotted you can't see that she's vicious, ruthless, self-centered, and manipulative. She's manipulating you right out of our friendship. No, wait, I'm giving her too much credit. She couldn't make you do that if you weren't willing." I finished, almost out of breath with the rush of angry words.

Coop stared at me for a minute. Then, in a voice that was so soft it was almost a whisper he said, "Goodbye, Leah."

He turned and left. I just watched him walk out the door.

CHAPTER 41

NICK ARRIVED about 15 minutes later. As soon as I opened the door, he said, "What's wrong?"

"Nothing's wrong. Why would anything be wrong?" Apparently my answer was not as bright and breezy as I'd tried to make it, because he set the pizza box down, put his hands on my shoulders, and leaned down a little so he could peer directly into my face. His touch was light, but my arm was sore and I gave an involuntary wince. He let go immediately.

"Leah? What's going on? What's the matter?"

"Oh, my arm's kinda sore. I got a little beat up the other day."

"What do you mean you 'got a little beat up'?" He was frowning, and I knew there was no way this explanation was going to go well. Might as well get it over with.

"You know that text I got at the party? The one from Isabel? Well, it wasn't from her. I lied, because I thought it was from Cole Granger to give me some information I need. And I thought you'd want to go with me or try to talk me out of it. So I, well, I just lied. I'm sorry."

I braced myself for my second verbal battering of the day. Oddly, it didn't come.

"My God, Leah, are you all right?"

"Mostly." I pulled up my sleeve and showed him. He gave a low whistle.

"It looks worse than it feels. Well, no, that's not true. It feels pretty bad, but it's getting better. They told me just to ice it and rest for a couple of days, so that's what I've been doing."

"How about this? I won't lay into you for lying to me, in exchange for you telling me everything you've been up to."

"Deal."

He took the pizza into the living room while I grabbed a couple of sodas from the fridge. Nick sat on the wingback chair, and I sat on the couch across from him. When we were settled, I launched into my story. I told him everything right up to and through the reaming out I'd just taken from Coop.

"So, now Coop hates me. And he's never going to help me help Frankie. And I won't be able to get within a million miles of Bergman, and Ross is not about to listen to me, and the most I can do is talk to Frankie's lawyer, who is not what you'd call a strong advocate. And so, everything is worse than before I started. If I'd left it alone, everyone would have thought Garrett killed himself, Jamie might still be alive, and Frankie Saxon's life wouldn't be in ruins. So that happened." I finished with what I'd intended as a bitter laugh, but it caught it my throat and sounded more like a sob.

"I'm sorry, Leah." Nick put his pizza down and came over and sat next to me on my good arm side. I didn't answer, because I was too busy blinking and sniffling, trying to keep from crying.

"Hey," he put a finger under my chin and lifted my face up. "You made some mistakes because you put yourself out there, you always do. That's not a bad thing. It's not always a good thing either, but it's who you are. You don't have to feel guilty about it."

I didn't say anything, just swallowed hard.

"You are so fearless. You just jump right in if you think it's the right thing to do. You fight for what you believe in, for yourself, and for other people as well."

"Don't stop. I'm liking this."

He shook his head. "I'm not joking. You're a good person, Leah. And you're smart and you're funny and—"

"Makes you wonder why you found Cherubim so attractive, doesn't it?"

But instead of responding in kind to my teasing, he said, "Yes. It does."

I quickly moved us back to the subject at hand. "Well, I'm not sure what I'm going to do to clean up the mess I made. If I could get to Cole Granger, I think he might be able to help. If he would. And I'll have to talk to Frankie and let her know maybe there's a little hope. I just don't trust her lawyer to do much with what I can give him."

"That's one of your problems, Leah. You don't trust anyone, not really. I understand why—you had a childhood trauma that still affects the way you see the world. I—"

"You know, I liked that other part of the conversation. You know, where I'm a good, smart person? I'm not up for a stroll through the darker recesses of my psyche. Why don't we talk about you? Tell me more about that paper you're presenting next spring. What's it called? 'Psychopaths Walk Among Us: The Rebecca Hartfield Story'?"

"Something like that. But you know, let's not. Let's watch a movie instead."

"OK. Here, you have the power. And that's not something I give up lightly," I said, handing him the TV remote. "Find something good on Netflix while I take care of our pizza leavings."

When I returned from the kitchen we engaged in a short debate over what constituted "something good" on Netflix, but finally settled on *Love Actually*, a romantic comedy. I wondered if he remembered that we'd watched it on our first date. We'd walked out of a really awful movie and decided to go to his place to watch a DVD instead. I had been secretly impressed that he showed no embarrassment about owning what most people would call a "chick flick." It was a good night.

And, despite the terrible fight with Coop that had preceded it, so was this night. When the movie was over I said, "Thanks, Nick. I feel much better than I did when you got here."

"Well, you know, Nick Gallagher's my name, mental health's my game."

"Nice. I'll get you a T-shirt with that on it."

"Please don't."

And then, because I didn't want to be alone, or I didn't want the evening to end, or maybe just because I remembered what it felt like to be crazy in love with him, I reached up and pulled his head down and kissed him.

I woke in the morning and took a cautious but satisfying stretch before opening my eyes. My sore arm still ached, but not nearly so bad. Extending my body from tip to toe felt good. I lay there in a pleasant stupor, gradually returning to full consciousness, eyes still closed. It was the sound of voices in the kitchen that made my eyelids pop open and caused me to leap out of bed. Memory came flooding back, helped along by the unfamiliar pair of shoes I tripped over as I scrambled into my robe and stumbled to the kitchen. But it was just as I feared and already too late.

Miguel and Nick sat at the kitchen table, laughing and eating scrambled eggs.

"Chica! *Buenos días*. I stopped to check on you on my way to work, but I can see everything is fine." His wide smile was innocent, but his eyes were alight with suppressed laughter.

Nick rose from the table and came to me, bending to plant a kiss on my cheek that I turned my head to avoid. He stepped back with a hurt look. I tried to cover the uncomfortable moment by making a major production out of pouring myself coffee and putting bread in the toaster, talking all the while.

"So, are you getting things under control at the paper? Rebecca settle down any? I saw Coop yesterday afternoon. Have you heard anything more about Frankie Saxon?"

Miguel's grin had faded, and he looked back and forth between Nick and me. Nick didn't say anything. Miguel stood, saying, "Oh, I forgot! I have to shoot a photo at the hospital this morning. Gotta go. Looking good, chica. *Gracias* for the coffee and eggs, Nick. See you later."

As the door closed behind him, I buttered my toast and took it and my coffee to the table, frantically trying to think of what to say to Nick, who deserved some kind of explanation for my ridiculous behavior.

"Nick." He was still standing in the middle of the kitchen, watching me.

"Nick," I tried again, "about last night. It was nice." The feel of his gentle hands on my back, the tenderness as he carefully—and athletically—avoided pressure on my sore arm flashed in my mind and mocked the inadequacy of the word "nice." I steeled myself and continued. "But it didn't mean anything."

Still he said nothing. And the less he said the wordier and stupider I got.

"I mean, of course it meant something. It's not like I go falling into bed with every good-looking psychologist I meet. And, well, I didn't 'meet' you. We were married, right? You're a different person now. Nick 2.0. The same great operating system, but with upgrades like sensitivity and honesty. And seriously, where did you learn to do that thing with your tongue? No, never mind, what am I saying? I don't want to know that. But, uh, you see, yesterday I was just. You were so. And everyone else was—" I foundered on my own inarticulateness and petered to a halt, staring at my coffee to avoid looking at him.

"Leah, it's OK." He pulled up a chair next to me and tucked a lock of hair behind my ear. I turned to face him, my cheeks flushed with embarrassment, my whole self full of confusion and regret.

"Last night was great. But I know what you're trying to say. You were lonely, upset, your support system wasn't there—your mother's away, Coop is angry, Miguel was busy, even Father Lindstrom was otherwise engaged. I wanted to be there for you, to help you any way you wanted." He smiled. "And I have to say, given choices like make tea, bring pizza, just listen—I liked the option you chose."

"You're making me feel worse. Like I used you."

"Well, maybe you did, but I was a willing participant. I knew what you were doing, and why. And I know why you're feeling strange now."

"Oh? Why's that?" I was slightly irritated at his presumption that he knew what was going on in my head. When I wasn't entirely sure myself.

"You're in a vulnerable place right now. You've lost your job, you're blaming yourself for Frankie Saxon's problems, you don't see a clear way to fix it, and the best friend who's always been there for you isn't. And you're still not sure you can trust me, and you don't want us to fall back into old patterns—great sex, terrible relationship. How am I doing?"

"Pretty good. You should look into this for a career."

"You're going to have to come to terms with all that yourself. But you don't need to add feeling guilty about last night onto your list. I wanted to be with you, and last night you wanted to be with me. We're adults, neither of us is in a relationship, and we didn't do anything last night we haven't done hundreds of times before."

"Well, there were a few new things," I said, and finally looked up at him with a small smile. "Why are you making this so easy for me? I feel like I'm the playing the jerky guy part of the morning after a hook-up."

He shrugged. "Maybe I'm just paying something on my karmic debt. Nothing has to come of this. No strings. Are we OK?"

"Yeah," I nodded. "Yeah, we're OK."

"All right then. I'll get out of your way now. Still have papers to grade, faculty meeting to attend. Are we on for the faculty Christmas party Friday night?"

I looked at him blankly.

"At Miguel's, I asked if you'd like to go, you said you'd text me later? I'm here now so—"

"Yes, sure, I remember. Yeah, OK, let's do it. What time?"

"I'll pick you up around 7. It's casual."

For a second I thought he was reiterating the state of our relationship, then realized he meant the party attire.

"Got it."

As he went back to my room to get his shoes and socks, I cleaned up the kitchen. In the old days, Nick would have pouted because I'd been so focused on a story that I'd forgotten to answer his invitation. I would've had to apologize a hundred times, and even then he might still feel aggrieved. Old Nick would have loved the no-strings relationship, except he would want to be the one deciding that, not me. Maybe people really can change. I had to hope so, because there were definitely a few tweaks that needed to be made to my character. He came back into the kitchen.

"All right then, I'll see you Friday. I'll be pretty much buried in finals and grades until then, but text me if you need anything."

Then he took my hand and turned it palm-side up and placed two shoe strings in it. I looked at him, uncertainly. He pointed to his feet, wearing brown leather shoes without laces.

"See? No strings."

"Leah, I was just going to your house to call on you. Are you sure you should be out and about?"

"Yes, Father. I feel much better. I just wanted to bring you a little thank you gift for taking care of me Saturday night."

"Nonsense. I was happy to do it. After all, it's my job to take care of my flock."

"Well, I wandered away from the herd quite awhile ago. I think you're excused from shepherding duties where I'm concerned."

"You know the story of the lost lamb, Leah. I'll always go searching for you."

When I looked in his eyes, I felt my own welling with tears. What was wrong with me? I was as weepy as John Boehner lately. I pushed the bag into his hand and as he opened it, he gave a delighted chuckle.

"Benedictine B&B!"

"I don't understand how you can like that herby brandy stuff, but I know you do. So, enjoy."

"Oh, I will, thank you, Leah. Someday I'll make a convert of you. Now, sit down for a minute, won't you?"

"Just for about that long. I've got some stuff to get done today. So, did you hear about the drug bust?"

"Indeed. It's the talk of the town. Someone said that Dr. Bergman had been arrested. So your suspicions about his drug activities were correct. Do you think that will help Frankie Saxon?"

"Maybe, but I've got to find out more."

"Isn't that a job for the police?"

"It would be, if they were interested in finding out who really killed Garrett and Jamie. But Frankie fits the bill as far as they're concerned. And you know my history with Detective Ross."

"Perhaps Coop could serve as a liaison?"

"Don't think that's going to happen. Coop is not exactly in my corner. He and my ex-boss have decided that I'm a vengeful screw up, and I'm probably lucky if they don't put out a restraining order on me."

"I see," he said, though he clearly didn't.

"Believe it, Father. But I don't really want to talk about it today. Like I said, I just wanted to tell you thanks." His phone rang then, and he excused himself to answer it. I stood and put my coat on, then popped my head in his office just to wave goodbye. He held up his hand and motioned for me to stay. I waited as he wrapped up his conversation.

"Yes. Yes, I see. Of course. All right. I'll see you later then."

"Betty Meier passed away. That was her daughter Deborah. Seems she wandered away from the nursing home yesterday. She died of hypothermia."

I flashed on Betty Meier, sitting at my desk in the newsroom, confused and a little frightened.

"Poor Betty. How could she just wander away?"

"I don't know exactly what happened. Deborah was quite distraught. I'm going to meet with her now to plan the service."

"Sure, yes. I'll see you later, Father."

CHAPTER 42

I WAS BACK HOME icing my arm, which had started throbbing after I left Father Lindstrom's, when the phone rang. The caller ID showed the *Himmel Times*, so I picked it up, thinking it was Miguel.

"Leah, did you know your crazy old lady friend Betty Meier died?"

"Yes, Courtnee, I heard Betty died. She wasn't crazy; she had Alzheimer's."

"Same thing, right? Anyway, her obit came in from Delaney's Funeral Home today, so I thought you'd want to know about the visitation." That was oddly thoughtful of Courtnee. "The funeral is Thursday at 11, but visitation is tomorrow from 2 to 4 and from 6 to 8 at the funeral home."

"Courtnee, how did Betty get lost?"

"My cousin Jasmine is a CNA at Valley Manor. She said there was, like, a fire and smoke and the sprinklers went off and the alarm and they had to get everybody out. All these old people with walkers and wheelchairs and kinda crazy, I mean Alzheimery. I guess your friend Betty, she just kinda walked away when nobody was looking. She was a wanderer, Jasmine says."

"How bad was the fire? Did people get displaced?"

"Well there wasn't one, was there? I said there was *like* a fire. Don't you ever listen, Leah? Just the alarm went off."

"But you said there was smoke—"

"It was just in a wastebasket. They think one of the old people got a cigarette and dropped it in the basket to hide it or something. They're not allowed to smoke. But Jasmine said you'd be surprised what goes on. She said that she walked into a room once and there was this grandpa guy and this old lady in bed, and they were—"

I tuned her out as I thought about Deborah, and how she must be feeling. After the fire at Betty's house, she'd had her mother admitted to Valley Manor to keep her safe. And it turned out she was less safe there than she'd been at home.

"And so she says to the grandpa guy, 'Get your pants back on Mr. Harris, and—'

"Thanks for calling, Courtnee. I have to go. Bye."

"Deborah, I'm so sorry. I know you're going to miss your mom so much." I gave her a hug. I had arrived early on Wednesday afternoon so I could talk to Deborah a little before the visitation got too crowded.

"Thank you. Everyone keeps saying she's not suffering any more, and she had a good life, and I know they're right. These last two years have been so hard. I thought it wouldn't hurt so much when she died, but it does." Her eyes were red-rimmed, and her voice shook a little.

I nodded, because I didn't have anything wise or helpful to say.

"Did you know she wandered away? It isn't just that she died. It's the way she died—alone, confused, frightened. They found her in the storage shed at her old house. We had the house torn down after the fire, but we left the shed. And that's where she was. She just wanted to go home." Her voice broke on the last words, and as she started to cry I put my arms around her again. After a minute she pulled away and swiped at her eyes and nose, and when she spoke it was in a firmer tone.

"I don't blame the nursing home, not really. She sometimes slipped out when we were with her ourselves. Well, you know that, right? My brother Keith called her the Houdini of Halston Street." She gave a watery smile. "But I don't understand how she could get so far. That's miles away."

"Alzheimer's is funny. Mostly people are in a fog, but sometimes they have startling moments of clarity. Your mother wanted to go home. And she did." I thought of the day Betty had gripped my arm so fiercely, and the bright light that had burned in her eyes for a minute. What had she said? *"We're all dying."* Well, she was right about that.

Just then an elderly man in a shiny brown suit walked up to talk to Deborah. I excused myself and went to look at the picture boards set up to highlight Betty's life. There she was, a little girl, leaning back on a swing, blonde curls flying, laughing over her shoulder at a tall man in suspenders pushing her. Her father probably. A hundred pictures of a happy life—First Communion, birthday parties, high school graduation, a wedding photo, pictures with her husband and children in the yard, on vacation, gathered around a Christmas tree.

The second board was smaller and clearly dedicated to her professional life. There was a picture of her graduation from college, and another of her resplendent in an old school nursing uniform— white dress, white shoes, white stockings, white cap with a black stripe. One photo appeared to be Betty instructing a LaMaze class, another of her getting an award. In one picture that looked like it had been clipped from a newsletter, Betty stood in front of a large "Happy Retirement" banner as a distinguished looking man handed her a gaily wrapped package. I bent in to read the cutline. "Retiring nurse Betty Meier receives congratulations and a surprise gift from Dr. Martin Rosen on behalf of the St. Cyprian's Transplant Center."

A voice at my elbow made me jump. "She was a real nice gal."

"Yes, she was." I turned and saw that I was speaking to a solidly built man, probably in his 60s, with light blue eyes under thick, bushy eyebrows. "I'm Ed Slade. Betty was a friend of my wife's." He held out his hand and I shook it.

"Leah Nash. I've known Betty for years." I started to withdraw my hand, but Ed held firm. I noticed his eyes were bloodshot and the large nose over his gray mustache was red-tipped and blotchy, as though he had a cold.

"I'm from Chicago. My wife Gail worked at St. Cyprian's with Betty. Alzheimer's. A terrible thing."

"It is. Is your wife here today?" I had managed to extricate my hand, but Ed gave every sign of being a long talker. If I could steer us in the direction of his wife, I might be able to make a polite exit.

He hesitated a second, then said, "No. No. Gail passed away six months ago." He cleared his throat and said, "It's why I came. Gail would've wanted me to." His voice broke, and he reached in his pocket for a handkerchief to mop his eyes.

"Oh, I'm so sorry." I felt like a jerk for trying to ditch him, and I touched his sleeve. It seemed to be the signal for him to unleash the sadness he was trying to contain.

"She was only 56. We were going to Hawaii for our anniversary. She went shopping for vacation clothes, and she, she—" I expected him to say she was in a car crash, or had a heart attack or a stroke. Instead he said, "She fell from a subway platform. You know, someone just goes out shopping, you don't worry, you don't say 'be careful,' like they were going on a long trip. You expect them to come back, they should come back. But the platform, it was just so crowded and everyone was pushing forward and..."

"Oh my God. That's so unbelievably awful."

He nodded miserably, tears streaming down his plump cheeks. He dabbed at them again.

"I'm sorry. I shouldn't have blurted it out like that. I think I've got it under control and then... well, and then I don't."

"Don't worry about it." I touched his arm as he took several deep breaths and pulled himself together. Just then Deborah walked up to us and said, "Ed, I thought that was you! I'm so glad you came. I'm sorry we didn't get there for Gail. When we heard about it, Mom wasn't doing so well. I just wasn't sure she could manage. I don't—didn't— ever really know how much she was taking in. Especially the last year, so—"

"That's fine, that's fine." He patted her on the back, and they both teared up. Now seemed like a good time to leave. "It was nice to meet you, Ed. Deborah, again, I'm so sorry." I gave her hand a quick squeeze and left.

At the moment I didn't have much to do. I had called Frankie's lawyer, but he was out of the office until Friday. I didn't want to bug Miguel again; I'd already asked him to find out anything he could about where Cole Granger might be, and I knew he was really busy as deadline day approached. Cole and Frankie's lawyer were the two major items on my agenda.

When I pulled in the garage I noticed the bag from my clean out of Miguel's Mini Cooper. I hadn't finished sorting stuff that day because Paul had called me to talk about my mother. I should get it done and return what seemed meaningful to Isabel.

I dragged the bag in and sat at the kitchen table, separating things into "keep" and "trash." I tossed out the old food wrappers, dried out pens, and other detritus. A couple of CDs, a book of poetry, and a copy of *On The Road* I put in the keep pile.

When I was done, I picked up the garbage bag I'd been pulling things from and turned it upside down to shake it out and make sure I hadn't missed anything. A jaggedly torn envelope came floating out. It was the one I'd found under the seat and tossed in the bag when Paul called. I picked it up and read the writing on the front. The return address was preprinted. *Garrett Whiting, MD, PC* with his office location. A yellow return-to-sender-not-deliverable sticker was just below the mailing address, which read:

Dr. Martin Rosen

4914 Howard Street

Willow, Wisconsin

I felt a start of recognition. That was the name of the guy in the newsletter photo with Betty.

When I looked at the postmark, a little shiver ran through me. October 13. This must be part of the mail that Elaine Quellman had taken to the post office for Garrett that Sunday when she left the office.

I googled the name and the town and found a Dr. Martin Rosen at 4194 Howard Street, not 4914 as Garrett had written. Where was the letter? Why did Jamie have the envelope? What had Garrett written to Dr. Rosen the day he died?

It was only 3:30. Willow was about three hours away. I felt the sudden urge for a road trip.

CHAPTER 43

I PULLED INTO THE DRIVEWAY of a two-story brick house flanked by tall fir trees. Light shone through gaps in the curtained windows on the first floor. The night air was damp with the promise of snow to come. I rang the bell. No response. I was about to press it again when I heard the slow thump and measured pace of someone using a cane or crutches. A man leaning slightly on a cane in his right hand opened the door. Despite the device, his posture was erect. He looked at me directly with beautiful cornflower blue eyes behind silver, wire-rimmed glasses. He had a full head of thick white hair.

"Yes?"

"Dr. Rosen, I'm Leah Nash. I'm a friend of Garrett Whiting's daughter Isabel. I wonder if I could speak to you for a moment?"

"You're Garrett's daughter?"

"No, I'm a friend of his daughter's. My name is Leah Nash. I wanted to talk to you about Dr. Whiting."

"I'm sorry. It's a cold night to keep you on the doorstep. Come in please. Can't get used to this damn hearing aid." He lifted a hand to his ear and fiddled with it, trying to adjust it. "Come in, come in."

He moved aside and then led me to a cozy study with a crackling fire burning in the brick fireplace. He gestured for me to take a seat on one of two upholstered chairs while he took the other, turning it slightly so he could face me directly. "You want to talk to me about Garrett?"

"I don't want to take up too much of your time. Garrett's daughter Isabel asked me to look into her father's death—I'm a reporter. She doesn't believe it was suicide."

"Garrett's dead?" He looked surprised.

"I'm sorry. I didn't realize you hadn't heard. Yes, he died in October."

"I had a stroke in September. I've been staying with my niece in Chicago for the past two months. I just returned home a few days ago. You said suicide? No, you said it wasn't. I'm sorry, my thought processes are a little slower these days. It was an accident then?"

"No. Dr. Whiting was murdered."

"Murdered? Who would want to murder Garrett?"

For the moment I ignored the question. "He sent you a letter the day he died, but it was never delivered, because he addressed it incorrectly. Do you have any idea why he wrote to you?"

"No. I haven't heard from Garrett in years. But you have the letter. What does it say?"

"That's just it. I don't have the letter, only the envelope. It was empty when I found it, in the car that belonged to Dr. Whiting's son, Jamie. And I can't ask him about it, because he's dead, too."

He was looking slightly alarmed, and I realized that I sounded more than slightly strange. I took a step back and started again, giving him a brief explanation of Garrett's death and what I'd turned up.

"But today, I was at the visitation for Betty Meier, and I saw a picture of you and her when she retired from St. Cyprian's. Then I saw your name on an envelope I found in Jamie's car, with Garrett's return address. It got sent back because he got the house numbers wrong. It was mailed the day he died. It just seemed, that is, I thought, if you had any idea what he wrote to you about, I felt I should talk to you," I finished a little lamely.

But Dr. Rosen, though he hadn't asked any questions, had been paying close attention. His eyes were bright and alert. "I don't know why he wrote to me, but I can tell you why he wrote to me."

OK, so maybe those bright eyes were deceptive. Maybe the stroke had affected his speech? He saw my confusion.

"I'm sorry. That was very unclear. What I meant was, I know why he communicated with me by letter. Quite possibly he called, but I don't have an answering machine. I hate the damned things. And of course I was away. So he could have tried several times and never reached me. If he really wanted to contact me, a letter might have seemed his only option."

I was thinking hard. "You don't have an answering machine, but does your phone track missed calls?"

"Yes, it does, but I don't pay much attention to the feature. My friends all know they'll have to call back if I'm not here."

"Could I take a look at it?"

"Certainly. It's on the desk over there."

When I scrolled through the call list, I found a number with a Himmel area code and prefix listed several times. It wasn't the Whiting's home phone. I pulled out my phone and googled Garrett's office number. It was a match.

"Garrett did try to call you, more than once. But you said you weren't in regular contact with him?"

"No. The only member of the team who stayed in touch with me was Neal Dawson, one of the nurses."

"Team?"

"Yes, the Kidney Transplant Team at St. Cyprian's. We—the first members—got things off the ground there. It was an exciting time." As he spoke, he leaned over and pulled out a drawer on the end table and sorted through some things in it. When he sat back up, he held a photograph out toward me. As I crossed the room and took it, he said, "That's our transplant team, as it was originally composed."

Seven people stood in a row in front of a sign that said "St. Cyprian Kidney Transplant Center." From the clothes and hair, it looked like an early to mid-90s photo.

"I know Betty Meier, and I recognize Garrett Whiting, but is this you?" I pointed to a man with thick gray hair and dark-framed glasses.

"Yes. Next to me is Gail Slade, our social worker. That fellow with the cocky grin is Neal Dawson, another transplant nurse, like Betty. Next to him is Bill Lessing, the nephrologist. The one on the end is Greg Lindstrom. He was chaplain at the hospital then. Not technically part of the team, but he worked with the families and the team quite often. Some decisions we had to make were extremely troubling."

I pulled the photo closer. I hadn't realized Father Lindstrom had once been a ginger. But beneath a copper-colored head of wispy hair, I identified his sweet smile. "Yes, I know him. He's a priest in Himmel. And I remember now, he did mention he'd worked with Garrett a long time ago."

"Nice fellow. All of the team were good people. But you said you were at a visitation for Betty?"

"She passed away just a couple of days ago. She had Alzheimer's." I felt like the angel of death's recording secretary, but figured I might as well tell him about Gail Slade as well.

"Gail Slade died, too. I met her husband at Betty's visitation this afternoon. About six months ago. An accident. She fell from a subway platform."

His eyebrows drew together in a frown of concentration. "But that would mean. That would be. I don't understand." His face had lost some color, and the fingers he put to his temple shook a little.

"Dr. Rosen?" I half-rose from my chair.

"No, no," he waved me back "I'm all right. I'm just having trouble taking this all in."

"Of course, I understand."

"No, I don't think you do." He looked at me with an odd expression on his face.

"Neal Dawson died of an allergic reaction last Fourth of July. I went to his funeral in Eau Claire. We used to go trout fishing in April every year. He's the only team member I stayed in touch with. Last March, I received a solicitation for a scholarship in Bill Lessing's memory. It said he'd died in a hit and run accident in January. Do you see what I'm saying? There are only two of us left."

My brain was racing. "*We're all dying.*" That's what Betty had said to me weeks ago in the newspaper office. That day there was a fire at her house. Five people in a group of seven, all dead in less than a year? Five people who had made "troubling" decisions. Life and death decisions.

"Dr. Rosen, you said some of the decisions the transplant team had to make were troubling. What did you mean?"

My abrupt change of subject didn't fluster him. "Organs are in such scarce supply that we had to make sure that a transplant would be a long-term success. We had to weigh not just physical matches, but also consider the financial and psychological state of the patient."

"Financial?"

"There is Medicare coverage available, but it only covers 80 percent of the cost for anti-rejection drugs, and then only for three years. The drugs are necessary for the lifetime of the patient."

"So you would turn people down because they were too poor?"

"With such a shortage of organs, we had to consider not only how sick patients were, but whether they could afford the anti-rejection drugs on a long-term basis. Or the kidney would essentially be wasted."

"You said psychological, too. Did you turn down people with mental illnesses?"

"It wasn't cut and dried. If a mentally ill patient was stable and compliant with his medication, that wouldn't be a reason to turn him down. But if he were noncompliant, again we had to consider the likelihood of long-term success. A patient who didn't conform to the strict drug regimen would endanger the ultimate success of the kidney transplant."

"I imagine it's very hard to give a dying patient the news that he's not eligible for a transplant."

"Yes. The entire team makes the decision. It's a very heavy burden. I'm convinced one of the decisions we made broke our team apart."

"Really? What was it?"

"A single mother. Amber Pelly. Very beautiful young woman. Her kidneys were irreparably damaged by a suicide attempt with a large dose of acetaminophen. She had a pattern of going on and off her mood stabilizer drugs. She was in financial distress as well. We turned her down. The repercussions of that decision took a toll on all of us."

"What repercussions?"

"She killed herself. She jumped from a bridge in her hometown. Sandersville, in the western part of the state. I remember because that's where I spent summers as a child. Amber's mother blamed us, the team, for her daughter's suicide."

"That must have been pretty terrible. For everyone."

"Yes. Despite the process we followed, we all felt some measure of guilt and regret. It was a very hard time. There was some adverse publicity, some accusations from Amber's mother that we had only rejected her because she was poor. That wasn't true, but as I said, it's a factor in every transplant decision." He sighed heavily, and I noticed his hands were still shaking slightly. I pointed to the crystal decanter and glasses sitting on a nearby table.

"Are you allowed to have alcohol? You look like you could use a drink."

"A small glass of brandy would be very good medicine for me right now, I think, my dear."

"Let me get it for you."

"Please, pour one for yourself. If you're not a brandy drinker, there's an excellent scotch there as well."

"Thanks, but I've got a long drive back to tonight." I handed him a small glass of "medicine." I waited as he took a sip and some color returned to his cheeks.

"It's so gratifying to match a patient with a donor organ. But it's devastating, every time, to tell a patient there is no kidney for them, for whatever reason. Garrett seemed to take it particularly hard. He was almost physically ill with the stress of Amber's death. He actually met personally with her mother, though our attorney advised against it. I always thought it was his deep sorrow that persuaded her to drop the legal action she threatened. He left the team not long after. Eventually everyone moved on." He took another sip and settled back a little in his chair.

"What about Amber's child?" An idea, fragmentary and bizarre, was forming in my mind.

He thought for a moment, then said, embarrassed, "It was a daughter, I'm sure of that, but I, I just can't recall anything else. It seems as though she was school age, certainly. But, perhaps younger? Is it important? I just can't retrieve information as readily as I once did, I'm afraid."

"That's all right," I said, although his memory lapse frustrated me. I knew that I was upsetting, even badgering, him, but I had to find out. "Do you remember, did she go to live with Amber's mother, her grandmother?"

"No. Amber's mother accused us not only of killing her daughter, but also of ruining her granddaughter's life. I believe the grandmother suffered from ill health and couldn't care for the child. My recollection is she was placed in foster care. Or perhaps adopted?"

"Do you remember her mother's name?"

"Yes, it was Wilson. Goldie Wilson."

"I just have one last question. What year did Amber die?"

"1994."

"All right. Thank you, that helps a lot. But there is something." I hesitated, not wanting to upset him any more than I already had. But I had no choice.

"I don't want to alarm you, but I think you need to take some precautions. You mentioned a niece in Chicago. Maybe you should go to her for awhile."

"What? Why would I do that? I just got back in my own home."

"I understand, but realize what we've been talking about. Five of seven people on your transplant team are dead. Someone is after you. All of you."

CHAPTER 44

IT TOOK SOME CONVINCING, but by the time I left, Dr. Rosen had been on the phone with his niece and told her he felt he wasn't quite ready to be on his own. She arranged to pick him up the next morning. I could tell from his side of the conversation that she had been requesting him to stay with her longer anyway.

"I have to talk to some people, but I'll get back to you as soon as I know something for sure. I may be wrong, this may be crazy, but I don't want to take a chance, and you should be fine with your niece."

I wished I felt as confident as I sounded, but in my car on the way home I knew this was a big fat mess. And a dangerous one, too. I reached for my phone and automatically started to call Coop, then stopped.

He wasn't going to believe me. I hardly believed me. But I knew I finally had it. Nothing else brought everything together. I'd made a huge mistake. I'd been looking at Garrett's death all wrong. He wasn't killed because of who he was as an individual or what he knew. He was killed because he was part of the transplant team that had killed Amber Pelly. Or so her daughter believed.

Betty had told me that in my office. *"We're all dying."* The funeral that Deborah had taken her to, not long before she showed up at my desk—it must have been Garrett's. In some elusively lucid part of her brain, Betty made a connection. Garrett was the fourth member of the team to die. Amber's mother had blamed the team, and Amber's daughter had absorbed that anger. It didn't matter that the team made an ethical decision. The end result was that Amber Pelly had died. Her young daughter hated the people she believed responsible.

I called Nick.

I told him about Amber and the daughter she left behind.

"Listen. This is what I think happened to Garrett and Betty and three other members of the original St. Cyprian Kidney Transplant Team. I think Amber Pelly's daughter killed them."

"I'm stunned."

"But you don't think it's impossible?"

"No. It's definitely not impossible. But if you're right, you're talking about a psychopathic personality. Someone with a strong sense of entitlement and an enormous capacity for narcissistic rage. She'd have to be high-functioning to have escaped detection, which means she's very, very dangerous."

"So she's smart. Angry, but not crazy, right? She wants to get away with these murders."

"Not only that. She positively thrives on the knowledge that she's more clever than anyone else. And, to give her due justice, she's pretty damn smart. A series of accidents in widely different locations, victims not easily linked—that's a good way to go. The only death that breaks the pattern is Garrett Whiting."

"I've been thinking about that. What if Garrett somehow stumbled onto the connection? Dr. Rosen said the team had split up and not stayed in touch, but he got a letter for a scholarship fund after Dr. Lessing died in a hit and run accident. Maybe Garrett did too. And in his case, maybe he had some other information that made him suspicious. He wanted to talk to Dr. Rosen but couldn't reach him, so he sent him that letter."

"Possible, but it still doesn't explain why and how Amber's daughter killed Garrett and faked a suicide."

"But she wouldn't want it to look like murder—it would ruin her clever planning. None of the other deaths were investigated as suspicious, because they looked like accidents. If Garrett discovered her identity and thought he was smarter than she was—which of course he would, because he thought he was smarter than anybody— he might have invited her to meet him. Maybe she even liked the challenge. She turned the tables on him, but she had to make it look like suicide. A murder investigation might have turned up something that could lead to her."

"And Jamie? Do you think she killed him, too?"

"I don't know. But the empty envelope was found in his car. If he read the letter from his father, he may have decided to take matters into his own hands. He didn't have much faith in the police, or in me. She agrees to meet with him, and when she realizes what he knows, he's got to go. That's a big risk. But then psychopaths are risk takers, right?"

"Yes. Now, your next call is going to be to the police, right?"

"Soon. Very, very soon."

"Leah—"

"Come on, Nick. You're only half on board, and you like me. Ross is going nowhere near this. I can just imagine what he'd say if I told him a mystery woman killed Garrett, and she's killed five people altogether. And I can't blame him, really. It's not like I have a great track record on this one."

"Hey, I'm fully on board. I just think you should expand your crew. What about Coop?"

"No."

"What are you going to do then?"

"I'm going to find Amber's daughter."

"OK, wait a minute. What about 'she's killed five people' makes you think it's a good idea to confront her?"

"I didn't say I was going to confront her. But I have to find out who she is, where she lives, what she does. Besides killing people."

"And then what?"

"Then I give the police something solid to go on."

"How will you do that?"

"Well, I know that her mother was from Sandersville. Her grandmother might still be alive. She might even be in touch with Amber's daughter. So, I guess I'm going to find grandma."

"Leah—"

"Thanks for everything, Nick. I'll talk to you soon. Bye."

I ignored the incoming call from Nick as I waited for Miguel to pick up.

"Chica! *Dónde estás?* Where are you? I stopped by your house, but nobody was there. And you didn't answer my text."

"I'm on my way back from Willow. And I need your help, bad."

I explained what I'd figured out.

"I have to find Amber's daughter, fast. First thing is to find out her name. Can you check online, the Sandersville paper, maybe the local library? Try to get the story that ran when Amber killed herself; the daughter's name might be in that. Also, see if you can find Goldie Wilson. I don't even know if she's still alive, but if she is, she could have some answers."

"Maybe the *abeula* knows where her granddaughter is?"

"That would make things easier. But Miguel—"

"I know. Don't let Grandma Goldie know I'm trying to find her granddaughter. *No problema.* If she knows, she'll tell me, and she won't even realize she did."

"I'm counting on you. There are only two people left on the team. I think I have Dr. Rosen squared away. But I'm worried about Father Lindstrom. I'm going to call him now, but I can't explain everything on the phone. Can you meet me at his house when I get back? If we tag team him, maybe he'll take it seriously. I should be there by 11 or so."

"*Por supesto.* For sure, I'll be there."

Father Lindstrom didn't answer his home phone, and I didn't bother to leave a message, because it was way too much to explain. I tried his cell without much hope. He does carry one, but he's not a big fan, and he's always forgetting to turn the ringer back on after he turns it off. I'd have to try later.

I drove as fast as I dared on the two-lane highway, but the snow that had threatened earlier had started to fall in big, wet flakes that gave my wipers a workout trying to keep the windshield clear. Then I got behind a car going 30 miles an hour on a long, curvy no-passing of road. I had my phone GPS reroute me, but instead of saving time, it took me onto a series of dirt roads that finally dead-ended at a lake. By the time I backtracked and got back on the main road to Himmel, I'd lost over an hour. At least the snow had stopped. But there was no way I'd get back to town by 11 p.m. I texted Miguel, told him we should skip tonight and meet at Father's at 8 a.m.

When I pulled into town I was about three adjectives past very tired. I really wanted to go home and go to bed, but I couldn't yet. I knew he was probably fine, and he might as well have one more night of untroubled sleep before I told him he was the target of a psychopath. But I had to go by Father Lindstrom's house, just to check and make sure that all was well.

CHAPTER 45

HIMMEL AFTER MIDNIGHT is pretty quiet. Most of the houses are dark; a couple of party stores and the bars are still open, but almost everything else is shut down tight. I like driving down the deserted streets, seeing the occasional light in a window, wondering if someone is up with a new baby, or a sick child, a new boyfriend, or a broken heart. The silence, interrupted only by the occasional bark of a dog or the wail of a passing train, is so peaceful, all the stress of the day temporarily stilled. It was so calm, in fact, that I felt a little silly as I drove toward Father Lindstrom's, but I couldn't not check on him.

The stoplights had already switched to flashing red and yellow, an acknowledgement of how the traffic slows at night. But as I turned onto Father Lindstrom's street, a car blew past me. A silver Miata. Rebecca. I couldn't see her face, but with that car and that entitled attitude, it had to be her. Probably going home from Coop's.

Father's house is a small brown bungalow on a corner. It's a nice location, because he's got an empty lot on one side, St. Stephen's on the other, and a parking lot that takes up a big chunk of the block. It's quiet and private, and he has plenty of yard for all the bird feeders he likes to set up. It's a buffet of sorts—for the neighborhood cats. As I approached the house, I saw smoke coming out of his chimney. Maybe he was up after all. But still, I thought I'd go home without stopping. I was so tired.

But when I pulled in the driveway to turn around, I noticed the windows were all dark. Why would he have a fire in the fireplace and then go to bed? Then I saw it. A red-tipped flame showing through a basement window. It was coming from the back of the house. Then a bright yellow flicker visible in the living room. My fingers shook as I called 911.

"A fire. A fire at 529 Church Street. There's a man. Father Lindstrom. I think he's inside." The phone slipped from my sweaty hand. I could hear the dispatcher talking, but I couldn't answer. I couldn't move, my breath was coming in short gasps, my heart was thumping so loudly I couldn't think. I stared in horror, but I wasn't seeing Father Lindstrom's house. It was our house, my mom and dad's house. And the fire roaring through it had ignited more than 20 years ago.

It started while we slept. I shared a room with my little sister Annie. She was 8 years old, just two years younger than me. Mom was holding the baby, Lacey, when she came to wake us up. Dad wasn't home.

Confused and stumbling with sleep, we held hands and followed her. She carried Lacey and shepherded us across the street to a house kitty-corner from ours. Mom pounded on the door, and Mrs. Nussbaum answered, wearing curlers and a purple velour bathrobe. Her hand went to her mouth as Mom told her our house was on fire. She held Lacey while Mom ran in to call the fire department. Soon other lights went on in the neighborhood, and a crowd began to gather on the Nussbaum's lawn.

We weren't scared anymore. We were excited to be up so late, to be so brave— that's what Mrs. Nussbaum said as she handed us each a cookie—we were such brave, good girls. Lacey started crying. Mom told us to stay put while she went in to change the baby's diaper. We could hear fire trucks and police sirens in the distance. Our eyes opened wide as we watched flames shoot out of the roof of our house. Annie tugged at my sleeve. She was worried about her cat, Mr. Peoples. I told her it was all right. He always went out for the night through the cat door in the basement. He wasn't even home.

David Cooper, a boy from my school, came up and asked me what happened. Breathlessly I told him how we had escaped, dodging flames with fire chasing after us. That wasn't true, but I wanted my story to match the keyed up atmosphere on the lawn. Then I heard my mother call. I reached to grab Annie's hand. But she wasn't there. My eyes quickly scanned the crowd in the yard. Mostly grown-ups standing in twos and threes, a few kids, but not Annie. I turned and saw my mother waiting on the doorstep. I looked across and down the street. The fire trucks had pulled up and in their bright headlights I saw a flash of pink squeezing through the tiny opening in the hedge that surrounded our yard. Annie!

I took off at a run, dashing between the chattering adults, dodging past Mr. Nussbaum who had reached out to stop me. I heard my mother calling me, but I ran faster than I ever had. I slipped through the narrow gap in the hedge. I started screaming Annie's name. Window glass had shattered and flames pushed out through the open spaces. Loud crackling pops rent the night air. I could feel the heat on my face. Annieeeee! Annieeeee! Annieeeee! I ran toward the back of the house. I heard the yowl of a cat and saw Mr. Peoples in the far corner. I looked wildly around the yard. Annie? Annie? I ran toward the back door, but someone scooped me up from behind. A firefighter carried me away from the fire as I struggled and screamed for Annie. Out in the street, Al Porter, the fire chief, was holding my mother and she was sobbing. When she saw me, he let her go. She swept me up in her arms, gasping and laughing with joy.

Suddenly her laughter stopped as she asked, "Where's Annie?" I stared at her. I couldn't speak. After what seemed like a long, long time, a fireman came out with a small pink bundle in his arms. My mother jumped up. Then she saw the limp limbs, the lolling head, the tears streaking the smoke-stained face of the fireman. And she began to wail.

All of that flashed through my mind in seconds as I sat there, sweating, panting for air, watching the flames move toward the front of the house, hearing the first shatter of glass from the basement windows, knowing Father Lindstrom was inside. I was crying now, sobs that came from deep within and rattled through my body, expelled in jagged barks of fear and frustration.

I have to do this. I have to go in there. I can't do this. I have to do this. I forced my hand to open the car door. I didn't let myself think. I ran to the front steps and up to the landing. I touched the door. It wasn't hot. That was good. I fumbled with the knob. Not locked, but the door stuck.

I twisted to heave my good arm and shoulder into it. As the door swung inward, a billow of smoke came out. There were no flames, but the hallway was filling with smoke. I dropped to my hands and knees, my eyes burning. I pulled my sweater up over my nose as a filter.

"Father! Father!" The thick yarn muffled my voice. I called again. No answer. The smoke was so heavy it was hard to see. I crawled down the hallway, my eyes glued to the baseboard to guide me. I turned the corner toward his room and saw him. Lying face down, one arm stretched out in front of him. *Please, God. Please, God. Please, God. Please, please, please. Not this time.*

I reached out and grabbed his wrist. I shook his arm. "Father, Father."

He coughed and turned his head slightly. He was still alive.

"OK. You're OK. It's OK. Come on now." I moved beside him. I put my arm across his back and tried to get him into a crawling position.

"Come on now, stay down low." I spoke quickly, in short bursts to save my breath. He struggled into position. I tugged to help him. My head jerked up. I felt the heat buildup above us. I knew what that meant. There's not much heat in a smoke-filled room. If you feel it increase, that's a bad, bad thing. When it gets hot enough, all the combustible fuel—wood, insulation, furniture, carpeting, everything—goes up in a flash. Including anyone who's in the room.

"Come on." This time I yanked on him as hard as I could. He was up on all fours and I said, "All right. We're moving now. You can do it."

He was coughing, weak and obviously confused. But he followed my simple commands. One arm, one leg, other arm, other leg. We were only inches from the door. I could see the smoke-free air outside. Then his arm collapsed. He sank down. "Can't. Can't."

"The hell you can't."

I moved behind him. He was still on his knees, though the front of his body had collapsed to the floor. I tucked my head down into my chest. I leaned back on my legs. Then I sprang forward, keeping my head low. I plowed into Father Lindstrom's backside. The force propelled him forward, but I'd knocked him off-balance. He lay crosswise at the threshold, his head and shoulders partially out of the opening. He was so still. I knew he wasn't conscious any longer.

I took a quick look up, then gasped. Above the thick gray shroud of smoke that surrounded us, black smoke was rolling back into the hall at ceiling height. Fire darted snake-like out of the blackness. I heard the scream of sirens coming nearer. It wouldn't be soon enough for us. We had about 10 seconds before the hallway flashed over and burst into flames.

I scrambled over him onto the outside landing. Still kneeling, I reached under his chest. I grabbed up the folds of his pajamas, his robe, and his belt. Then I held tight as I launched into an off-kilter sideways somersault that sent us tumbling down three steps. We landed in a heap at the foot of the stairs. The fire flashed over inside the house, shooting out a wall of flame. Father Lindstrom wasn't moving. I didn't know if I'd saved him or killed him. I reached for his wrist. His pulse was thready, but it was there. I stood up and started tugging him away from the house. I was coughing and wheezing as firefighters and two paramedics came running up.

"I'm OK," I managed to cough out as I pointed in Father Lindstrom's direction. "He's not doing so well."

The little priest was lying on his back, breathing shallowly, his shock of silvery-white hair coated in soot and ashes.

"Is he going to be all right?"

Neither answered. They got him on a gurney, covered his face with an oxygen mask, and quickly wheeled him away.

"He's going to be OK, right?" I called after them.

"Don't worry. They know what they're doing." Al Porter, the fire chief, was standing next to me. I didn't even see him walk up. "Come on, Leah, you need to move back, let the guys get in here. That house is fully engulfed." I looked back then and shuddered as I saw orange flames shooting out of every window.

Al half pushed, half pulled me away. I stumbled, and he put an arm around me. I leaned against him gratefully.

"You OK, Leah? You know you did a really brave, really stupid thing going into that building. A few more seconds and... "

"I had to. I had to make a different ending. I couldn't just watch, not again."

He shook his head. "Leah, your sister. That wasn't your fault. You were a little girl. There was nothing you could do."

"But I'm not a little girl anymore. And there was something I could do. This time I got it right."

We had reached the street where the scene was controlled chaos as firefighters in turnout gear, helmets, and masks grabbed equipment and set up hoses. More trucks continued to arrive.

I saw an ambulance pulling away. "Al, my car, I have to get to the hospital."

He shook his head and pointed toward the garage and driveway. His crew was already shooting hundreds of gallons of water at the house and garage out of huge high pressure hoses. "You're not gonna get anywhere near that little car of yours. Tell you what, I'm gonna give you to Janice over there; she's gonna check you out."

"But I don't need—" He was gone before I finished. Janice, a paramedic with a no-nonsense haircut and the sturdy appearance of a beef-fed woman, appeared at my side.

"Hi there, I'm Janice. Understand you had a close call with a fire tonight. Let's just get you checked out here. What's your name?"

"Leah Nash. I'm OK, if I could just have a little water?" My throat felt so dry and tight it hurt to swallow.

"We'll get you some real quick there, Leah. Just let me look over a few things. Why don't you hop up here." She had produced a gurney as if by magic, and I scooted myself up onto it. Her voice was calm and slow, but her hands were quick and efficient as she checked my pulse, my blood pressure, my breathing, looked in my nose and down my throat. Finally, she handed me a bottle of water. "Take it easy."

I took a long, slow drink. It was the coolest, sweetest tasting liquid I'd ever had. I might not ever drink anything but water again. "I love you, Janice."

"I get that a lot. Now, how long were you in the house?"

"I don't know, maybe four or five minutes. Felt like four or five hours. I'm not sure. But I'm OK. And I really have to get to the hospital."

"Now that's a real funny thing. That's just what I'm thinking. I'm just gonna have you lie back here, get this oxygen mask on you. That'll get some real good fresh air right into your lungs. You're a pretty tough little cookie, but we want to get your CO and CN toxicity checked, just make sure there's nothing going on."

She deftly slipped the mask over my face and gently pushed me into a prone position. I gave up protesting. It was one way to get to the hospital fast.

"Leah! Leah!" A shock of happiness zipped through me as I turned my head and saw Coop running toward me. As he reached the gurney, I sat up and pulled off the mask.

"We have to quit meeting like this," I croaked.

He stopped in front of me and grabbed me by the shoulders, bending down to look into my face. "I heard it on the scanner. The fire. You were in the house. Are you all right? What were you thinking? Jesus, Leah!"

"Don't be mad at me again. I had to do it. I couldn't let another goddamn fire swallow up someone I love. And I didn't. I was so scared, but I did it Coop. And I'll never let myself be that scared of anything again."

He hugged me then, bending down and smooshing my face into his chest. When I pulled back I saw that I'd left a wide smudge of dirt and ashes on the front of his jacket.

"I'm sorry. Looks like I ruined your coat."

"You're quite a hero, Leah. I admire your courage. That was an amazingly brave thing to do." I hadn't even noticed Rebecca, but at the sound of her voice Coop dropped his arms and stepped back.

Before I could say anything I'd regret, not that I had many regrets when it came to insulting Rebecca, Janice reasserted herself.

"Sorry folks. I need to get this gal to the hospital."

"Leah, we'll meet you there."

"No, Coop. No need. I'm good. I just want to check on Father Lindstrom. I'll talk to you later."

"She's right, David. We'd only be in the way. And I have to get some photos and talk to the fire chief. Miguel chose a bad time to be out of town."

I laid back down with a secret smile on my face. Miguel, I knew, was busy working for me.

CHAPTER 46

WITHIN MINUTES OF ARRIVING at the hospital I was in an examining room. No waiting time, I guess, when you arrive by ambulance. But none of the people who came in and out would admit they knew anything when I asked about Father Lindstrom. That worried me.

Then the doctor, the same guy who'd treated my arm the week before, came in with the lab results. "You're a lucky girl. Your blood work is fine. I think we can let you go. I have to say, I had no idea writing was such a dangerous profession," he said in a deadpan voice.

"What about Father Lindstrom? Is he going to be all right?"

"He's in intensive care."

"Will he be all right?"

"He has significant carbon monoxide saturation in his blood—the result of prolonged smoke inhalation. There's some airway injury and respiratory compromise. He's receiving high flow oxygen and an IV. He's been intubated as a precaution. Airway obstruction is a possibility over the next 24-48 hours. He'll have a series of chest radiographs because of his exposure to the toxins in the smoke. He has a second degree burn on his left forearm."

Each piece of the information I had been so hungry for hit me with the force of a blow. A heavy weight had settled in the middle of my chest. My eyes must have shown the bleak fear I felt, because the doctor patted my hand.

"For a man his age, Father Lindstrom is in very good health. He is conscious and responsive—though he's not able to speak just yet. He's not out of the woods by any means, but he's holding his own."

"Can I see him?"

"He's not allowed visitors—"

"I—"

"But," he continued smoothly, "I think we might make an exception. Very briefly. For the person who saved his life."

The intensive care unit was dimly lit and eerily quiet, except for the whoosh and soft beeps of various medical equipment. Two people were working at the nurse's desk, which provided a clear line of sight to a series of small glass-walled patient rooms that encircled the area. One of them looked up as I approached.

"You must be Miss Nash. The doctor said you can see Father Lindstrom, but you can only stay a few minutes. He's sleeping right now, so please don't wake him."

"No, I won't. I just need to see him."

He was lying in a hospital bed with tubes coming out of his nose, his mouth, and his arm. A blood pressure cuff attached to one arm periodically inflated and deflated. A machine beeped off each beat of his heart, its screen tracing the electrical pattern. The only light came from a small fixture over his bed.

"Oh!" I gave an involuntary gasp at the sight of his pale face. His beautiful silvery-white hair, usually fluffing out in multiple directions, was matted and dull. Without the sparkle of his light blue eyes, his face looked old and worn.

"He's doing better than when he came in." I had forgotten the nurse at my side.

"Can I stand by the bed? I won't disturb him, I promise. Just for a minute."

She nodded and left me alone with him.

I stood and stared down at him through tear-filled eyes.

"I'm so sorry, Father. I should have left a message. I should have tried harder to reach you. I know why this happened. And I'm closing in fast. You rest, and you'll be better before you know it." I paused to give my voice a chance to steady. Hard to impart confident optimism when you're choking up.

"And guess what? I'm signing both of us up for the St. Stephen's talent show. I think we've got a real chance of winning with our new stunts and tumbling routine. But next time we'll use dry ice for the smoke and no flames."

I might have imagined it, but I thought his eyelids fluttered.

"It's time to go," said the nurse who had again appeared at my elbow.

"Yes, OK."

I turned back to the bed. "I'll see you tomorrow, Father."

On the way out I asked, "So, do I need special permission to get in tomorrow?"

"No, you're on the visitor list now, and unless there's a no-visitors order, you can come by. But visits are restricted to 10 minutes."

"How many nurses are taking care of him?"

"We have a 1:1 staffing ratio here, so each patient is assigned a nurse. We're monitoring all the time. If he shifts position, we know it. If his blood pressure drops a millimeter, we know it. If his stomach starts to growl, we know it. We'll take the best care of him. He's pretty special to you, isn't he?"

I swallowed hard and just managed a husky, "Yeah, he is."

"Well, don't worry. Nothing is going to get past us. We'll take very good care of him."

"You have no idea how comforting that is."

Father Lindstrom was about as safe as he was going to get, short of having a personal bodyguard. Which, if he got out of here and I still didn't have Amber's daughter, I was perfectly willing to get for him. No one was going to get in who wasn't on the list. And I really didn't see the killer trying again tonight. It would be impossible to go unnoticed in the ICU. So while I wanted him out of there as fast as possible, at the same time, it wasn't a bad place for him to be.

I had to get in touch with Miguel, but I'd dropped my phone in my panic attack in the car. There was a visitor's phone in the hospital waiting room, and I used that, but his cell went straight to voicemail.

"Don't have my phone. Come to the house. Go on in, the door's not locked." OK, now I had to find a ride home. There is no taxi service in Himmel, and the city-run Dial-A-Ride shuts down at 8 p.m. My usual go to people—my mother, Coop, Miguel, Father Lindstrom—were unavailable for various reasons. My second-string favor granters, Jennifer Pilarski—she had little kids, there was no way I'd roust her at 2 a.m.; Miller Caldwell? No, a non-emergency middle-of-the-night phone call was pushing it too far. I needed to work on my friend-making skills.

Isabel. I hated to wake her, but I knew she'd be glad to do it. And, actually, given everything that had happened in her life lately, she probably wasn't sleeping too deeply anyway.

"I feel bad getting you up in the middle of the night," I said, sliding into the passenger seat of her car.

She took in my bedraggled appearance, my stained and smelly clothes. "What happened? You sounded terrible when you called, and you look even worse. No offense," she added.

"None taken."

"Are you all right? What's going on?"

"Listen, Isabel, I found out something today that changes everything. Frankie didn't kill your dad, Bergman didn't kill your dad, Jamie didn't either. It wasn't anyone from his present. He was killed by someone from his past."

"I don't understand."

"You will." As she drove toward my house I tried to lay it out coherently, but between my exhaustion and the urgency I felt, it came tumbling out in a way that I feared made no sense. The pictures at Betty's visitation, the empty envelope I found in Jamie's car, Dr. Rosen, the transplant team deaths, the suicide of Amber Pelly, the fire at Father Lindstrom's. By the time I finished I was almost breathless, my mouth was unbelievably dry, and we were standing in the kitchen of my house. Isabel looked shell-shocked.

"I don't know what to think. Some stranger killed my father and all those people? But why, what would she gain?"

"Revenge. Satisfaction. A warped justice for what she thinks the members of the transplant team took away from her. She's had a lifetime to hate everyone she blames for her mother's suicide. Why should they have happy lives? Why should they have wives, children, husbands, love, a good life? They took the possibility of all that away from her mother and from her. They went on with their nice little lives, and she was left with nothing."

She was shaking her head. "I don't know, Leah. What do the police think?"

"I haven't told them. And judging by the way you're looking at me, that's probably just as well. I know I'm not helping you take me seriously, standing here ranting and waving my arms. But you have to, Isabel. You could be in danger too. Who knows how warped this chick is? Look, can you stay a little while? I just want to hop in the shower, get into some clean clothes, and I'll try it again. With a touch less crazy, OK?"

"Sure, I can stay. Go on. I'll make some toast and eggs for you. And some tea."

Suddenly food sounded like a great idea. I couldn't remember the last time I'd eaten. "Thanks," I said, as she found a knife in the drawer and started slicing bread for toast from the loaf Miguel had brought on Monday.

CHAPTER 47

I STOOD UNDER THE HOT WATER, scrubbing the ash and grime off my body and out of my hair. The water ran black for a few minutes. When it was clear, I raised the temperature and turned the nozzle on the shower head so that a hard stream of hot water hit my shoulders. The steam rose around me, and the only sound was the beat of the water. It wasn't hard to let my mind float. For 10 minutes. But then the hot water started to run out; the air was chilly outside the shower, and my "moment of Zen" began to dissipate. I toweled myself off quickly, ran a comb through my hair, and went into my room to pull on jeans and a sweater. The light on the cordless phone was flashing. Miguel.

I pressed the voicemail button—my mother's antique cassette tape answering machine had finally died, and we now had the latest technology. From 15 years ago. Voicemail accessible from all the extensions.

I played the message twice, unable to take in what he said the first time. It wasn't any easier the second. I called him back and it went to his voicemail.

"I'm here with Isabel. Come as soon as you get this."

I walked slowly back to the kitchen. Isabel was just closing the kitchen door.

"I just ran out to roll up my window. I left it down to get rid of the smoky smell, but now it's starting to sleet." A plate of eggs and toast sat at my place. "Let me get that tea, you look like you need it."

I sat and didn't say anything. Her back was to me as she put a tea cup in the microwave. I noticed then that she was wearing a hoodie. She half-turned and saw me looking at her.

"Hope you don't mind. This was hanging on the hook, so I just grabbed it to keep the rain off. How many minutes for the tea?"

"Two."

She turned back and began punching in the digits on the microwave keypad with her left hand. As I watched her entering the numbers, wearing my hoodie, identical to Jamie's, a montage of half-registered memories surfaced and fast-tracked through my mind.

The crime scene photo showing Garrett's computer mouse on the left side of his PC, though he was right-handed, like Jamie. The ATM slip in the pocket of the hoodie Isabel had "accidentally" switched for mine. Jamie's friend Keegan, telling me Isabel "helped" him remember when Jamie left the party. Her repeated referrals to Jamie's past drug use and relapse, though I'd seen no signs, nor had Frankie. How she goaded Jamie into confronting me by telling him I found the ATM receipt.

Her story that Jamie had misread her note and gone to the wrong park to find her the day he was killed. Ivah at the insurance office telling me Isabel's car was hit by a deer in Michigan last January. And that she was in Eau Claire July 4th, the day Neal Dawson died. Cole's cryptic remark about the left hand not knowing what the right hand was doing. All those clues, half-noticed or ignored, because I was sure Isabel needed a champion. The angry words Coop had hurled at me, that Isabel was manipulating me, that she was always lying to me. Lies that I excused, because I was giving Isabel what she really needed. Not a champion. A chump. Me.

I was so lost in my thoughts that I jumped when she set the tea down for me. She waved her hand in front of my face.

"Hey, anybody in there?" She smiled.

"The day's catching up with me, I guess. I'm a little slow on the uptake. Thanks." I pulled the tea closer, knocking over a vase filled with chrysanthemums. I grabbed it before all the water ran onto the floor. Isabel jumped up and got a dish towel as I righted it.

"Hey, you're kind of wobbly, aren't you? Do you want to call it a night? We can always talk tomorrow," she said, mopping up the spill.

"No, I'd like to talk awhile." How long would it be before Miguel got my message?

"All right. Just take it slow then. Eat something, why don't you?" I hadn't touched anything on my plate.

"I'm not as hungry as I thought I was."

"It's probably the smoke. Drink some tea. I put some honey in it. I like it that way. It'll be good for your throat." She took a sip of her own.

I nodded and lifted the cup to my mouth and swallowed.

"Leah, I've been thinking about what you said. I guess if this daughter really believes the transplant team killed her mother, I can understand her anger. But the idea that she could get away with killing five times, and no one caught on? Could she really be that smart?"

"It wouldn't take a mastermind."

"You're kidding. Someone kills five people and doesn't get caught, and you don't think she's super smart?" She laughed, shaking her head, but I could tell she was irritated.

"It's just a riff on the plot of *Strangers On A Train*. How do you get away with murder? Kill people you have no obvious connection to. No one on the team knew Amber's daughter. The members themselves went their separate ways 20 years ago. So when the individual team members began dying "accidentally" one by one, with no common cause of death, no red flags went up."

"If you're right, I think what Amber's daughter did took an amazing amount of intelligence. She'd have to be really clever."

"Look, if she has the IQ of a potato and an internet connection, it wouldn't be hard for her to find the team. And just google 'accidental deaths,' and you've got a hundred different ways to go. I'm not saying she doesn't have nerve, but smarts? Not buying it."

"But she got away with it."

"Almost, but not quite. And that's thanks to you."

"Me?"

"Sure." This was starting to be fun, playing cat and mouse with her as she tried to figure out if I was the cat or the mouse. I wanted to goad her narcissistic self into such a fury that she'd blurt out the truth. And she had no idea Miguel and Coop were on their way. *At least you hope they are.*

She took several long drinks of her tea before setting it down. Her brown eyes fixed on me, but they were now the hard, shiny color of a cockroach's shell.

"If you hadn't wanted justice for your dad, to prove that he didn't commit suicide, nothing would have come out. Amber's daughter had already killed three people. But she made a mistake with your father. Instead of an accident, she tried to make it look like suicide. But you saw through it."

"But that doesn't mean she's the killer. Don't killers stick with a pattern? Why would she switch from accident to fake suicide?"

"Maybe she had to. Maybe somehow Garrett found out what was going on, and she had to improvise. And that might have worked. It was very well done, I admit. But she didn't count on you. You knew your father, and you knew he wouldn't kill himself. And I finally got lucky, finding that envelope in Jamie's car. Otherwise, I wouldn't have connected Betty and Dr. Rosen and the rest of the team to Garrett's death."

"The envelope was empty though. The letter could have been about anything. I don't see how that matters." She got up with her empty cup and my untouched plate of food. She tossed the eggs and toast into the trash can, then turned to the sink, her back toward me as she started rinsing the dishes.

"If it didn't matter, why wasn't the letter in Jamie's car? If it wasn't anything important, why didn't he just crumple it up and toss it in the back seat with the Burger King wrappers? No. I'm sure Garrett was trying to tell Dr. Rosen what he suspected. That he was warning him. And when Jamie read it, he realized what your father knew. That's why he went to the park, to meet Amber's daughter. That's why he called Frankie, so she'd know where he was and what he was doing, in case anything happened."

"You haven't told anyone else your theory yet?" She raised her voice slightly over the running water.

"No. Not yet. I just figured it out, and I've put so many wrong theories out there, I want to at least find out who Amber's daughter is and prove the connection. I don't think it will take long, now that I know who I'm looking for. Then I'll give up everything I know."

When she turned around, the bread knife was in her hand. And she was pointing it at me.

"Oh, I think you know who Amber's daughter is, Leah."

"It took me long enough, didn't it? What are you planning to do? Go full Manson on me in my own house? How do you think you'll get away with that?" *Where the hell was Miguel with my reinforcements?*

"I'm sure I'll figure out something. I always do." She took a step toward me. "You know, I always liked you, Leah. This isn't personal. You just know too much, and you never stop. You just can't help yourself, can you?"

"I don't know as much as you think I do. Why don't you tell me more? How did you find out Garrett was your father?" I was stalling, hoping she couldn't resist the chance to demonstrate her brilliance.

"Last Thanksgiving a water pipe burst in the basement. I went through the boxes that were water damaged. I found a picture in one of them. A woman, who looked a little like me, holding a toddler, who looked a lot like me. On the back it said, *Amber and Lynette, Sandersville Centennial, 1991.* I already knew I was adopted. It wasn't that hard to figure out who was in the picture. I went to the Sandersville library, looked through the high school yearbooks. There in the Sandersville 1988 *Tiger Tale*s was a picture of Amber Pelly, Homecoming Queen, with her mother Goldie Wilson.

"It's a small town. I didn't have any trouble finding my sweet Grandma Goldie. She was finishing a fifth vodka when I got there. She could hardly stand. But she could talk. I told her my name, and she said she'd been waiting all these years for me to find her. Right. She told me all about my mother, and that bastard doctor who got her pregnant, and the transplant team he was on that killed her. Then she had a crying jag, then she passed out.

"I looked through the house. Found bank statements with regular deposits from my father's bank. It was all pretty clear then. I wasn't sure what I was going to do then, but I warned Goldie to keep quiet about my visit, or the money would dry up. I think it's time for me to visit her again."

She blinked rapidly, then squeezed her eyes tight for a moment. She gave her head a shake, as though trying to bring something in focus. Then she took two quick steps toward me and stuck the point of the knife in the space between my ribs.

"Get up. Get up!" If I made a sudden move, she could slice right through me.

"OK, OK, I'm getting up. You have to move back, I don't have room to move my chair out."

She inched back a little, but the knife tip still poked at my side.

"So how do you think you're going to get rid of me?" I said, as I slowly rose and pushed the chair back with my knees.

"Shut up." Only she slurred her words, so that what came out was "Shub ut." I felt her wobble. I turned abruptly. She stumbled. The knife skittered across the floor. We both lunged for it. I grabbed it first. I pointed it at her, suffused with primal rage and the urge to hurt her as she'd hurt someone I loved.

"You tried to kill Father Lindstrom." Anger coursed through me, and my hand clenching the knife shook.

"Wha. Wha gonna do? Gonna do abou, about it?" She swayed. I sprang forward. Then her eyelids fluttered and she gave a soft sigh, like air leaking out of a tire. She slumped, and as she hit the kitchen floor, the door flew open. I turned, the knife still in my hand.

"*Díos mío*, chica! You killed her!"

CHAPTER 48

"*HÍJOLE*, CHICA, YOU SCARED ME. When I saw that knife in your hand and Isabel lying on the floor—" Miguel shuddered. It was two hours later, and Isabel was in the hospital sleeping off the Klonopin dose she'd intended for me. We were in the conference room at the Himmel Police Department, waiting to sign the statements we'd just given.

"I can't believe you'd think I'd kill her in my own kitchen. I'd at least do it somewhere I could hide the body." I was giddy with relief that Isabel was at least temporarily out of the picture, and when I had checked, the hospital said Father Lindstrom was showing signs of improvement.

"You did so good tonight, Miguel. You found Amber's mother, and you got her to talk. I can't believe she told you so much."

"Chica, you know the ladies, they love me." He grinned. Then he got serious. "I found the story online about Amber's suicide, then I got an address for the grandma, but no phone number. I used a reverse directory and found one for a neighbor. I called her, and she told me Goldie goes to the Comet Tavern every night. So I drove to Sandersville."

"Now that's good reporting, my friend. Most people wouldn't drive two hours at eight o'clock at night on the off chance of finding someone."

"You would," he said. "And that's my mantra, WWLD—What Would Leah Do? I knew I'd be late, but then I got your text, so I knew it didn't matter. And the *abuela*, she had a lot to say."

Despite the extremely late—or was it early?—hour, he was energized. Chasing down a lead can make you feel that way. I could tell he wanted to relive his reporting prowess for me, and he deserved to.

"So tell me again what happened."

"OK. You know, the grandma was at the *taverna*. And she was pretty *borracha*. Pretty drunk. She was crying, crying. The bartender told me 'Goldie is either cryin' or cussin', no in between.' I bought her a drink and asked her about Garrett Whiting. She said he was a *bastardo* who took her granddaughter. '*Dígame*, tell me why did he do that?' And she said—" Here he paused to add some dramatic tension to his tale. He resumed with a deep frown, a sweep of his hand, and the solemn intonations of Darth Vader, "Because, he is her father!"

I doubted Goldie had delivered it with such flourish, but Miguel does tell a good story.

"I didn't know everything, chica, but I knew you needed to know. So I called your cell and no answer. And texted and no answer. And I called your house and no answer, but I left a message. Then when I came into town I saw the fire, so I had to drive by."

I nodded. It's in the blood. You have to check out a fire.

"I saw your car. Chief Porter told me you were at the hospital with Father Lindstrom. But when I got there, you were gone. I was getting worried. Your call came in when I was checking with Coop but it went to voicemail before I caught it. After I listened, we came right over. And saw you trying to stab Isabel."

"I could have. I thought the Klonopin she tried to give me would never kick in. I switched the cups when I knocked over the flowers, and she drank the whole thing, but she didn't go down easy."

The door opened and Coop came in, followed by Detective Ross and Sheriff Dillingham.

I had to go over everything again for them.

"Once I put it all together, I knew Amber's daughter had done it. And I thought Father Lindstrom might be next. And I was sure none of you would believe me without more evidence. I had Miguel check out Amber and her mother. I drove straight to Father Lindstrom's. When I got there, his house was already on fire. It wasn't until I got home and heard Miguel's message that everything fell into place."

"So you're sayin' that you've been withholding information that would've helped me find a serial killer?" Ross leaned menacingly across the table. He had held in his anger and resentment for as long as he could. But then, so had I.

"No. I'm saying that Christopher Columbus with a GPS couldn't help you find your own ass. I knew there wasn't a chance in hell you'd listen to me, unless I could give you Amber's daughter on a silver platter. So that's what I did."

Ross slammed his hand down on the desk so hard that Miguel jumped. The sheriff intervened.

"That's enough, Charlie. Nobody's covered in glory here. In fact, it looks like we got a world class FUBAR to try and figure out. Let's calm down. I'd like to have something in my back pocket when the prosecutor gives it to me in the neck this morning. Miguel, you want to tell me what you did tonight?"

After Miguel finished, Ross didn't say anything, and the sheriff just nodded and sighed. Then he said, "OK, Leah, now did Isabel Whiting confess to you tonight? Seeing as you had her at knifepoint as I understand?" For just a second I thought I saw a flash of laughter in his weary blue eyes, but that was probably just a trick of the light.

"How we gonna prove any of this stuff?" His tone was belligerent and his cheeks were bright red from the effort of holding in his hostility. I felt no such constraint.

"Geez, Ross, isn't there any part of your job I don't have to do?"

His beefy face reddened even more. Coop stepped in.

"I think everybody's pretty tired. Leah, why don't you and Miguel go home, get some rest. The sheriff and I need to get ahead of this thing as much as we can, and we've got a lot of catch up to do."

CHAPTER 49

WHEN ISABEL WOKE UP later that morning, the first thing she did was ask for a lawyer. When I woke up that afternoon, the first thing I asked was, "How's Father Lindstrom?"

"Much better. They moved him to a regular room a little while ago." My mother was sitting on my bed, having just woken me up by asking me if I was still sleeping.

"Leah, I don't know whether to kiss you or smack you." She settled the question by doing a little of both, planting a kiss on my cheek, enfolding me in her arms as I sat up, and then hitting me lightly on my arm.

"Hey! That's my sore bicep."

"You don't want to go there. Why didn't you tell me you'd been beaten within an inch of your life?"

"Because I wasn't, there wasn't anything you could have done, and you'd only worry."

"With good reason."

I had groggily promised when she had arrived home at 10 a.m. to tell her everything, if she'd just let me sleep. But I dreaded the thought of going through the whole complicated story again. She read the look on my face.

"Don't worry. I've got the gist of it. I talked to Coop and Miguel, and I went to see Father Lindstrom early this afternoon—though he doesn't remember much." Abruptly, she turned serious. Her dark blue eyes searched my face. "Honey, how did you manage to go into that burning house?"

"I don't know, Mom. I just kept thinking about Annie, and, and, and—" I took a breath to stop my voice from quavering and tried again. "I felt like I was right back at our house. The night of the fire. I couldn't fail again. This time I had to do it."

"Oh, Leah." She took hold of my hand. "Honey, you did everything you could. Just like you did last night. But you were a little girl then. And now you're a grown, amazing, brave woman, and you saved Father Lindstrom's life. I am so proud of you."

"He wouldn't have needed saving, if I hadn't been so stupid."

"All right, now. That's enough of that. I can tell you need some four-cheese macaroni, a nice green salad, and apple crisp for dessert. Fortunately, I've got all three going in the kitchen. You get up, get showered, get dressed and there will be no more talk of what you could have or should have done. You did wonderfully well." She hugged me again, and I did as I was told.

A lot happened over the next week; unfortunately none of it involved Isabel confessing to multiple murders. Father Lindstrom got steadily better. The *Himmel Times* ran a huge story on the drug bust and Dr. Bergman's involvement and a small story about the fire at Father Lindstrom's. The sidebar on my "heroism" in rescuing him was a little embarrassing. I'm sure that was Miguel's idea, not Rebecca's. I spent some time that week helping my mother and some of the other St. Stephen's parishioners fix up a little house for Father Lindstrom, so he'd have a place to go when he got out of the hospital.

On the night before his release, she and I went grocery shopping to stock his refrigerator and cupboards for his return home on Friday.

347

As we worked together putting things away, I tried once again to get her to talk about how things were going with Paul. I'd made several attempts since she got home, but she had adroitly avoided my questions by parrying with questions of her own, about what I wanted for Christmas, or whether I was going ahead with my freelance story for the *Milwaukee Journal*, or if everything was set for my book release in February. If she were really desperate to get me off the topic of her and Paul, she'd ask me how Nick was doing and what our long-term plans were. A sure way, she knew, to get me to leave the room.

But she hadn't seemed any less tense or stressed than she'd been before she went to Michigan. She was still preoccupied, a little short tempered, and sometimes I caught her staring into space with a worried look on her face that she always briskly denied when I pointed it out. But we were alone at Father Lindstrom's new place and there was nowhere for her to run.

"OK, what's going on with you and Paul?"

"Nothing. Everything's fine."

"Then why haven't I seen him all week? Why hasn't he called?"

She busied herself putting cans of soup in the cupboard before she answered. When she did it was in a forced, breezy voice. "Nothing's wrong. We've both just been busy."

"Mom."

She sighed but still didn't say anything.

"I'm not going to stop asking, and you're not leaving this room until I know."

"All right. Fine. Paul asked me to marry him. And I said no."

"What? Why? Why would you do that? You're perfect for each other."

"No, we're not."

"Mom."

"Leah, I don't want to talk about it."

"Paul is wild about you. You guys love spending time together. It may not look like it, but seriously, I can take care of myself. It's about time I got a place of my own anyway. And—"

"Stop it."

"But you're just being—"

"I can't marry him, that's all." Her eyes were bright, and I realized she was trying hard not to cry.

"Yes you can, Mom. Paul must be crushed. You have to tell him you changed your mind. Well, at least you told him there wasn't another man, right?"

She looked like a deer caught in the headlights.

"Mom? There's not another man, right? That's not why you can't marry him?"

"Enough. I'm not talking about this with you anymore. I don't want you asking me, and I don't want you talking about this to anyone else. Do you understand? Do you promise?"

"All right! OK, I promise. I promise." I let it go, because she was as upset as I've ever seen her. Later that night, she was in the shower for a long time. And mixed in with the noise of water beating down on the fiberglass tub surround was the unmistakable sound of heart-wrenching sobs. And worse than hearing them, was knowing that she wouldn't tell me why.

CHAPTER 50

ON SATURDAY MORNING Coop called and asked me to meet him at the Elite. That I was surprised and that he didn't just drop by the house to talk to me were both indicators of how far apart we'd grown.

He didn't notice me as I came through the door, and I had a chance to look at him unobserved. He wasn't wearing his usual HPD cap, and I could see that he'd grown his hair out so that it was a little longer on the front and shorter on the sides. It looked good. Rebecca's influence, no doubt. He was staring into his coffee cup, and he looked tired. He glanced up then and smiled, and for a minute it was like the last few weeks had never happened.

"Hey. I got you a chai latte," he said, pointing to the cup in front of me as I sat down at the table.

"Thanks." We sat in silence for a minute, then both started talking at once.

"Coop—"

"Leah—"

"No, me first."

"All right."

"OK. I want us to be friends. I'm sorry I made such a mess of everything—Garrett's murder, Isabel, the DEA investigation, you and

Rebecca. Sometimes I get so focused on the way I see things, I forget everyone else doesn't share my vision."

"Oh really? I hadn't noticed."

"Yes, really. So, anyway, I've made a lot of mistakes. Bad ones. I'm sorry. I'll try to do better. No, I will do better. I've missed you."

"Same here."

"Wait a minute. I had to do a whole mea culpa, and you get away with ditto?"

"You wanted to go first. Then you said it all. Like usual."

"Shut up."

And we were back. Maybe not the same way. There was Rebecca now, but that was something I just had to accept. I would do better. I would.

"So, what's going on with Isabel?"

"That's the second reason I wanted to talk. Charlie Ross arrested her for Garrett's murder about an hour ago."

"Just Garrett's? What about Jamie?"

He shook his head. "The prosecutor didn't think there was enough evidence."

"Cliff Timmins is a politician, not a prosecutor. He doesn't want any case that doesn't come with a signed confession."

"He's got a decent chance of winning on Garrett's case. There's just not enough on Jamie. Yet, anyway."

"What about the rest of them?"

"Come on, you know jurisdiction is in three different places. There's not much Cliff can do about that. We're sharing information with the other departments, but so far they're not overwhelmed by the evidence. There isn't anything solid linking her those other deaths."

I slumped down in my seat. "So she'll get away with all those?"

"Maybe. She did cross state lines though."

"Yeah, so?" And then I got what he was driving at. "That means she could be prosecuted in federal court. The FBI could assume jurisdiction and link all the murders together." My voice rose with excitement.

"Take it easy. The operative word is 'could.' Doesn't mean they will, but it's possible. Right now, be happy she's going on trial for killing her father."

"Who's her attorney?"

He grimaced. "It's Aiden Kennedy."

"That's bad. He's good. Probably the best criminal defense attorney in the state."

"No doubt. But Isabel had two of the top five motives for murder: money and revenge. Ross dug up cell phone tower records that put her within three hours of Himmel when she talked to her father. And there's a security camera at a toll booth near Hammond, Indiana, with a nice picture of Isabel's car to corroborate that she was actually in that area. She had enough time to get home and kill him within the window the ME gave."

"That's good news," I said, my spirits lifting. "And there's the video from JT's and the ATM slip."

"Yeah. There's a lot a jury's gonna like. And if Cliff can get in that Isabel tried to frame her own brother, that's going to have an impact. Though there is one tricky part to this case."

"What's that?"

"Convincing a jury that Isabel set up a fake suicide for Garrett, then tried to make it look like murder. The defense may argue that if she'd killed her father and got away with a suicide verdict, there's no way she'd focus attention back on the crime. After all, she's the one who pushed to have the investigation reopened. Kennedy could argue that it doesn't make sense. Why didn't she leave it alone? That's the question Cliff will have to answer."

"But that's easy. She thought suicide would be the cleanest way, but she slipped up. She either forgot, or didn't know there was a suicide clause. Or she didn't realize the two years hadn't run out on it yet. She went through Garrett's papers after she killed him, and oh-oh, she's not going to get the money she thought she was. And Isabel is a greedy girl. So she created a murder scenario on the fly. She worked backwards to re-stage things, and as an added bonus, to implicate Jamie, so he'd get the blame."

"Good argument. I like it."

"Thank you."

"But Ross didn't follow her plan. It looked like a straight up suicide. He made a classic error, and he didn't investigate it the same way he would a homicide. I'm not sure I would have either."

"Yes, you would, Coop."

"Well, it's easy to second guess. Anyway, he didn't, and nothing Isabel set up panned out. He didn't find the clues. She was too clever for her own good."

"So then she calls me, because I'm like one of Pavlov's dogs, salivating at the sound of injustice. I jump in with both feet and do exactly what she wants me to do."

"Not exactly, because she definitely didn't want you to go beyond suspecting Jamie. But she didn't realize that Leah Nash never does what anyone wants her to do. She's pushy, know-it-all, stubborn, and she won't be bossed. And she's maybe the best reporter I've ever seen."

"OK. Now I want to thank you and to punch you in the arm. Why do you have to tangle up a compliment with a list of my flaws?"

"Take 'em where you can get 'em. You did a good job, Leah, you really did. You made some mistakes. So did the rest of us. But you got there in the end."

"Thanks. Hey, Frankie's out, right?"

"Yep. This morning."

When I checked my phone after leaving, I saw an email from Jane Barstow, the forensic document examiner. I stared at it blankly for a second. With everything that had happened the last few days, I'd forgotten all about the portfolio.

I finished the indented writing tests. I'm FedExing the original materials back to you, as well as my formal report. Attached is the text I was able to recover. Interesting. Best, Jane.

I clicked the attachment open.

To the investigators of my death—

I have taken my own life. I apologize for the unfinished business I'm leaving.

My daughter Isabel Whiting, born Lynette Pelly, is a multiple murderer. Isabel is my natural daughter, the result of a brief sexual liaison with a woman named Amber Pelly. I didn't want the child; Amber didn't want anything but the child. We parted. She never contacted me. However, in 1994 while I served on the St. Cyprian Kidney Transplant Team, Amber was a candidate for transplant. I was ethically obligated to recuse myself from the decision process. I didn't. No one on the team knew of my connection to Amber. She was turned her down because of mental instability and financial problems. She killed herself shortly after.

Her mother, Goldie Wilson, threatened legal action against the team and the hospital. Then she met with me personally to say that she would report me to the medical board unless I agreed to her conditions. Exposure would have ruined my life. I did as she wanted, paid her, and took the child she didn't want to raise. I had no further contact with Goldie Wilson other than recurring quarterly payments until recently. She phoned to tell me Isabel had learned her real identity and my role in her mother's death. In her drunken state, Goldie had concluded I would pay her for that information. I allowed her to think that. I had already determined I was going end my life. But what she said disturbed me. An unsettling suspicion began to take hold. After some research, it became a conviction.

Isabel discovered the truth of her parentage, and the fate of her mother, last January. Last spring, I learned a colleague on the transplant team, William Lessing, was killed in a hit and run accident jogging near Grand Rapids, Michigan. A few months later, another colleague, Gail Slade, was killed in an accidental fall from a crowded subway platform in Chicago. Last month I heard that Neal Dawson, yet another team member, had died in Eau Claire on the 4th of July, the result of an allergic reaction. Isabel was in each place at the time the incidents occurred, and she had lied to me each time about where she was.

Lest you think my conclusion is histrionic, please know that Isabel was an accomplished liar and manipulator from an early age. Her beauty and intelligence hid a ruthless nature. People who thwarted her suffered—accidents, damage to reputations, loss of treasured possessions. I suspected, and I sometimes knew, she was the cause, but I did little. Parenting was never an interest of mine. However, I never imagined she was capable of what I am convinced she has done.

Still, I didn't want my brief time left taken up with investigations and infamy. You have the information now to do with it what you will. In any case, I've ensured that Isabel will suffer some punishment. By committing suicide, I void my life insurance. Isabel will get nothing from that source. Neither will my son, Jamie, but it will do him good to stand on his own.

There is one other matter. Dr. Hal Bergman, my associate, is involved in prescription drug fraud; how deeply I'm not sure. Elaine Quellman can provide the information we have. I leave on my own terms, without regret.

Garrett Whiting

Holy shit. Holy shit. Holy shit.

Isabel hadn't committed the only crime she was arrested for. She really didn't kill Garrett. He killed himself.

Charlie Ross had been right all along.

CHAPTER 51

ON MONDAY, I received the FedEx package with the originals and the document Jane had recovered from the indented writing on the portfolio pad. I still hadn't told anyone about the report. If I gave the material to the prosecutor, it would mean Isabel would go free. If I didn't, she could be convicted for the one crime she didn't commit.

When my phone rang at 11, it was Miguel telling me Isabel had been arraigned, but she was still in jail. She couldn't make the $500,000 bond the judge set. Then I made a phone call of my own.

"Hello, Leah." Isabel said it as though she were receiving me in her living room, not sitting at a beat-up table wearing handcuffs. Even in the standard jail uniform, without make-up, she was stunning. Her big brown eyes were warm and guileless, her dark blonde hair framed her face. She looked like the angel on top of a Christmas tree.

"I'm surprised you agreed to see me."

"I was curious. What do you want?"

"I'd like some answers."

"I didn't kill my father. That's the only answer I'm prepared to give."

"Yes. I know."

"So now you believe me? What changed your mind?"

"I have your father's suicide note."

"You can't have it! I de—" She stopped abruptly.

"You what? Destroyed it? Yeah, I'm sure you did. Have you ever heard of indented writing, Isabel?"

Her expression was wary, her eyes narrowed and calculating. "No. What's that got to do with anything?"

"I have your father's portfolio. The one you gave to Elaine Quellman. There was a pad of paper in it. Miss Quellman put it there herself the Sunday Garrett died."

"And so?"

"So it's the one he wrote his suicide note on."

"There's nothing there. I—"

Again I interrupted. "You checked, right? Yeah, I didn't see anything either. But that's the thing. Indented writing isn't always visible. I sent it to a forensic document examiner. She was able to bring up the impressions his pen made on the pages beneath the one he wrote on. That means I have a copy of your father's suicide note. It's pretty clear you didn't kill him."

She made a sudden move to grab my wrists and was brought back to reality by her shackled hands. She settled back in her chair, but her voice was sharp and commanding when she spoke.

"You have to give it to my lawyer, now!"

"Actually, no, I don't. See, I'm the only one who knows it exists. Well, the expert who examined the portfolio does, but I have the original materials. Maybe she could testify on your behalf, but it would be pretty hard with the originals gone." I paused for effect. Her knuckles were white from the effort of controlling herself, but she didn't say anything.

"I have to tell you, I'm not the most careful person in the world. Anything could happen. Maybe I'd set the documents on the roof of my car. And then I could forget and drive away. They'd fly right off, maybe into the river if I was crossing a bridge, and never be found again. Then again, I'm a little clumsy too. I might be looking at them while I was drinking a cup of tea and then oops, I spill it all over them. The paper would be ruined. Nothing could be recovered from that."

"You can't do that. I'll tell the prosecutor and my lawyer what you just said."

"Oh, I wouldn't do it on purpose. But like I said, I'm very careless. But even if nothing happened to the documents, and I turned them in, you might not be home free. Remember the note? Your father says that you killed all those people on the transplant team."

"That doesn't matter. I can't be prosecuted for a crime that never happened. He wasn't murdered. He committed suicide. Anything else he wrote is just a product of his damaged mind. The Parkinson's, the Klonopin he took, the stress he was under, it all affected his thinking."

I knew that's what her lawyer would argue. And she'd make a very attractive defendant—young, beautiful, bereft. Hell, Lizzie Borden got away with it, and she wasn't half as appealing as Isabel.

"Could be. But without Garrett's note, Cliff Timmins has a pretty good case against you for murder, you have to admit. And juries don't like kids who kill their parents."

"What do you want?"

"I want you to tell me what you did. And I want you to promise that if the murder charge is dropped, and you manage to escape the consequences for the other murders you committed, you will never, never come within a hundred miles of Father Lindstrom again. Or Dr. Rosen, either."

"No matter what I say here you won't be able to use it, even if you could prove it. You're extorting a confession from me. You're making me admit things I didn't do, in exchange for evidence that will prove I didn't kill my father."

"That may be true. But no one is going to see the documents if you don't tell me what you did. And if no one sees them, you might just go away for first degree murder. I think I can live with that. Do you want to risk it?"

"Give me the documents first."

"No. You tell me what you did. And you promise me that you will not hurt Father Lindstrom or Dr. Rosen. Then I'll turn them over to Cliff Timmins and to your lawyer."

"How do I know I can trust you?"

"I guess you'll have to take a chance. Just like me."

Surprisingly, she laughed.

"I do like smart women, Leah, and you're almost as smart as me. I think I can agree to your terms. Father Lindstrom and Dr. Rosen are both old men. I can let nature take its course. But I have a condition, too. You agree that your next book will not be the story of my father's death, and you will not write anything that tries to link him, or me, to the transplant team deaths. I'd like to put this chapter of my life behind me. A book by you would make it hard to do that, even though I'd sue you for libel and win."

So, she was a little rattled, despite her cool demeanor. That was a good thing. In truth, I had no plans to make the Whiting case the subject of my next book. She'd been too smart—though I would never tell her that—and too lucky. There was almost zero chance of finding evidence that would hold up in court linking her to the transplant deaths. But if she was just a little worried that I might keep trying, it might be enough to keep her away from Father Lindstrom.

"All right. Agreed. Now, let's hear it."

"First of all, I want to say that you don't have any idea what my life has been like. It was no fairy tale, growing up in the Whiting house. Once my father agreed to my sweet grandma's blackmail terms, he deposited me with Joan and never gave me another thought. He was too busy with his women and his practice. Joan hated me, and she treated me like dirt. Plus, she was strung out on prescription drugs most of the time. They were quite a pair of parents. I had to fight for the right to exist. And Jamie, that whiny little brat. The only fun I ever had in that 'family' was setting him up for things I'd done. He was so trusting and stupid, he fell for it every time."

"That's a really sad story, Lynette. I can see why you had to kill six people. Let's get back on track with what happened. Start with the night your father died."

I saw the flash of anger in her eyes at my use of her "real" name, but she controlled it quickly.

"All right. This is all hypothetical, and I'm not admitting anything. I'm just going to tell you how things might have happened. Hypothetically."

"OK, fine. Just get to it."

"I told you that I was driving home from the Adirondacks that Sunday, that part was true. But I said that I stopped outside of Cleveland for the night. I didn't. I drove as far as Hammond, Indiana, and stopped there. I was less than three hours away when Garrett called me. He didn't even know I'd started for home. He thought I was still in New York. I didn't tell him any different. He told me he'd been diagnosed with Parkinson's, and he didn't see any point in living if he couldn't be a surgeon. I was surprised he was confiding in me, because we didn't really have that kind of daddy-daughter relationship. But then he also told me that he knew what I'd done. He was so proud of himself for working things out, and even prouder that he'd figured out a way to destroy me. He told me he was leaving a note for the police telling them everything. And then he laughed. Because he knew I wouldn't be able to get home from Blue Mountain Lake before the housekeeper found his body in the morning and the police were called—not even if I drove all night. Then he hung up, leaving me helpless to save myself—he thought. But the joke was on him. I had plenty of time to get home and destroy his suicide note, because I was three, not 14 hours away.

"When I arrived around 2:30 a.m., Jamie's car was there. I went right to my father's study. The light was on. He was dead. I read his suicide note and realized Garrett had tried to outmaneuver me to the very end. By killing himself, he voided his insurance policy. I wouldn't get any insurance money, and he owed me that. He died thinking he'd checkmated me, but that was never going to happen. I destroyed the note, and I decided to make his suicide look like murder. And to let Jamie take the blame. I'd get all the money, and Jamie would get payback for being Joan's precious favorite. $100,000 to him and nothing to me? He deserved to suffer. I went to Jamie's room, found him passed out, and I knew he wouldn't be a problem.

"I set up the Hook's cheese, ordered the book, flushed an old Klonopin prescription I had down the toilet, and put the bottle in Jamie's room. Then I drove Jamie's car, sideswiped that nosy old bat's mailbox, and went to the ATM wearing Jamie's hoodie. When I got back home, I hid the ATM slip in Jamie's desk, and waited. Everything pointed to Jamie. At 8:30 I woke him up. I told him I just got home and found Garrett dead in his study.

"He couldn't take it in. He was confused, couldn't remember anything except he went to a party with Keegan. He didn't know when he got home."

She paused for a second, and looked at me expectantly. When I didn't say anything, she gave an impatient sigh.

"Don't you see? This part was pure genius. He didn't remember, so I knew if I worked it right, I could make him think he didn't get back until much later than he did. And he'd tell the police that and use that moron Keegan as his alibi. All I had to do was convince Keegan that it was 4 a.m., not 2 a.m. when they left the party, and tell him it was important for Jamie that the police knew it was 4 a.m. I knew Keegan wouldn't be able to keep the story together if the police questioned him. Then I had another piece of 'evidence' that Jamie was guilty. His alibi wouldn't hold up. He could easily have left the party much earlier than he said, killed Garrett, and made a run to the ATM.

"Then the police came, and everything fell apart. That detective, Ross, he was sure it was suicide as soon as he saw the body. He believed Jamie's story, he barely questioned Keegan, they didn't search Jamie's room, so they didn't find the ATM slip, so it didn't lead them to JT's, or the security camera footage, or Mrs. Wright's stupid mailbox. And when I tried to convince them it was murder, Ross just dismissed me. I didn't have any choice. I had to call you.

"And that worked out perfectly, at first. You followed the clues beautifully. I wanted to get that ATM slip to you, but I had a hard time figuring out how. Then your mother dropped it into my lap by asking me to bring you your hoodie. I zipped back home, put on Jamie's hoodie, stuffed the ATM slip into the pocket, and then I pulled the switch at the paper. It was so fun to watch you try to convince me that my brother was a murderer, when I was trying to convince you of that very thing. It was all coming together.

"Until Jamie picked up the mail that Saturday. He opened the letter I didn't even know my father had sent to Dr. Rosen. He went to the county park—I really did leave a note, but I said I'd gone for a hike at the county park, not at Patmore's Ridge like I told you. I rode my bike out, and he saw it parked at the start of one of the trails. He found me, and he confronted me. He really didn't leave me a choice. But even that turned out all right, because he'd made that call to Frankie. And you found out about their affair, which I didn't even know about. When Detective Ross arrested her for both deaths, I thought I was home free.

"But I admit, I made a mistake. I should have stopped then. If I hadn't gone ahead with Betty, you never would have put things together. But I thought she would be so easy, and she was. I just put on some scrubs, set a small fire in a wastebasket at the nursing home, and pulled the alarm. In all the confusion, I took Betty to my car and I drove her home. That's where she kept telling me she wanted to go. I had to come back in the morning and unlock the shed she was in, to make sure she was dead, but that was no problem."

"You're a monster."

"And the people who killed my mother weren't? They took away something that belonged to me. They had to pay, that's all."

"Why did you go after Father Lindstrom? He just advised the team. He wasn't part of the medical decision making."

"He let them kill my mother. Probably told them it was all right, they were doing their duty, making the hard choices. But it wasn't all right. And it wasn't fair. They had happy lives. They had families. They had what I deserved. They took it away from me, so I took it away from them. It was justice."

"What about the others? How did you get rid of Dr. Lessing?"

"It wasn't hard to find out he's a jogger. Hit and run accidents, they happen all the time."

"Gail Slade?"

"She was on Facebook. Not good with privacy settings. Said she was going shopping at Neiman Marcus. I knew where she lived, and I knew the subway line she'd take."

"Neal Dawson?"

"That was tougher. But his daughter is on Tumblr, and she tells the world everything. It took a little effort, but I managed to switch his coffee for one laced with peanut oil. It only takes a tiny amount. It was so crowded no one even saw me. But then that insurance bitch had to call my father. Every step of the way my planning was perfect, but my luck didn't hold up, that's all."

Her narcissism was boundless.

"But now my luck's changed. You found the note that's going to set me free."

"We're all through here," I said as I got up and knocked on the door. The guard opened it immediately and walked over to Isabel.

"You're going to do what you promised, aren't you?" I enjoyed the fearful suspicion in her voice.

I shrugged.

She twisted away from the guard, but he grabbed her quickly and shoved her roughly forward. "What are you going to do, Leah? You'd better keep your promise." She hissed out the words.

Now it was my turn to lie.

"I don't know, Lynette."

CHAPTER 52

BUT I DID KNOW. I turned everything over to the prosecutor. I had played God once before, and I still wasn't easy with what I'd done. This time, I couldn't do it.

I did, however, have an ace up my sleeve. An old friend of mine, Jess Patterson. I'm pretty good at finding people, but Jess is the best PI and skip tracer I've ever met. And Jess owed me. Big. It was time to collect. Through Jess, I would always know where Isabel was, and what she was doing, no matter how far away she went or what she called herself. I'd be able to keep my eye on her for years. And she'd never know.

I pretty much avoided people for the rest of the day, not wanting to explain myself, or listen to Miguel's upbeat chatter, or even to Coop's commiseration or Nick's comforting words. I went to McClain's for a burger by myself before the evening rush started.

I was enjoying the solitude in my dark corner booth. Then Ross walked through the door. I tried donning my cloak of invisibility. It didn't work. He spotted me and came over.

"Mind if I sit down?" That was a switch—a polite inquiry instead of an aggressive demand.

"Suit yourself."

"Isabel Whiting got out this afternoon. Prosecutor dropped the charges. I heard you turned over the suicide note." I waited for him to tell me what a dumbass I was, how I let a killer go free.

"Yep."

"There was nothin' you could do. You had to turn it in, but it hurts like hell, doesn't it?"

"Yeah, it does," I said cautiously. I wondered what the catch was. Surely such empathy didn't come for free?

"We're still investigating Jamie's death. Doesn't look good though. No witnesses, nothin' at the scene. Well, the DEA surveillance guys did put Bergman near the park, like your goofy friend said, but not at the right time and he never even got out of his car. That empty envelope you found in Jamie's Mini Cooper? Timmins says it's 'suggestive,' but we can't prove anything."

"And the other deaths?"

"Betty Meier belongs to HPD. Coop musta told you; they can't find anything but some crazy old guy at the nursing home who saw her walkin' away with a nurse. The other three deaths belong to three different departments, and nobody's very interested in trying to dig up new evidence on cases they already ruled accidental. Maybe if we had a serial killer slittin' throats, we might be able to get the FBI to take an interest, but we don't." His shoulders sagged, and I knew he was as frustrated as I was.

"I talked to the fire marshal. He said the fire at Father Lindstrom's house started in the basement. It could've been set, but it could've been that the stacks of old newspapers down there were too close to a gas water heater. They can't tell for sure."

He shook his head. "We can't make anything stick to her. It's like she's made outta Teflon."

I didn't say anything, just took a bite of my burger and chewed it slowly. Though as I tried to accept the reality of Isabel walking away, I had a hard time swallowing. I took a sip of my soda.

"Look, Nash. I think we both got some things wrong here. But, uh, in the big picture, you know, you were more right than I was. You didn't totally screw up." His face was sweating, no doubt with the effort of giving me a semi-compliment.

"Well, you didn't either, Ross. In fact, you saw Garrett Whiting's death for what it was from the beginning. I got distracted and taken in by all the fake clues Isabel was strewing all over the place. Your instincts were right."

"Yeah well, like I told you, if it walks like a duck and quacks like a duck, it's a duck. And that duck—"

"Yeah, I know, was 'quackin' suicide.'"

"Still, I missed that portfolio. I mean, we looked at it, but there wasn't anything there. I made a mistake. I should've had it tested. But it looked like suicide—"

I interrupted. "Because it was suicide. Everybody makes mistakes. Don't beat yourself up."

"You, either." He sat there for a few seconds, then put his hands on the table and used it to support his slide out of the tight confines of the booth. As he stood he said, "Yeah. OK, then. I just wanted to say that you, uh, weren't all wrong. And you did good with the Father."

I looked at him, a stocky middle-aged man with little squinty eyes and a too-tight collar pinching the fat rolls on his neck. And for some reason, another one of Father Lindstrom's favorite quotes popped into my head. *"Everything that irritates us about others can lead us to an understanding of ourselves."* Ross was stubborn, and didn't let people in, and held fast to his own point of view, and he made a lot of mistakes—just like me. Maybe there was something to that. Maybe.

"Thanks, Ross. See you."

"Yeah, see you."

"Hey, Father. You would've been proud of me last night."

It was Tuesday evening, and like any wild and crazy woman in her early 30s, I was having a drink with an elderly priest. Various people in town had donated items to furnish his new living room, and the result

366

was definitely eclectic. I sat on a posh leather sofa provided by Miller Caldwell. Father Lindstrom was enthroned on a plaid recliner that was a gift from the high school football coach, whose wife had declared there was no room for a king size chair in her new family room. Someone else had donated a glass-topped coffee table and a Tiffany style floor lamp.

The little priest's color was good, and his light blue eyes had regained their sparkle. But sitting in the big chair that threatened to swallow him up, he looked very small, all of his 70-years and then some.

"Leah, you saved my life. I'm more than proud of you. I'm indebted and grateful for your bravery."

"Yeah, well, OK." I reddened slightly and continued my initial thought. "No, seriously. It's like I was channeling you." I told him about my conversation with Ross at McClain's.

"I'm very glad. But you weren't channeling me, you know. You have a very deep vein of loving kindness inside you."

"OK, no. I think you see people the way you want to see them, not how they really are."

"You're quite wrong. I have exceptionally clear vision where human nature is concerned." He wasn't in a reclining position, but his short legs barely touched the floor. He took a drink.

I did the same from the glass in my hand. And made a face. "You know that conversion thing? To Benedictine B&B? It's not happening."

He smiled but didn't answer, and I took another sip of the nasty stuff to please him.

"Do you think you could turn your 'exceptionally clear vision' on my mother?"

"What do you mean?"

"Something's wrong. I promised her I wouldn't talk about it to anyone, so I can't say specifically. But it's really upsetting her. I heard her crying the other night. I don't know what to do."

"Sometimes there's nothing you can do. I know that's hard for you to hear, but you can't solve everyone's problems, no matter how much you want to."

"Do you know anything about it? Has she talked to you?"

The look he gave me was kind and full of concern. So full, that I was sure he knew the truth. My mother had told him, and he couldn't tell me.

"You know, don't you?"

He took a sip of his drink and didn't answer.

"Father, please. Give me something to go on, something I can use to help her. Please."

"The only way you can help her is to respect her wishes. Your mother is in good health. She is not in trouble, nor is she in danger. Beyond that, there's nothing I can tell you. I'm sorry. You must be patient. When she's ready, she'll tell you herself."

There was no point in badgering him. He's small, but he's mighty when it comes to protecting confidences, in the confessional or otherwise. I had to let it go. So we talked quietly and laughed some. In the soft glow of the lamplight, I began to feel that things were finally righting themselves in my world.

Coop and I were friends again. Rebecca and I were civil to each other. My first book was coming out. Nick and I were doing surprisingly well. My mother was troubled, but she was healthy and she was safe, and she would tell me, eventually, and I would help her. And everything would be all right.

I had no premonition then that in the months ahead, everything I thought I knew about myself, my family, my life, was going to change forever.

ACKNOWLEDGEMENTS

IT TAKES A VILLAGE to edit a book. I'd like to thank my all beta readers and proofers who gave their time, attention and insights willingly and cheerfully.

Also, thanks to Jane Lewis, MFS, D-ABFDE, forensic document examiner nonpareil, who generously shared her expertise about indented writing and also allowed me to appropriate her first name for my fictional forensic document examiner. Any mistakes with reference to forensic document examination are entirely my own.

And it goes without saying, but never should, thanks to my husband Gary Rayburn for his unflagging encouragement, patience, and love.

DISCUSSION QUESTIONS

1. What's the most important part of a mystery/thriller to you—characters, action, plot, dialogue? Which aspects does the author focus on in *Dangerous Mistakes?*

2. How important is setting to *Dangerous Mistakes?* Is Himmel a place you feel like you've been—or would like to go? Why?

3. Besides the main character, Leah Nash, which other characters in the book stood out? Who was your favorite? Why?

4. Part of the fun of a mystery is guessing "whodunit." Who was your prime suspect early in the book? Did your guess change as you read further?

5. What red herrings threw you off the track of "whodunit?"

6. Leah experienced loss and abandonment at a young age. How does that affect her relationships with others and her approach to life?

7. Do the characters in *Dangerous Mistakes* act consistently with what you learn about their personalities? Were their motivations believable?

8. Is Leah any different at the end of the book than at the beginning? If yes, how?

9. *Dangerous Mistakes* has a small element of romance. Did it add to or detract from the story?

10. Leah has to make a choice at the end of the book. How did you feel about the choice she made? In her place, what would you have done?

11. What did you enjoy, or dislike, most about *Dangerous Mistakes?*

12. How did you feel about the ending? Would you have preferred a different conclusion? Why?

13. If you could tell the author one thing about *Dangerous Mistakes,* what would you say?

AUTHOR BIOGRAPHY

SUSAN HUNTER is a charter member of Introverts International (which meets the 12th of never at an undisclosed location). She has worked as a reporter and managing editor, during which time she received a first place UPI award for investigative reporting and a Michigan Press Association first place award for enterprise/feature reporting.

Susan has also taught composition at the college level, as well as written print, radio and television advertising copy, newsletters, press releases, speeches, web copy, academic papers, and memos. Lots and lots of memos. *Dangerous Mistakes* is the second novel in the Leah Nash mystery series. The first, *Dangerous Habits,* is also available on Amazon.

Susan lives in rural Michigan with her husband Gary, who is a man of action, not words.

Visit Susan's website http://leahnashmysteries.com to read her biweekly blogs, see a map of Himmel, and learn more about Leah's world. You can also email her at leahnashmysteries@gmail.com. She'd love to hear from you.